HAUNTED

A YOUNG ADULT FANTASY NOVEL

Library of Congress Control Number: 2021905257
Ebook 978-1-7356641-5-6
Paperback 978-1-7356641-3-2

Front Cover Art by Diletta De Santis
Cover Design by Lesley Worrell

Black Glory Publishing House
https://blackglorypublishinghouse.com/

HAUNTED

A YOUNG ADULT FANTASY NOVEL

NATALIE C. ZIEGLER

Outlands

O

Outlands

Outlan

KÄHARI

Väike

Lîla Sea

CHAPTER
ONE

As I thread through the open-air market, I see it—a soul's trail.

The knife lies, dull and unassuming, in the vendor's cluttered cart, yet I hear the jarring hum, feel the tingle in my fingertips, and see the solemn aura hovering in the air. I curl my fingers tightly into my palms. I know I should not touch it. A body dies, but the soul remains relentlessly alive. I can see the souls, speak with them, and experience their memories. Some say it is madness, but I know it's magic. Magic is forbidden, but it hovers around me; lifting me up, filling my lungs. The magic, ancient as the realm itself, burns in my veins and tickles my skin.

In this underground street market, called Arufin, the vendors are cutthroat, unscrupulous, and vague about their goods' origins. They lie. They loot. They'll steal the tunic off your back before your body cools and unflinchingly hawk it the next day. This sandstone street is also the one place in Kähari where magic abounds, rushing around as living energy, shimmering in the air like heat. Of everything I have seen today, this knife practically vibrates with it. I do not know precisely what will happen if I touch it. If I lose myself completely, someone might notice.

Someone who might tell my mother.

After hesitating another breath, I reach for it anyway. One day, my curiosity will kill me, mother enjoys harping. Maybe she's right.

As soon as my fingers curl around it, my muscles freeze, my fingers whiten, and black shadows swirl across my eyes. The chatter and noises of the market fade, and a vision sweeps in like a summer storm. I am dragged helplessly into it, eyes squeezed shut.

When I open my eyes, I am in an unfamiliar body, still feminine but older and softer. I stand inside a strange house with thoughts running through my head that are not my own:

I will die today, and it is not the death I expected for myself. I thought I would grow old and drift away, awash in scented oils and surrounded by candles and several children and grandchildren. They would sit around me, chummy and nostalgic, passing a bottle of wine while declaring their adoration for me in happy, convincing voices. Every year, they would visit my grave on the anniversary of my death with fresh flowers and fuss just enough over removing the matted leaves from my final resting place while I look in satisfaction upon them from the ancestral realm. Alas, I will die today with no scented oils, no wine, and no reverent grave for visitors. No one to remember me.

Under the saber-toothed moon, the heavily-armed attackers descend upon the village, and the rumors of their brutality prove unexaggerated. From the window, I flinch as the attackers set mud and straw homes ablaze, moving hastily down the row. As the flames lick at the sleep-disturbed inhabitants, they dash into the streets where shadowy figures with crossbows and sabers wait to sow death among them. On a mission of discretion, the foes also rip holy beads from dead necks, dump incense into the dirt, and bash the modest temple into dust with their heavy blades. The screams and wails shake my nerves, and the smell of burning flesh sends my stomach tumbling, but I force myself to calm. Volatile emotions mean unstable magic.

I push away from the window and into the arms of my partner and love, Jaali. He presses his forehead against mine, raking his hands through my coiled hair. I close my eyes for just a moment, savoring the closeness and his smell, knowing the finality in it. Between us, cradled to my chest in a basket, is our daughter.

"Jaali," I choke, unable to stop my tears.

"Amaka," he whispers my name like a song. "Run."

He releases me. Eyes burning, I charge out the garden door and into the scrubby brush. As quickly as I can, I dart through the trees. Somewhere in the distance, I hear smashing and shouting. Heat flashes at my back. Our home is on fire; my partner's death weighs on my heart. I trust Jaali offered me enough of a start to reach the gully and the river with our little girl, who has begun to wail loudly in fear. I will not fail either of them.

With every crack of a branch, my chest squeezes tightly. The countryside, thinned by the recent winds, leaves us exposed as the roaring wall of fire scuttles after us. Before long, I hear the mad thrashing gallop of sharp-fanged warcats moving at neck-breaking speed.

An arrow pierces my shoulder, sending me stumbling and gasping, but I have reached the river. I delicately place the basket with my only child into the water and fight against cooing and comforting her as she cries even harder, her eyes round with alarm. I put my hand to her forehead, feeling the magic in my veins stir to life. She quiets as I touch the blood leaking from my side and smear it onto her round cheeks. Then, I give the basket a little push, and it begins drifting downriver in the green water. I trust my magic will guide her to safe hands. Still, I observe her hopefully, praying to our ancestors, until she floats out of sight.

"Please, protect my Nuri," I whisper, putting my fist to my chest.

With a jolt, another arrow hits me, and my body jerks. This time, it lodges firmly in my side. I collapse into the mud on the bank. The arrows must be steeped in poison; from the first, a coldness works through my blood, leaving me writhing and wheezing. As my consciousness begins to float away and black spots dance arrhythmically across my vision, I take shallow gulps of air.

Heavy footsteps stomp through the brush, closer to me. Flames whip around and consume a nearby tree, sparking in the sky as it burns. I cover my face with a wet sleeve to protect my blistering eyes from the flying embers. Then, my hands twist into fists as I hear a man (or breast) move heavily nearby. Despite the crackle of the flames, I overhear each branch snap as he moves closer and closer still. I inhale another shallow breath and close my eyes. For comfort and with considerable effort, I jam my hand into my pocket and rubbed my thumb against my knife's sharp edge, though I do not have the strength to wield it. Heavy footfalls land nearby again. So close by, they scatter my pulse in every direction.

Through the smoky haze, I finally squint into the paranormally bright hazel eyes of my attacker, a young brute by his build wearing black—black armor, cloak—and a crass collar of stained bone and teeth around his neck. He shoves his crossbow into a casing on his back and pulls out his sickle. Behind him lurks a red dragon with its lone yellow eye, prowling, fixated on me. I cannot move; the poison paralyzes me, leaving me unable to draw in a breath, as though pinned to the bottom of a lake, stones tied to my wrists and ankles. My heart pounds with the intensity of a thousand bougarabou drums as I await my fate.

My attacker grins widely, and it turns my stomach. Despite the paralyzing poison, I tremble; my tribe is reduced to ash by this evil brute and his ilk. I turn away, gasping and blinking rapidly. I want him dead with every fiber within me, but I do not have enough magic left. I smile through the unbearable pain, hoping it haunts him until his dying day.

He lifts his sickle, but I do not give him the satisfaction of the kill. I call upon what little pops of magic I have left. As it becomes concentrated, it glints off my skin and flirts with the air.

I stop my own heart before the blade can pierce me.

Blinking rapidly, I drop the knife. My frozen heart warms to beating again.

There only a moment ago, the river shifts back into Arifin's sandstone street. The burning, crackling trees swing into life as vendors, selling an eclectic collection of goods from their stores and carts. The sounds and smells of the Kähari marketplace push in from all directions, growing louder and stronger until my vision dissipates into the air. I suck in a breath as my hands meet the reassuring silky fabric of my purple and gold print dress. I exhale the sea-laden breeze deeply as everything around me hazily falls into sharp focus. Directly in front of me, the long-bearded vendor with a scar down his cheek is waving his fingers to jolt me. His red-bellied parrot, perched on the cart, glares at me too. I hope I have not been haunted for long.

Then, the vendor squints, and his expression snaps in alarm. He eyes my finely-made dress and sandals and closely examines my thick, coiled locks and uneven pattern of freckles. Nausea flutters in the pit of my stomach.

"Daughter Mäzzikim *Ka* Kähari," he guesses, unsure.

"No," I say, pasting on a smile. I borrow the name from my vision. "My name is Nuri."

Typically, neither vendors nor customers on Arifin Street notice or question me; they attend to their own indecent business. But this man is shrewder than his colleagues. He sets his jaw and glances this way and that for an escort, nanny, servant, or guard, but finds no one. He knows a woman as young and important as a Chieftain's daughter would not be alone. Luckily, I ditched my annoyingly intrusive guard before I ventured into Arifin.

Tilting his head to the side, he addresses me again. "Your eyes—"

"It is a rare health condition," I cut in smoothly with the excuse my mother prefers. "Sometimes the heat makes me feel ill, but I am fine now."

Edgy about his line of questioning, I avoid his gaze. "Where did you find this knife?" I inquire, gingerly picking it up again and feeling the magic prickle at my palm.

"Pretty piece, isn't it?" the vendor replies, his eyes aglow with the prospect of a sale. "I found it in the Outlands, washed up in a river."

Probably a lie, but I expect as much from an Arifin vendor. It only makes the mystery—the adventure of discovery—more thrilling. I wait for him to name his price.

"It is yours for only two pieces of silver. Quite the bargain," the vendor declares.

Quite obscene, frankly, but I reach for my coin purse. The knife practically hums with the soul intertwined with it. I cannot leave it behind. He eagerly counts his profit and then wraps the knife in thick paper. After thanking him, I pocket the knife and move back into the crowd. With a lightness in my chest, I hurry to Nadu, the next street over, where it will be more acceptable to be noticed by someone who matters. It is also more crowded, and despite the heat, the merchants remain relentless. They hover, sweat, and hawk brightly colored linens, fruits, salted meats, intricate bursts of flowers, gowns, vases, hair oils, and sandals.

"You'll never find brighter colors!"

"Curry that even your mother will love!"

The buyers, more subdued and skeptical, mill around the carts and weigh needs and desires against the coins in their purses. I already bought what I need from this part of the market, so when I reach the corner, I whistle. From a nearby alleyway, my outsized melanistic panther, Helissi, lumbers up.

I clamber onto my warcat and command him through the unruliness market. In spite of the bedlam, eyes linger on me. They stare at me because I look like a noble; gawk at me because I am riding an animal meant for warriors. So long as they do not notice my magic, I do not mind. Today, I am lucky they cannot see it. The vision sits with me; the death in my body, vibrating beneath the skin where the arrows buried their hilt, the poison drifting through the blood towards my heart—even with the knife wrapped in parchment and buried in my pocket.

Then a noise louder than the market hubbub raises the hair on the back of my neck to attention. I pause Helissi and look over as four heavy-set camels pull a prison wagon—sleek, stark, and gray—into view. The stony-faced patrolman rings the heavy bell so that people step aside. Naturally, most scurry away like cockroaches at first light. However, even while clutching their purchases to their chests, some curious people try to peer into the tiny, barred windows. A few heckle and hiss at the wagon; children follow suit, tossing stones from the road. Feeling my leg muscles tighten, I start to guide Helissi to a side street to keep my distance.

To my alarm, the patrolman abruptly pulls the wagon to a stop. Everyone freezes and flinches as he stalks through the crowd towards an older woman selling miracle ointments. She trembles as he picks up her potions one at a time. He pauses with a bottle of a violet liquid in hand. His eyes remain fixed on the woman as he takes the bottle, uncaps it, and pours it into the street. Hazy purple steam rises from the ground. I do not know what that proves, but the patrolman thinks he does.

"*Magic!*" he declares loudly, smashing the bottle on the cart.

The terrified woman cries, claiming innocence, begging for mercy. I know she will be afforded none; she was too brazen and should have stayed in Arifin, where the buying and selling are subtle and subdued. Patrols usually do not openly raid the market, but lately my father, Chieftain Oko, has been adamant about cracking down on the rise of dangerous magic in our clan nation. Mage or not, the woman will be taken to a place called Iboji, where she will live as a slave, die—or both. I want to leave, but I cannot stop watching.

The patrolman grabs the older woman and drags her to the wagon. He binds her thin wrists to the bars and then returns to the gaudy cart with his club. He smashes the other bottles, which explode in clouds of every color of the rainbow, while the crowd looks on, jeering their approval.

A priest bellows from the steps of a nearby temple. "Shame! Shame and damnation! Magic is the work of demons!" he chants. Others join in.

I am sure I saw that priest frequent the woman's cart before. Say something, my heart implores as I move jerkily away from the scene. But I have magic much more potent than the potions in those bottles; the class of magic that sparked the Chaos. I may be the daughter of a sovereign ruler, but in Kähari, fear of magic runs deeper than loyalty to the crown.

My mother taught me that, and the scars on my back remind me of those lessons.

I swallow my protests and urge Helissi to move faster.

I move farther from the street markets into a rural, less affluent area— Omiki, my birthplace. I smell and hear the sea rushing up against the nearby shores of rock and sand. As I ride, I pass a determined trio of men heading for the fishing boats. Outside round tents and modest clay homes, women cook and gossip. Children pick fruit in between chasing and teasing each other. A handful of nosy elders look on, offering unsolicited critiques of all they survey.

"Good afternoon, Mazzie!"

My grandmother, Funani, greets me warmly when she opens her wooden door with one hand and leans heavily on her hued cane with the other. A disease called quell forces Funani's use of the cane (though certainly at her age, my grandmother likely also struggles with other yet unnamed health conditions). Though I worry about her, my body relaxes, and the anxious buzzing in my mind dulls as I step into her home.

My grandmother's house can fit inside my chamber at the Palace; however, she strongly prefers living in Omiki in near anonymity. A small house is better suited for intimate conversations, she would say often. Frankly, my grandmother's house has many structural shortcomings beyond its size, but her floors, made of special wood, warm gently to the touch of a bare foot; her furniture, painted and carved whimsically with rainbows and suns. When I was a very young girl, my grandmother claimed that she bought it for a single copper piece from a band of traveling faeries—one of her many entertaining stories. My grandmother's home is a sanctuary; her soul, refreshingly bright, fills it whole.

She peers curiously behind me. "Where's your guard? Does the poor man want something to sip?"

I blink innocently. "Oh, yes, *him*. He would not have approved of the vendors I frequented today, so I ditched him in the market. I trust he'll find his way home."

"Maze, you promised me that you would do that slightly less. You're going to make this one twitch, too." My grandmother massages a little line in her forehead. "And Nanny Ododo?"

"Oh, she quit weeks ago. Described me wickedly. Tossed about words like 'odd' and 'ornery' and 'too old.' Mother must have *finally* decided I was old enough not to have a Nanny. Or she ran out of people to hire. I am not certain of which..."

My grandmother tuts but smiles. "Mazzie, you cannot run off on your own no matter how old you get. It's not safe. Not when you are Daughter of Chieftain."

"No one recognizes me anyway," I quip.

With a shrug, Funani does not press on my lie. I clear my throat and unload most of my purchases onto the table. "I've brought rice bread, fish, and rum, and that tea you like."

Leaning heavily on her cane, my grandmother hobbles over and picks up the bread. She holds the loaves to her nose with her dark, wrinkled hands and breathes deeply.

"Praise the gods, new *and* old."

There are lots of gods in the realm. Old (fallen) gods, the ones followed by the ancient tribes. Sun gods, moon gods, god of love, god of rain, god of fertility—so many gods. New gods, people—powerful humans—immortalized by history. My grandmother once told me that the gods created human beings to serve them, but the realm of the living held too many challenges for them. In turn, the old gods created mages in their likeness and blessed them with unique strengths and powers to fully embrace the realm's bounty.

I never really believed that story, having seen how mages suffer. Either the gods forgot about their special creations or they never existed. Because of my magic, my grandmother talks often of Kipporah, goddess of death. She believes Kipporah blessed me with this magic. As it certainly has never felt like a blessing, I am not convinced of the existence of a single god, but my grandmother praises all of them "just in case."

My grandmother exhales happily. "You must have bribed the baker for loaves this fresh. Please, do not tell me how or with what. I wish to enjoy them properly and without guilt."

"I cannot keep secrets from you. I showed him my tits—one for each loaf."

"Know your worth, I always say."

While I make tea, my grandmother carefully smears both sides of the bread with honey and goat butter and fries them in a pan. I wish she would let me do it for her, but she always insists. Once finished, she puts the basket of hot sweet bread on the table while I fill the tin mugs. It is our ritual.

I ask, "How are you feeling?"

Smiling, my grandmother answers in a similarly casual and elusive way. "You can only expect so much reward in this life, and I feel nothing but pure bliss while I eat this bread."

"Father is worried about your health," I warn, clearing my throat. "I heard him talking to mother about it. He prefers that you live with us at the Palace."

Truthfully, it was an explosive argument, the most recent battle in a long, cold war. My grandmother's refusal to move to the Palace when my father was anointed as Chieftain *Ka* Kähari is a constant source of contention between my parents. The tension grows with my grandmother's declining health. Grandmother Funani wrinkles her nose and smacks her lips thoughtfully. "That worrying son of mine. You will tell them that I am fine."

"Oh?" I raise my eyebrows. "Is that the truth?"

"It is *a* truth." Smiling, she polishes off her piece of bread and just as swiftly changes the subject. "Now, what *else* did you find at the market today?"

This is also our ritual. I reach into my dress pocket, pull out the knife, and unwrap it. "A street vendor had this in his cart. When I picked it up, I experienced a vision, a bit more involuntary than usual, and there were other oddities about it."

"How do you mean?"

"Just parts that did not make sense. It was a woman, and there were attackers and a *dragon*. I don't know. It is already a bit foggy." I wrinkle my nose. "Dragons don't exist. At least, not anymore—if they ever did."

"There are plenty of dragons. Your mother, for instance. You witnessed her blowing fire many times, wouldn't you agree?" My grandmother grins wickedly.

I roll my eyes and snigger.

My grandmother picks up the handle and examines the markings. Then, she reaches into her dress pocket and pulls out a pair of wired spectacles. Looking very much like an owl, she turns the knife over and over in her wrinkled hands. A flicker of recognition crosses her face, but it disappears so instantly I think I may have imagined it.

"I wish I could tell you what these symbols mean, but I'm just not that well-read." My grandmother puts the knife back on the table and slides it over to me. "Perhaps ask your new tutor when he arrives? What's his name again? Bean? Lentil?"

"Letaro." I am more focused on the vision. "No one has seen anything resembling dragon in centuries upon centuries, just vague hypotheses. Even if they once existed, the science is clear: people and dragons, they never *coexisted*," I declare firmly. "Further, the dragon, it was as it if was working on behalf of the attackers, as if it were controlled by them. If this took place during the Chaos, which I suspect, I imagine the *magicians* would control the dragons."

"Another lesson important to your rapidly impending adulthood. Not witnessing something *yourself* does not mean it does not exist." Grandmother Funani wiggles her eyebrows. "You of all people should know that."

"But not just me," I protest, pressing my palms to the table. "Renowned scholars—"

My grandmother's eyes dance and sparkle. "Renowned by whom? Mazzie, history is kept by those with access to the fastest pen and the darkest ink. While I have no doubt that a dragon would not prefer to lurk around a well-populated nation, I would not be overly surprised if they live, relatively unbothered, in the Outlands—and dragons are certainly *not* extinct in the Trench."

I sigh in frustration. "I am far too old for tall tales."

"Indulge me, dear. I am a sick, old woman, and I do what I like."

"I'm sure you've told me this story already," I protest.

She clears her throat theatrically. "Then perhaps you'll hear something new this time."

My grandmother leans forward. "Once upon a time, humanity and mages peacefully co-existed. Then came the Chaos; forever wars without clear enemies or purpose. Wild. Messy. Upon witnessing the Chaos, it is said that the old gods abandoned their creations—leaving humans to reign this brutal world. To prevent the return of magic, the practicing tribes were banished to the southernmost point of the realm, a place far below sea level—referred to in tales as the Trench of the Demons. Tough to find. Hard to get in. Thought to be impossible to get out."

There is something undeniably enchanting about my grandmother's voice. She reminds me of the traveling storytellers—griots—who share news of the realm with the poorer villages, where most cannot read. Unable to help myself, I hang off her every word.

"In the Trench lived fire-breathing dragons, hulking mammoths, dire wolves, and other magical beasts and peoples. They all fought and pinned for escape, prayed to their lost gods, but there they stayed for centuries until they forgot they were imprisoned," my grandmother continues with animated hands.

"One day, a powerful little "demon" found his way into the Trench and reminded them. He used his magic, bestowed upon him by the gods, to lift the Trench and free the people. However, it was not the homecoming their ancestors sought. Upon setting foot outside the Trench, they lost their magic and could not defend themselves against the greatest predator of all."

She pauses for a sip of her tea (and likely dramatic effect, as is her style).

"What's the greatest predator?" I ask, indulging her.

"So-called civilized humans, of course." My grandmother winks at me and pours some rum into her tea. "Told you it would be different this time, didn't I?"

Again, I roll my eyes, and fear they may roll out of my head altogether by the end of this visit. I have heard so many versions of this story. Sometimes, the Trench is a refuge. Sometimes, a cage. Sometimes it is in the stars; sometimes it is underwater. Sometimes there is a happy ending; other times, the story ends with blood. I trust my grandmother with my magic. I wish she trusted me with the truth.

"You're pulling one on me again," I complain.

"Perhaps I jest, my dear, with just another old tale from an old woman. But I will remind you of this: your vision is the woman's *memory*. A memory is never absolute truth—only one version of it. Just because she *thinks* her enemy was a dragon does not necessarily mean it *was* a dragon."

"I mean, I suppose."

"She could've been fighting an enormous goat with spicy breath for all you know."

I snort out my tea.

We talk about politics of other clans (pondering the cause of the water crisis in the Ohia nation of Ganju, lamenting the anti-mage laws recently passed in Ogun), bread, and funny names for a pet dragon (hotly debating Spark as an option and then dismissing it for being too on the nose). My grandmother asks about my older sister, Ewatomi, and whether plans had been made for her coming-of-age Hathi celebration. She asks about her son, my father, and I tell her that he is grumpy as usual. She does not ask about my mother, and I do not mention her either.

"You should be getting home, Mazzie. Plenty of other beasts to be worried about out there—most of them on two legs," my grandmother warns after considerable time has passed.

She's right. I ditched my guard ages ago and it will be dark in a few hours.

Once outside, I climb back onto Helissi, who had been sunning himself on the sandy front stoop (and frightening the neighbors' goats and chickens).

"If your guard boy comes, I am telling him you went home. Don't make me a liar, Mazzie," my grandmother calls before closing her door.

I glance northward. In the distance, I see Kähari's potentate Palace rising out of the rocky crag above the confluence of the sea and northern river. The Palace, the most distinctive, sprawling homes in the Käharian empire, features grand, sand-dusted white stone, intricate gold trim, blue-green mirror pools, and stone statues commemorating past monarchs and gods—all surrounded by coconut palms swaying gently against the pastel-tinted skies.

My eyebrows furrow as I look to the west—toward the Outlands, and perhaps if I ride far enough, answers to the questions raised by the knife. The sun has not dipped too low yet—there might be time for an adventure. My mother rarely seeks me out (thankfully); my father's advisors, council and other influential nobles require his constant attention; and my older sister thinks I am a bore because I prefer books to people.

I suck my teeth with indecision. If I discover evidence of a dragon, it would be a stunning discovery for science—and a gateway to the life in academia I had always envisioned for myself. Perhaps that particular dragon would appear in books as the *Mäzzikimia Doenisis*. I will tell the story of its discovery in a nonchalant, humble way while students and other scholars (in some academic community far, far away where public discussion of magical creatures is allowed) alike hang on my every word. Afterward, they might offer to buy me a drink in a local tavern (I will demure humbly but eventually agree, I decide).

The woman from the vision might have hailed from one of the lost tribes. Maybe the discovery would lead to the infamous Trench of Demons. I would turn the realm on its head to put facts to that old tale. Maybe I would discover the origins of the Chaos, the mysterious event that shaped the realm as we know it, but historians have yet to adequately explain. In moments, I am caught up in the possibilities. So, pulse quickening, I travel westward.

Helissi and I ride for a while, through fields of fruit trees and then through a hidden underpass, a little-known mining tunnel that dwarf spirit showed me years ago (granted, the dwarf had died in the tunnel, so I always proceed with caution). The tunnel enables me to bypass the front gate, where a guard would certainly recognize and stop me.

We press through the brambles at the other end and cross into the Outlands, which warrant some explanation. The Outlands are extraordinary because they are tainted with magic from the Chaos. The magic runs deep in the soil, and so the mountains, valleys, rivers, and lakes—they *move*, transform, wobble, and wrinkle with the moon cycles. The land is only still under the full moon; when the moon changes, the Outlands change with it.

So, I could travel to the same coordinates but at the next full moon, instead of a canyon, I might find a river delta. Instead of a jungle, I could find myself wandering in a desert. Mapmakers eventually gave up; a map will tell you if you are *in* the Outlands and when you are *not*—and little else. Further, the Outlands are home to bizarre, biodiverse species of fauna and flora, some outsized and dangerous, not seen anywhere else. Thus, it is uninhabitable (particularly by humans who apparently wilt when forced to adapt abruptly).

I recognized the wide, choppy river I saw in the vision because I saw at least part of it before, years ago. At least, I know where it *was*; I have no idea where it is now. It might not even be a river anymore—in the Outland ripples, perhaps it dribbled into spurting brook (I pray not, as locating it will be impossible). But the moon should still be full tonight; if the merchant found the knife recently, perhaps the river isn't far from where it used to be.

My eyes scan the countryside, looking for the distinctive clearing from the vision, which I hope will offer a clue. Things change in the Outlands, but some elements stay fundamentally similar. The appearance of the trees, for instance, no matter what kind; the magic travels through the phloem and bursts into the outer bark as a glistening layer, omitting a muted sparkle when caught in the light, and when Outlands trees shift, they move together like a family as in a free-flowing dance.

Sweat beads and rolls down my forehead. Helissi starts to slow and growl in discomfort as we move through the muddled wilderness in the rapidly dwindling sunlight. I face long odds in finding the location of the vision, but waiting even one more day may mean I have lost my chance because the moon is changing. Still, the Outlands can be quite dangerous at night and the sun sets quickly, so there is never enough time; today may be no exception. Although my rarely family dines together, eventually someone will notice I am not at the Palace; sooner or later, my guard will confess he lost track of me.

"Just a little longer," I murmur, stroking Helissi's fur.

Then, I see a small child, lying face down in mud some distance away. Heart sinking, I immediately pull a skittish Helissi to a stop and slide off his bare back. To my relief, I shakily pick up a flax-threaded wooden doll from the muddy ground. Although the doll's yellow dress is pristine, one of her brown glass eyes is shattered. Then, glancing around, I observe tents, torn like slaughtered beasts, with their innards spilling onto the ground.

No birds chirping or locusts droning. The air sits perfectly still. Rooted to the spot, I peer around cautiously. My primary concern is wild dogs, secondarily a humpback lion even; but nothing emerges from the brush and golden ferns. Enchantment hums in my body, so I hold the doll to my chest, close my eyes, and prepare to reach out to any lingering spirits. They rush to me; soul-curling screams fill my head, and nausea rolls up my throat.

"What are you doing here?"

I practically leap clear from my skin and the impending vision. A man with a naturally scowling mouth, a scar from the top of his left eyebrow down to his cheek, and long, dark dreadlocked hair stalks towards me.

"Who are you? What do you want?" I counter defensively.

"What do *I* want?" he practically spits at me in disbelief. He towers over me intimidatingly, his large hands twisted into fists. "I want *you* to *go*."

I bristle. "Do you know who I—"

He scowls. "Who *you* are is not germane to what *I* want. Go. It's not safe here."

My eyes dart over the man's aggressive tattoos wrapping around every visible part of his enormous body. This man is an Ojo, an anointed class without alliance to any clan nation that protects the Ohia Realm. Ojos are beyond human—superhuman—in knowledge, deduction, and combat. Some people have never seen one; they move almost invisibly through the realm. However, given my father's position, I see them quite often—usually for testimonies before the realm's Congress of the Great Clans or Kähari's elder council. Never like this, in the Outlands where I am not supposed to be. Sweat beads on my lip. Will he tell my mother?

Forcing the quiver from my voice, I raise my chin. "I demand to know what happened here!"

Two dark eyes glow from his face and rake over me as he smirks in amusement. I am the daughter of the Kähari Chieftain; he will not dare hurt me. Yet, a tiny flicker of doubt shoots up my spine. Would he? I draw in a trembling breath, and my loyal warcat Helissi lets out a low growl behind me. If I command it, Helissi will attempt to rip the man's throat out; but even if Helissi managed it, severe consequences wait for those who harm an Ojo.

"Go home," the Ojo advises decisively, ripping the doll from my hands. "You shouldn't be in the Outlands. Nothing will protect you—not your cat or your title. Understand?"

When I did not move, he snaps, "Go—before I drag you back myself!"

Forcing my legs into action, I stiffly mount on Helissi and urge him forward. Over my shoulder, I see the Ojo examining at the campsite. He looks calm and calculating as he takes in the scene, and he moves like some sort of giant predator come to life. He has killed, indeed, for the good of the realm. He has seen things—seen death, perhaps more than I have.

Atop Helissi, I ride back to Kähari at break-neck speed, putting as much distance between myself and the ruined camp and hostile Ojo as I can.

CHAPTER
Two

When my family first moved into grand Kähari Palace, I was young. At the time, I did not understand the significance of my father, a mere fisherman, being selected as Chieftain *Ka* Kähari. When we arrived, I was captivated. After all, it is an enormous four-hundred-year-old Palace with hundreds of rooms, each more decorated with elegant furniture and bold art than the last, several gardens filled with fruits, trees, fountains, and flowers, and a park for field games—a home of dreams. As we walked through the tall doors, I understood that my family was forever changed.

My enthusiasm dulled slightly when my mother warned me not to poke around. What was the point of so many rooms, then? But I cheered again that first evening when a servant, dressed smartly in a new uniform, brought chicken, fresh bread, and curry to eat along with hot tea. I ate my fill with food leftover, a novel experience, while the servants rushed around to clean after me, calling me "your grace." I held my chin a little higher.

Then I met my first (I say first as I have been through quite a number) nanny, Nanny Okeya, a large, disagreeable-looking woman with pale skin, thin, graying hair, and gray eyes. My mother nearly wept with joy when she learned she no longer needed to care for me, but I did not like Nanny Okeya at all. That first night in the Palace, she attempted to braid my disagreeable hair, which ended in a tearful tantrum. When the nanny tucked me into bed, she tried to kiss me on the cheek, but I squirmed out of reach (in my defense, she smelled like dirty clothes and fish, and her lips were dry as parchment).

After the nanny left the room, I turned over to gaze out of my expansive windows. It had just begun to rain, and water streamed down the panes, almost poetically obscuring the view of the sea. Even though I was Daughter of Chieftain Mäzzikim *Ka* Kähari, and as important as a person as I would ever be in my life, and living in a grand house with hundreds of rooms with family and more servants than I could count, a thickness grew in my throat. It did not feel like home. However, Kähari, and especially the Palace, might be a lonely place for me—but it also means safety.

You need more context, I think. Here it is: Centuries ago, tribes of humans built walls and mastered the enclosed land and its elements. We built lives; raised banners; created order called Clans. However, in the Outlands, we found limits. Sometimes we forget these limits, having solved the mysteries within the walls of the stable lands. Growing bored, we venture into the Outlands only to have the ground shift and shake ceaseless beneath their feet until our grip is lost.

Perhaps the ground did not shift on me today, but the abandoned camp and the angry Ojo certainly shook me. So, I race back towards the Palace, moving through the countryside atop Helissi. My thighs burn with pain and sweat pours, without prejudice, down my forehead. I do not slow; my heartbeat sets our pace. I curse myself. I am sixteen years old, nearly an adult, but my childish curiosity continues to plague me.

Maybe my grandmother is right. I should stop ditching my guard.

Finally, I reach the garden entrance, where I encounter my guard, Abrar. He mutters to the other guards and the bearers of my palanquin in low, harsh tones—until he spots me. Despite his apparent strength, Abrar sags in relief when he sees me. Then shock, anger, and bewilderment crisscross on his hawk-like face while the other guards exchange knowing glances. Everyone knows how slippery I am—everyone but Abrar, an incredibly skilled but a newly minted officer of the royal guard, which is part of why he got the difficult assignment of protecting me in the first place. My parents felt positive, upon his hiring, that Abrar could handle me. Now, Abrar has learned not to allow my warcat to accompany my outings.

By the color draining from Abrar's face, and I am assured he will not tell my parents he lost track of me. Such an admission would put him considerable danger, and he knows it.

Abrar hisses, practically spitting. "Your grace, I searched the market for you all——"

"Not now," I insist, climbing off Helissi and pulling down my hood. I try in vain to pat down my hair. "Return Helissi to the stables, please."

Without waiting for a response, I hurry away.

"You're going to get me killed!" Abrar calls after me. "Your damn cat doesn't like me!"

"In that case, do try to hurry—Helissi is famished, and you know how he gets tad nippy when he's hungry," I reply sunnily, pulling open the door.

I tear into the bustling kitchen with twigs in my hair and mud and sweat staining my dress. The servants do not notice me (or do not care); instead kept to their chopping, spicing, and frying. They often witness my bizarre interruptions and entrances from the serving door, which I often used to avoid my mother. Before striking for the backstairs, I claim a banana from the fruit bowl and drop it into my other pocket.

"MÄZZIKIM! I know you're in there!"

My jaw clenches; my mother's roar, unmistakable. Sweating copiously, I will myself to be either be faster or invisible or both. I hear my mother, Chieftess Farida *Ka* Kähari, burst into the kitchen. The power of invisibility instead of necromancy would be useful now, so I sink down, hastily praying to the gods I barely believe in.

My mother twinkles like a brilliant emerald star in a green and gold gown that glows against her bronzed skin. Around her neck, a high, diamond-adorned collar, and atop her head, a matching turban. From the excessively ornate collar, I know Clan Kähari has guests for an engagement that I forgot about, that these guests are important—and that I am *horribly* late. I hope against hope that she does not see me.

My mother rarely enters the kitchen. Once my father Oko was chosen as Kähari's ordained chieftain and ruler, even *seeing* household chores became *far* beneath her. Thus, the shocked servants immediately stop all cooking operations and bow or kneel, sinking low to the floor. I must have prayed to the wrong gods; their movement makes it that much easier for my mother to see me on the stairs. Her eyes, scanning the room, find her prey instantly. Awkwardly, I stand, tottering a little on the stairs, a baby antelope unable to defend itself from the coming slaughter.

"You're a mess," my mother snaps in annoyance. "Your hair—what are you wearing? Weren't you supposed to be at the temple? What, have you fallen out of a damn tree? You're not clean enough to spit on! Where have you been? Look at you there, hiding like a fool-born coward! You're too old for this, Maze!"

A less knowledgeable person would take my mother's words as a virulent assault. I consider it a greeting. I theorize my mother was never a child; instead, she had burst into the world fully grown, a bit bitter, and very determined. As the story goes, my mother, Farida, was the most beautiful woman, a lesser kind of nobility, in our village. My father dared ask her parents for her hand; her parents reluctantly consented because at least Oko owned a boat. Very romantic, don't you agree?

Anyhow, I respect and love my mother, in that precise order. I am also fully accustomed to my mother's rage; I know to let my mother finish her tongue-lashing before bothering to respond.

Glaring, my mother crosses her arms. "I want an explanation, Mäzzikim!"

Knowing full well that no explanation will satisfy, I hang my head in disgrace and hurriedly stammer, "I'm sorry, mother. Very sorry. I went to the market for Funani, and then I lost track of time visiting her."

My mother's eyes narrow further. "I will speak to Abrar. It is his duty to—"

"Please do not blame Abrar. It is my fault, and it won't happen again," I gracefully interrupt, standing back up. "I'll go wash up."

Then, I realize that my mother is not alone. A young man wanders into the kitchen, following her (or her outburst). My mother follows my gaze and seems mildly surprised that he stands there but recovers quickly. I cannot help but smile. I will not be further admonished in front of a guest, especially one unrelated to family or belonging to our clan. It would be unseemly, and reputation is everything to my mother, who clears her throat and forces a smile onto her exquisite face (a smile that, notably, does not reach her cold eyes).

"Bosede, this is Mäzzikim, my youngest daughter. Maze, this is Bosede, eldest son of the Chieftain of Ogun," Chieftess Farida explains reluctantly.

I search my mind, recalling that the Ogun clan are known for metal, iron, coal, and frighteningly efficient weapons. For his part, Bosede, tall and well-built with curly with black hair, matching beard, and cynical but laughing eyes, wore a neatly-pressed blue and gold tunic with slacks and a wry smile. His eyes met mine, mirroring my half-hearted scrutiny.

"Charmed," I offer, bowing my head slightly.

Embarrassed, actually. I smell like a woolly elephant.

"The pleasure is mine," he answers politely.

"He came to observe his father in Congress and meet *Ewatomi*," my mother adds pointedly.

My sister Ewatomi has an ethereal bearing impossible to ignore. Some even say that she is the most beautiful woman in the realm; a kind of beauty that happens only rarely so as not to destroy everyone else's self-esteem. Contrary to me, she takes after both of our parents, but *only* their most attractive features. Our mother's long legs and command of a room. Our father's high cheekbones and charm. I got the bits that Ewatomi refused to claim in the womb—my mother's flat feet and my father's large nose, for instance.

I reply, "I apologize for my appearance. Again, nice to meet you, Son Bosede *Ka* Ogun."

"No apologies needed, Daughter Mäzzikim," he answers smoothly with his ghostly blue eyes boring into mine. Bosede clears his throat and changes the subject. "Tell me, was that *you* racing along the countryside, bare-back on the panther? You are a very talented rider. I've never seen one move quite that fast without tossing its rider."

I freeze in horror as my mother swings her gaze to me and narrows her eyes, resembling a snake. Immediately, I force an innocent beam to my lips and sputter unconvincingly. "No, your grace, certainly not. I always ride at a slow and cautious pace to prevent injury and only in the yard. I was with my grandmother this afternoon, saying prayers."

The servants do not flinch, but I know they will gossip about my lie later. Bosede also senses the temperature in the room drop and changes tack. "Ah, my mistake then. Now that I think about it, the rider looked quite different from you."

Swallowing a raspy breath, I manage to say, "No harm. Please excuse me, I must go wash."

Suspicion drains from my mother's face. "Yes, go wash up, dear. Don't be late *again*." She turns away from me and back to the young man. "You absolutely must hear Ewatomi perform. She has the most wonderful singing voice. Where is that Titus? He will arrange it."

I exhale and sag against the wall. Bosede raises his eyebrows and smirks knowingly at me before following my mother back into the hall. The servants resume their cooking while I, completely and utterly shamefaced, resume my way up the stairs, and journey to my chambers.

After all these years, the Palace still feels astonishingly massive even though my chambers are towards the front, not the back. The upstairs hallway goes on and on with doors to various living chambers, all with their own bedrooms, sitting rooms, closets, wet rooms, and pantries. A few even have their own kitchens. The floors vary from wood, colored tiles, and lush carpets—clear evidence of the many previous owners and their difference of opinion in style. In addition to the noble family, several others of importance live in the Palace: the appointed assistants to the noble family, assigned servants (the remaining help lived in a separate and more modest dwelling beneath the Palace), and several of the top advisors and religious officials too.

"Titus!" I exclaim, seeing my mother's assistant pacing outside my chamber door. "My mother is looking for you."

Titus's gaze swings upward from the floor and he lets out a breath. "Nothing to say for yourself. Perhaps, sorry for stopping your heart, dearest Titus?"

I swallow hard as he casts a heated glare on me.

"Farida is looking for me because *I* was looking for you and failing spectacularly at the tasks," snaps Titus. "Your mother planned an introduction to Bosede *Ka* Ogun, the eldest son of the Chieftain of Ogun, who is perhaps the most powerful man in the realm—"

"I already met him."

Titus halts mid-lecture, and wide-eyed, he shakes his head and twitches a little.

"The Son of Ogun met you in front of your mother with you looking like you napped all afternoon in a field with digestively-distressed cattle?"

I laugh shakily. I often struggle to tell if Titus is truly upset with me or mildly amused.

"You're so dramatic!" I mock, patting Titus on his meaty shoulder. "Yes, I met the Ogun. Mother is taking him on a tour of the Palace, and I happened to be in the kitchen—"

At that, Titus covers his face with his hands and moans.

I sigh and fold my arms. "Are you finished?"

"Are *you*? Praise the *gods* Bosede is not here for you. Your mother wishes to arrange a romantic affair between him and Ewatomi. He is noble, wealthy, and …"

Titus trails off. "Noble and wealthy, and that is what your mother wants for Ewatomi."

"What does she want for me?" I ask, only half-joking.

"If I had to guess, a compulsory bath and a comb."

"Gods, it was not *that* bad. I kept my distance, and she was distracted. I'll bathe and change." I open my door. "I'll be ready before they announce the guests at supper."

"Excellent, thanks, be doing us all a *grand* favor," Titus replies, very sarcastically.

Sighing, I step into my chamber, my beautiful cell in a luxurious prison. It opens onto a broad verandah with a perfect view of the rolling sea through the large windows draped with cream-colored muslin curtains. My feet revel in the soft, thick rug embroidered with rosebuds and intricate gold leaves around the borders. The bed, chairs, and lounges—furniture in Kähari is famous realm-wide for precision and beauty. Each piece is carefully carved from rich cherry wood and then layered with supple cushions. I call it a cell because my mother confines me here like a pet that has yet to learn not to urinate on the carpet.

There are separate but adjoining apartment features rooms for my assigned servants. I have two house girls: Hanya and Imvula, two girls working for free in exchange for room, board, and education at a creche accessible to Kähari nobles.

"Your bath is cold," Imvula frostily greets me. "There is no more hot water."

I have a bell in each room that I can shake when I need something, but I try not to ring the bell for Imvula. By and large, Imvula wears an expression that implies she would shove it, ringing and dinging, down my throat.

Accepting my fate, I enter my wet room and strip. I grimace at the chill but bathe without complaint in the icy perfumed water. Hanya arrives not a moment too soon with a silky robe, which I gratefully shiver into.

"Who are the guests tonight?" I ask Hanya through chattering teeth.

"Your father invited a few of the Great Clan nobles here for a special dinner. Congress actually starts tomorrow, but I hear the real negotiations will be *tonight!*" Hanya squeaks excitedly. "Have you heard about the water crisis?"

I have, but I suspect I know much less than Hanya. Hanya hears everything because no one ever notices her and speak too freely. As such, Hanya is the perfect source for gossip. She adds, "By the time they have the session tomorrow, it will all be decided. Perhaps your mother will let you stay?"

I have never been allowed to stay past dinner, but there is a first time for everything. "Perhaps," I answer with much less optimism.

After some confused muttering about how to tame my hair, Imvula and Hanya set to work to make me presentable. There is not much they can do about my looks, but at least I can vaguely resemble nobility with the right hair, makeup, and clothing.

To pass the time, I wander in my head, pondering the vision again—mostly the bit about the dragon (or abnormally large goat) and my grandmother's mention of the Trench. I suspect—*know*—that perhaps some of my grandmother's tales are not fictional. Maybe they would be dangerous to repeat as a fact. Because otherwise, why wouldn't she just—

I jerk out of a rough grasp. "I've grown quite fond of my hair. Please refrain from pulling it all out."

Lip curling, Imvula pauses in the middle of the scalping and glares at my reflection. Imvula makes an imposing figure, tall and thick as an old tree, and her dark eyes glitter like a fire. Despite our difference in class, I shrink a little in my seat.

"I suppose I can do without a few strands. Carry on," I mutter.

Imvula repays my outburst by roughly dabbing the purple clay around my eyes and across my forehead. I grit my teeth and bear it.

"You need to hurry, your grace," Hanya insists as she rushes up underneath a yellow cloud of a gown. "They're going to serve soon, and your mother will be *furious* if you're late," she adds before ducking into my spare room to find a pair of sandals.

"More furious," Hanya realizes. "Your mother does not smile much."

"Well observed," I agree wryly.

Imvula begins putting the combs and ties back into the basket. "Get dressed, *your grace*."

With a lot of effort and much lacing, Hanya helps me scramble into my dress. She adjusts it carefully to hide the stark white scarring on my back.

"See if your mother got any of those delightful brown butter cakes, your grace," Hanya says as she follows me to the door. "Bring us some please, if that wasn't clear!"

I hurry down the hall, down the stairs, towards the grand hall. Though my mother abhors talk of magic, Chieftess Farida *Ka* Kähari spun the Palace into a mystical place for the dinner. The grand hall opens brightly with a welcome wave of floating twinkly candles high in the vaulted ceilings, thick white powdering of flowers, and gleaming silver goblets and plates on top rows of long tables. People dressed in bold hues, rich fabrics, and glittering gems gradually fill the grand room. The highest society and clan and religious leadership and their offspring, people differing widely in age, character, and dress, from across the realm are in attendance.

I twist my way through the crowded hall, making awkward conversation with the older nobles. As usual, faces light up when they recognized me but then drop with disappointment when I speak. Some avoid me altogether, remembering our previous encounters. Paranoid that they sense my difference, my words come out in stutters and shakes.

Bosede appears at my side. "If I may borrow Chieftess Daughter Mäzzikim?" he asks, smiling broadly, interrupting my clumsy chat with an overly talkative Chieftain Son from one of the smaller clans. Bosede towers over the poor boy in both height and social status. He offers no protests as Bosede firmly takes me by the arm and guides me away.

Although my heart still pounds from my chest, I break into a relieved grin. "Thank you."

"That's twice, your grace." He winks at me and pulls back my assigned chair from the table. "You can repay me by introducing me to the girl I saw riding the panther."

He does not wait for my answer before going to take his seat further down the table. I sit towards the middle of the table between the leaders of the various clans and their younger children and nannies. Ewatomi and Bosede, as the eldest children, sit next to the other realm leaders. It is an honor only enjoyed by the firstborn.

Towards the front of the room, a small troupe of acrobats in sparkling costumes dance, buck, flip, and fly through the air to the rhythm of drums and flutes. The servants serve supper, a true feast of roast wild boars and chickens, salted and buttered rice, roasted tomatoes layered with thick goat cheese, and twisted flatbreads. Unfortunately, I can barely eat any of it with my gown of layers of cascading yellow tulle laced skin tight. Already, my head aches from the tight braids and elaborate violet-colored head jewels that Hanya and Imvula put in my hair, which makes it harder to stomach the bickering conversation with the bratty noble children of other clan nations.

I watch jealously as Chieftess Udo *Ka* Amẹci, an albino woman wearing a headdress resembling a white bear's head, speaks in low tones to my parents, who nod as they sip their wine. I should probably explain—Amẹci is unique. There, humans and mages dared to build a nation together, not by choice, not due to a morally-motivated alliance, but out of pure *necessity*. They needed to build a barrier between them and chaotic shifting elements and landscape, and they required shelter to protect against the brutal cold. If they continued fighting each other, they would all die, so, they stopped. In spite of its unusual roots, Amẹci also has an abundance greatest, most valued commodity of the realm—functional water. Accordingly, Udo is possibly the most powerful person (and certainly the most powerful woman) in the entire realm. For that reason alone, I wish to be in earshot.

Nearby, the ruler of clan Ogun, Chieftain Gye Nyame, with his square jaw and squinty eyes always darting, grumbles inaudibly to his wife. With dull-looking eyes, she nods behind her silk veil now and then. She is his third wife and youngest yet, though I am not sure how I learned that fact in the first place (a passing griot's cloying song, perhaps?). Gye is known to be tight-fisted, sharp as a knife, and ambitious. More significantly, Gye is the third in his family to be named a ruler of his clan, which is a suspicious coincidence considering the rulers are supposedly selected by the demigods via the priests and priestesses. I know little about politics, and I am not religious, but it seems plainly apparent to me that Gye is grooming Bosede to become the next chieftain of Ogun.

My sister nods in the conversation—as if she is *perfectly* comfortable amongst the most important people in the realm, and is not bothered *at all* by the tight lacing of her violet gown. Atop her head of curly hair, Ewatomi wears an exquisite hood of diamonds and gems. I recognize it—one of our mother's headdresses. Ewatomi seems to be moving intentionally so she can sparkle in the light, but surely even *my* vain sister could not be that calculated.

"To what demon have you sold your soul for such exquisite beauty such as yours, Daughter Ewatomi?" Gye asks, leering at Ewatomi's bronze shoulders and pert breasts.

His wife, glancing all over the room, pretends she does not see it.

Uncomfortable or not, Ewatomi does not let on. Instead, she tosses her head and laughs. "No, impossible! But I could say the same about your son. I must assume his beauty is a wicked trick, and he is actually a toad."

Bosede raises his eyebrows and smirks a little into his plate after discovering my arched eyebrow. "You're too kind, Ewatomi."

Bosede, upon closer examination, *does* have a wicked beauty. Firm features, strong chin, striking eyes. He sits straight and tall like a warrior. His lips usually form either a smirk, a line, or a cynical frown but rarely an outright smile—as if he is aware of too much hardship in the world to fully experience joy. He cannot be much older than Ewatomi, but he moves and speaks with the cautious air of someone who has lived a long time.

Gye laughs and points at Ewatomi. "Oho, what a delightful young woman!"

I am distracted from the show when a little boy next to me spits out a chewed up twig of dried thyme. "This food is awful," he declares.

"It is a *garnish*," I correct, recoiling. "Don't they teach manners in your clan?"

"No." He glares at me with his beady little eyes. "In Ogun, manners are for *girls*."

"Sounds like a barbaric place," I mutter under my breath.

"Who *are* you anyway?" the same little boy rudely asks me. He cannot be more than six or seven years old but examined me critically. "Never seen you before. Are you a Nanny?"

"Do I *look* like—" I clench my jaw. "No. I am Mäzzikim *Ka* Kähari, daughter of Chieftain Oko *Ka* Kähari. This is my nation."

"I didn't know Ewatomi had a sister. She never said," he scoffs in disbelief. "It's not *your* nation anyhow. It's your father's and only until he dies. That's why Ogun is so much stronger than Kähari, as a clan and nation. Monarchy—that is the way of the future."

I blink for a moment before realizing who he is. "You're Bosede's little brother. Kwame. Aren't you an... outspoken prat—er, delight?"

Kwame opens his mouth, but thankfully his surly retort is interrupted by the servers, who enter carrying precariously tall cakes of doughy dumplings drizzled in honey and sugar and giant jugs of coffee.

"Yes, well, the water crisis—" I hear someone say, and my ears perk up.

"I'd *hardly* call it a crisis. More of a situation," Chieftain Gye Nyame interrupts, shifting from his flirtation with Ewatomi. A coldness undercuts his light reply. "We have *sent* water."

The polite conversation sharply ends, and jovial sensibilities evaporate from the room. In point of fact, it is funny that words 'politics' and 'polite' share so many similarities, yet the reality of the conversations seem so different I tense, waiting for my dismissal. Based on my seat, I sit right on the line—not a child but not officially considered an adult. Where would I fall today? With little prompting, nannies rush the smaller children away from the table and into a separate room for games; servants begin rapidly clearing the plates. No one removes me.

"Bye, Kwame," I nettle Bosede's younger brother, who glares at me. "Shame about dessert."

Holding my breath, I look at my mother, who shrugs, and I fight a happy beam. Not exactly a glowing endorsement, but, finally, I can stay and listen. I can only hope it means my mother is also considering my Hathi.

"It is gone. It has been an *exceedingly* hot, dry summer. You of all people know that, Gye," Chieftain Hasir *Ka* Ganju replies tensely.

Noticing he has the room's attention, Hasir addresses the table, "People are *dying*. We need to extend a water line—perhaps a man-made river—from Ogun, and we need to do it quickly. Ganju is desert and volcanoes.

We do not enjoy the sea or rivers and our nation does not cool in the winter."

"The economies of the other clans have improved. We'll never find the people willing to build anything stable in the Outlands—not without great expense," protests Chieftess Udo.

"So, you will sentence my people to death because of *the great expense*," Hasir replies scathingly.

Evidently prepared for this conversation, Chieftess Udo straightens up and crosses her heavily ringed fingers in front of her. "Don't be crude, Hasir. It will become you," she warns.

Even I know that Hasir's only chance is to turn one of the powerful clans to his side. The smaller clans will follow like lemmings. I have seen it happen before; just one powerful clan—such as Ameci, Ogun, or even the slightly smaller Kähari—to place itself as an ally of Ganju.

"How will Ganju pay the debt?" Gye asks Hasir sternly as if talking to a disobedient child.

Hasir looks thin and haggard in his cream-colored robes. "We cannot. Not at first, but we will supply the labor. Prisoners. We need supplies, materials, lodging along the waterline..."

I fully expect the other clans to immediately come to Ganju's aid, but they dodge it spectacularly.

"Prisoners? That is *slave labor*," protests the plump Chieftess of Väike. Tossing up her hands, she turns to Udo. "If we provide waterline funds, we will also be inadvertently supporting mass graves for all of those people—on our land, no less."

Hasir bristles. "Our system of justice—"

The Congress of the Great Clan members begin to trip over themselves, asking leading questions, doubling back on Hasir's answers, defining their terms or conditions in such complicated ways that Hasir is forced to admit he does not understand or cannot provide an answer. They bring up old scandals and long-settled disagreements and trap Hasir in contradictions that he does not understand. It seems everyone knows how this conversation will go—except for Hasir. As Hasir grows more cornered, the conversation becomes even tenser and dissolves into familiar tropes and finger-wagging.

"There comes a time when Ganju must help itself—"

"Certainly, we don't want to enable a culture of *welfare*—"

"Perhaps we should focus on the larger problem. It is clear the realm is warming-"

"—forget the actual desperate murderers and thieves and mage enchanters who would be sleeping next door to our families and loved ones—"

I glance at my father, who sits in grim silence. My father, Oko, began life as a warm and optimistic child turned warm, optimistic partner and father who was calm in temperament, satisfied with a modest life, and morally upright. After his selection, a difficult transition for anyone, I suppose, my father became withdrawn and quick to anger. He shed his nativity and warm love of souls like a worn cloak and, instead, put on a crusader's chainmail armor of nationality, power, and justice for Kähari nation.

As the conversation grows increasingly vile, I wait patiently for an opportunity, as I was taught to do as a child, to perhaps share my views and ideas. It is a feminine and youthful art, staying silent. Ewatomi, meanwhile, looks disinterested as she sips her coffee and twirls her hair.

My father used to tell me there is no space for neutrality when someone is suffering. If the space sits empty, darkness fills it. I expect he will say something, but I am disappointed. Eventually, I watch as he leans over and whispers something to my mother. After, the Chieftess Ka Kähari abruptly rises and loudly excuses herself (pointlessly as nobody notices her rise). She makes a beeline for me, and I realize my time has dried up. My dismissal confirms I am not a child, but my mother does not consider me an adult either. Honestly, I do not understand it. If we lived in the fishing village, I would be married by now—perhaps with children on my own (I mean, to be frank, I do not want either of those shackles—but my point stands).

"Maze, come," my mother hisses, grabbing me roughly by the arm. My mother's bony fingers clench like iron cuffs. Wincing with embarrassment, I follow her from the room.

"Please," I beg, once we are on the other side of the door. "You're letting Ewatomi stay!"

I curse myself internally. Sounding like a whining, jealous child will only solidify my position outside the door. I fight myself from declaring

"It's not fair!" and stomping my foot even though I really, *really* want to do it. I believe that's called growth.

"Ewatomi needs to be aware of these politics and make nice with those with influence over the realm. If anything happened to your father and I, gods forbid it, she would have to temporarily serve as Kähari's chieftess until another is chosen and coronated."

I bite my tongue. I am no fool. My mother hopes Bosede and my sister will bond.

My mother, fully committing to her lie, shudders. "Believe me—a country—a continent—the realm can be destroyed with one poor decision. That pressure will never be on you. Consider yourself lucky in that."

I gripe under my breath. "Yes, I am so lucky to be ignored and powerless."

Wistfully, my mother pats at the little lines by her eyes unconsciously. "You should enjoy being young. Youth is so fleeting."

I raise my eyebrows. "So, I should... run along and play then?" I ask lightly.

My mother's eyes dart back at the closed door and then examines me.

"You will go to your chamber. Sleep is good for the complexion," my mother directs.

"Yes, mother." I swallow my final appeal, withering under my mother's heated gaze. No matter how old I am it always affects me the same way, but not long now until I can leave it all behind and start my life as an academic. I must stay patient.

I cannot stop myself from asking, though: "Will there be a waterline to Ganju? Do you think father will support it?"

"Go, you vexing little goblin." My mother goes back inside, closing the door firmly in my face.

CHAPTER
THREE

he next morning, the Congress of the Great Clans is officially in
session. All the leaders of the realm—from chiefs to advisors—gather
in the south wing of the Palace for formal discussions that could take
days. Congress always meets in Kähari; as the first established clan nation
in the realm, it is a well-honored tradition. During each Congress session,
all the guest houses and the Palace overflows with influential people and
their subsequently relevant families.

For most in the realm, it is also high holiday—a celebration of Umoja,
the unity that ended the era of Chaos. It is celebrated with special dinners,
parades, fireworks, and prayers at the temples. My house girls went home
to be with their families, leaving me to figure out how to climb into and
lace my complicated gowns on my own. A problem of privilege, I can
admit, but a problem nonetheless.

After unsuccessfully flopping around like a fish for a while, I opt instead
to wear a buttery yellow jumper and wrap my hair in a silky turban. A
relaxed smile crosses my face. With the clan leaders and their staff observing
Congress, it is peaceful and quiet throughout the Palace—just the twitter
of the birds flitting around by the windows in most of the sunlit rooms. I

do not have any lessons or engagements to attend and the servants serve a hearty breakfast buffet-style, of which I plan to take full advantage. I time it carefully, of course, so I can eat alone and read my book.

"Good morning."

I utter a foul troll curse under my breath. My lips press together in a slight grimace as Bosede *Ka* Ogun strolls into the dining room. "Chieftain Daughter Mäzzikim *Ka* Kähari, we meet again."

"Good morning," I reply awkwardly, shifting my plate, which is stacked embarrassingly high. "Aren't you meant to be in the guesthouses?"

Frankly, I hope it sounds rude. How dare he ruin my solidarity breakfast?

Bosede laughs a little and smiles winningly. "Yes, perhaps I'm *meant* to be. But your mother, she insisted I stay in the Palace proper as her special guest."

I put down my plate at the table and an eager servant scurries over to pour coffee. I wave him off. "I can't imagine why," I reply dryly.

As if on cue, Ewatomi parades by the kitchen entryway in a brand-new gown. with her gaggle of companions and servants and guards in tow. The dress is exquisitely made; dangerously long, blue and purple, trimmed with glittering gems and beads, with feather-like sleeves and matching headdress. She looks like an arrogant peacock.

"Haven't an idea," Bosede replies with equal dryness before tucking in. His plate is also heavy, but with eggs and fried potatoes with curry. I put my book aside and we eat in awkward silence for a few moments. Or rather, Bosede eats. I nervously push my food around the plate and tap the tabletop with my finger.

I clear my throat. "What did you think of the waterline discussion last night?"

Bosede chews thoughtfully before replying. "Complicated."

"Where do you think Ogun will fall? In the official vote, I mean."

"Not in favor."

He grabs a jar of garlic tomato relish and pours a copious amount on his potatoes. "My father never liked that Hasir. Neither do I, if you want the truth."

"I adore the truth, but it *is* the hottest summer on record," I object. "Hasir—he volunteered the labor. If all the nations pool coin together, from where I'm standing—"

"Outside the door?" Bosede asks, raising his thick eyebrows.

He chuckles at my reddening face. "I joke. You're right; it *sounds* simple."

"It does, but you are about to tell me why it's not."

"If you'll allow me."

I shrug and roll my eyes. "Please."

"Much of Hasir's labor is slave labor," he explains patronizingly, either ignoring or not noticing my tone. "In Ganju, people go to prison, sometimes for life, for the most benign, harmless things. We all *know* it but cannot do anything about it. Not our nation. Not our concern."

I cock my head to the side and shake it slightly.

"So, if we provide the funds for the waterline, we will also be inadvertently supporting mass graves for all of those people. They have no rights; he will work them to death, and don't forget the delinquents who will be your neighbors while the line is being constructed."

I open my mouth, but he holds up a finger. I blink and fold my arms across my chest. Punching guests in the face over breakfast is not good diplomatic action.

"So, let's say *we*, Ogun, as the closest to Ganju, provide the labor instead. The economy there and in several of the nations is healthy—simple economics. Not many people want to take on that type of back-breaking work in a healthy economy. We'll need to shell out significant funds, and that increases the cost of the waterline dramatically."

"All right," I say slowly. As annoyed as I am by Bosede's arrogance, I suspect some of the things he describes are true and reasonable. "I'm following."

Pleased to have an attentive audience, Bosede clears his throat; his breakfast temporarily forgotten while I gaze woefully at my eggs and potatoes, wishing there was a graceful way to eat it.

"Furthermore, Hasir has continued to borrow and spend, living a life of splendor in that obscene Palace of his instead of improving his infrastructure and helping his people. Never paying any of the realm back for a lick of it putting the rest of us at risk for his fate."

I open my mouth to argue but stop short. "Complicated," I agree.

"Yes, but I didn't say fair or right because it isn't. It is not the *people's* fault that they were born in Ganju or that they have a corrupt leader." Bosede exhales pompously. "But they will be punished for it, some of them with their lives. It's just the way of the world."

Easy for him to say, but I am unprepared to argue with him. I can admit that I know too little, and he could easily back me into a corner. Worse, I suspect Bosede would find my discomfort satisfying. "So, you're not going to Congress today?" I ask, changing the subject. "I would think your father would have you sitting in—as his eldest son."

"I have an engagement with your sister," he replies.

With light sarcasm, I ask, "Pun quite intended?"

He chuckles and points at me, looking like his father for a moment.

"Your mother arranged a game of umagodi and then I will attend temple with the rest of congress for evening prayer."

"Better let Kähari win. Ewatomi is competitive and carries long grudges."

Bosede laughs. "I'm no fool. I've already advised our team. How will you spend your afternoon?"

"I plan to visit my grandmother and take her to temple for services—if she's up to it. She doesn't care for the prayers, but she enjoys singing."

Afterward, conceivably, I can look for the clearing from the vision and find evidence of a dragon—completely ordinary afternoon activities.

He observes, "You sound close."

"She is like a second mother to me. We spend a lot of time together in her village."

Bosede blinks in surprise. "Your grandmother doesn't live here in the Palace?"

"She refuses. Nothing changes her. It is my favorite thing about her."

Bosede shrugs. "It is just interesting, being she is a noblewoman. My father would never allow that."

I force a smile. "I should go."

"Really?" Bosede glances at my plate. "You've barely eaten."

"I wasn't as hungry as I thought," I answer lightly.

My stomach growls loudly in the *ultimate* betrayal, and an unkind smile crosses his face.

"Enjoy your game," I grumble, rushing away with my book clutched to my chest. I'll sneak back for a biscuit later.

That afternoon, the air shimmers from the heat and intelligent creatures sprint for shelter in whatever shade or hole in the ground that could be found. Heavy, dark clouds quietly shift in from the southern coast. I hire a chauffeured camel-coach knowing my grandmother cannot walk well, and bring Abrar in tow to appease my mother. For Umoja, I will be a dutiful daughter and granddaughter to make up for the disaster yesterday.

As my grandmother lives in a slight gully, the elaborate-wheeled coach (pulled by a small team of camels) cannot make it to her door. My grandmother slowly makes her way down the dirt path with her multicolored cane. With my free hand, I desperately fan myself with a palm leaf I found on the ground. It is dirty but effective.

"Grandmother, I am so hungry," I complain, wiping sweat from my brow with the back of my arm. "Could we please skip temple and get some curry?"

"It's a high holiday, Mäzzikim. Of course, we must attend temple today! We must pray for peace, unity, and prosperity of the realm," my grandmother replies cheerfully.

"Besides, didn't you have breakfast? Breaking your nightly fast is your favorite part of the day, followed by your mid-day meal, then supper—"

"You make me sound like a greedy hyena, to which I take mild offense. Yes, I *went to* breakfast, but I was having a conversation with someone and did not eat very much."

My grandmother smiles knowingly. "Must've been riveting. With whom?"

I mutter my reply, so my grandmother makes a show of putting her hand to her ear. "Oh, I'm sorry, dear. Who?"

"Bosede, Son of Chieftain Gye Nyame *Ka* Ogun." I shake my head. "We were talking about politics—that Ganju waterline—and not for long. Did you know mother has her sights on him for Ewatomi? She even let him stay in the Palace last night."

"Is that so?"

"Yes, can you believe it? I mean, I like him for Ewatomi. He is a bit older but seems bright and well-read. A bit rude and old-fashioned, actually," I ramble.

"I can tell by the tint in your cheeks that he is as beautiful as you are," my grandmother finishes kindly.

I grimace. "Yes, Bosede is a beautiful jerk."

"Most of the beautiful ones are." On cue, my grandmother imparts her wisdom. "Be careful, Mazzie. They may have their Hathis, but boys take much longer to turn into men than girls into women. Everyone is just too scared to tell them so."

I smirk. "Is that a fact?"

"Just the personal observation of every woman to ever live and die in the realm and the next," my grandmother replies wryly. "Besides, your sister Ewatomi—she is a very determined young woman. Much like your mother. Unless you're prepared to—"

Abruptly, my grandmother stares at me in alarm, and then wincing, stops mid-stride, and clutches her chest.

"Oh, dear," she whispers faintly.

"Funani?" My heart tumbles in a freefall.

"Funani, are you—"

Her cane drops into the dirt, and my grandmother falls with it. I rush to kneel beside her and put my hand to her cheek. My magic immediately surges to my palm and a burning pain rages through my body. Funani is dying and I see in her eyes that she knows too.

THE AFTERNOON IS A BLUR. THE GUARDS AND I RUSH MY GRANDMOTHER BACK to the Palace. My father calls in the most excellent doctors in the Kähari from their holiday and shoos everyone from the sick chamber. Outside the chamber, I pace with my father, who looks pale and drawn. Ewatomi holds our mother's hand, and they silently watch the pacing from their perch on a chaise. Two of the doctors offer their empathy and leave. The quell, it settled in Chieftess Mother Funani's vital organs, they say. There is nothing they can do besides make her comfortable. My mother and sister wince and sigh. My chin trembles, and I stare down my hands. A strangled moan escapes my father's throat.

The doctor allows Chieftain Oko to see Funani first; my father goes into the room with his jaw set and fists clenched at his side. My heart breaks. I cannot think of my own pain or cry. My father needs me to stay strong. Letting my heartbreak for him distracts how fractured my own heart feels.

Finally, it is my turn to see her. I take a deep breath, straighten my dress, and go inside.

I move into the dark, stuffy room but nearly cry out in shock when I see my grandmother, thin and pale, lying against thick pillows. Her skin seems nearly translucent, and her chest jolts slightly with every breath. Then suddenly, her large, dark eyes open and focus on me.

I offer a quivering smile and my tears spill down my cheeks.

"Mazzie, your face looks like boiled cabbage," my grandmother scolds.

I snort through my tears. "Sit with me," she commands, gesturing to a lone stool next to the bed. "Mäzzikim, take care of your father," she murmurs once I am seated and slip my hand into hers. "He will need you."

"He has—"

"He will need *you*." My grandmother wets her lips and coughs; we both ignore the alarming little splatter of blood on the sheets.

I rarely speak to my father. It is not that I do not like him, I love him, of course, but I do not *know* him. It is an odd thing to confess not genuinely knowing one's father, but it is the truth. Before being selected as chieftain, my father had been a fisherman. He was warm and kind back then. He smiled more. But now, his advisors, council, and other influential require his constant attention. Chieftain Oko rules the clan and the family as a stone-faced authoritarian who rarely shows emotion besides anger. How could I possibly care for *him*? What did I have to offer?

Death stalks this room. I gaze at my grandmother's discolored fingernails and listen to her labored breathing. Although the magic tingles at the tips of my fingers, I do not need necromancy to know she does not have much time left in this realm. A couple of nights; maybe even less. I bit my lip as I feel my tears burning again.

"I'll take care of him," I promise, finally.

"Good. Now, I am curious. Last night after you left," my grandmother mumbles, her mouth barely moving to form the words. "Where did you go?"

I sniff, wipe at my nose, and try to smile. "For a ride in the Outlands. I saw a ruined tribal camp and an Ojo."

My grandmother's lips upturn. "Was *he* handsome?"

I let out a soft, tearful laugh. "He was scary."

My grandmother struggles to take in another breath, and her eyes roll a little in her head. All of a sudden, she also seems to realize she doesn't have much time left, so she briskly changes the subject, "There's something I'd like you to find. It is for you. You are ready for the truth.

The truth about what? I lean forward to hear her better. "What? What is it?"

"There is a library hidden in the Palace that will help you understand, but you must be careful…no one must know it's here…"

She couldn't be referring to the main library; there had to be another. "Where?"

"Learn everything you can."

"Where is it?" I ask again.

Except it is too late, at least for now. My grandmother's eyes close, and she snores gently, overcome by the opium-laced tonic that the doctors gave her for pain. Her nurse politely shoos me away.

I OPEN MY GUMMY EYELIDS IN THE DARKEST PART OF THE NIGHT BECAUSE I hear singing. I stare at the ceiling for a few moments and then begin to look around the room. Although my first thought is a spirit trying to commune with me, I do not see anyone. Still, I hear someone singing low and beautiful. Curious, I pull on a thin robe over my nightgown and try to follow it. The sound vibrates from deep inside the Palace, echoing through the vast halls. The source is unclear, and I find myself walking in circles.

I go to Ewatomi's chamber and into her bedroom, where my older sister is snoring like an enormous bear. I shake her gently. "Ewatomi, do you hear that?" I whisper.

Ewatomi swats at me as if I am a pesky mosquito. "Go on, go away, noisy little troll," she mutters. "I'm asleep."

"Liar," I quip, but let my sister be.

When I leave Ewatomi's chambers, the singing quiets, and I hear voices downstairs. I wonder if they finally called in a healer, given my grandmother's aversion to 'new-fangled doctoring.' I creep down the stairs, careful not to make a sound, and expertly tip-toe down the hallway until I reach the back parlor. Then, I carefully peer around the corner.

Nanny! My heart drops in shock and horror. Nanny Ododo had quit weeks ago, but there she sits across from my irritated-looking mother at a table. Between them, tea and a conversation that had long gone cold. Why had she returned? Oh god, had she changed her mind? I am not sure I have the energy to terrorize the woman again. I am getting too old for it.

Happily, the former nanny sounds irritated. "She's very different."

My mother crosses her arms defiantly. "Get on with what you came here to say."

At her words, I notice there is no one else in the room; not one servant. My mother never takes tea without a band of servants to boss about. When my nanny speaks next, I understand why. Nanny Ododo clears her throat. "Chieftess Farida, Mäzzikim has exceptional abilities. I believe she could be mage—at least, in part."

I stifle a gasp and put my fist to my chest as if I mean to hold my heart inside, but my mother's reaction is muted. "That's impossible," she states.

"It's possible, Chieftess, even if you are unaware of a known ancestor. Mage people and humans are tangled roots! Surely you've noticed."

"No," my mother dissents. "She has a rare health condition. That is all. A doctor cared for her when she was young, but she is much better now at controlling herself."

"The nocturnal visions—"

"Nightmares, and she no longer speaks of them."

"With respect, your grace, that does not mean they've stopped. It simply means she has stopped telling you," Nanny Ododo offers gently. "Even the tonics—"

"You speak of magic in the chieftain's house. The very thing Oko has been dedicated to eradicating—"

"Your grace, if Maze does not learn how to embrace her power, it could lead to severe mental and physical illness," Ododo protests. "That is why I have come. Funani, she is Maze's outlet. When she passes, I'm afraid—"

"Be careful, Ododo," my mother warns. "You do not know what you say."

Ododo scoffs. "Your grace, please, you misunderstand me. Maze is exceptionally gifted, but she is not *safe* here. She will be considered an adult soon. I could take her somewhere. A special place where she could safely—"

My mother coldly interrupts, "Your fears are unfounded and dangerous, and I forbid you to mention them again. They will put my daughter and my entire family at risk."

"Please, for her sake, you must consider—"

My mother stands, nostrils flaring. "I'll no longer dance around this. Maze does not have a drop of low blood. But you—are *you* admitting that you are a mage, Ododo? That you know of such abilities. Of such a place? Say the word."

It is a thinly veiled threat from a woman experienced in issuing them.

Another long silence endures before Ododo replies carefully, "Of course not, your grace. I'll just be on my way. I know this is a difficult time, and I did not mean to offend and apologize for my forwardness, Chieftess Farida."

It is not good form to be caught standing there, so I rush from the doorway and tie-toe up the stairs, wincing at the creaky ones. I hear Ododo leave the parlor, closing the door behind her, and making her way down the long hall. My former nanny exchanges nervous pleasantries with the guards at the door before exiting. I fight the urge to chase after her. Instead, I wander back to my room, where I stare into my looking glass, scrutinizing my appearance for any physical characteristics of a mage (pointy ears, a long nose, maybe a special twinkle in my eyes) and finding none. Eventually, I climb back into bed, which had gone cold in my short absence, and drift into restless sleep.

Just before sunrise, I thrash awake, shouting and crying in pain. Hanya rushes to my side with an herbal tonic, which dulls my senses. Slowly, I catch my breath, and the pain gradually disappears, leaving my body weak and drained.

"It was just a bad dream. It's over now," Hanya whispers soothingly as she dabs at my sweaty forehead with a cold cloth.

Except it was not a bad dream, and it is far from over. In my vision, Ododo's hired buggy veered off the road and rammed into a tree, crushing her until her life drifted away. It was a sudden and painful death. Quick. Over as soon as it began. Over before Ododo even knew she was dying. Ododo died, and she wasn't the only one who passed last night. I dismiss Hanya, and draw my limbs close to my cold body.

Later that morning, Chieftain Oko *Ka* Kähari stoically announces that his mother, Funani, had died, just before the early morning. Her nurse found Funani propped up in her bed, smiling and eyes closed as though experiencing a delightful dream. At least, that's what he says.

As my father makes his announcement, I let out a strangled cry, and do not care who hears me. My heart breaks, and a crushing emptiness fills my body. Ododo's death, which I cannot confirm without revealing myself, shifts to the back of my mind. I can think of nothing else but my grandmother. The broken pieces of my heart travel up to my throat, and I expect they will stay there for months, always ready to escape in uncontrollable bursts of weeping. I cry until my eyelids swell almost shut, and then I cry some more. When there are no tears left, I lay in my bed, drawn and defeated.

I have only one comforting thought: How wonderful it would be to be so content that you are *singing* just before you pass? I am sure it was my grandmother, and I try to remember the words to the song, but they remain out of reach in my brain's recesses. Some of the singing sounded like a different language, one that wasn't familiar, and that makes me surer that there is more to my grandmother's stories than she'd ever let on. Perhaps my grandmother was using her voice to guide me to the conversation between my mother and Ododo; so that I would know there is a safe place for me somewhere. A place I can live and learn without fear. But where is it? My grandmother spoke of a library—where is that?

I can speak to the dead with my magic. Unfortunately, I am not sure where to begin. I barely understand how it works. I have never tried to conjure a *specific* person or vision before, and my grandmother never thought the middle (living) realm was worthy of her—she will not linger. I need to move quickly. Maybe I have to find an object, a place—something fundamentally crucial to *Funani* as a person. It seems like a reasonable plan, and my mood lifts.

There are distractions for much of the morning in preparation for the seven days of fasting and mourning. Vibrantly-colored clothes are put away in exchange for black, silver, and gray; wreaths of white roses and black hollyhock hang from the doors and windows; sheer, black silk curtains obscure paintings of my grandmother. A conscripted sculptor begins work on a statue for the ancestral gardens, where a portion of her ashes will rest, and the temple is bright with candles lit in remembrance of Mother of Chieftess Funani *Ka* Kähari.

All day long, relatives and the Congress of the Great Clans members visit the Palace to offer their condolences. Bosede visits with his family. He joins the line of well-wishers and looks as though he wants to say more to me, but leaves it as a simple, "may she join her ancestors" in a flat voice and a bow. A modest wave of disappointment slips through me.

There are people everywhere, and I am annoyed by them. They make me relive my sadness over and over, asking questions about Funani and how she died, offering empty words of comfort, and looking at me in tearful pity. I take to a corner, pulling on my hood and tightening my veil for invisibility. My sister Ewatomi handles things more gracefully. She offers sad smiles from behind her black veil and seems to have heart-warming conversations with each person who greets her. My mother, who quite transparently never liked or respected Funani, disappears into the task of planning the period of mourning. My father, drawn and brooding, retires to his study and avoids people altogether. I want to go to the study with him, but I fear we would both blubber uncontrollably at the sight of each other.

For a brief respite, the Palace quiets. Relatives and friends wander home. Congress members depart hastily for their corners of the realm. So, that afternoon, I ride Helissi to my grandmother's house with my reluctant guard Abrar in tow. The temples teem with mourners, but the streets in the villages are unnaturally quiet and empty. The way that the country handles a noble death is eerie—the living essentially feign death for an entire week. I can hardly tell the difference between the living and the spirits lurking around. By comparison, everyone else throws a party complete with feasts, bonfires, and dancing.

I pause at the graveyard by the temple to speak briefly with Funani's old friends, two women, Tolani and Healer Abaku, who had been friends with Funani since they were all born under the same jackal moon. They passed away years ago—Healer Abaku from quell; Tolani of another malignant disease known for a spiking, unbreakable fever. Neither had children, so at Funani's request, I keep their gravesites neat and visit now and again.

"Might I have a moment of privacy?" I ask Abrar solemnly, as I disembark from my panther. "I would like to pray."

Abrar looks understandably skeptical, but also knows better than to argue with an emotional woman. He nods curtly. "I will watch from the tree over there—with Helissi."

Helissi bares his teeth and growls in apparent disagreement, but I nod my assent, and the big black cat relents and follows Abrar to a tree slightly uphill.

I find the flat gravestones and kneel in front of them, grasping my hands together and whispering. My magic tingles at my fingertips, and I exhale.

With a shimmer and a pop, the spirits of Healer Abaku and Tolani appear. They make an odd pair. Healer Abaku is exceedingly tall and slender, while Tolani is short and squat. It is difficult to describe how a spirit might look to someone who could not see them, but if forced, I will say they look as though they are alive but sculpted from fog. They both kneel, flip open fans and flap them at their nearly translucent faces, and smile as they set their eyes on me. Immediately, Healer Abaku's smile drops.

"Darling, you look vexed. What has happened?" Healer Abaku asks.

"Funani is dead." I choke back a sob and clutch my arms tightly around my body as if the approach might hold my emotions inside. I hope it works; the swelling in my eyelids just subsided. "Quell."

The dead women exchange glances.

Tolani ultimately replies, "Oh, how dreadful. I know she was like a mother to you. That quell is a beastly thing. It has ravaged the village—it is getting crowded here!"

Healer Abaku cuts in, "Thank you for telling us. I know you feel pain, darling, I know, but I hope it comforts you that she will never feel pain again. It is not so terrible, being dead, I mean. Being alive, that is the difficult thing."

"Where will her body be laid to rest? Here, I hope. I should like to say hello before she passes," Healer Abaku adds.

"You know she will pass—this realm has never been kind to her," Tolani agrees.

I shake my head. "I am on my way to her house now. I need to find a way to speak to her. She mentioned something about a library. Maybe she mentioned it to either of you before?"

Healer Abaku wrinkles and taps her long nose. "No, I do not believe so."

"Sorry, love," Tolani confirms. "Never, and Funani is infamous for providing far more information than anyone ever wanted to know about everything."

I snort in laughter and wipe at my eyes. "You two have never passed onto the ancestral realm. Why? Will you now?"

"Oh, it is a simple explanation. We are cowards," Healer Abaku says bluntly.

"You lie," I accuse.

"No, she is right. We are cowards. Every year we have the opportunity to pass on, and we never take it. We do not know what is on the other side," explains Tolani.

"What if it is nothing? What if our religion was wrong? I mean, there was one set of gods. Now there is another. If it is right, did I live in such a way that earned a comfortable rest with my ancestors or did I earn hell dogs chewing on my loins?" Healer Abaku gestures vaguely. "Instead, I am here with my closest friend."

"It is grand! And I get to haunt my fickle partner and his new young wife," Tolani puts in gleefully. "It brings me such delight. I keep moving her kettle around the kitchen. She thinks she is losing her mind—"

"Oh, yes," Healer Abaku laughs. "Your last crack was quite the rib-tickler. The poor girl may never sleep again."

"You think Funani will not choose the same?" I ask. "Maybe she will want to stay here with you."

They instantly grow more somber. "Funani is not afraid of anything," Tolani says thoughtfully. "And her curiosity—"

Healer Abaku nods her head. "Always getting us into trouble!"

The two friends chuckle again.

"Funani will go to the ancestral realm just to see what it is, and if it turns out to be an assemblage of demons munching on her intestines, she will still be glad she found out."

I sigh heavily. "Well, I should go. I need to go to her house and find something I can use as an ingress to speak to her."

"Do you know how to do that, dear? What an advancement in your abilities!"

"Oh, I do not have the slightest idea," I reply honestly, glancing up the hill to make sure Abrar is not watching me too closely. "I will figure it out."

"With that attitude, your future cannot be anything but brilliant," Healer Abaku comments kindly. "Somewhere, your grandmother is glittering with pride."

Then, Tolani asks, "Have you celebrated your Hathi yet? I know you have been waiting."

"No," I answer.

"In ancient times, a Hathi had nothing to do with age or your parents. It was a celebration of first experiencing your magic, your *nature*," Tolani adds blithely.

"It has been relegated to some misogynistic birthday thrash," Healer Abaku agrees.

Now I am even more depressed. "Ewatomi will have hers soon, but my father has not declared that I am ready. It is my mother's doing."

"You are ready to be released to the world," Healer Abaku proclaims, gesturing to the sky. My mother disagrees, and I am not sure she ever will.

As Helissi, Abrar, and I make our way to my grandmother's house, I discover several royal guards removing my grandmother's furniture and loading it into a cart attached to a team of bored-looking donkeys. My eyes bulge, heat floods my face, and I take a couple of steps forward. I mean to tell them *exactly* what I think about them disturbing my grandmother's things so soon—when my father walks out of the house and sends mouth falling open. He has not left his study since he made the announcement. My father, solemn and distracted in his black robe, and overlooks me at first. Then he looks up, and our eyes meet.

"Mäzzikim, you should be at the Palace with your mother and sister."

"I wanted to say good-bye to Grandmother Funani's house. Why are you moving Funani's things?" I return, swaying slightly.

"A few precious things will be buried with her in the catacombs," he answers, watching the guards, who are wearing the ceremonial black masks shaped like phoenix birds and heavy gloves, carry out a small dresser. "Upon death, all of our family will be placed there in honor."

"But her *things…*?"

"It is a religious rite. Funani was the mother of the ruler of the clan. A sacred, noble position in society. All of her most prized belongings must be put in her tomb with her," my father explains gently. "It is Kähari's will."

"Well, it is not *Funani's* will. She did not *want* her position." My voice wobbles. "She hated it! She hated all of it!"

My father winces and hangs his head. I try to force myself to stop there but cannot. The words tear out of me. "She didn't even live in the Palace! Who can say she would even want to be buried in the catacombs? I can! I spoke to her more than you! She wouldn't. She wouldn't want it!"

My father surprises me by pulling me into a tight embrace until the fight drains from me. Tears involuntarily stream freely down my face. I take several hasty breaths to quiet myself.

"We are chosen, and we sacrifice for the clan," he murmurs sadly into my hair.

CHAPTER
FOUR

spend the evening determinedly searching my closet for anything Funani gave me recently. I never organized it—not since I started collecting things that sparked my magic years ago; I merely add to my collection. In my haste, I plunge my hand into a broken teapot and, with a shriek, withdraw to see blood smeared across my fingers.

Hanya opens the closet door with one hand and holds a candle in the other. She yawns widely and leans against the door jamb. "Daughter Mäzzikim, are you all right?"

"I am fine." Snorting impatiently, I toss aside an old locket and peered at a military badge with a seabird emblem. "Just looking for something."

Hanya's eyes skims over my bloody fingers.

"You should go to bed," she advises softly. "Or at least let me wrap your fingers."

When Hanya takes a step forward and my shoulders tense.

"Leave me, Hanya," I snap. "Now."

"Yes, your grace," Hanya whispers, closing the door behind her. I listen as my servant's bare feet pad away before resuming my task.

Sometime, long before sunrise, I admire my handiwork; piles sorted into weapons, dishes, books, diaries, maps, paintings, old clothing, and jewelry. I wonder what my mother would do if she found it all. Probably burn it.

I found several items that my grandmother had given me. A wooden flute, a collection of shiny stones, a few dolls. Desperate, I hold each and wait, but no magic, and nothing comes—not one memory. I groan heavily and slump to the floor.

There is a soft knock at the door.

"What is it?" I ask wearily.

Hanya opens the door, this time with a tray balanced on her bony hip. "I have bone broth and tea," she offers nervously. "Shall I…"

I gesture vaguely and sigh. "I'm sorry for snapping earlier."

"It is fine, your grace. You are in mourning; it is expected."

Hanya places the tray next to me on the floor and goes to leave, but I stop her. "Have you ever heard of another library? Here in the Palace?"

"There are the main library and the personal stacks that your parents keep in their quarters. I could ask some of the servants—if you'd like."

I press my fingertips against my forehead. "No, don't. What about a place called the Trench? Anything about that?"

"The Trench of Demons?" Hanya shrugs her skinny shoulders and sits on the floor by me. "Just old tales from the village. Stories that parents tell to get their children to behave in the temple. My mother used to say: be good or I'll toss you in the Trench! That always shut us up. Your mother never told you those stories?"

"No." I pull my knees to her chest. "She doesn't quite have the stomach for tales. She's very practical in every sense."

"Not even when you lived in the fishing village?" Hanya asks, partly curious and partly envious. "Before your father was chosen?"

I understand Hanya's curiosity. I once felt it. What was it like to go from a village girl—a fisherman's daughter—to a noble family? When my father was chosen by the priests, the whole family rose with him. However, the grandeur is all temporary. My grandmother understood that better than anyone and refused to be caught up in the entrapments. Would Kähari, our founding deity, choose someone from the family to succeed my father?

Maybe, but most likely not. Soon after my father passes, the priests will select someone new.

If you could manage it, your star never falls; at least that is what my enterprising mother told us right after our father's selection. Obviously, being a child, I did not know what it meant then. I do now. Lands, investments, gowns, renowned tutors and mentors, handsome sons and beautiful daughters—everyone barters to curry good favor with the noble family. Families chosen to serve are almost always better off than the rest even after the sun sets on their titles. When the gods smile upon you, so does everyone else. A tale of triumph.

"Never. My mother believed she was always destined for this life. I suppose she was right." I pause for a moment. "Where is Imvula? I haven't seen her since before the holiday."

Hanya's eyes widen. "You didn't hear? Her father was detained. He is a Zain mage, Giant tribe, and he was using his magic on his crops to make them grow faster and larger, violating the peace treaty of the Great Clans. *Everyone* is talking about it."

"Huh," I reply, stunned.

"Your mother won't allow the daughter of a mage to work here, especially so close to one of her daughters. Besides, Imvula had to get a job that paid more coin, so, she is working as a servant instead of a house girl. It's hard work, but pays," Hanya rambles on, but then pauses and shakes her head. "I am certain the guard will be watching the whole family."

Now that Imvula had a known mage in her bloodline, members of the guard will look for an excuse to arrest and expel her. Hatred for mages infects every corner of Kähari like the quell. Perhaps Imvula could go someplace overseas, but Imvula's father—if he even looks vaguely like a Giant, there will not be a suggestion of a fair trial. I do not need my necromantic sight to know he will die.

My brow furrows and my muscles tighten as my magic presses lightly throughout my body. I should help him, in honor of my grandmother. Imvula already lost her mother—she needs her father. She needs *someone*. Tears threaten me again. Gods, I am such a mess! I try to focus: what would Funani do? I sigh and glance at the congealing bone broth.

"I know we are supposed to be fasting, but I think your grandmother would prefer we eat cake tonight, your grace," Hanya comments, misinterpreting my gaze.

A quiet whisper fills my head and an idea begins to pull together.

"Actually, I *do* need cake," I suddenly declare.

When Hanya goes to move, I stop her. "Wait, I'll go, and I have an odd request. Might I borrow your clothes?"

I PASS THROUGH THE KITCHEN TOWARDS THE HEAVY WOODEN DOOR TO THE servants' quarters. Dressed in Hanya's gray servant cloak, hood, and prayer veil, no one gives me a second glance. I am invisible. It is late, and there are just a few servants wearily washing the bowls and broth pots. They have one intent—finish washing so that they can return to their quarters to gather strength to do it again tomorrow.

I open the door, revealing a dark stairway. As I head down the stairs, I enter a hellish place. The air is cold and musty with sweat. I reach the bottom of the stair and look down into the long, stone hall. It is nothing like the Palace I know. There are no beautiful carpets or paintings or plants or grand windows with sun spilling across bright wood floors. It is devoid of color, made of stone, and there are doorways but no doors, and all sorts of crude sounds of life spill forth—a baby wailing, a couple of men loudly bantering, and two lovers going at it like a couple of wild dogs.

A chill passes through me. Death lives here too.

The guard at the bottom of the stars, with a generous belly straining his tunic, stops me. He frowns at Hanya's uniform. "You're a house girl. What are you doing down here?"

"I am visiting a friend," I explain carefully. "Do you know where I might find Imvula?"

"The big one, yeah? She shares a room with a couple other women down the hall on the left. Make it quick."

I hurry away from him and promptly find Imvula's quarters. With her head in her considerable hands, Imvula sits on the edge of a cot in a cramped, stone room. In one corner, an old woman winces and massages her bleeding feet. In the other corner, a woman (not much older than either Imvula or I) bathes with the aid of a rag and a bucket. I swallow hard.

"Imvula."

Imvula looks up, eyes widening. "Daughter Ma—"

I put my finger to my lips. "*Daughter Maze* sent me down to speak to you."

"What are you doing down here, house girl?" the old woman snaps angrily, pausing briefly from nursing her feet. "Why don't you go upstairs and enjoy your tea and cake?"

"Let her be. Everyone is in mourning. No one is having cake," the other woman puts in as she scrubs as her small breasts with the coarse sponge. I try to avert my eyes, and she smiles at me as she continues to wash, unfazed. "Don't mind her, love. She just had a rough day in the fields. The heat does things to you."

I mouth a brief thank-you to the kinder woman (though she probably cannot see it under the veil) before returning to my task. "Imvula, if I might have a moment in the hall?"

Imvula grudgingly follows me out.

"You look shaken," Imvula observes, a tint of glee in her voice. "Is the décor not to your liking?" she asks mockingly. "I would've put out the good silver if I'd known you were coming."

"I heard about your father. I want to help. You can't work down here, live down here."

I wrap my arms around myself and hug tight. "It is *horrible*," I add in a hush.

Imvula lets out a baffled scoff. "What did you *think* it looked like?"

I never thought about it. I am ashamed for never thinking about it.

Imvula sighs. "To be fair, it pays enough to take care of my family. I'm assigned to the kitchen. It's hard work—harder than taking care of your hair—if you can believe it."

"You flatter me. Why is there a guard?"

"Some of us are workers. Some are property of the crown." Her eyes flicker downward. "*Abeds.* Slaves until debts to society are paid. They are chained and guarded at night."

I swallow hard. It is crass, my mother always said, to speak of the abeds. I did not even know the Palace uses them. Unlike in Ogun or Ganju, the slave market in Kähari handles the practice discretely; most have never seen an auction. It seems that many of the abeds are mage. For those that survive years of being bought and sold, you can see the evidence in their emaciated, bruised bodies and dull eyes. I've felt the anguish of those who did not. I feel it now.

"I want to help you get out of Kähari," I hear myself say.

Imvula's eyes narrow suspiciously, and her face flushes slightly. She licks her lips before her reply. "Why do you care? I may have served you, but I have treated you with nothing but contempt—hopefully, you noticed."

"Daily, you did excellently, but now I understand why you hate me."

Imvula's face darkens.

Coldly, she replies, "No. You do not, your grace."

"I do."

"Don't tell me how I feel!" Imvula snap, her dark eyes flashing.

My smile wavers and I bite my lips closed.

Imvula explains, more gently, "My mother, Atiti, was a revolutionary of sorts. She was a human, but fighting for fully-recognized citizenship for all—including mage people. She was making in-roads too, convincing people with this elegant, passionate voice. She'd even been invited to speak at elder council a few times to discuss her views, and it seemed like the powers that be in Kähari were finally willing to consider a change."

"My mother was walking home from a session of elder council one day. Alone, as she always did, but it was daylight and people were all around. Still, a group of men with large rocks, followed her, jeered, threatened her and her 'half-breed' children."

Imvula's voice catches in her throat for a moment before she soldiers on. "She told them that that she was not afraid. That she stood with Zain, and her god would protect her."

"They threw the stones, battered her, and people—people all around, they just *watched*." Imvula's face remains stony, suppressing any visible emotion. "They watched as those men beat her until she wasn't breathing anymore and then left her. In the morning, they tossed her body in a ditch and washed the blood away—as if nothing had happened at all."

Goosebumps lift on my skin.

Imvula's face shifts slightly to outright anger. "So, *Hanya*, how would I *brush the locks* of the privileged brat who sits at the head of the snakes who tolerate...*encourage* these ungodly things—with a smile on my face? Who, despite that privilege, says nothing as people suffer? Forgive me if I do not believe that a human as foul as that would come to the aid of a family of Giants."

"Imvula, *I'm*—" I catch herself. It would be foolish to admit that I might not be, in fact, fully human. Imvula is angry; she could do something rash.

"Sorry," I finish.

"No. You—ahem, *Maze* feels guilty. She has finally taken her head out of her perfumed ass. She is just now realizing she lives a golden life of privilege—wealthy, human-blood with all of her limbs and senses. Her biggest concern is how quickly she can leave behind her bitch of a mother and go to university, which she can easily afford."

I open my mouth to protest, but Imvula is not finished. "*Maze* never worried about her next meal. She does not even need to wear the same gown twice! She has all the best tutors and mentors that money could buy and all because of what and who she was born as."

Cheeks burning, I hang my head.

Eyes softening, Imvula relents, "If her guilt compels her to help me and my family..."

Before I could lose my nerve, I grasp Imvula's forearm and push a folded piece of parchment in her hand. On the paper, there is a name and an address of an odd old man, a clockmaker and companion of my grandmother, who told stories about the daring man. If the stories are true, the man smuggles people and property in and out of Kähari. Funani told all her stories for a reason. This plan is her reason; I can feel it in my bones. "Please, leave here tonight. Gather your family. Go to him," I urge, closing her hand. "He will help you."

"We won't leave until my father is free," Imvula warns.

"I will free him," I say confidently. "I have a brilliant idea, but I require a cake."

"A brilliant idea?"

I relent. "A ghost of an idea that could possibly be brilliant."

Imvula frowns deeply. "And a cake? But the mourning period—"

"It is for the Daughter of Chieftain Oko," I scold. "If that spoiled girl wants cake, she shall have it."

A smile tugs at the corner of Imvula's downturned mouth, but a worried crease appears between her eyebrows. "I appreciate this, more than you know, but this won't bring back your grandmother."

Tears threaten me again. "I know, but I will feel her pride in my heart if I do it."

CLAD STILL IN HANYA'S GRAY SERVANT CLOAK, HOOD, AND PRAYER VEIL, I hurriedly leave the Palace. The timing is perfect given the distraction of the mourning, and I marvel again at how no one looks at me while wearing a house girl's garb. Even the guards just grunt in a half-hearted greeting as I move past. I do not matter. I am invisible.

I briskly cross the bridge and breathe in the salty morning air. The sun has yet to rise, and the streets in the capital are still and quiet. The only light comes from the torch-lit street lamps and the temple, which shines brightly against the dark blue sky. Some very devout Käharians, professional grievers, slowly make their way towards it; the only sound is a gentle salty breeze shifting the palms.

The business district and the market slowly open for the day. The more modest street vendors roll up their carts while the wealthier, more established merchants open their shutters and adjust their window displays. A few buggies overloaded with bushels of fruit rattled up and pass me. At the edge of the business district, I hire a chauffeured camel-coach. The driver is a kindly old man with a crooked, toothy smile, who matches his equally kindly old car with a twisted face. To my surprise, he does not question why I want to go to Iboji.

We bump down the streets of Kähari for about an hour and I fiddle with my sleeve, my veil, and the top of the cake box.

"Driver, are we nearly there?" I ask nervously.

"Nah. Iboji is far from any seaport. Got a way to go. Might as well sit back."

I sit back into my seat and jam my fingers under the cushion as my bravado begins to wear off. I am starting to have second thoughts about my brilliant plan. I should go back to the Palace. There are pillows there.

Soft ones. Besides, this is mad. I cannot help Imvula. She is doomed to the same fate as her father; the same fate as me if I am discovered.

The whisper comes to me again. My grandmother would want me to try. She would reassure me and tell me that it is possible. Still, I swallow the lump in my throat. My grandmother might be proud of I am attempting to do, but my mother will scrounge up her whip if she finds out (probably my father too, honestly). Admittedly, Imvula is not my favorite person, but Giant or not, Imvula does not deserve the sad past behind her or the depressing future ahead of her. If I am ever in a similar position, I hope somebody would also stand up for me instead of running to hide in their bed.

The driver glances back, sees my cloak. "You work at the Palace with the noble family?"

I wince inwardly.

"I wonder what you think of the proposed bans on mage people and other low born working in the Palace, ministry, and military positions."

With eyes like steel, he looks back again for my reaction.

I stare pointedly out the window and pray for the conversation to end with haste. I agree with him, of course, but talking about such things would reveal too much and make me far too memorable. "I doubt many work in the Palace now."

"No, and it is a pity. Those positions are one of the only chances at upward mobility," the driver replies, coughing a little. "The bans would make it impossible."

"Well, I'm not on the elder council clearly. I don't have a say," I try nervously.

"Elder council is elected—"

"Too young to vote, I'm afraid," I quickly rebut. "I haven't celebrated my Hathi."

He seems unsatisfied with my answer and we endure the next leg of the trip in tense silence. The air changes as we move farther from the coastline and closer to Iboji. Even with the buggy's windows tightly closed, it is thick and heavy and smells funny—likely due to the clouds with poisonous fumes from the large, gray-stoned factories.

Several of the streetlamps are unlit, so I am unsure of how the driver sees the way, but apparently, he has made the drive many times. I take deep, slow breaths as souls swim at the edge of my consciousness— darkness, pain, strangled breathing. No escape, no escape, the voices cry. Their emotions, rolling fear, searing horror, seep over me, massive waves in a stark white ocean. I would know we arrived if I were blind; the cries of the souls grow louder.

"Who are you visiting?" the driver asks, glancing back. "You don't need to tell me if you don't want, but you got to tell them."

He gestures ahead as he pulled his camels to jolting a stop.

"I'd rather not say."

"Well, I don't like to get no closer to evil than this," he replies with a shudder.

"Could you wait here, please? One now. Another later."

I put a gold coin in his palm.

His eyes widen as he reluctantly replies, "Surely, miss."

I step out of the buggy and look ahead at the front gate operated by several guards with helmets and phoenix masks. Each cradles a gray-colored repeating crossbow the size of a small child. I have never seen weapons that large and wonder about their necessity for guarding a prison of battered, unarmed people. I stand in a line with other road-weary people, some of whom are turned away, and when it is finally my turn, I clear my throat.

"Identify yourself," the tallest one says gruffly, raising his weapon slightly. "Now."

"My name is Imvula," I say confidently with magic tingling at my fingers and toes. "I'm here to see my father, Mobo Omfemi."

I hold up a honey cake. "For his day of birth," I explain.

Glaring at me, the guard sticks his clearly dirty finger into the cake. I flinch but stare right back at him as he drags his finger slowly through it. Then he rubs his fingers together while the other guards chuckle darkly behind him.

"We don't take many guests in here," he replies finally. "Not worth the trouble."

"Then, perhaps you'd be more amenable to the visit if I also had a gift for *your* birthday?" Praying everything my grandmother has told me about Iboji guards is true, I drop a small pouch of silver coins into his open palm. "To make up for the trouble."

Raising his eyebrows, he opens the pouch and counts it. I know it is probably more than the man's yearly salary. He raises his dark eyes and examines me.

"You'll make it quick?" he asks at last.

I lift my chin. "You have my word. Take me to my father, please."

The guard reluctantly leads me into one of the many gray concrete buildings. As soon as he opens the door, I hear yelling and weeping and breathe in the horrible odor hanging in the sticky, sickly air. Though the guard did not seem to notice, I nearly gag and begin to panic that I am in over my head. Death lingers there. The souls raise bumps on my skin and make my bones shiver to my bones. Souls howl and whisper to me, together forming a low, unintelligible hum. It unsettles me, stretching deeper into my body than any vision I have experienced before.

In the cages, behind iron bars, shells of people—battered and miserable—hunch together in clumps near barred windows. Fear seems permanently etched on their faces, and they flinch and cower as the guard passes.

"Unsettling, isn't it," the guard comments, noticing my face. "Good lesson for you, being part Giant. My father used to say magic is like a disease. It starts with just a tickle in your belly and ends with vomiting your intestines into a tin bowl."

"That's quite the metaphor," I choke.

"Hurry up. Special cage for those big brutes," the guard explains as he leads down the dimly lit hallway with a seemingly endless, suffocating row of iron bars.

I put my free hand to my mouth and nose, try not to breathe, and push down the urge to admonish the man for his ignorant commentary. It will not help Imvula's cause to get thrown out (or thrown in the cage, for that matter).

"Small little thing. You must not have gotten the blood, looking at you," he observes, looking up and down my body with a leer.

"Good on you," he adds before coming to a stop. "I'll give you a moment, but you need to get out of here before the next shift."

He lumbers away, his boots clomping across the stone floor and occasionally splashing through a puddle. Probably of urine. I shudder and turn toward the cell.

My face whitens and I grip the cake box so tightly I worry it will bend. Mobo Omfemi is tall as tree; his hands are larger than a beater, and heavy, wrought-iron chains, stained with blood, wrapped around his thick angles and long legs. As a child, I heard stories from other children in the village—old stories—of Giants ripping people limb from limb with their bare hands, but it is hard to imagine that from this man. He hunches in despair, consuming the cage, with his face in his dark hands.

"Are you...Imvula's father?" I stutter.

He looks at me, confused.

"I've brought you a cake. For your birthday."

Trembling, I push the cake under the door slot.

I raise my eyes back to his large ones. "The best part is at the bottom."

He understands immediately; I can tell by the way his eyes widen when his thick fingers run over the lockpick wedged discretely into the bottom of the platter. I got the idea from a book about a prison escape in Ogun. While I know most of the guards probably cannot read, I am shocked I wasn't found out at the gate. Thank goodness for their gross mixture of arrogance and ignorance.

"Every evening at sunset, the guards all have a nightcap at the northern entrance while the next shift is just arriving. Get out by the southern entrance, meet your family, and go north to Ameci," I hiss, looking around to ensure the guard is out of earshot.

"She said you would come," Mobo utters in disbelief.

It is my turn to look puzzled. "Who said?"

"Oy, Giant girl, time to go."

The guard, standing impatiently farther down the hall, jerks his thumb back towards the dark, horrible corridor. I wipe my clammy hands on my cloak, draw up my shoulders and follow him. "Costs too much to feed them if you ask me," the guard growls crassly. "They're useful in the fields though."

My eyes flash. I want to avenge his assault on my ears, but not today.

In a show of arrogance, the guard spits on the floor. "Time to go! If you want to come back and visit, bring more coin, eh? The price goes up daily."

Trembling, I inhale my anger, but follow him out. I return to the coach without incident and pray that the rest of the plan will work. My part was easy. Mobo will need to free himself from his cage, escape Iboji, and meet up with Imvula. For a man as tall as a tree, it would not be easy. As we ride farther and farther away from the prison, the buzz of blistering pain from lost souls slowly recedes from my body. I sag against the seat in relief.

But I notice that it does not disappear; the coldness of blood leaving the body, the sharp, searing pain of shattered bones. It settles in as a dull hum, as the souls continue to plead with me. I am not naïve. These were not peaceful deaths, surrounded by family, prayers, and candles. They were deaths of terrible violence—some long ago, some more recent, but the souls have awakened, erupting and suppurating as hives on my skin.

"That bad, eh?" the driver observes after glancing back.

"Worse," I admit.

He looks at me, his eyes like bright volcanic glass. "Something should be done."

LATER THAT DAY, A CROWD, CLAD IN GRAY AND BLACK, GATHERS AT A LOCAL temple. My grandmother's body is entombed in the catacombs, an eerie tunnel far beneath the Palace. I do not witness the resting—only her children and spouse (if he still lived, which he does not) can attend. It is for the best. I do not know what will happen if I enter a tunnel full of the dead. I am still shaken by my visit to Iboji. I could barely function in that tragic place.

Outside the Palace, thousands more adorned in mourning robes grieve with traditional dancing, food, and music for Funani's journey to the next life. Sadness floats all around me, but I do not have any tears left. I merely float through the motions with wet, dull eyes.

A few days after the ceremony, I return to my grandmother's house and sit on the kitchen floorboards. I sit there for hours, waiting for the familiar tingle of magic, but nothing comes to me. Abrar gently tells me that the sun is setting, and it is time to return home. Later, a maid offers me a silver bracelet she found in my grandmother's sickbed, but nothing comes to me (it turns out that it belonged to someone else). Taken all together, it all meant that my grandmother left my life with a finality that I do not understand and cannot accept. What was the point in being a necromancer if I cannot speak to the one person with whom I desire to communicate? My grandmother is dead, and I cannot summon her memories. A heavy pain settles in my body. I am a failure.

When saving Mobo and Imvula, I felt close to her energy again. Yet, the glow quickly drained away. My actions were dangerous—what had gotten *into* me? If the guard discovered the lock pick, I would have been arrested immediately and never released (probably killed). My family would have lost our royal status. Now, there is a thousand-coin silver price on the head of whoever helped the Giant and his comrades escape. A thousand-coin silver—on *my* head.

Except, not exactly my head. I, in my foolishness, identified myself as Imvula and had been wearing the cloak of a Palace servant, making my former servant the primary suspect in the conspiracy. So, in addition to my own family, I put Imvula and her family in danger with my genius antics. If Mobo did not escape, if Imvula did not find a way out of Kähari—

Will any of the guards identify me? I do not think so. I wore a mourning cloak and veil, they were distracted and drinking, there were lots of visitors, and it had been days. I toss in my bed, worrying about the prisoners there. So many doomed people. So many tortured souls. I tried to save one—reluctantly, if I am honest with myself, and not selflessly—but left all the rest behind.

Eventually, one bright note—no one finds Mobo, Imvula, or any of their family members in Kähari. Hearing the news, I want to speak with my grandmother so badly that my heart aches. I wanted to ask my father to free Mobo, but I knew could not. Why? I already have a mother who cannot stand me; my father is all I have left. And, although they are vastly different people, it is clear they share similar views. My kind father upheld several anti-mage laws, including several recent regulations restricting aspects of their public and private lives. I love my father, but it makes me feel differently—uncomfortable—about him.

Hanya comes in to check on me. She says words I do not hear. She takes my arm, gently, and pulls me up. She walks me to my bed and firmly shifts my body into it. She says more words, but I do not hear them. This is too much. It is too much for me to bear. I will never speak to my grandmother again. I will never find that library, if it even exists. My magic failed me the first time in my life it would have been exceedingly useful. Hanya hands me tea, and I sip it until she is satisfied and leaves. I slump down and stare into space.

Oh, how I long to go back to being *satisfied* with being fed, sleeping soundly soft bed, waiting to go and share each bit of knowledge I learn, each part of life I experience, each emotion, every scar with my grandmother. I want to sleep for a long time. Instead, I am crippled with the knowledge of the dark underbelly of Kähari, forced to relearn everything I thought I knew. I bend forward, laying my head on my arms and sob. Is this nonsense part of being an adult? If so, I do not like it.

CHAPTER
FIVE

bury the pain of my grandmother's death with distractions. While any distraction will do nicely, it us increasingly difficult to find a proper one. With her death, I lost my excuse to habitually leave the Palace. My mother eyes me with suspicion whenever I ask to go into the market and appoints Ewatomi and several guards to accompany me. With Ewatomi's Hathi coming up, her only interests are dressmakers, with her close second interest of shoemakers and a third interest of hatmakers. When I ask to ride Helissi in the countryside, my mother insists that I stay on the Palace grounds under the watchful eye of the potentate guard.

Until I celebrate my own Hathi, my mother reserves the morning for studying literature and arithmetic with my governess. The afternoons are determinedly for arts and sports, which I find to be frivolous and a waste of what little energy I have. However, at my mother's insistence, Ewatomi and I are working towards a mastery with a saber. It initially is a welcome reprieve from dancing and painting but my relief doesn't last long. Ewatomi, who had initially showed open distain to the sport, quickly finds that she quite enjoys the practice. Or, rather, she enjoys beating me— swiftly and consistently.

"Again, Maze! This time, move with more purpose. You're hopping around like a coward with no survival instinct. A terrified mouse in the cage with a cape fox!"

I yelp as Ewatomi manages to jab me in the stomach again. Ewatomi grins wickedly and hops out gracefully out of the way when I counter. She growls playfully and jabs again.

Our trainer Akachi, a round little man, sits at the edge of the sparring pit. He observes our every move carefully, occasionally barking out corrections mostly directed at me. We spar with rubber, paint-tipped sabers, which leaves marks—the points—on our stark white tunics. I have no points. I have never had any points. It is unlikely I will ever score any points.

"You are not protecting yourself." Now Akachi sounds bored and annoyed. "Look for an opportunity. If the opportunity is not there, do not attack. If it is, do not hesitate."

"Ha!" Ewatomi jabs me again, this time on the shoulder. "Ha!" And on the back.

Another two points for Ewatomi, whose tunic glares white while I am covered in bright blue splotches. I pant and struggle to catch my breath, feeling an uncomfortable heat rising in my cheeks.

Akachi calls warily, "Stop, stop!"

Still grinning, Ewatomi drops her saber in the dirt and stretches. "You'll manage one of these days, little mouse," she teases cloyingly as she circles me.

"Thanks," I grumble back.

"Do you enjoy my half-pirouette to the left, Master Akachi? I thought it was perfect, but I welcome a second opinion as long as it is as accurate as mine." My sister smugly calls to the instructor.

"Your arrogance tickles catastrophe, Daughter Ewatomi. You're dismissed," Akachi replies with a sigh.

Unfazed, Ewatomi grins and sashays back towards the Palace. Meanwhile, I groan and drops my saber into the dirt. Frustrated, I rub at the blue paint all over my sparring tunic and trousers. All it does in response is smudge and spread.

"I'm not going to beat her. She's faster than me and more graceful," I complain to Akachi.

Akachi does not disagree with me. "You're nervous. Irritable. Distant."

"A genius observation, Master Akachi," I reply wryly. "What would I do without your incredible insight?"

"Jest if you like. But it is why you lose. Learn to focus your intention."

I HAVE GROWN WEARY OF LOSING. FOR THAT REASON, I AM VERY MUCH LOOKING forward to becoming the history apprentice of a clever but stern little man called Professor Letaro. According to credible rumors, the height-challenged Professor Letaro is over a hundred years old, blind in both eyes, and wears mirrored spectacles. He is widely considered an expert on languages, history, politics, and religion.

In Kāhari, children in the village learn trades from family members or in limited, costly creches taught primarily by the most educated in the field. In some cases, exceptionally gifted older children and adolescents are selected to learn advanced trades and industry in proper schools. Very talented young adults (who could afford the costs) consider universities, colleges, or academic communities across the realm.

As my mother regularly tells me, I am *not* academically gifted (I respectfully disagree), but I am from a powerful family. So, instead of studying with my governess, I will spend the next year learning from Professor Letaro, who is on a sabbatical from a prestigious research position in Amęci. I requested him, carefully. Every perspective university student must write an essay on a topic of interest. Then, from the essays, the universities choose tributes to present on their narrative. It had grown competitive indeed, so the more unusual the topic, the better. One might assume I'd garner a special advantage being daughter of a chieftain, but academic has its own titles and classes. Coming from a family that never attended high education, I rest somewhere near the bottom. That is my strategy in choosing Letaro. He is considered radical by some, yes, but any topic I determine under his tutelage will stand out.

My mother would not approve if she knew his reputation. Lucky for me, my mother did not bother to learn to read when she became Chieftess. Still, I couched my justification using vague language and tried not to appear too eager. I need Letaro. I am an avid reader, but the records I am allowed will not help me develop an enlightening historical perspective. From my visions, my conversations with spirits, my "nightmares," I know there is more to understand. Imagine a thesis on the Trench of Demons. Imagine it!

Finally, Professor Letaro arrives in Kähari, with little fanfare, and unobtrusively takes up residence in one of the plusher guest chambers. He commandeers an office in the Palace library, which he grudgingly calls 'moderately adequate.' I meet him in the library for the first sessions, and Letaro spends much of the first session asking questions about my previous apprenticeships and what my governess covered, cryptically saying "hmmm," and scribbling things down.

I am curious about a great number of things. What happened before and during the Chaos? Where did the tale of the Trench of Demons originate? Ojos—how did they come to be? I want to know more about the original founding gods—or as some said, the fallen or lost gods—and the ancient tribes. Further, the Congress of Great Clans—I know it was not a perfect union created by larger than life, godlike heroes, but what was the truth? How did the Ohia Realm arrive in this era, where mages are destructively disregarded? Why had so many tribes simply vanished for decades, well after the Chaos, without explanation? Letaro is over a hundred years old (allegedly). If anyone knew the answers, wouldn't it be him?

That said, it does not seem prudent to pepper the man with a lot of questions right away.

"To understand the tradition of the quarterly Congress of the Great Clans, you must first understand what came before," Letaro drones on.

I intelligently jot down 'understand what came before.'

"No one can exactly pinpoint when the realm came to exist. Was it a thousand years ago?" His mirrored spectacles flash as he shifts his head.

I blink. "Yes?"

"At least," Letaro snaps impatiently, lighting so many candles on the desk that I flinch from the heat and brightness. "Based on ancient cave drawings, skeletal remains, and other such evidence, but we don't know how long such evidence lasts. So, for all we know, the realm has existed for one hundred thousand years.

The realm is a living thing, covered in living things, and living things *change*. We know that life, from one perspective anyway, was once more primitive. In the stable nations, we've learned to tame water and material elements in ways that make our lives simultaneously easier and harder."

"Yes," I agree uneasily, although I have little idea of what he means.

"As we discovered these things, some of us discovered a desire for more and found that there was a limit to resources. That's when life became more barbaric. Wars. Fighting. Boundaries drawn. Rationale for why we deserve; why they do not. Us and them. You understand?"

"I—"

"Then, there was a need to control the Chaos lest we all perish. Thus, political systems. Congress. Order. That is the simplistic explanation."

Professor Letaro drops several heavy books onto his desk. "You'll read these to start."

"All of them?" I ask, sagging into my chair.

"Oh, no, my dear. Only the ones you'd like," he replies kindly.

I look up hopefully.

Letaro sighs heavily. "Yes, all of them, and you will attend the next session of Congress tomorrow."

"My mother has never let me stay for a full session of Congress," I note nervously.

"You will not be there for the petty gossip this time, so I think Farida will understand," he mutters as I redden. "You will be there to learn politics. Read. Observe. *Think.*" The professor taps his head as if I do not know which organ is responsible for cognitive thought.

Perhaps next time I will summon the courage to ask one of my questions, but I certainly do not have it today. This professor is undoubtably different from my governesses. He will not tolerate a toe out of line. He is preparing me, he says, for an enlightened life.

Well, I asked for it, I suppose.

My courage does not increase as the lesson continues. Professor Letaro lectures about the different political bodies in Kähari. I know about the chief potentates, properly called the Chieftain and Chieftess, the most powerful positions in the country. The chief potentates have advisors, who are selected purely by their credentials and helped manage the many branches of the ministry—taxation and coin house, military, economy, education, religion, health, safety and general welfare of Kāharians; there is also Elder Council, made of elected assembly of representation from each village, big and small, in Kāhari. The members of Elder Council bring their grievances to the chief potentate, the Chieftess or Chieftain, and petition for their causes. They also usually sit in Congress of the Great Clans to observe and hear news from across the realm.

"But the temple—the religious congregation—it still has control over Kāhari because they select the Chieftain. These other institutions play a role, but their power is an illusion. You understand?"

I scribble as fast as I can to keep up with it all and try to write even faster when Letaro casually mentions an oral examination to assess my retention.

Finally, Professor Letaro pauses, plainly mentally grappling. On the one hand, his apprentice (me) is evidently clueless. On the other, the sun had set and it is nearly supper time. Seeing the opportunity, I offer us both an escape.

"Next time?" I ask eagerly, bringing a shaky hand to my forehead.

"Next time," he confirms grimly.

THE NEXT DAY, I WANDER AROUND THE FIRST FLOOR OF THE PALACE LOOKING for a quiet place to read my assignments when I hear arguing in the front hall. My curiosity and procrastination win over my sense of responsibility, I head in the direction of the raised voices. I could do with hearing a bit of gossip.

"You will *not* lecture me on irrigation theory. I have an advisor for that," my father replies. "I only want the facts. What exactly did you see? Don't speculate on what it means."

My heart nearly stops—the Ojo from the Outlands.

"With all due respect, your grace," the Ojo says coldly. "It is far from speculation. Perhaps we could discuss this matter someplace more private?"

The Ojo's gaze shifts to me. If he recognizes me, his dark eyes give no indication. Instead, he continues speaking in low tones to Chieftain Oko and four of his advisors. I move closer, slowing my pace and pretending to head towards the kitchen.

"No, we will finish it here, Ojo Mezu. You have come unannounced, and I have many appointments to attend. So, you say—the camp was abandoned?" my father asks crossly.

"No, as I've already said," says Ojo Mezu, crossing his arms. "All evidence suggests that the camp was attacked, and the people forcibly removed. It is the first of several I have found. I brought my concerns to Chieftain Gye—"

My father pinches his lips together. "Those mage tribes—what's left of them—never stay in one place for long. Maybe they stepped away for a hunt, and their camp was ironically met with its own hungry predator. That area is heavy with wild dogs."

His advisors, men and women of different hues and sizes in violet and gold robes and tunics, murmur their agreement.

"Or perhaps a dragon," one quips mockingly.

I frown. Where was the appreciation and respect that Ojos usually enjoyed? They are treating his man, who had sacrificed everything for the realm, like a stupid child.

The Ojo's jaw noticeably clenches. "Your grace, if you just send—"

"It's true," I blurt out. Why am I like this?

My father and his advisors turn to me. The Ojo drops his intense gaze to the floor. I swallow and continue, "Sorry. Pardon me, I didn't mean to interrupt. It just meant… it is true what he said about the campsite. I saw it too."

My father raises his eyebrows. "Don't be ridiculous, Mazzie. You cannot possibly know what campsite we're talking about. It's not within the bounds of Kähari—it is in the Outlands."

"I saw it. I was out riding Helissi." I trail off nervously as my father's eyes grow wide and his face reddens. "Outside the, uh, gate."

"Where was Abrar? How did you pass through the gate unnoticed?" my father asks in alarm.

Well, I had certainly just cost my guard his position. "It's not Abrar's fault," I offer weakly. "I…lost track of him in the market."

Chieftain Oko's dark eyes narrow as he takes a step towards her. "How did you—"

"Never mind that." I clear her throat. "At the site, there was a cookfire. It wasn't put out. There was a child's toy—a wooden doll—discarded on the ground. I looked it up after. It is a standard toy used by children in the Tofuli Elven tribe. They did not leave on their own accord. They—"

"You're basing your assessment on the state of a child's toy and one book you once read," scoffs one of my father's advisors.

It is better than basing your assessment on nothing, I think in annoyance.

My father silences him by lifting a finger. The advisor scowls at me, which is completely unnecessary as my cheeks are already flushed with embarrassment.

I look desperately to the Ojo, who does not acknowledge my presence. Not mild surprise. Nothing. He stares straight ahead, an obedient warrior of the realm. Or a man who did not want the Chieftain to know that he'd already met his youngest daughter—alone in the wilderness.

Fair, I decide grudgingly.

"Mäzzikim, we get our intelligence from the *Ojos*. They are trained for this. You are not and you put yourself in grave danger," my father says grimly. "I know you are nearly an adult, but you will always be my daughter, and the Outlands will never be a safe place for you. Your mother will not be pleased. Go to your chambers and wait there."

It is not safe in the Outlands, but my father focuses on the wrong dangers. Wild dogs did not drive that tribe away; I am much more threatened by whatever did.

But not as threatened as I am by the thought of my mother knowing what I did.

I panic. "Please, I'm meant to attend Congress this evening. It is part of my studies with Professor Letaro."

"Until you have learned to follow basic instructions and mind your elders, Mäzzikim, I highly doubt you could grasp the complex issues we grapple with in Congress. Go."

My father waves me away.

So, I miss Congress that evening, and Professor Letaro accuses me of not taking my studies seriously. While I certainly do not consider myself the most diligent scholar at times, that had not been the case. Maybe I shouldn't have said anything to my father. Next time, I will carry on my merry way. Except, deep down, I know I will not. I know what I saw. Something must be done.

I am unnerved by her father's quick dismissal; I am used to being dismissed quickly by my mother, but not by my father. He usually holds a soft spot for me. Normally, he might've humored me.

In between apologies, I try to explain what happened to Professor Letaro, but I cannot tell if the professor believes me. His mouth never moves, and his spectacles reflect my earnest expression.

"I assure you, sir, I do take my studies seriously," I insist as a sheen of sweat begins to dot my upper lip.

Still, Letaro says nothing.

"There is something I'd really like to understand. The tradition of Ojos. Perhaps since I missed Congress, we could cover that instead?"

I say it more as a distraction from his anger towards me, and it works beautifully.

"Ojos existed on this continent since before recorded time," Professor Letaro answers briskly. "They are selected by elder Ojos as children—just boys and girls around the age of five—and separated from their families."

"Really?" I ask, disturbed. "That young?"

"It is important that they have no emotional connection to family or country—just to the higher order of the realm." Pleased to have my attention, he clears his throat and sits down behind the desk. The library candlelight flickers against his spectacles.

"They learn to fight. They learn to think. They learn to negotiate. No one besides an Ojo knows exactly what the training entails, but not everyone finishes or survives the training. The few that make it are anointed and marked. Are you listening?"

I rush to write my notes. "Yes, professor."

"Ojo is a highly respected title and a source of pride for the clan nation that produces the most Ojos in a given year. Many years ago, before the nations, individual tribes made offerings to support them. Today, they are paid and housed by all of the nations—through Congress. But still, many tribes make offerings."

"Sounds lonely though," I comment. "No family. No roots in a clan."

"It is an honor."

Professor Letaro taps the desk with his fingers. "I have another book for you to read."

My lips press tight into a grimace.

"It appears you've learned two lessons today. The second—don't ask a question without expecting a full answer," Professor Letaro says, as if reading my mind. "Don't expect me to ladle the full answer into your mouth as if you are a dim-witted infant. With all of these books, resources, and people available to you."

He gestures at the full shelves all around them. "Your ignorance is a choice."

I pale and suck in an offended breath, but he is not finished.

"Try not to upset your parents so that you're able to attend the next session Congress or I will have several longer books. Perhaps written in an ancient Elven language. Translation is a healthy task for the young mind."

I force a pained smile. "Understood."

A FEW MORE DAYS PASS WITHOUT INCIDENT, AND AT FIRST, IT SEEMS THE admonishment from Professor Letaro will be my only punishment. It is shocking actually; neither of my parents mention my wayward ride over breakfast, which features a rare appearance by everyone in the noble family. Instead, they make small talk about the slightly cooler weather and the remaining crops to be harvested. The tension I have been holding in my shoulders slowly relaxes.

Once the meal ends, Ewatomi and I spend a rare moment in each other's company on a large balcony with salty coastal breezes and a distant view of the sea. Sitting with my knees drawn up to my chest, I carefully pick my way through my texts, reading some lines several times over.

Upon the formation of the Clan of the Ohia Realm, all magic was forbidden for the safety of the citizens. Anyone caught practicing magic or magical rituals would be henceforth imprisoned. Blood magic, defined as the magic used against another person or persons, was deemed an offense punishable by death.

"Still true," I mutter to myself.

Suspected mages are not entitled to vote in Elder council elections or be selected as rulers of any nation.

Frowning, I thumb to another page, confused by why I'd never learned any of this history before. Letaro is not my first tutor. I've had several as I advanced academically. None of the books he presented are in our stacks either.

Mages are not permitted to marry or have sexual relations with non-mages to prevent the spread of dangerous genetic mutations associated with mage races.

Mildly depressed, I lean back from my text and glance over at my sister. Pretty brow furrowed, Ewatomi concentrates on the needlework on a satin fan, a spray of the Kähari colors of purple and gold. I wonder what it feels like to be human like Ewatomi—at least one less worry to wrinkle her face; no concern over hiding a potentially deadly secret. No ghostly whispers in her head.

Ewatomi is notably dressed more casually than usual in a silky black jumpsuit, a sweater in a splashy print, and a gold headband. I hardly recognize my sister without tulle and glittery fabric. "I presume you're going to tell me why you're staring at me so hard," Ewatomi murmurs without looking up from her stitch. "Or don't. I honestly don't care."

"Sorry." I flush and looked back down at my book. "I was thinking that I liked your sweater. I do not think I have ever seen you wear one."

"Do you?" Ewatomi smiles a little and shrugs her slender shoulders. "All the girls dress like this at Natal," she says, referring to Kähari's most prestigious (and only) college.

Natal is a vibrant place—always alive, packed with the country's brightest who spend their days in lectures and libraries and their nights in parties and taverns, but it is not far enough away from my mother.

"Do you plan to go there?"

"Good glory, no. I could do without reading that much."

Ewatomi expertly pushes her needle through again. How does she do it without pricking her fingers? The last time I handled a needle, I lost too much blood for my liking.

"It cannot *possibly* be more than Professor Letaro makes me read," I complain. "He wanted me to attend Congress, but I missed it. Was there any talk of the waterline at Congress? Was it decided?"

"The situation in Ganju has gotten worse," Ewatomi offers generously, briefly lowering her fan. "No water or bread. There are calls for Hasir to set down—violent demonstrations. People have fled it and disappeared into the Outlands and into nearby tribes that will take them."

"Will we take any exiles? We're not far from Ganju.".

"Far enough, and no, we won't. Father was positively adamant. There's the issue of different cultures, for one." Ewatomi resumes the needlework with vigor.

Seeing the subject is closed, I move on.

"Was *Bosede* there?" I tease good-naturedly.

"Of course. Accompanying his father." Ewatomi smiles to herself. "Isn't he a handsome brute? He looks like he could command the *stars* with those blue eyes."

Smitten but on guard, Ewatomi clears her throat. "He'll be back. Our mother has volunteered to host the charity gala in Kāhari to support the less fortunate in the Outlands. I'm getting a new dress made for it. And then there's my *Hathi*."

I stifle a yawn.

Either not noticing or not caring about my disinterest, Ewatomi sighs, sulks prettily, and sprawls herself across the chaise. "I am fortunate my mentor does not assign nearly as much reading like yours does. I certainly don't have the time."

"Yes, I can see you're terribly busy," I mutter.

There is a quick rap at the door before our mother joins us on the sunny balcony. Both of us straighten up and hastily stand to bow. "Maze," Chieftess Farida says, by way of a greeting.

She clears her throat and my heart drops. Ewatomi grins and gracefully sit back down.

"Your father and I have decided that you should have an escort and companion. Please welcome Kala, daughter of Mother Puli and Father Naco *Ka* Väike—the Small Lands."

Kala pads in behind my mother. Kala is young, perhaps slightly younger than me, with very dark skin like the night, eyes like stars, very long, wavy black hair. She wears a lovely blue and gold dress, flared at the waist, and matched turban with gold pins in it. It is probably her best dress, meant to impress. It does not distract from her eyes, which are dark, wide, and scared. Kala wrings her small hands into a tight ball while she awaits my response (and while Ewatomi grins wickedly into her needlework).

"Mother, I am supposed to choose my friends. You're assigning a nanny even though I am far too old for one," I complain. "Nice to meet you, Kala, but I have not selected any companions."

My mother clears her throat again. "Kala will be your friend and confidant. I think you'll quite like her. She is a quick wit, athletic, and well-educated—for a Väike girl."

"No offense, of course," mother adds quickly, grasping from Kala's taunt face that some offense was indeed taken.

"Of course not, your grace," Kala replies, rearranging her face back into place.

I continue my protest, "I don't much care for having a vapid cow follow me—"

Maybe that was unfair and prejudiced, but I don't care.

My mother purses her lips. "Oh, my apologies. I am sorry, dear. I must have said something confusing. Did I give any sort of impression this arrangement was optional, Mäzzikim?"

My mother smiles but her tone drops low. "If I did, again, I sincerely apologize."

My mother controls my Hathi. I will never escape if she decides she does not want me to leave. Heart pounding in my ears, I visibly bite back another objection and instead decide to try to appeal my mother's vast ego.

"Mother, while I much appreciate your effort and Kala, dear, you seem lovely—"

"Yes, a lovely vapid cow," Ewatomi murmurs under her breath, smirking to herself.

"I will not have you lurking about the Palace like—like some lonely, goose-eyed goblin," my mother snaps, moving offensively forward.

I flinch. "Please, mother, see reason!"

My mother crosses her arms over her chest. "It will be a very long year—or two or three—if you say one more word!"

The silence is sticky and uncomfortable. Kala's lips purse even tighter. My mother stands rigid as a board with her eyes bright with rage. A vein in my neck pulses. Ewatomi watches each of us in mild amusement as if she is watching a show at the theater. I'm on pins and needles, her expression seems to say.

Finally, smiling tightly, I politely say, "So sorry, Kala. Where are my manners? My name is Mäzzikim. It is a pleasure to meet you."

"Hello, Daughter Mäzzikim *Ka* Kähari," Kala practically whispers as she dips into a highly unnecessary courtesy. "It's a pleasure to meet you."

Ewatomi snickers quietly into her needlework.

My mother grounds out, "Kala, you are her *companion*, not her *servant*. Get up," and the shame-faced Kala rises immediately.

"Show Kala to your chambers. She will stay in the bedroom next to yours. Take her on a tour of the grounds and the gardens. It is best she be familiar with it all as she will be *living* here—for a year," My mother instructs before leaving the room.

As the sound of my mother's footfalls fade away, I drop my smile and turn to Kala. "I'm sorry, but you're only here before my parents found out that I went into the Outlands. You are my punishment. They want you to spy on me."

"You did?" Kala's eyes widen. "How far did you go?"

"I'm not telling you anything, spy," I say sharply, sitting back down and picking up my book. "In fact, tell my mother that you are perfectly useless. I will not confide in you in the least. Perhaps she'll send you back to Väike, where apparently the people are drooling, fat dolts."

"Excuse me?" Kala sputters.

"Oh, this is quite the show," Ewatomi quips, putting down her needlework to watch.

"Daughter Mäzzikim, and I mean this as disrespectfully as possible, I will tell her no such thing. This position ensures me access to proper education and will pay my way for university and out of ruddy Väike."

Kala's eyes bore into me, but I refuse to flinch. "I'm staying. I'd like it if we could be friends. It could help pass the time."

I fire back, "Oh, would you? Why do you even want to be my companion? You know nothing about me."

"I know that you are a great rider, you like studying history, and must be clever if you're studying with Professor Letaro for your entrance exams. He's legendary. I have training in languages—"

"Pardon my interruption, but Letaro thinks she's a moron," Ewatomi cuts in helpfully. "So, I wouldn't count that as evidence of her intelligence."

I seethe. "Shut it, Ewatomi."

Kala grasps, "People talk of your beauty and your hair, which is known to be very…"

"Untamed? tangled?" suggests Ewatomi. "Wild?"

"Fun. It is fun," Kala decides.

"Fun! Like a jester!" Ewatomi claps her hands and laughs prettily. "Oh, I am *dead!*"

I am unamused. "I will do you the courtesy of politely ignoring you. I trust you'll be satisfied with that," I say softly before getting up and leaving the room.

"Oh, that was *horrible*," I hear Ewatomi chortling as I storm away. "*Fun?*"

A FEW WEEKS PASS. A DRY HEAT SETS IN KÃHARI BUT KALA AND MY RELATIONSHIP remains frosty. We study and dine in near silence while Ewatomi and her ladies, by comparison, had flighty, fun conversations full of giddy gossip. I am suffocating. So, one morning before joining Kala for our obligatory breakfast, I hurry down the hall to Ewatomi's chambers and knock on the door.

Osata, one of Ewatomi's timid house girls, answers. Speaking only above a whisper, she says that I can join Ewatomi at the receiving table in the front room. I roll my eyes at the formalities but follow Osata into the room. Ewatomi, still in her night silks, sits at the table picking through a bowl of figs. To my surprise, she looks up at me and breaks into a bright smile.

"Sister, Bosede brought me an elephant of my very own!"

I have never seen my sister quite that happy over an animal. It nettles me.

"He bought you an elephant," I say in disbelief, sitting down across from Ewatomi.

"Ah, yes, he did," Ewatomi says distractedly, as she critically examines a raw fig. "I may have mentioned it was my favorite animal, so he bought one as a pet for me. Very thoughtful."

Ewatomi has a favorite animal? This is completely new information to me, *her sister*, with whom she has lived with her entire life. I suspect

Ewatomi has an entire persona expertly crafted for Bosede. The poor boy, he does not stand a chance.

"We don't *believe* in owning elephants as pets," I remind Ewatomi gently. "We consider them a higher level of animals who—"

"Yes, yes—but the Ogun are *different*. It's a different culture! They believe *humans* are the highest of races. Animals are the lowest and exist for our enjoyment. Something like that. I'm not sure. Besides, we *eat* animals when we care to do so. Not sure we should be judging."

It is a fair point. "It was a thoughtful gift," I concede. "You're not taking breakfast downstairs?"

"I will not chance visiting with Bosede before I've put my face on. I look like the dead."

I frown skeptically. "You look fine."

My sister glances upward as if asking the gods how I could possibly be related to her. "Dear sister, never underestimate a man's shallowness."

Ewatomi daintily bites the fig, wipes her hands on a cloth napkin, and turns to her house girl. "Osata, it tastes quite queer. Take it back to the kitchen and bring me something that tastes less like a worm-ridden lump."

Osata bows her head and practically runs from the room with the tray.

Once the door closes behind Osata, Ewatomi smirks at me. "It was a perfectly fine fig. I've sent her down four times. That will show that idiot barnacle to let me leave the room with a wrinkle in my gown."

"You're cruel, sister."

"Oh, don't be such a bore." Ewatomi reaches for a glass canister of juice and pours it into a stout glass. She raises the glass as if toasting. "I do what I like when I like. It is my way of life. I highly recommend it."

We both look up when Osata rushes back into the room with a plate of stewed lamb and mashed vegetables. I am honestly impressed. The sprint down the stairs, into the kitchens, and back again—it must've been some sort of record. Osata puts the plate down in front of Ewatomi and grasps her hands in front of her as if in prayer. Perhaps she is actually praying; the Palace stairs are not for the faint of heart. Sweat beads across Osata's brow, I notice sympathetically. Ewatomi sniffs and takes a bite. She chews carefully.

"Osata, I—well." Ewatomi frowns.

Both Osata and I hold our breaths.

"Actually, it's quite good," Ewatomi says grudgingly. "Go away, Osata. I've no further need of you for now. I'll call you back to dress."

Delighted, Osata bows and leaves the room.

I ask, "She doesn't speak much?"

Ewatomi shrugs. "When necessary. I prefer they don't get too familiar."

I wrinkled my nose. "Ewatomi, do you remember the village?"

A shadow crosses over Ewatomi's face.

"Not very," she replies unconvincingly. "It was a long time ago."

She lies. We will never forget the sweltering hot days in our small home. The evenings when we were unsure if supper would be on the table. The days when our father could not pay our fees, and so our studies would be halted for months at a time while we joined him on the fishing boat until our hands bled and skin peeled. Ewatomi and I were closer back then, joined together by our misery. Without it, we drifted apart.

"If our father hadn't been chosen, we would've been house girls—if we were lucky."

"But he was. And we aren't. Am I supposed to feel guilty?" Ewatomi asks defensively.

I shake my head. "Not guilt. Empathy. It's a new emotion you could try."

Ewatomi groan. "Why does every conversation with you descend into preaching? You're one to talk, as horrid as you are to Kala."

When I startle in offense, Ewatomi sighs, and her face softens a little. "This world is hard. If you do not armor yourself, it will destroy you."

"Poetic. I shall embroider that on a pillow."

Ewatomi sniffs and shrugs. "If that will help you remember, have at it. Now, why are you here? What do you want? You never just stop by to chat. You always want something."

I wince. "The Väike girl. How can I be rid of her? She's like a nanny, following me everywhere I go. I must drive her away before I lose my mind."

Ewatomi smirked. "I thought you might eventually like the vapid cow."

"I like goat cheese too, but if I have it every day for every meal, it gives me painful winds," I blurt out in frustration. "Please, Ewatomi."

"Bold of you to reprimand me for cruelty and then request it."

"Yes, a little," I confess, flushing with guilt. "I thought you might help me discover a *creative* solution to my problem."

As a wide, mischievous smile slowly crosses my sister's pretty face, and I realize I've made a terrible mistake.

I WOUND UP REGRETTING THAT CONVERSATION. KNOWING MY IMMENSE discomfort, Ewatomi splashes around in my uneasiness.

"I am too hot," Ewatomi complains as she enters an airy sunroom where Kala and I set up to study. "How can you two bear it? I might move north to Amęci,"

Flashing a cold smile, Ewatomi fans herself with a spray of peacock feathers.

"Must you murder every animal on this planet for your comfort?" Kala mutters under her breath. Loudly, she says, "It's hotter in Ganju, and there is very little water there."

"Well, that's bad luck. Pity for the Ganju. Thoughts and prayers and all that," Ewatomi sniffs, dropping down onto one of the thick floor pillows. "Fetch me some lime water, Kala."

"Bug off, Ewatomi," I reply without looking up. "Get it yourself."

"Feisty," Ewatomi retorts, elegantly lifting her frame off the chair. "I don't suppose you two would be up for some umagodi?"

"We're learning about the establishment of Congress of the Great Clans, and then we have our translations of ancient texts. We will hardly have the energy," I banter back.

"Kala, you?" Ewatomi needles. "Don't be a lonely, goose-eyed goblin."

I glare daggers at Ewatomi.

"N-no," Kala replies quickly. "Thank you. I am enjoying my time with Mäzzikim…conjugating these exciting verbs…"

My mother is right about one thing—Kala is incredibly well-educated. Not for a woman from Väike, but as a person from anywhere, really. Kala speaks several languages quite well (apparently, she'd taught herself how to read using her father's discarded papers). Her natural intellect certainly helps with the challenging Elven translations that Letaro assigned, so that, at least, is a benefit.

"Are you really? I thought you'd be the owner of at least one good quality, vapid cow," Ewatomi says with a smirk and a sniff.

Grimacing, Kala disappears behind a curtain of her hair. With a final little wave, Ewatomi disappears to go play a game of umagodi with her gaggle of giggling friends. Kala stares after them, fiddling with the pages of the book in front of her.

I clear my throat and pointedly dip my pen.

"Feel free to go," I mumble. "My fun hair and I will be fine without you."

Kala flushes even redder. "I'd rather stay here," she replies firmly.

I roll my eyes and glare at her. "I truly wish you were a better liar. Or at least could tell a good joke."

"Really," Kala insists unconvincingly, looking back down at her book. She absently turns a page. "We should go to the next passage."

It is not Kala's fault that my mother had brought her in as a spy. And the poor girl, with no social skills, so far from her family; Kala misses them horribly. I hear it; the Väike girl sniffs and sobs into her pillow at night. While I have no intention of ever trusting or befriending the Kala, surely, I can be slightly less of a misery to be around. I close my book and hope my mother is right about the Kala's athleticism as well.

"I suppose I do not feel like studying anymore anyway. Come on, let's go play," I say grudgingly.

"Have you ever played a game of umagodi?" I ask.

We approach the vast, green field. Several girls already changed into their playing tops and flowy skirts and were swinging around painted beaters—wood slats with handles. Ewatomi, gracefully stretching her arms, stands in the middle of them.

"No. We don't have much time for that sort of thing on the farm," Kala replies sadly. "And I've never been to a tournament."

"It's simple." I open a box of balls, each a different color and weight— blue, red, green, and yellow. "You take turns. One person hits the ball with their beater into the field. Then they put their beater on the ground like this. The person closest to the ball runs to get it and then tries to roll it back to hit the beater. If they miss, they're out and the hitter gets points. If they hit the beater, then that player gets points and get to hit next."

"The blue balls are worth one point, red balls are two points, green are three points, and yellows are four points. They've got different sizes and weights. See?"

Kala blinks and nods a lot through the explanation. "So, it's an individual game?"

"No, you have teams." I bend down to tighten my shoes. "You want to try to hit the balls towards your team members so that you have the most opportunities to get points."

"I understand. And the colors on the beaters?"

"Oh, no particular significance there. People tend to paint their beaters." I pick up mine, painted blue and dotted with stars, and spin it in my hands. "The official national teams—their beaters are painted in clan colors."

Because of the unbalanced numbers, two of Ewatomi's friends grudgingly join Kala and my team. Although no one is in the stands for this 'friendly' game, nervous butterflies flutter in my gut as I take my place on the field. I hate team sports. I hate the idea of letting anyone down, I hate losing even more, and team sports offer the opportunity for both.

"We're going to win!" Ewatomi calls from the hitting mound. She twirls her rainbow-painted beater in her hands and grins. "But let's try to play a nice fair game to give my little sister and her farm friend a chance!"

Ewatomi expertly tosses the yellow ball in the air and belts it towards Joche, a girl who looks to be half horse with a very long face and close-together eyes. Joche effortlessly rolls the ball back and it hits Ewatomi's beater. Four points.

Joche, less talented than Ewatomi, tosses the second yellow ball in the air and appears to try to bunt it to another teammate, but it rolls to a stop in front of Kala instead. Kala rolls it back and hits the beater. Joche is out. Four points for my team! I cheer as Kala runs up to take a hit. Kala, with her plain wooden beater, hits the green ball *far*.

A loud crack and it shoots down the field like a shot from a crossbow. Ewatomi and her prissy friends, who are *not* inclined to run and muss their hair, hesitate, so I take off for it. I charge down the field as fast as I can and scoop it up. I carefully crouch and wind up to throw it back. There are a few tense moments as the ball slows down and rolls towards the beater.

Finally, it gently nudges it. Kala shouts happily while Ewatomi fumes and barks at her teammates.

Even though there are two other people on our team, Kala and I clearly dominate. We hit the ball skillfully to each other without leaving many opportunities for stealing, and rake up the points. Sometimes, Kala intentionally hits the ball towards one of Ewatomi's teammates—long and far—so that they would struggle (or be too lazy) to return it. Eventually, Ewatomi, the only one left on the field from her team, gets so angry that she storms off in a cloud of profanity and heads back to the Palace.

I grin in satisfaction and toss my beater to the ground. Kala beams ear to ear as the other girls congratulate her—they'd never seen someone hit a ball that far (that wasn't on an official clan team). I cautiously admit that anyone who can help put Ewatomi in her place couldn't possibly be my enemy. Kala beams at me, and I offer a half-hearted smile back.

Perhaps not an enemy, but not a friend though either and certainly not a confidant (to be perfectly clear).

CHAPTER
SIX

One morning, I wake to the sound of the approaching caravans carrying the chieftains, their families, political entourages, and servants. A full moon appeared last night; it is time again the Congress of the Great Clans. Hopefully the Ogun left that annoying Kwame behind.

I climb out of bed, pull back the curtains, look out my window. The Ogun noble family, traveling by their traditional elaborate caravan full of elephants, camels, and decorated coaches, arrives. The uniformed military, a sea of red, green, and black with the occasional glint of their gold eagle emblem, march alongside the caravan with careful precision and stony faces. The more modest procession of Väike follows close behind, flying their more modest banners bearing a fig tree. Having the farthest to travel, Amẹci will be the last to arrive—with their flags of silver and blue, bearing a fierce white bear.

Groaning, I ring Hanya to help me into an appropriate gown (one that would not anger my mother but also not overshadow the Ewatomi). Kala, the perpetual early bird, already dressed and went to breakfast a while ago. I know if I take too long to join her, Kala will come back looking for me.

"I asked Ewatomi, could she help me ditch my ruddy shadow," I quietly relay to Hanya, who patiently folds my hair into pretty knots at my dressing chair. "I thought, you know, perhaps she could do me one favor..."

"Kala is still here, so I suppose she didn't oblige," Hanya muses without looking up from her task. Her long and elegant fingers expertly move through, looping and twisting. "Besides, you two seem to be getting along."

"Ewatomi made the point that she has to co-exist with me, so she does not owe me any favors. She's completely useless."

Hanya makes empathetic noises. "Some sisters are, I find. About half."

Finally, Hanya clenches my hair with a gold halo and pats me on the shoulder. "There, you're ready. I got the gown from your spare closet. Would you like me to lock it again?"

I nod glumly. Now that one of my spare bedrooms belongs to Kala, I lock my 'closet' full of 'treasures' and seemingly abandoned my mysterious quests (to Hanya's obvious relief). It is near impossible not to stir the interests of Kala, who does not seem fooled by my theatrical snores. One might assume I have finally moved past my grandmother's death. The truth: I know that I cannot visit my grandmother's memories, look for a hidden library, or find the Trench of Demons with the Väike mosquito Kala buzzing around me day and night. The girl never seems to sleep. I have to be rid of her first.

"GOOD MORNING, DAUGHTER MAZE," KALA SAYS BRIGHTLY, LOOKING UP from her nearly empty breakfast plate as I pad into the dining room. "You're just in time. The biscuits are still warm."

Beaming, Kala passes the basket to me.

"Thanks," I mutter, taking one and smearing it with the whipped nutty spread. I look around at the empty table. "Where—"

Perhaps everyone was eating breakfast in their chambers. Ewatomi had the right idea.

"Your father meets with Congress early today—there is an emergency, closed session in the morning—and your mother has gone into the village with your sister for her Hathi portrait, surely an all-day affair," Kala says rapidly. "You seem disinterested in temple, so I thought perhaps we could tour the Kähari countryside."

"Not much there. Besides fruit groves... cotton fields," I reply, mind reeling. Though Kala seems ignorant to its significance, I know closed Congress means something awful is happening in the realm; those sessions only happen in times of crisis. "Goats."

"Then perhaps farther...into the country." Kala raises her thick eyebrows. "I haven't seen much of the realm. My homeland is called 'Small Lands' for a reason."

"Well, what's the reason?"

Kala blinks. "Because they're...oh, I see. Very witty. But I'd like to go. Get out a bit."

I continue chewing my biscuit. "No, thanks," I reply with false gaiety.

"If we both go without Abrar and we get caught, wouldn't we both get in trouble?" Kala points out in barely veiled annoyance. "Would I risk that if I was your mother's spy?"

A reasonable argument, but I do not trust her.

"We don't have time. We have a session with Letaro today," I dissent.

"I am just trying—"

"I am not interested in your transparent attempts to catch me in a transgression."

As she balks, I smile sweetly.

Through the window, I watch a couple of grim-looking Congress members leaving the Palace and heading for the guest residences. It must be a recess. Although my parents seem unconcerned about Ewatomi flitting around ignorantly, I have no doubt Gye would've insisted on Bosede being present and, if I know my mother, Bosede is staying in the Palace.

"Excuse me. I need some air," I announce, standing.

Briskly leaving the dining room, I wander into the hallway and pause for a moment in front of a large decorative looking glass. I adjust my oversized sleeves to a more flattering angle on my shoulders, but the red color of the dress suddenly seems too bright in the late morning sun. The little blue butterfly wings carefully etched into it also seem childish. And, once again, I find myself making mental comparisons between my sister and I—and coming up short. If only my legs were longer. If only my curls hung loose and long. If only my waist was smaller (I suddenly regret my breakfast biscuit. Several biscuits, if I am being honest).

Determined, I pass through several stylish sitting rooms, which are vacant besides the occasional servant feverishly cleaning. I charge down corridor after corridor. Though I tell myself that I am only looking for Bosede to obtain information about the closed-door Congress, I redden nervously with the thought of seeing him.

Having no luck, I head outside and into the gardens, where the branches of the naked fruit trees rustle and whisper in the breeze. A mortifying disappointment settles in my stomach. I assumed based on the gifted elephant that he would be around, but perhaps Bosede did not accompany his father to Kähari this time.

Just then, carrying a relatively full basket of fruit, Bosede comes out from behind a particularly thick grove of trees, and my heart dances a little.

"Ah, Mäzzikim," Bosede acknowledges me charmingly, strolling up. "Mäzzikim, daughter of Chieftain Oko, who rides her panther at a mild pace to avoid injury but looks a lot like a girl I saw racing at breakneck in the Outlands."

"What are you doing?" I sputter curiously. "You don't have to pick the fruit."

At this point, I must advise myself to stop spitting on him. It is unseemly.

"I don't mind. We don't have gardens like this in Ogun," he replies without offense. "Besides, my options included stare blankly at a wall in the guest house or discuss historical preservation with my grating tutor."

"Does my sister know you're here?"

I wince inwardly at my accusatory tone.

"Actually no, I haven't seen her today."

Bosede smiles, and I hear pounding in my ears and my magic zipping around like lightening in my gut. He winks at me, a motion I will replay in my head a thousand times over. "Am I in trouble here?" he asks.

"I mean, I can arrange that if you like," I say in what I hope is a teasing tone.

"I will see Ewatomi at her Hathi tonight." He gestures to the trees. "Do you want to help me? It's for a tart. You all served it at a congressional dinner a couple of sessions ago. One of the cooks said she'd make it for me if I brought her the fruit. I couldn't find a servant."

"I beg your pardon?"

"Help me pick the berries. You were in the gardens to garden, I presume," Bosede replied, amused. "Or maybe admire the trees before the winter sets in?"

"Of course," I answer stiffly. "That's exactly why I'm out here. I enjoy trees. Big ones...and, uh, ones with those flowers."

I try to keep a straight face, but it is difficult; I sound so stupid.

"Did you...see a big tree you like?" He also seems to also be struggling to maintain his composure. "Or perhaps...one with flowers."

"You're mocking me!" I declare, releasing the air from my lungs.

"A bit." Bosede laughs but abruptly stops. "I'm very sorry," he adds after cleaning his throat. For the first time since we'd met, he looks wrong-footed and I am not sure what to say. Bosede moves closer, so close I can nearly touch him, and lowers his voice more. "I'm sorry about your grandmother's passing. I wanted to say more that day. I know she was important to you. I just didn't know what to say that would help."

"Thank you, she is," I reply in soft surprise, acutely aware of how close we are standing.

"It gets easier," he offers. "Not easy. But easier."

I manage a smile. "You say that with unreliable conviction."

He reaches out, clasps my hands and squeezes tightly. He does not tell me a story of someone he knew that had passed. Someone he loved deeply. He does not need to tell me. My magic hovers in the palms he holds; the painful memory radiates from his body. We look at each other glowing with a shared pain. At last, Bosede breaks the silence in a sandpapery voice firmly saying, "You should get inside. It's cold."

I turn and hurry away, smiling tearfully to myself as I go. For the moment, I have forgotten about the emergency congress.

I GO THROUGH THE KITCHEN, WHERE THE COOKS ENGAGING IN HAVING SILLY banter and discussing their own Hathi ceremonies. It is funny how someone else's Hathi always stirred everyone's memories.

"...It was so hot that day, and I was sweating through my tunic," one of the chefs is saying. "'Course, it was my mother's idea to have it outside..."

"...my mum made my gown. In the wrong colors, but it was beautiful..."

A dedicated few will not be distracted as they cut sugar and butter into intricate shapes for the coffee. I wonder if I can sneak one of the sugar butterflies without anyone noticing.

"You are flying too close to the sun."

I jerk my hand back and turn to see Kala, sipping from a steaming cup of coffee.

"What do you mean by that?" I ask crossly, thinking that Kala saw me eyeing the sugar sculptures. "I wasn't going to eat one," I lie unconvincingly.

Kala grins knowingly and leans forward. "I mean, I saw you with *Bosede*," she says in a sing-song hush, putting the coffee down and standing. "In the garden, you looked like an infatuated school girl. You know Ewatomi would cut your throat."

Mortified, I continue towards the stairs with an amused Kala trailing close behind. "I just needed a bit of air, and he happened to be in the garden."

Kala nods, "Sure. That's why you checked all the rooms in the Palace first. For the *air*."

I sigh heavily. "Don't you have anything better to do than to follow me?"

"Honestly, not really," Kala admits as we walk together towards our shared chambers. "I would be careful, he—"

"I did not *ask* what you think. Is this what friends do? Is this how friendship works? No wonder I've never wanted to pursue it," I snap at Kala.

A stunned Kala opens her mouth, closes it, and stares at the ground as we walk the reminder of the way.

INSIDE THE CHAMBER, HANYA HAS BEEN BUSY FOR MOST OF THE DAY PREPARING the gowns, paint, jewels, and dangerous-looking headdresses. I am in a poor mood and sit stoically as Hanya carefully paints the traditional Kāharian purple and yellow markings, glittering against the candlelight, on my face and arms.

"Do you think Bosede will propose marriage to your sister tonight?" Hanya asks, trying to break the uncomfortable silence. "It's what everyone's saying."

I stiffen in irritation and nearly admonish Hanya for treating me as a familiar. It is something I've never done before and would've immediately regretted. Hanya works hard nearly every day—even harder now that Imvula has left. The least I can do is treat her with some respect and avoid spilling my sour mood all over her. My angry retort dies on my lips. To my relief, Kala casually replies, "I'm much more curious about what happened in the closed-door session of Congress."

"That had something to do with Ganju. I heard a servant—the one who served the tea and water—talking in the kitchen," Hanya replies excitedly. "Something about refugees."

"Refugees? People are leaving the Ganju nation?" Kala asks in surprise.

"They *have* to leave." Hanya seamlessly moves onto braiding my hair. "There's not a drop of water there. It is completely dry. They're better off in the Outlands."

"Congress must've been voting on emergency aid," Kala suggests optimistically.

I am not so sure about that but say nothing.

I eventually notice the white dresses hanging in the corner. "Is that what we are supposed to wear? They look ridiculous. Where is the color?"

"Haven't you attended a noble Hathi? The boys and girls wear white. The men and women who have celebrated their Hathi wear their clan colors," Hanya explains as she mixes more paint for Kala. "It's tradition."

Actually, I hadn't. I'd only attended Hathis in the village, and they are vastly different celebrations. It begins with a mass at a local temple and then the village comes together to throw a modest celebration with food, each family brings a dish, wine, and dancing. Sometimes there is cake. The honored guest wore her nicest dress for the occasion, but no one owns a white dress in that backwater village—it simply isn't practical.

After I dress, I examine myself in the looking glass for the second time that day. The bodice of the gown is sheer, delicate, full of swirling lace flowers just above my nearly visible skin. The bottom silver-white ballgown skirt wraps tightly around my waist and flares out from my narrow hips. As my topping, Hanya jams on a headdress, which forces a spiked, glittery semi-circle around my face. According to Kähari tradition, the headdress is meant to deter boys from stealing my virginity too soon, although now it has become more symbolic and an opportunity to show off crystals, diamonds, and pearls.

The chamber door opens and the Chieftess Farida enters in all of her splendor in an elegant violet gown dripping with gold diamonds. "Let me have a look at you," my mother demands in way of a greeting. "You're representing the family after all."

Obediently, I smile, turn on my toes as I was taught in dance and etiquette class, and end with a flourish.

"You'll do fine," my mother says grudgingly. "Hanya, you are a lamb, darling."

A relieved Hanya releases her arms and beams proudly. Then my mother examines Kala, who also wears a white gown, albeit a muted one. "Stunning, Kala. Your parents would be very proud."

Kala offers a small bow. "Thank you, Chieftess Farida. I am honored to be a part of Ewatomi's Hathi. What a privilege!"

I heave a sigh.

"Remember," my mother says, wagging her long, elegant finger at me. "This night is about *Ewatomi*."

I fight to keep my smile from wobbling. "Of course, mother," I grind out graciously.

"I'll see you downstairs."

With that, Chieftess Farida Ka Kähari leaves to attend to the night's festivities.

EWATOMI'S HATHI FEAST IS A GRAND FEAST INDEED. NO MATTER WHAT I desire, it is there, cooked three ways with several delicious accompaniments, sauces, and smears. But my nerves march, stomach turns, and, even after Kala and I sit at the table with the other Chieftess daughters, I contemplate claiming illness and returning to my chamber. Ewatomi hasn't made her entrance yet though, and my sister will consider my absence a personal affront.

I watch Bosede, who sits across the grand hall. He banters comfortably with the other guests. When he notices me, he smiles and then looks away. So, do I. Until I notice that, every now and again, his gaze slides right back. A heat rises up my neck, and my magic expels from my skin as stinging sweat. I fan my face with both hands.

"Are you all right?" Kala whispers in my ear. "You look sick."

I try to answer, but my tongue is like cotton. Darkness begins creeping into the corners of my vision. I am cold, chilled as Amęci ice. There is a spirit in the room fighting to speak to me, and the more I fight it, the more the magic and energy spills from me. I have not experienced a vision in months, and I had forgotten how disconcerting it feels when it rushes in on its own—especially after I'd learned to control and summon them myself. I haven't experienced a completely involuntary, unprompted vision (while conscious) for years. To be fair, I have also never gone months without summoning one.

Sweat beads on my forehead as I try to will it away. I fail, and gasp as it takes me.

Panting, I find myself in the woodlands, bordered on one side by a thick, dazzlingly frosted wood and a frozen lake on the other. The heavy clouds carrying ice rain loosen their wrath in full and the chilly air coats and squeezes my lungs; the nearly frozen droplets burn my cheeks. In the distance, I hear the treble of a heavy-footed and chanting army. They are coming. They will kill us all, but I kill as many as I can first. Gritting my teeth, I raise my saber to my shoulder and charge forward as the magic shifts the ground beneath me.

"Daughter Maze? Your grace?"

I inhale and Kala's concerned face swims in front of me. We sit together on the tile floor of the powder room off the kitchen. Kala gently pats my sweaty forehead with a wet hand towel. I pull in a breath and then release the air.

"Thank the gods. Are you okay?" Kala whispers. "Gods, I did not know what to do."

"How did we get here?" I manage, closing my eyes against another wave of nausea.

Kala explains, "I thought you were going to vomit, and I thought I'd protect you from the wrath of your mother."

"I stare at my trembling hands. "Did I say anything?""

"You weren't blinking, and your pupils were like plates," Kala says in a hush as her eyes dart nervously. "You just looked...What happened?"

"It was nothing," I reply quickly.

Kala's eyes narrow. "I still think we should call a doctor. Maybe take you to the sick chamber or medicinary."

"Not necessary, but thank you," I declare, trying a different tack. "I sometimes have these...attacks. They're nothing really, but they frustrate my mother."

Kala raises her thick eyebrows. "So, this was one of the epileptic fits?"

I frown in confusion. "How——"

"Your mother. She told me to watch for them," Kala fesses up, looking nervous. "I'm sorry that I didn't tell you. Honestly, I thought it would be much worse..."

I know that saying anything to the contrary could be deadly for both of us. I think of Nanny. Poor woman. Kala may have little idea of my mother would do to keep my necromancy a secret, but I know well. Too well. "I wouldn't mention this to her. It worries her, and they don't know how to treat them," I add hurriedly.

Kala bites her lip. "Are you sure...I feel like——"

"Please, Kala. Please don't tell her. You don't know what my mother is like. Please."

Kala relents. "As long as you're all right, let's just hurry back."

"You can't tell her." I gulp, unconsciously putting my hand up onto my cheek. "Please."

At last, Kala replies kindly, "Tell her what?"

A SPIRIT IN THE ROOM PASSED RIGHT THROUGH ME. A MAN, JUDGING BY THE hands in the vision. He is tall and powerful, ruthless, and he suddenly decided he wanted to be heard or seen. Would he do it again? Did he want to speak to me? I bit a nail nervously, but Kala and I return to our places not a moment too soon. Dressed in elegant robes, Titus announces the guest of honor in his most pompous tone.

"Ewatomi *Ka* Kähari, daughter of Chieftain Oko and Chieftess Farida *Ka* Kähari," he calls dramatically before opening the grand hall doors with a flourish.

My mouth involuntarily falls open as the Daughter of Chieftain Ewatomi *Ka* Kähari sweeps into the room. As Ewatomi moves, her elaborate white gown slowly brightens into a glittering gold and purple, Kähari nation's official colors. Ewatomi positively drips in jewels and does not seem the least bit weighed down by the astonishingly large, feathered headdress. The paint on her skin seems alive, moving and curling with every step. She walks as a phoenix from the ashes, power personified, the goddess Kähari herself.

I am proud of her. I am jealous of her. I am a lot of things right now.

The awestruck room erupts in thunderous applause, which Ewatomi acknowledges demurely with tiny dignified nods. She makes her way to the altar, where a line of priestesses awaits her. One of the priestesses removes Ewatomi's headpiece, hands it off, and gestures for Ewatomi to kneel before the gold basin of blessed water.

The priestess scoops water with her palm and smears it across Ewatomi's forehead.

"*Busisa gameni lika Kähari, lunkulukazi ezithelo nokuzala,*" she sings, blessing Ewatomi's in the name of the clan's founding demigod of life and fertility. "*Iyin, Kähari. Bukun, Ewatomi ka Kähari.*"

Ewatomi stands with her chin high, an adult in the eyes of people, the world, and the gods. "She'll be intolerable now," Kala grouses.

"May the gods help us all," I agree ruefully, joining the applause.

Already people are passing around the dishes, eating and talking. The servants, dressed quite nicely in gold-tasseled black tunics for the event, rushing around clearing used plates, replacing them with clean ones, and serving the traditional buttery coffee.

I can grudgingly admit that the dancing is lively and fun to watch. As a musical group with horns and drums strikes up a lively tune, all the young men, mainly sons of other chieftains and other officials, take turns dancing with Ewatomi, who seems deliriously ecstatic from all the attention. The Chieftain and Chieftess *Ka* Kähari watch with pride and whisper amongst themselves. My father smiles for the first time since grandmother died, which warms my heart just a little.

Bosede steps up to Ewatomi for a whirl on the floor, and suddenly my tongue feels too big for my mouth. Bosede and Ewatomi look like a beautiful couple. Surely, everyone in the room agrees. While the noble daughters of the other nations and their ladies chatter like chickens around me, I stare down at the table instead and admire the china and silver sparkling on it. Every available place setting must've been on the tables. I am a little nervous to touch any of it; what if it triggers another vision? No, that's foolish; the spirit probably isn't imprinted on the place settings.

It isn't long before my mother strolls up and puts her hands on my shoulders. "Oh! Just look at them," she squeals happily.

I force her eyes up. Bosede dips Ewatomi close to the floor, pulls her back up, and spins her beautifully across the room. People applaud. Annoyance rises in my throat.

"Rather dizzying work though if you ask me," Kala quips.

Kala earns an annoyed look from my mother. Poor girl winces into her wine while I hide a smile.

"Ewatomi will be a Chieftess *Ka* Ogun one day. We have signed the marriage contract, and Oko will announce the engagement tonight." My mother scans the room, which is good—she didn't see my eyes go wide with shock and my heart drop into my sandals.

"They do things differently there, you know. In Ogun, the gods—they choose a divine *family*. There is a *natural* succession. Monarchy—that is the future." My mother sounds wistful.

My mother had done it. Ever the opportunist, she had ensured Ewatomi's star would never fall. Ewatomi will never be the wife of a fisherman. Never wonder if she could feed her family or keep a house. All of my mother's greatest fears. From my mother's point of view, it is quite an accomplishment. Ewatomi has little interest in academics and no professional aspirations. Ewatomi wants to be a wife and mother. Now, she will be a wealthy and powerful one. And Chieftain Gye Nyame; his eldest son Bosede would be married to the most famously beautiful woman in the realm.

"...and, I think, he would be perfect for you," My mother finishes. "After Ewatomi's wedding, we'll plan your Hathi. I already have ideas for the gown, something to hide your—"

"Wait. What?" I startle. I really must stop drifting off. "Who? *What?*"

In a fairly jubilant mood, my mother patiently explains again, "Chieftess Udo—she has a cousin called Korambo. Only a few years older than you. Nice young man. A commander in her impressive army. He probably will not ever be Chieftain *Ka* Amęci, but he is plenty well-off."

"I can appreciate that, but, mother, I don't want to be married," I protest, getting up from the table and guiding my mother away for a more private conversation.

I just want to leave; my heart and mind declare in unison.

"Mäzzikim, it is a competitive marriage market, and you are nearly of an age—"

"Not yet, and not this way. I thought maybe I could study history or science at a university for a few years. Maybe conduct research and write about history," I dissent quietly. "Perhaps become a scholar or lecturer or noble advisor one day. Someone useful."

"Why?" My mother asks, baffled. "Darling, you must live for the present and future. You have also been too obsessed with the past. Don't you want to *enjoy* your life? Besides, what better use is there than to bring *life* into the world? There is no one more useful than a mother!"

"I find learning about the past enjoyable," I insist carefully. I think about the vision earlier. Already, I want to know who the man was; who was he protecting? He contended with ice and snow. Was it in Amęci or the shifting Outlands? If Amęci, why and how did the vision come to me? My curiosity is killing me. "It is important work. The past helps predict the future."

My mother's mouth twists into a frustrated little knot.

"At least meet Korambo," mother replies finally. "Before you make any decisions."

"I have a choice? Thought you might've sold me off to the highest bidders by now."

"Don't be crass. The Amęci people frown upon arranged marriages. They are so...*liberal* there," she replies glumly.

I blink.

"Yes, I thought you might like that," mother acknowledges wryly. My mother offers me a rare smile, so quick I nearly missed it. "Carry on with your companions."

I raise an eyebrow.

"Companion," my mother corrects. "Carry on."

AFTER MOTHER MOVES ON TO HER NEXT SOCIAL TARGET, I ALSO MOVE ON— outside to get some air. After claiming illness and chatting reassuringly with Kala, I wander into a balcony and lean against the tier of cabbage roses. I am not sure how long I stay there, staring out at the garden and watching the strings of twinkly candle lights shifting in the breeze.

I hear a cheer rising inside the Palace (likely my sister's engagement was just announced) and decide to bail on the ball. Everyone is occupied, and by some miracle, Kala hasn't followed me. Perhaps she has given up on me doing anything of interest.

After grabbing my hooded cloak, I discreetly pass through the mostly unguarded gardens and wander to the stables. I whistle, and Helissi immediately approaches and gently nudges me.

"I am so sorry. I missed you, too," I whisper, stroking his fur. I grin. "Come on, let's go for a real ride."

We avoid the busier, more populated districts and villages and instead make a path through the lush, green fields distinctive to Kähari. The closer I get to the wall that separates Kähari from the Outlands; the more stars are visible in the sky. The stars above the Outlands twinkle a little brighter, in my opinion.

At last, something very familiar comes into view; the small fishing settlement, Omiki, on the sea-edge of the Kähari. Omiki had grown organically against beaches of the sea, where fishing boats launch each morning. The salty, wet smell tightens my nostrils in a way it never has before. That isn't too surprising; I have not returned to my birth village since shortly after my grandmother's passing. Frankly, I am not even sure why I rode back tonight. I did not set out with that intention.

The village is quiet save for the crickets and the comforting sound of the waves. Quite unlike at the Palace in the capital, security seems to be of little concern to everyone who lives in Omiki. Still, I pull up my hood a little tighter. No sense in having this little adventure reported back to my mother.

Finally, I reach our family home again, and it looks the way I remember—mostly. Its sun-bleached mud bricks are streaked, a couple of windows are broken and the vegetable garden hangs limp and brown in a severe state of despair. Gnarled weeds, sticky white sand, and dark moss-covered blanketed everything.

I climb off Helissi and find myself struck hard by a gust of emotion. The place is in ruins, however; for a moment through my wet eyes, there is almost no change to the place at all. The edges soften, the sandstone brightens, and green ivy climb up and down the walls. On the front step, my grandmother sits, singing and knitting.

"Funani?" I whisper hopefully.

Was this a vision? Her spirit?

But when I wipe my eyes with the back of my hand, it all disappears. It was just a memory—my own. I exhale in disappointment. This isn't my home anymore. It was just a shell, a skeleton, haunted by memories but no souls. I mount Helissi and ride swiftly back to the Palace, which still does not seem like home either. The thought depresses me.

As suspected, nobody noticed my absence, and nobody notices my return. Another depressing thought. I do not know where I belong, but it is not here.

Though it slows, the party continues late into the night. The older crowd say their good-byes and return to the guest houses and villages, but the young and saucy play a game called Orwi, where two players leave the room and secretly decide upon a word. Then they return and carry on a random conversation between themselves to give the other players cues about the word. Everyone tries to guess. Whoever guesses correctly winds up joins the conversation while the rest continue to guess. Sparkling like a star, Ewatomi moves in the thick of it.

I hate games. Groaning, I head straight to the quiet and empty kitchen and pull out a bottle of wine and an old clay mug with the full intent of filling it to the brim. I fuss with the corkscrew, jerking and yanking while the cork stubbornly remains stuck in the bottle's neck.

I nearly jump out of my skin when I hear someone say hello.

"Sorry," Bosede says, laughing a little. "I didn't mean to scare you again. Making a habit of that, aren't I? I came in for a nightcap myself but couldn't find one."

"Just startled," I stammer, catching my breath.

"Here." Bosede takes the bottle and, with a little ingenuity and a knife, removes the cork. "Mind if I join you?"

Without waiting for an answer, he finds another mug and fills both.

"Should we toast to your engagement?" I ask lightly.

Was it lightly? More tightly? I grimace internally as we sit at one of the prep tables.

He heaves a sigh, smiles a little, and raises his mug. "It's been a night. Where were you?"

So, someone noticed my absence after all. I hide a pleased smile. After guzzling half of my mug, I tell him that I'd gone for a ride back to my birth village. It made me think about my grandmother, which I had been trying so hard not to do for months.

"It was depressing to see it look so broken."

Bosede winces. "It hits you out of nowhere sometimes—the grief."

After taking a deep breath, Bosede admits his mother died two years ago in some sort of accident. "It broke my heart like nothing ever had before. I thought I was past it, but then I saw you at your grandmother's services—you looked destroyed. It brought all of it back."

It does comfort me, knowing someone else understands exactly how I am feeling.

We move to good memories. We describe our childhood homes. Bosede grew up in the capital of Ogun because he was born the son of a Chieftain. As a child, Bosede learned to read while I was hunting fish with a spear and harvesting fruit and vegetables (he had a great laugh at the thought of Ewatomi doing any of that).

"Ewatomi called baba 'a pox-marked defacer of her beauty' behind his back and sometimes right to his face," I confirm with a laugh. "She was meant to be a daughter of a Chieftain, honestly, since the moment she crawled from the throne in my mother's womb."

It is very dark in the kitchen, so Bosede lights a few candles, which glow charmingly. "When I saw you riding, your movement—it strikes me to this day as *preternatural*. Have you ever fallen off—" he probes, pouring himself more wine. "What did you say its name was?"

"Helissi, and yes, a few times." I pull up my sleeve to show him a long scar, a striking white line against brown skin, on my forearm. "I thought he could leap this stone ledge. Maybe he could've without me on his back, but we were moving so fast and all of a sudden, the ground rushed up to smack me. There was so much blood—my mother thought I was dying."

But I knew I wasn't dying because I know how death feels.

After a beat, he reaches out and runs his finger along the scar. I hold very still, feeling all the blood and magic in my body rush to my face. Our eyes meet for exactly one heartbeat. Then, finally, his hand drops back at his side.

"Wow," Bosede replies in awe, continuing as though the world did not just pause. "That's mad. I imagine riding one of those warcats has ruined you any other form of travel."

"Nearly, but it is beautiful to travel on water. You wouldn't believe it."

"On the contrary, I believe everything you say."

I smile hazily. By now, we sit on the stone floor with our legs nearly touching; a third bottle opened between us. "We should get back to the party," I declare suddenly, sitting up straighter.

He chortles. "It is over now, I hope—I'm tired of playing that game."

"It's some loathsome rubbish," I agree defensively. "But it's *our* loathsome rubbish."

Bosede stands and outstretches his hand to help me up. I grasp tightly and stand, feeling the hair from his arm tickle my wrist and a fluttering in my stomach. He holds my hand just a beat longer, and I freeze with my heart slamming against my ribs. He leans forward, our foreheads meet, and his lips hover just above mine. I can hardly bear it, and apparently, neither can he.

Bosede takes my face in his hands. He presses his warm lips softly against mine, and my eyes drift close. My hands find their way into his dark hair while his hands slide onto the nape of my neck. He moves his lips to my cheek, my ear, down my neck. When he finally pulls back, I hear myself breathing embarrassingly hard. Happily, he seems to be having a similar response. He regards at me with his pupils dark before he leans in again. He deepens the kiss, and this time, his hand wanders down to my thigh, lifting my white gown, and drawing a small circle on my skin. I close my eyes as warm wave of a pleasure I've never felt before rushes through my body. The kitchen around me disappears.

CHAPTER
SEVEN

n the morning light, the merrymaking from the night before seems more severe. It was the wine, I decide firmly, and I will never drink again. I remember enough about the night to know what had happened would not reflect well on me.

My cheeks warm as my mind flashes back to the night. I shake my head, hoping it will shake the memory away. Would my sister find out and murder me where I stand? Would my mother find out, resurrect me from Ewatomi's murder, and murder me again? Would my father die in horror at the thought of his whorish daughter? Was Bosede somewhere in a guest house thinking she was a naive little fool? "I could have either of the Kähari Daughters," I imagine Bosede boasting to his noble society friends, "but of course I chose the *beauty*."

Of course, I hope Bosede does not feel that way. When I look at him, something rises deep within me that manifests into flushed cheeks, hot eyes, tangled words, and the nearly overwhelming desire to trace his jaw. Obviously, these sentiments are inconvenient given his engagement to my sister, but last night, he showed me that my feelings are not one-sided. Was there a chance, albeit a small one, that Bosede might choose me? Would he go against his family? I do not know. Probably not. Ordinary families are complicated; noble families are hopeless.

I worry the thoughts running through my head will be evident to anyone who looks at me. Luckily, my mother sends breakfast to my chamber (primarily because I had claimed to be sick the night before, and my mother worried the illness would spread and alarm the guests). So, for at least the morning, I can avoid my problems.

Kala and I sit at the little table in the sitting area while I push my breakfast porridge around my plate and ignore my pounding headache (and the pleasant mental picture of Bosede ravishing me in the white Kähari sand to the rhythm of the sea). I close my eyes and bite my thumb.

With a heavy sigh, Kala takes up looking at me in suspicion as a hobby. "How are the travels you're taking in your head? Sunny, I hope."

I grunt and reach for my tea. I will avoid Bosede on account of her sister Ewatomi, she decided. While I do not feel particularly close or indebted to my sister, we are blood. That meant something surely; it means I'm a monster.

"Oh, are you back to politely ignoring me?" Kala asks brightly as she passes the vat of sugar. "I thought perhaps we were becoming friends."

"Kind of presumptuous." I take the vat and dump half of the contents into my porridge.

With a start, I remember to be grateful that Kala did not mention the 'attack' from the night before, especially within earshot of any servants who happily traffic in information. Perhaps Kala would pretend it never happened. Say something to appease her, you twit.

"But we're not *not* friends," I allow grudgingly.

"How exciting for me! I'll write to my mother and tell her the good news."

I roll my eyes but smile a little.

Kala chews and swallows. "Your sister's ladies are a dim-witted bunch of cackling hens. I would've claimed sick too if you hadn't already. I thought it might look fishy if we *both* left the party. Or maybe we could've blamed the fish? It looked like they grabbed it from the ocean and tossed it on our plates."

I snort. "How did the game end?"

"In utter chaos. A bunch of people disappeared a couple rounds into it; Bosede, for one." Her dark eyes carefully watch me for a reaction.

"I don't think they play those sorts of games in Ogun," I reply casually, feeling my toes curling in my sandals. "They're into physical games. He probably wasn't interested."

"Hmm. Perhaps not," Kala replies unconvinced.

"Did *you* like the game?"

Kala sighs. "Of course not, Maze. Your sister was drunk with wine *and* ego. I wanted to toss myself from the window."

AFTER BREAKFAST, WE GO TO THE LIBRARY FOR OUR ACADEMIC SESSION WITH Professor Letaro, who was strangely nervous and skittish. He rushes through his lecture, misidentifies locations on a map, and keeps losing his place. It is wholly out of character for the usually stoic, brilliant (and kind of mean) man. He begins to discuss a time before the clan nations came to exist, a history I have never heard before—a time when there were various tribes, each following one of the original founders turned prophet deities. Kala has a lot of questions about the ramifications of the tribes dissolving and evolving into clans and nations, which is great for me. I am paying very little attention to any of it and staring out the window instead.

"It seems to me that there remains a bias against certain tribal people, interwoven into the new realm's origins and laws, is that accurate?" Kala asks intelligently.

I did not need to complete the required reading to know that. Only a fool could not see it. Still, Professor Letaro hesitates for a moment before speaking. "In the majority of cases, there is no true difference—besides perhaps some slight variations in physical architecture."

"Some of it is nonsensical—simple stereotypes infected minds and twisted into something ugly over time. Sometimes insecurities and jealousy became hate. Hate always comes to violence and discrimination eventually, which brings death."

He clears his throat. "I've got more books for you to read."

I stifle a yawn. "Oh, wonderful."

"I'm sorry, I must correct this—I must also warn you of only using the word 'mage' to refer to other peoples," Letaro suddenly admonishes, deepening his tone.

Both Kala and I blink in surprise.

"Using the word mage to describe a person...it allows space for fear and hate and cruelty." His voice rises angrily. "These peoples are not a monolith."

I never really thought about it. It is how things are, and I have never heard anyone condemn it. Then again, this is why I wanted to learn from him (pity that it is such an embarrassing process). The history I learned does not fit with the visions I see. I want answers that *fit*. Maybe if I understand, it will help me feel less lost in the world we live in now.

"Oh, I'm sorry," I splutter in surprise, feeling my eyes burn but also a small bit of solace moving within me. "I didn't realize it. I didn't mean. Everyone—"

Professor holds up his wrinkled hand. After a pause, he begins speaking again, more calmly now. "No two people are alike. In other parts of this world, there are humans with pink skin, blue eyes, and red hair."

"I find that hard to believe. What a peculiar combination," Kala whispers to me.

"There are people who are very short-statured and very, very tall. Some are fast; some are slow. Some who could cure the quell if given the education and resources. Others that would not invent the wheel if they live a thousand years," Professor Letaro continues. "I say all that to explain that even amongst people who share the mage ancestry, there is enormous diversity."

"Not unlike the heredity traits that cause dark skin, the mage traits *express* differently in everyone. Some can do things that others without the gene cannot. Some with mage genes have no special abilities at all. We use races—Elf, Faerie, Giant, Dwarf, Goblin, and such—to broadly define specific combinations, but it is not that simple, and these races have been intermingling with humans for years, despite society's best efforts against it."

Clearing his throat, he retrieves several thick texts and drops them onto the desk. Kala and I jump nervously. "In Kähari, you believe science, which is not so different from magic if you really study it," declares Professor

Letaro, daringly. "Certainly, the whole realm participates in religious rituals that an outsider would find bizarre and strange. *Mystical,* even."

I exchange glances with Kala. What is the difference between magic and religious miracles, I wonder? How has that distinction been made? Kala has a version of the same question. "So, forgive me, professor, but where's the conflict?" Kala asks with her pen hovering above the ink well. "If everyone is basically the same."

"Put far too simply, self-preservation." The professor sits back down and folds his hands in front of him. "Imagine, if you will, that there are dozens of original tribes, but only enough founding elements for the survival for a few."

He taps the books. "Read these. Remember, no matter what you think about what happened, it is why certain clans in the realm are as prosperous as they are today, and others are not. You, generations later, have benefitted from the strategy that came before."

The way he said 'strategy' sounded very ominous. Kala and I exchange nervous glances again.

"One day, the Ohia Realm will reckon with its past. I pray I will have passed on by then." Professor Letaro glances at the windows again, stands up, and straightens his robe.

"Professor, if I may ask one question—have you ever heard of the Trench of Demons?"

Kala gives me a sharp look; Letaro's mouth twists.

"That's enough for today. I leave tonight for Ameci. I trust you'll continue your studies in my absence. I'll write. Sometimes. I might write. I probably will just see you when I return." Professor Letaro insists.

"You're leaving already?" I ask in surprise.

"Yes, I must go—to address a purely academic crisis." He smiles tightly and clutches his materials close to his chest. "Best continue with your reading assignments and university essays."

Academic crisis? Was there even such a thing?

"Of course," Kala answers quickly. "But when will you be back? Before the essay submission ad tribute selection, I hope? Acceptance rates for women, well, historically—"

Professor Letaro lobs a vague answer at us ("sometime after the new year") before saying his goodbyes and hastily leaving the library. We stare blankly at the closed door.

"Do you believe him? What he said?" asks Kala after several moments passed. "The new year celebration is still weeks away. What could possibly be so important in Amẹci?"

I twist my hands. Did Letaro notice something odd about me? Worse, did he confide my mother? Perhaps he fled for his life. I hope that he will be more successful than poor Ododo, who is buried in the back of my mind.

When I do not respond, Kala leans forward and lowers her voice conspiratorially, "I think there is more to worry about than people are letting on about the Ganju refugees."

"He was being a bit strange," I agree, stuffing my parchment into my textbook. "Maybe I just offended him with the whole mage thing or my question about the Trench."

"He's a bit radical in his views, isn't he," Kala replies carefully. "But the Trench is just an old tale, that's all. They tell it all the time in Väike to scare children into behaving."

I sigh.

Kala moves on. "We should try and find out more about the emergency congress; maybe we will figure out why he left so abruptly."

"Maybe another time," I respond quickly, thinking about how terrible it would be if I saw Bosede or worse, I see Bosede and Ewatomi together, giddy about their fresh engagement. I squirm uncomfortably.

"How about temple? I notice you never go…the services at the temple in the Palace are actually quite moving."

I have to get out of the Palace. "We should go into the business district and find gifts for the new year," I suggest instead, shuffling my feet.

"I mean, I suppose it is almost Onyanka. In all of the excitement, I nearly forgot," Kala concedes reluctantly. "You never want to leave the Palace, so I suppose I must take advantage."

I sniff in annoyance.

Kala stands and neatly piles her books. "I need to make travel arrangements—and buy gifts here in Kähari. What can I buy for my parents back? Another goat?"

Kala thinks for a moment and glumly admits, "I mean, they'd love it, but it's not very original."

WHAT A JOY THERE WAS IN BEING OUTSIDE, AMONGST PEOPLE, AND IN THE daylight!

I did not realize how dark and small my world had become since my grandmother's death—sorting through old things in dark closets, holding up in sitting rooms with heavy texts, crying until my eyelids swelled shut, and in general, avoiding the world, which turned out to be worse than I ever imagined.

I trained myself into thinking that study and distraction were somehow vital to my preservation. If I could just understand the past, it would solve everything, but maybe my mother was right—I had become a lonely, goose-eyed goblin.

Now, it is like I am seeing the marketplace for the first time. Kala and I travel stylishly by palanquin. Abrar and two other guards march besides it down the glimmering stone road to the heady allure of Kähari commerce. The merchants at food stalls hurriedly swap hungry customers' coins for fragrant meat and dumplings cooked in the open air and wrapped in brown parchment. Other stalls and storefront advertised books, beers and wines, hats, flowers, candles, tribal rugs, toys, religious artifacts, and imported gowns. The merchants are all boisterous and merry. Although it is still early, Onyanka gives new life to their cause. Kala buys gifts for her entire family, including her three older brothers. "In case they earn their leave from the military," she explains, choosing several little wooden games.

For her mother, Kala purchases a silk scarf. For her father, she finds a historical book of Outlands maps. I am reluctant to buy anything but find a pretty spray of lavender, Ewatomi's favorite, and a striking clay vase. I pick up a pair of sequined slippers, which I know Ewatomi will love. I swallow hard and take a pained breath. It is *not* just an ordinary day. I cannot just continue as if nothing had happened. I will have to talk to Bosede. Or Ewatomi. Or...my mother?

Moving beyond the merchant and warehouse district, Kala and I go to a special place called Ifa, with its chandeliers, glass place settings, cloth napkins folded into animal shapes, and servers in white linen. Kala appears in awe, having never enjoyed a meal in such luxury outside the formal dinners at the Palace. The wait staff fawns over us, practically giddy that someone from the Chieftain's family chose to dine at their establishment.

While Kala hums along, happy and content. I find it impossible to eat my lamb, and my left eyelid begins to twitch.

Was it *my* fault? Was it his? After all, he is the one who is engaged by contract. Further, am I supposed to be a good sister *every* day? That seems excessive.

"Are you all right?" Kala asks as we walk back to the Palace with the guards trailing behind. "My...*non*-friend?"

"Yes, of course," I reply lightly, fighting a chin quiver.

IT CANNOT BE AVOIDED ANYMORE. KALA AND I BEGIN THE FINAL ASCENT UP THE stairs of the Palace. Since we'd gone and returned, the Palace doors are already decorated in purple and gold paint for the engagement announcement. Craftsmen on the grounds are set to work building an elaborate wedding arch, and several vendors struggle to carry bunches of exotic-looking flowers and fabric samples. I take deep breath as Kala and I pass through the large front doors. A servant marches up to take our headdresses, cloaks, and packages.

"Good glory, Maze," Ewatomi calls, poking her head out of one of the sitting rooms. "Where have you been all day? Come here now," she demands.

She disappears back inside.

I swallow hard again. Does my sister *know*? What was her tone just then? Light and airy? Full of suspicion? Mild annoyance? My heart begins rattling around my ribs. Kala, who probably assumes I only fear my sister's shallow conversation, gives me an encouraging smile and then follows the servant. I walk into the sitting room as though I am walking to her execution. It'll all be over soon. Ewatomi is quite skilled at sparring and I am not. I plaster on a smile.

Ewatomi pounces on me. "Hello! Where have you been? Come, let me show you. Well, you will stand to the right of me—wearing a custom gown of violet and silk flowers in your hair, which should be braided just so—I've drawn a sketch," Ewatomi explains, speaking quickly. "You must collect the gifts and pile them in such a way that it looks like they are *infinite*. Oh, I have frightened you. Well, hello, anyway."

I exhale. "I—"

My mother greets me. "Mäzzikim, I trust you are feeling better."

As I nod, my shoulders sag in relief. Bosede is not in the room, and Ewatomi seems to be in great spirits. My sister is oblivious to what transpired the night before.

"Don't slouch, dear," mother admonishes.

In her excited babble, Ewatomi explains Bosede returned to the guest house with his family after breakfast to begin preparations to return to Ogun. Later on, the Ogun Chieftain and his family would travel back to Kähari to pay the bride price before the ceremony. That means, for now, I only have to contend with my mother and sister.

My relief is short-lived.

Overnight, Ewatomi became quite the high-strung young woman, skin glowing like gold, one hand with a prominent, glittering collection of engagement rings. She is eager to plan the wedding, which in Kähari equates to at least three days of feasts and celebrations, and speaks quickly with very few pauses or breaths. Our mother, who is normally quite opinionated and outspoken, receives the onslaught politely whilst sitting complacently at attention. Finally, my mother interrupts to call in Titus, who hurries in looking harassed and sweaty in his slightly too tight tunic.

Apparently, Titus had already begun to make the arrangements, and he rattles them off as he rocks in place. The invitations will be handwritten by hired calligraphists (instead of sent to printing press). After the bride price negotiations, the wedding ceremony will take place at the largest temple in Kähari. Ewatomi chose the brightest flowers and finest silks and satin for the decorated spread, which will be covered with symbolic items to help bring the marriage luck. After the ceremony, fireworks in the square and a reception with dinner and dancing in the Palace—and that is just the first day.

Our mother nods while Titus scrambles to take additional notes from Ewatomi on each item. Sweat pools in the small of my back. "I'll consult the coin advisor straight away, your grace," Titus gulps finally, rubbing the back of his neck.

"Tell that currish man to spare no expense," Chieftess Farida *Ka* Kähari states crossly. "We wouldn't want the noble family of Ogun to think we're *poor.*"

"Of course not, no. *That* would be a travesty," Titus replies, catching my eye in exasperation. The Chieftess agrees, completely missing his sarcasm.

"Oh, and dresses!" Ewatomi's mouth forms a little 'o.' "That modiste from Amęci. I must have at least one dress and headdress by him."

"As a member of the noble family, it is a tradition for you to wear dresses by a native Käharian for your wedding ceremony," our mother gently reminds her, pulling out a few drawings from royal modiste.

"Oh, I never get what I want!" complains Ewatomi, who is indeed getting nearly everything she wants.

Our mother gives her a warning look. "I've narrowed down the top contenders. Any one of them—"

"Fine," Ewatomi pouts, glancing over the drawings.

"Magado, and he should make Maze's dress too."

"And your companions?"

"I only want my sister beside me," Ewatomi replies firmly, turning and smiling graciously at me. "Only Mäzzikim."

I blink. Sisterly love, will you look at that! I did not think Ewatomi capable, which had, at first, assayed some of my guilt over the night before. While our mother looks like she might sob with pleasure at her two daughters *finally* bonding, the lump in my throat grows so large it threatens to choke me.

"I'd be honored," I declare, forcing a smile as my cheeks burn. Perhaps Magado can fashion a dress heavy enough to hide my shame. Is there enough fabric in the realm for that?

"I've another matter of importance, Titus," Ewatomi says briskly, ignoring my emotional response. My sister regards all emotions as suspicious and never entertains them. "I want to send a letter. By a competent postman, not a starling. Take this down."

The passerine birds with black, purple, and green feathers called starlings are trained to fly between post stations in all the villages and clan nations. However, it isn't a system without flaws. They are birds, after all.

Titus stifles a groan and flips to a fresh piece of parchment.

Twisting one of her rings around her finger, Ewatomi stands and walks to the window. "Start with …Dear Sabari, I am writing to tell you of my impending nuptials."

Mother and I both freeze and exchange nervous glances, and I start biting my last nail. Sabari, a son of one of the members of elder council, had courted Ewatomi for a short time—an embarrassingly short time. Ewatomi took it poorly. Very poorly.

Mother sighs. "Ewatomi, darling, I don't really think—"

"We were once quite close, so I do not want to have any secrets from you. I am marrying the son of a Chieftain who rules one of the wealthiest nations in the entire realm." Ewatomi continues, ignoring our mother. "Titus, new paragraph and dip the quill! I want him to be able to read it."

"It hurts me terribly that I had to dismiss the house girl that you were so interested in, and, even more so, to learn that she was part-nymph! To conceal such a secret, that must have been a shocking betrayal for you and your family. Still, I hear the faithless, blue-eyed beauty is struggling quite a bit in Iboji as she awaits her trial. It puzzles me that you have not written to her. I refuse to believe your passion for her, which proved so distracting to your courtship of me, petered out so easily."

Ewatomi knows very well that Sabari cannot write to a prisoner of Iboji even if he wants to do it. His family distanced themselves; as a high-profile family, they could not afford to be painted as mage sympathizers. They would lose everything. Even if Sabari does not care for himself, he wouldn't do that to his family. I stare at a little crack in the wood floor and bounce a curled knuckle on my knee.

Finally, Ewatomi pauses and turns back to them. "Did you get all of that, Titus?"

"…petered out so easily…," Titus mutters grumpily as he scribbles.

"It was a year ago, Ewatomi," Mother tries gently.

"With love, no, with my *deepest* respect," Ewatomi finishes with bright eyes, ignoring mother. "Ewatomi, Daughter of Chieftain Oko *Ka* Kähari."

"Vicious, your grace," Titus comments, signing her name with a flourish. "A soul-withering message to be sure."

"An open rebuke invites revenge, Titus," Ewatomi replies coldly, which sends a shiver down my spine. "Post it."

ONCE DISMISSED, I HEAD FOR MY CHAMBER WITH VOMIT RISING IN MY THROAT. I avoided the confrontation for now. Is it possible to avoid it forever? Perhaps if I stand far, far away from both Ewatomi and Bosede at the wedding, no one would ever have to know.

Or would Bosede tell Ewatomi? No, I decide, surely no one was *that* stupid. I briefly imagine Ewatomi's reaction, which involves reaching through Bosede's chest cavity and ripping out his still-beating heart and then pushing it into my throat.

Kala sprawls comfortably in front of a roaring fire, reading a book and eating from a small bowl of nuts. "There's a box for you on the table," Kala says, without looking up from her book. "What did your sister want?"

"Wedding talk. What else?"

"I should've known she'd start planning already."

"Start? She's practically done with it," I exclaim as I undo the ribbon on the box. "Several small villages will likely be rearranged to accommodate it."

I lift the lid from the box and expel a little gasp. On a pillow cushion sits a long, delicate gold necklace; at the end of it, a tiny ivory panther with little emeralds for eyes. An early Onyanka present from my mother! What a strange day! Mother always hated that I rode Helissi. Has her mind changed? Would wonders ever cease? I cautiously drop it around my neck and then pull out the slip of paper almost obscured by the pillow. After reading it, my heart stops for a moment.

Mäzzikim, you've ruined me for anyone else.

Meet me in the garden.

Come alone.

With love, B

"I have questions," Kala sighs.

"I mean, I don't know who—I, it could be from anyone," I babble nervously, tripping over my words. "I didn't—"

"What?" Kala looks up. "No, I meant questions for Professor Letaro." Her dark eyes brighten when she sees the necklace. "So, it *is* a gift."

I manage a nod.

"Very nice. Must be from the Oguns," Kala comments, looking back down at her book.

"Why do you say that?" I ask defensively.

"They're the only ones that fashion that still use ivory. Elephants being sacred and all that," she replies, turning the page. "Creepy Gye probably gave gifts to your whole family because of the engagement. It's tradition, before the bride price."

Wonderful, that will be my explanation should anyone see it. I tuck the necklace inside my gown. "That makes sense. Well, good night."

Gods, that wasn't awkward or suspicious at all.

But Kala doesn't look up. "Goodnight."

Inside my sleeping quarters, I sit in front of the mirror and brush my long, coiled hair one hundred times, as Ewatomi once advised. I admire my face from different angles and pinch my cheeks for color. Then I wait, listening for Kala, who eventually tires of working on the assignment and also pads to her sleeping quarters.

I take the service stairs all the way down to the kitchen, which has closed down for the night, and then wait for the sleepy patrol guard to pass to the outer perimeter. I let myself out into the kitchen garden and shiver a little in the surprisingly brisk air.

He is waiting. He is gorgeous, and my resolve shakes when he smiles. Oddly, my magic spins like a top in my belly. Falling deep into his eyes, I press into him and he runs his hand down my face and a thumb across my lip, leaving my body humming happily. His blue eyes never leave mine.

Stop. Stop! At the sound of a bird chirping nearby, we remember ourselves and break apart. "Did you like it?" he asks, touching the necklace.

"I love it, but…" Overwhelmed, I hang my head and stare at the ground.

"I'm sorry," Bosede says in quick retreat, and my heart begins to freefall.

Gods, he barely fought for me at all! I am not sure what I expected him to say, but I hoped it was not that. I hug myself tightly, rubbing my arms.

His shoulders drop. "I didn't mean to—it wasn't right to—," he stammers.

"It's fine," I cut him off, shuffling uncomfortably. "You don't have to explain."

He avoids my eyes at first but then forces himself to look at me. Bosede takes my hands in his decisively. "I can speak to my father—"

Panic hits me like a wave of cold water. I squeeze my eyes shut and drop my chin to my chest. *Did* I love him? What is love? Does love have anything to do with it? Was it worth the pain it would cause so many people? I could ask my grandmother, but I do not need a vision or a deep conversation with her spirit to know what she would say. *He's a man, the realm is lousy with them.* Bosede searches my face, looking for a reaction as I battle internally. I want nothing more than to leap into his arms and ride off. Maybe find a cave somewhere...

It takes everything in me not to reach out and put my hand to his chest. Settle in his arms again. I hear myself say it before I realize I'm saying it. "Don't do it."

Immediately, my chest loosens. Love or no love, I do not want to marry him. Marriage is so *binding*, and I am on the verge of freedom. I meet his eyes with my bright ones.

Then, I hear myself calmly, "I think we should pretend as if this never happened."

"Is that what you want?" he asks in surprise, although I also detect a tiny bit of relief.

We could run away, my heart begs. *Don't be ridiculous*, my mind chides.

"Yes," I say lightly. "It is."

"I'll write you," he offers.

"Then you alone will be responsible for my murder at the capable hands of my revengeful, jealous sister," I laugh a little, thinking of the letter that Ewatomi dictated earlier. "Please, don't."

He touches me gently on the arm and pretends to hold up a mug of wine. "To secrets."

"To secrets," I agree, turning away so he won't see the tears threatening me.

After taking a breath, I walk away—back inside; back up the stairs to my chamber. As I walk, a heat creeps across my cheeks, and I stare down at my clenched fists. I see little sparks of magic—little sparks of energy—dancing upon my palms. Once inside my chamber, I sit on the floor next to the fireplace, which is down to its final embers. I keep looking, wide-eyed, at my hands as my heart speeds up and tears drift down my cheeks.

My magic. Its power is always here, waiting. I am waiting too. Will I wait forever? Why am I waiting? My mind churns. Everywhere I turn, shackles—ornate shackles, handsome shackles, familial restraints, iron gates and prisons filled with weeping souls. That is what the realm has to offer me—offer mages—now that the magic is gone, contained to the Outlands and squashed almost everywhere else.

What if you bring it back?

Perhaps that is what my grandmother wanted me to do. Instead, when she died, I threw myself into the frivolous with abandon, unconscious of want, care; the family ignored, meals untasted, sleep unsatisfying. I ignored my magic. Then, I had a frightening vision without touching a thing, without seeking it—like a gasping, hurling breath of a child rescued from drowning. It is not a coincidence that I rode back to my childhood home afterward or pure happenstance that I was vulnerable to Bosede's charms that same night. I wanted something—someone—to anchor me. But my magic *is* my anchor.

There must be more to my necromantic abilities than visions and visits with spirits. What else I can I do? How could I use it to my advantage? Are there other people like me? How can I find my tribe? *Start by finding that secret library. Start with finding yourself.*

Jittery, I gaze into the crackling flames, feeling several sentiments coursing through me; my magic runs in tandem with my emotions. The power of my magic surges through me and sparks at my fingertips. I do not need Bosede, Korambo, or any other man; I need power.

CHAPTER
EIGHT

Amid some mild fanfare, Bosede and his family returns to Ogun, and I am relieved. We are awkward with each other; stumbling over our words, making conscious efforts not to stand too close. Perhaps the time apart will be enough to ease the tension. We can pretend it was nothing but a particularly lucid dream, and if I return to it in my head now and then, that is just harmless fun.

Onyanka draws closer, and the clan is abuzz with excitement for it. The economy happily hums along as people rush to buy gifts and pack their cold boxes with foods for their family feasts. Kala and I continue gathering information for our essyas, though with much less dedication without Letaro. Ewatomi remains focused squarely on planning her wedding but also seems distracted and dimmed. I assume it is because Bosede left. Or maybe my sister assumes the new year's celebration overshadow the wedding plans. Probably the latter.

I am excited too, but not for Onyanka. I have not spent much time searching for clues to guide me to the hidden library, creche, or the Trench. Frankly, I have been so busy with my studies that I flinch in direct sunlight and probably glow in the dark. With Letaro gone, I can begin my search in earnest.

As Ewatomi and I stroll towards the sparring ring one afternoon, my sister says something to me. I see her lips move but I do not hear her. "Pardon, what?"

"I *said* you look pale," Ewatomi comments. "Then, I said I asked three of my companions to leave the Palace—Joche, Ode, and Imani."

Who? What? "When? Why?" I ask aloud in surprise, as I lower my saber into the green paint jar. "But you adore, er, Joche, Zulu and, uh—"

Gods, I did not bother to learn the names of the others.

Ewatomi effortlessly twists her hair into a knot on top of her head. "Can't be too careful."

My sister dips her saber into the purple. "Ogun men have a wandering eye. I don't care what kind of business his father gets up to, but if Bosede thinks he's taking a second wife or a mistress—"

My body goes cold. "You're worried that Bosede...with one of your ladies?" I ask in a high-pitched voice and then clear my throat. My heart thuds so loudly in my ears that I grow concerned that Ewatomi can hear it.

Ewatomi sniffs dismissively. "I think one of them—I think Bosede has something going with one of them. I've nipped that quite soundly."

Sweat begins pooling on my palms and I fumble with my saber. "You are probably just being paranoid."

"I'm not. I can tell. Bosede is distracted."

"Maybe he is distracted by something else."

"Take your positions," Akachi commands.

"Why am I even talking to you about it?" Ewatomi scoffs, rolling her eyes. "Mother does not even think you're mature enough for a Hathi, and she had to *buy* a friend off a farm for you."

I take a deep, angry breath as my magic prompts goosebumps to slide along the back of my neck. I lift my saber as Akachi declares, "Strike!"

My magic moves differently inside of me, forcefully, controlling. I am in my own body, but I do not feel myself. *Let go.* I do not hear Akachi when he comments kindly about my sharp parry. *Point.* Ewatomi shouts something and tries to jump away as I strike again. *Point.* I watch, calculating, as everything around me slows down. After my sister would strike, she freezes for a second before moving again. My opportunity. Point. I block Ewatomi's next strike, spin, and strike again. *Point.* I move like a warrior.

In amazement, Akachi stands up from his perch. "Stop," he calls, waving his thick arms. "Stop!"

My extremities go numb and then release. Breathing hard, I drop my saber in the dirt and looked down at my tunic. Stark white, I realize smugly.

Panting, Ewatomi looks in dismay at her tunic, covered in green splotches, and throws her saber down with a clang. "What has gotten into you, feral little beast?" Ewatomi snaps.

"Daughter Mäzzikim, I haven't seen fighting like that in well—ever," Akachi declares. He lumbers over and puts a heavy hand on my shoulder. "Well done."

He turns to Ewatomi, whose eyes blaze and nostrils flare.

"It appears *you* have drastically underestimated your opponent," he comments to Ewatomi, a little too gleefully.

Based on Ewatomi's expression, I will pay for Akachi's comment later.

A COUPLE OF DAYS LATER, I STEP INTO THE LAUNDRY, WHICH IS IN A STATE OF chaos as the laundresses prepare for the upcoming holiday and nuptials. A group of young-looking laundresses vigorously wash clothes in a large basin. Like much of the hidden help, they (at least partly) represent one of the ancient tribes, half-dwarves they seemed like based on their height, and babble rapidly to each other in their native tongues. I wonder if they will be affected by the anti-mage laws. How much dwarf blood is too much? Half? One drop? I know my mother's answer.

Titus strolls in and heaves a sarcastic sigh of relief. "Oh, good. Hanya isn't completely useless; you're here on time. Praise the realm of the deities for small miracles."

I ignore the jab. "The modiste has arrived already?"

"Yes. He's settling into the guest house as we speak." Titus heaves another sigh. "The sooner these nuptials are over, the better. Get up there so Zegala can get your measurements."

A dour-looking female dwarf with thin blue-black hair tied in a severe knot steps up and expertly whips out a needle and thread.

"I've been meaning to ask you," I say casually to Titus as Zegala moves around me. "I'm working on an assignment for Professor Letaro. I'm looking for literature on the original founders of the realm and the old gods."

"Letaro assigned it?" Frowning, Titus pauses in his scribbles. "Well, worship of the old founding gods is strictly forbidden, so, you won't find those books in our stacks."

"Of course not," I agree quickly. "But if someone wanted to learn for purely *academic* reasons? I'm working on a theory for my university entrance, and I want to have something that makes me stand out."

Titus strokes his chin thoughtfully. "A lot of those stories are passed down through oral tradition. Probably best to find people from a minority tribe."

"How do I find them?"

"There are a number represented in the workhouses in the villages and a few halflings working here in the Palace—for now," Titus adds, glancing around in disdain and then back down at his parchment scroll. "Good luck finding one that speaks any of the common tongues. They seem reluctant or unable to learn."

I swear I sense Zegala bristle. I suspect she speaks a common tongue quite well.

"Titus," I scold.

"Might not be politically correct, but it's true." Titus grimaces, and with a dramatic flourish, turns on his heel and leaves the laundry.

"It is fun watching him struggle to speak with us. He speaks many languages very badly," Zegala says suddenly in a raspy voice after a few quiet moments.

The other girls in the laundry laugh and nudge each other.

I grin widely. "I don't suppose you could narrow down which tribe I'm trying to find? If I explain their magic?"

"It is forbidden to talk about such things," Zegala replies in a monotone voice. "We are lucky to find work in the Palace. We would never risk our jobs or our necks."

The other girls nod solemnly. They are right. I should not put anyone (else) at risk. Especially not anyone with a life much harder than mine. I pass as human; I am a noble, but they might be imprisoned—or worse, killed—to make an example.

"You will need to find someone with nothing to lose," Zegala continues, standing on her toes to add another pin. "Or someone outstandingly stupid."

Nothing to lose. You've got nothing to lose if you're already dead.

Suddenly, I have an idea. "I've got to go," I say, step off the podium.

"I am not done," Zegala protests as I wiggle out of the slip. "Your sister—"

"Don't fret. I will tell her that I felt ill." I push the unfinished slip into Zegala's hands.

"Of course, as long as you don't tell Titus we speak a common tongue," Zegala begs me. "It is our one pleasure."

"And I will not spoil it for you," I agree.

A SPIRIT LINGERS IN THE GRAND HALL. OF ALL THE HUNDREDS OF ROOMS IN the Palace, it is the one with the most robust presence. I walk up and down the hallway, wandering until there are only two servants left. Practically buzzing with excitement, I approach one of them, the older woman polishing a vase with slow, deliberate movements. Her queer gray eyes are heavy with sadness, which shift to anxiety when I approach her. "Daughter of Chieftain," she greets me hesitantly, bowing. "How may I serve you?"

"Is there an event in the grand hall today?" I ask the servant.

She nervously shakes her head. "No, your grace."

"Then, here is a silver piece," I offer, pushing it into her wrinkled and scarred palm.

The servant stares down at it in confusion.

"I'm working on a surprise for my sister's wedding." The lie rolls smoothly off my tongue. "There's another gold piece in it for you if you keep anyone from entering the grand hall until I come out. Understand?"

Brightening, she exclaims, "Yes, your grace."

I pull open the large doors. Empty and magnificent, the grand hall of the Palace is a hollow, mysterious place when it is without people. With a deep breath, I slip inside and close the doors behind me. My heart beats fast with excitement; I wander to the middle of the grand room and sit down on the glossy floor. Above me hang chandeliers holding hundreds of little candles and a mural of Kähari's history, which strangely enough I never really noticed before. I observe the gay Onyanka kites floating above the sea, the woods, and the Palace in the far distance painted on the ceiling. Then I take a deep breath and close my eyes.

I whisper the ancient incantation and the world disappears in waves around me. A tingle jogs down my spine and a strange gust of wind whips through the room, extinguishing all the lights. I fight the urge to shriek from fear. This feels different than anything I've experienced before. Am I summoning a helpful spirit? Or a demon?

Suddenly everything stands still again. Nervously, I open my eyes.

There stands a pearly white shadow of a man, young, tall, and well-built with coarse hair twisting and coiling down his back. He wears a plain tunic underneath massive crocodile skin armor and a frightening war mask with horns. "I knew you were *Kakipporah*," he states grimly, by way of a greeting.

I totter a bit as I stand. "I don't know what that means."

"Of Kipporah Elf *blood*. Natural-born necromancer. Blessed by Kipporah."

I gulp in a breath in excitement and fear as he confirms what I suspected. If he is right, that is my tribe: Kipporah. "Are you sure?"

"Neither of us are speaking a common tongue now; we are speaking the ancient language of our clan. You haven't even noticed because it is in your blood."

"My vision the other night—that was you. I saw your death," I reply, standing up and taking a tentative step forward. "And that was you— helping me in the sparring pit against my sister, wasn't it?"

"Yes."

"Who are you?"

"I was an Elf. A Kipporah tribe warrior called Adin Munduhaka. I died in the Chaos. But in death, we are all the same. Spirits."

"Where were you when you died? In Ameci? I saw ice and snow."

"You do not care how I lived or died. You wanted to determine which tribe was yours and find the library that your grandmother told you about. So, you found somebody already dead. With *nothing to lose*. Is that right?"

I blink in surprise. "Have you been following me?"

He tilts his head to the side. Behind the mask, I imagine he is smirking.

I clear my throat. "Fine. So, if we're dispensing with pleasantries, where is the hidden library?"

"What is my motivation for telling you?" he asks coldly. "While I might have nothing to lose, I also have nothing to gain."

"I want to know what happened to the Kipporah, Tofuli, and the other missing tribes. I have these awful visions and they are getting worse... crowds of tortured souls in my head," I explain. "I can't figure out how to stop it unless I understand what came before."

He lets out a bark of a laugh. "You sound like a lost little girl."

I bristle, but honesty is best. "I am lost, but *you* must think I can help you somehow. Otherwise, you would've ignored me or kept spying on me," I argue.

He stays silent.

"Please, tell me where I can find the library," I beg.

He responds thoughtfully, "Now that I hear you speak; I believe you're practically a child. You seemed much older when you were silent."

"I'm all you've got," I shot back. "When do you think there will be another of Kipporah blood in this noble house? Or any mage at all for that matter if they keep passing anti-mage laws? Will there be any left at all?"

Adin falls silent for a few moments.

"Maybe you want revenge for what happened to you. Besan; that's why you're here and not in the ancestral realm," I try in my appeal. "Well, I—"

"No," Adin interrupts sharply. "Do not presume to know me."

He removes the shoulder covering from his armor, and I startle at the large, gaping black hole. Silver blood trickles out and wraps down his arm, drips from his hand and pools in a silver puddle at his feet.

"Long ago, humanity and magic peacefully co-existed. Then came the Chaos. I died here by the hand of what became the Kähari clan. Not in this hall, but on the bones upon which is Palace was built."

"I don't understand how humanity won. How did they wind up on top if magic—"

"They divided us. They used us; they used mages to help bury the ancient power; to destroy their own; to steal magic. Humans are one race. Mages are not. Humanity used that to their advantage."

"I see."

Adin continues, "As for me, I was not laid to rest by proper traditions. I was tossed in a pit with my other dead comrades, burned and buried, and the enemy built a house over our bones, disrespecting the memory of those who suffered and died here. My fury keeps me tethered to this Palace."

I challenge him, "Then it should be a Palace full of souls. Where are the others?"

Adin shrugs. "This is a well-haunted nation, but not many of the dead enjoy observing, firsthand, the beneficiaries of their torture. Perhaps they were not as angry as me and rest in peace. I do not presume to know."

"And you have a thing for punishment?"

"I have been waiting to play my part in the prophecy."

"Oh! A prophecy!" I put my hand to my mouth in shock. "What prophecy? Am I the *chosen one*?"

My purpose! I have found it!

Adin sighs. "I certainly hope not."

I deflate. "Well, I find that insulting."

"I intended it that way, yes. The prophecy, in the words of high priestess Cilmi, anointed in Kähari: Under the New Moon, a holy trilogy burst forth into the world to do the will of the gods. To defend ancient nations and chiefdoms. To destroy. To build and to plant."

I frown. I do not recall my birth, obviously, but I feel my mother might've mentioned the New Moon when she recounted the story (she makes a point of telling me that she crossed her legs to prevent my entry to the world). "Trilogy—so, there are three."

Adin crosses his thick ghostly arms. "Perhaps you are *one* piece. You are a bridge between the three worlds: the upper realm of deities, the middle realm inhabited by the living, and the ancestral realm. As I grow increasingly impatient waiting for whoever or whatever the other pieces or people are, I will show you the library."

"Thank you. In return, I will find your descendants," I hurriedly promise. "I will tell your story, so you can be free of the Palace and this realm."

"I am not concerned with myself. I refuse to be free until everyone knows what happened to the Kipporah here on this land. *Our* land. That is my beṣan," he counters. "But it would be a beginning."

"I hear the beginning is an excellent place to start." I pause. "And thank you for helping me beat my sister in the pit."

I knew it was him. I practically feel his smile in the air. "It was a pleasure."

CHIEFTESS FARIDA KA KĀHARI HOSTS AN ELABORATE FEAST WITH OUR extended family to celebrate Ewatomi's engagement. The servants spin the grand hall into splendor for the occasion, plates and glass goblets glittered with the light of hundreds of purple and gold candles on every table. Several long tables crowd with aunts, uncles, cousins—young and old and all somehow related to my parents—from every corner of the nation.

I play my role as the dutiful sister well, smiling kindly and engaging with every relative, even the ones that smelled like fish and horse dung. Ewatomi plays it even better. She floats around like a stunningly beautiful golden angel in her tulle and silk. She even sits on the floor (carefully so she doesn't wrinkle her dress) with the children, who giggle and squeal at her charm and wit.

I do not mind. Throughout the evening, the chill of Adin rests at my back. It reminds me that I have another purpose, even though I'm not precisely sure what it is.

First, I found the hidden library. My search began in main library, where I counted until I reached the eleventh shelf. Under the floorboards, I found the rusty key, and underneath the fraying carpet under the librarian's nook, I found a trap door. I opened it up, and a looping, cobweb-ladened iron staircase lead into darkness.

With a lantern in hand, I made my way down three floors, connected by a looping iron staircase. Along the walls of the first floor, there were hundreds of paintings in varying sizes and covered in a film of dust. On the second floor, cases overflowed with old books that clearly had not been touched in years. They are books about the original tribes and the old gods, and they are illegal in Kāhari. If they were found, they would be immediately burnt. The literature of heretics, the priests would say. I could be hanged just for reading it, but for some reason that only thrills and pushes me to read faster.

Half-melted candles rested everywhere, and the only light came from a small elevated window revealing just a patch of blue sky. Some books were left flung open to specific pages as if someone had been reading but was then called away for supper. The scene offered the impression that the library was frozen from another time, which also made me wonder what had happened to the person—or people—who used to frequent it.

As I moved around the room, I vibrated with excitement. I spent the first afternoon digging through the stacks, and discovered at least one of references I need almost immediately. Since discovering the treasure trove of books and history, I would disappear into the hidden library as often as I can and poured over it by the light of a lantern.

The book, handwritten, loosely bound together, contains a colored sketch of Kipporah, a beautiful demigod with sharp features and icy eyes. Kipporah appeared to many during their last moments and performs miracles. The demigod brought people back from the dead (at a price to the living), decided on when and how lives end, and summoned spirits to the realm of the living to do her bidding. Breathing quickly, I came across an enlightening passage, which I loosely translate to this: 'strong emotions—fear, anger—tie souls to the living realm.' Peace enables the souls to voyage to the ancestral realm in the same way peace brings me control with the magic within me and in nature around me.

Still, even with access to the books, I struggled to understand what happened to the Kipporah Elves. Where are they *now*? I searched for answers, reading one page and then another. I hurriedly translated when needed, muttered incantations to myself, and tried to ignore the ringing in my ears.

Adin checked my progress regularly. He seemed pleased that I am taking my "studies" so seriously, but did not offer much in terms of help. Even in life, he had not been gifted in the same way as me. He was Kipporah, but at most he experienced a vision or two. "I celebrated my Hathi when I was ten, but I understood that others had a more powerful connection with the magic in their bodies and nature," he told me during one of his visits.

I could not see his face behind the mask, but I heard envy in his voice.

"I'm not sure I'll ever be able to keep all of this straight if my life depended on it." The stubborn little spider that I had been trying to kill for days crawls aimlessly around its jam. "Incidentally, it does."

"You can't learn it all in days," Adin tells me.

I know he meant it as an encouragement, but my spirits sank a little lower. I tap my lips with a shaky hand. "My former nanny mentioned a place I could go to learn. Some sort of creche."

"Ask her where it is."

Heat rising to my cheeks, I mutter, "She is dead."

"Promising lead then," he replies dryly.

I speculate on the day's lesson, "Magic must work through a vessel to perform work. It can be converted, but not created or destroyed. Converting it is an internal process that sometimes comes naturally and sometimes is a struggle for me. Maybe suppressing this energy my entire life has rendered it practically useless."

His tone is sharp. "I tire of your self-pitying."

"Adin, rude."

"Daughter Mäzzikim, your ancestors were enslaved, slaughtered, and yet, you are here." Adin exhales in frustration. "You must fight for them as they fought for you to survive. You do not need to *learn* how to be a Kipporah. You are a Kipporah. Reach deep inside yourself and find it!"

"Don't you have somewhere to be?" I ask in annoyance, rubbing her forehead. "Go haunt my sister for a spell. Pun *very* intended."

Even behind the mask, I can tell that he rolled his eyes before disappearing. To my surprise, as soon as he leaves, a weight settles in my chest. In a short time, I daresay Adin and I are nearly friends. Nearly. I don't use that term as loosely as others.

I sigh and turn back to the pages of interest. There is a specific Kipporan prayer, *mulo kudla*, which I have loosely translated to mean "souls of prey." If I could cast it, I would be able to summon lost souls to defend me against live threats. It comes with a cost, of course; I am realizing most magic does. I take a sewing pin out of my pocket and poke one of my fingers. As the spot of blood bubbles up, I wince and fight to clear my head from other distractions. I whisper the incantation and watch the spider. At first, I think it is working—the spider pauses and appears to gaze at me. But then he resumes building his web. I groan in defeat.

I try another prayer, called *huleko*. From what I understand, the spell allows me to gather natural 'elements' to force a death, again, at a cost. It is not a prayer I plan to use except in self-defense, of course. I've read enough to know that exerting too much blood magic would result in a cursed existence. Yet, my curiosity drives me to look at that damn spider and try again anyway.

He pauses in his web and looks back at me. I'm pretty sure he's laughing.

With everyone consumed with preparations for Onyanka, the realm's new year celebration, the international umagodi tournament, and Ewatomi's wedding, hardly anyone notices my regular absences—besides Kala. As an interest, Kala notices everything all the time.

"Where have you been?" Kala asks as she pours tea. "You missed your second dress fitting, and Ewatomi is furious."

"Please send my condolences." I sip my tea.

Kala puts down the tinpot and wipes her hands on her dress. "I told them that your stomach turned foul again, but no need to send for a doctor because you are on the mend."

Kala continues cheerfully, "Kept your mother at bay at least. I think she has a thing about bodily fluids. Bear in mind, they might start to think you're seriously ill and send you to the sick chamber or quarantine you for quell if you're not careful. You have gotten rather thin."

I glance around. "Where is Hanya?"

"In the kitchens. The servants required additional help to serve the modiste in our mists. He's apparently quite demanding."

"Huh." I take another small sip.

Kala raises her eyebrows. "You seem relieved for a daughter running so short on house girls. Shall I ask Titus to send another? You probably need more than one."

"It's quite alright. I don't need the help," I return, avoiding her eyes.

Kala shrugs and disappears into her own bedroom to continue packing her trunk. She will leave for Väike in a day or two for the holidays, and I will not see her again until the umagodi tournament. I will be alone again. Frankly, it will be a relief to go to the hidden library without fear of being followed. I am just getting to the good bits, gaining a better understanding of magic and how to ignite its energy like a spark, an intentional metaphor—I set my spider on fire by mistake while attempting a calming meditation.

I wonder what spirits might be in the room with us now. Probably Adin—though I cannot feel him, and I usually can. Perhaps he has gone to haunt Ewatomi. The thought cheers me.

Even though I now have some answers, I am very much in over my head with even more questions. How am I descended from Kipporah blood? Both of my parents are purportedly (proudly) of *Käharian* blood. In fact, it is a clan requirement to be native to Kähari to be part of the noble family. Then again, the Kähari clan is a blend of tribes. *Tangled roots.*

Further, I have not found a single mention of the Trench—and I've read several books in the library. Was the Trench just a fairy tale meant to instill hope that some of the tribes had survived the otherwise swift and violent death raids of the Chaos?

I need help, but without my grandmother, where can I turn? Whom can I trust?

"What are you thinking about?" Kala inquires when she returns to the room. "You've gone off somewhere in your head again. It must be nice there; you've been distant."

"No, I'm fine. Just thinking about that assignment that Letaro gave us about what happened with the ancient tribes," I say, only half-lying.

"I'm struggling too," Kala confesses. "I read about how the more powerful clans enslaved the least powerful tribes. A bit about the rebellions. Liberation. Then there's just a gap of history on the ones that died out. Not sure how I'll write that essay..."

A gap in history. An intentional, shameful gap, if the souls I've encountered throughout my life are any indication. Undoubtably, the books available in the stacks only contain the episodes and injustices captured by whomever wrote them. As my grandmother said, the ones with the *darkest ink and fastest pens.* What about the other stories? I am the only one who can see and hear them—and now read about them in the hidden library.

While Kala prattles on, I say silent, twisting the panther necklace in my fingers.

CHAPTER
NINE

A few nights before Onyanka, screams, cries, and chants fill the night. Ganju refugees carrying torches gather in droves at Kähari's gates. How many? No one knew. Perhaps hundreds of them along the road. Maybe more on their way; apparently, Ogun violently turned them away, back into the Outlands. At least, that is the rumor.

In our nightclothes, Ewatomi and I huddle on one of the chaises in the communal living quarters. Veins beating visibly in his neck, my father debates what to do with his war generals and my mother frets and paces around with her silk nightgown and robe swishing around her thin, brown ankles.

"No, we can't take that chance. Put four auxiliary squadrons on the wall. Titus, send word to the elder council immediately," thunders the Chieftain. "To the other clans too."

Titus rushes from the room, barking commands to the servants and guards. Next to me, Ewatomi flinches and slaps hand across her mouth to hide her whimpers.

"It's not a full moon; how did they even survive the Outlands travel?" My mother continues to pace. "Congress won't be here for a week, if they can gather here at all. What will we do until then? House them?"

"Good gods, no, we cannot house all of them, Farida." My father exhales and his shoulders drop. "We can accommodate a few of the most vulnerable."

"The priority should be given to *humans* from Ganju," my mother insists. "We don't know how danger—"

"My first priority is to protect our districts and villages. Especially the ones closest to the wall," my father cut her off, to my relief. "I will send our squadrons there and every royal guard."

"*All* of them? What about us?" my mother squawks in dismay. "Oko! Be reasonable."

"Farida, I am the Chieftain. I must protect my clan," he roars back, leaving my mother flinching and blinking rapidly. "Besides, we're far enough south. They won't be able to reach the Palace without meeting significant resistance. As far as we know, they are mostly unarmed."

"What about our squadrons returning from overseas?" Ewatomi asks, pulling her robe tighter around her slender shoulders. "Where are they?"

"According to the last post we received, they encountered a storm. They weathered it successfully, but they are several days out," Oko says grimly.

Mother clears her throat. "Girls, you might as well go back to bed. Do what you can to ignore the noise."

"That'll be impossible," Ewatomi mutters, tugging nervously at her hair.

"Kala is headed to Väike for the holiday right now. She left just a short while ago," I realize suddenly as I stand.

"Caravans were stopped at the gate and sent back. Kala might be a bit disappointed but safely back at the Palace soon." My father pats me on the shoulder. "Go to bed."

For the three days, Kāhari remains under siege. Every day, my father sends his advisors to get news from the gate. How many Ganju refugees are there? What are they demanding? What do they need? Oko does what (he claims) he can—he sends provisions, tents, food, water, and supplies—but they shout and plead for more. The Kähari most-skilled military squadrons, made up of the men, women, and everyone in between, guard the gate and make liberal use of their hooked sabers to prevent anyone from crossing the border. The roads, the only safe path through the Outlands, between Ganju and Ogun and Kähari become unsafe even as the full moon approaches, and the next session for Congress is postponed indefinitely.

Usually, on the days leading up to Onyanka, music fills the Palace. Several crates of oranges, limes, lemons, and strawberries arrive from every fruitier. At the serving door, servants would busily unload loaves of bread, potatoes, rounds of cheese, and bottles of gin, rum, firewater, and wine. Decorators drag in enough candles to replace all the stars in the sky and canvas tablecloths splashed with bright and beautiful color.

Nearing this *Onyanka*, we huddle around the breakfast table, flinching at noises, while my father debates plans with his advisors at one end. The servants prepare and serve pineapple, notably thin sausage, hard biscuits, and coffee. The imports from the other nations have stopped and the villages are thin on farmers; most of them have been called to defend the gate.

"Ogun drove them away with their military," my mother comments over the hum of Ganju hoard chanting, loud enough to reach us at the Palace. "Can't we do the same? Strike now before more arrive. Discourage this!"

"Attack innocent people with blades and crossbows?" My father sends mother a warning glance, one of many lately. "We'll send the most enterprising, desperate, and angry survivors racing onto the practically defenseless Väike."

I glance at Kala, who just stares stoically straight ahead and keeps her elbows pressed tightly to her side. Kala has been quiet since her forced return to the Palace. She must be heartbroken not to be seeing her family. She already spent so much time away from them—and with *me*. I know I am not pleasant company.

"The Ogun should have warned us that they were coming," my mother complains, shooting a quick glance at Ewatomi who has been strangely silent. "Perhaps you should send a starling to Bosede...?"

"Mm?" Ewatomi looks up blankly from her runny eggs.

Her normally radiant face looks gray. "Oh. Yes, I write to Bosede. He is well."

"Helpful," I grumble.

Ewatomi blinks and glares at me.

"Things are happening that you can't possibly understand," Ewatomi whines shrilly, before getting up and leaving the table in a huff.

"Well, there's no sense fighting amongst yourselves," my mother admonishes me before standing up to follow Ewatomi. "Haven't we enough to concern us?"

THE SITUATION WORSENS. BY THE NEXT MORNING, NEWS ARRIVES THAT A member of the Kähari military took the life of a Ganju woman when she tried to climb the gate with her starving child. Bad optics, my mother flippantly called it. I find that an unusual way to describe a slaughter.

I know what had happened at the wall. I experienced it. The woman, called Fili, fell in and out of blackness and pain as she dropped from the gate. Her mind did not register that her hands were gone, only the incredible pain. She screamed and cried as she looked into the empty eyes of her son, who had not survived the fall. Then her soul left her body too.

I'd woken up in a cold sweat that left my silk nightwear stuck to my skin. I say a prayer for Fili, but know that—with the anguish surrounding in her death—the woman's soul will probably roam the realm for a very long time, crying out for her child.

Throughout my life, I have met so many souls. Determined warriors, frightened children, desperate mothers, the near-victors, the clear losers, young and old, sickly and expectant, and the utterly surprised to find themselves out of time. Each memory is different, indeed, very different, but they also are not peaceful deaths, not one of them. What is my role? Is it to console? Guide? Help them find peace? Or do I focus on the living?

Once Fili's blood spills, more follows. The refugees shift from desperate and pleading to teeming with rage. Small scuffles and then larger ones as the refugees realize they have nothing to lose. I begin to drink a sleep tonic to help keep the visions of death away. I am unnerved by how the same guards who wave a cheerful hello to me in the morning can proceed to be violent and aggressive towards others.

In response to the spike in violence, my father sends more guards—with heavy weaponry now—to the gate and into the villages to protect the nation from breaches of the wall, which were becoming more and more likely. If the wall is breached, Ganju may wind up being the least of our worries as the unstable Outlands magic oozes into the soil of our nation.

Until reinforcements arrive from the other clans or the squadrons return from sea, my father decides Ewatomi will be immediately be evacuated to Ogun to prevent any delays to her pending nuptials. I suppose Ewatomi's wedding contract to Bosede already has value. For better or worse, Ogun is considered an impenetrable fortress.

"Perhaps we should bring Maze to Ogun too," my mother suggests nervously, as we again huddle in the communal living quarters (except Ewatomi, who is packing a rumored seven trunks for her voyage to Ogun). My mother looks smaller in her thin robe than she had only a few days before. "With Kala, of course," she adds, meeting Kala's eye.

"No. You'll go to Ogun with Ewatomi and her companions. We will send Maze and Kala to Ameci. They'll be safer there."

I suppose with the signing of the engagement, Ewatomi belongs to the Ogun now.

My father looks very troubled, which terrifies me. I have never seen him this way. Will this night lead to the end of the realm?

"This is only a precaution in case the refugees breach the gate before the other militaries arrive. I need to be here to monitor the situation. I have a safe hideaway, do not fret," my father tells me. He leaves the room and motions for Titus to follow.

My mother clears her throat and stands. "Go, pack your trunks. Not too much."

"And no one should leave the house without a guard until further notice." My mother looks directly at me. "Is that understood?"

I nod and exhale shakily.

I GO TO EWATOMI'S CHAMBER TO SAY FAREWELL. WE ARE NOT OVERLY CLOSE, not anymore, but it feels prudent given the circumstances. I do not have many people in this world, three, and one gave birth to me.

When I arrive, I am surprised to find my older sister wearing her nearly-finished ceremonial wedding dress—a voluminous gold, violet, and cream patterned gown of satin and lace. The dress wraps gracefully around Ewatomi's tall, slender body, and the bright color makes her skin glow. Delicate crystals glitter around the revealing sweetheart neckline and the matching turban. Yet, Ewatomi stares at herself in the mirror with a sorrowful expression.

"What's wrong?" I ask in alarm.

"Those invaders," Ewatomi grounds out with her voice trembling as she pulls off the turban and shakes out her curly hair. "They'll ruin it."

I frown, wondering if my sister truly thinks her wedding takes precedence over starving people and violence between clans. However, knowing that I can be preachy, I choose a comforting route.

"Ewatomi, you'll still have your wedding. You'll still be with Bosede. We're only leaving for a few days."

"This is bigger than you *know*, Maze," Ewatomi declares mysteriously with a loud sniff.

Then, my sister's eyes narrow and the mood of the room shifts.

"What's that?" Ewatomi asks, pointing at my chest.

My hands fly to my chest and realize that I'd forgotten to take off Bosede's Onyanka gift—the necklace with the panther. I usually wear it tucked under my gown, but my night clothes do not cover me as completely.

"Oh, I bought it at the market," I reply carefully, pulling it out so that Ewatomi could get a better look. "Isn't it lovely?"

With some effort in the substantial gown, Ewatomi steps towards me. I freeze, rooted to the floor. With a fluid motion, the bride-to-be rips the necklace from my neck and examines it more closely. When she meets my eyes again, her eyes are hard.

"This is a necklace from *Bosede*. They don't sell ivory in the Kähari."

"I—"

After a quick flex of her fingers, Ewatomi slaps me across the face, sending me shrieking to the ground with stars in my eyes and ringing in my ears. My mind immediately flashes back to my beatings at the hands of my mother every time she knew I saw a vision. I find myself struggling to take a breath as the memories roll over me.

"You slept with Bosede," Ewatomi hisses. "It was *you*."

She drops the necklace onto me.

"Please, Ewatomi," I beg. I scoot away from her as the metallic taste of blood faintly fills my mouth. "I didn't! I swear it! It was just—"

"Get out of my chambers," Ewatomi snaps coldly, turning away. "I'm going to Ogun tonight. To Bosede. By the grace of Kähari, neither of us will ever see you again."

Tears streams freely down my cheeks as I stand up. "Ewatomi, I'm sorry—"

"Do you know why I chose you to walk with me on my wedding day? Instead of all my *beautiful* ladies? Do you know why I suspected one of my ladies—and not you?" Ewatomi sneers, lurching back at me.

"It is because you are an ugly little witch. I shine *that* much brighter beside you."

Blinking back tears, I swallow and clear my throat.

Don't say it. *Don't say it.* But I lift my chin.

"Once again, you have underestimated your opponent," I reply

A dangerous silence hangs in the room as we glare at each other, breathing hard.

"If you say one more word, I will *end* your time in this world, you cock-eyed bridge troll. Get out," Ewatomi growls quietly, her elegant hands twisting into shaking fists at her side.

I rush from the room so quickly that I nearly lose what is left of my uneven breath. As I scramble blindly down the hallway, I more or less collide into my mother, who is on her way to Ewatomi's chamber.

My mother puts her hands to my face to briskly wipe away the tears. "Calm down. Hysterics cause unsightly wrinkles."

I swallow the blood in my mouth, wipe at my eyes, and hug myself tightly.

"Horrible mess. Congress will never make it safely here. We'll miss celebrating Onyanka...the umagodi tournament...the march of the Ojos," my mother agrees with a furrowed brow. She sighs heavily. "Pack your trunks. If your father can get safe passage earlier, he will. Ewatomi and I must go now. I'm just going to fetch her."

"Yes, mother."

My mother thoughtfully brushes a lock of hair from my face. "No matter what happens next, you go to Ameci. Don't look back. You find your godfather, and you stay with him until I send for you. Understand?"

I swallowed. "Yes," I whimper.

"I have a lot of regrets, Mazzie," she says suddenly. "A great many, I'm afraid."

I stare at my mother in surprise. Is she about to apologize? If so, it would be quite out of character. Perhaps the Outlands magic already seeped into Kähari.

"I will never regret doing everything I can to keep us safe."

My mother squeezes my hand and continues down the hall. I wonder fleetingly if Ewatomi will tell our mother what I've done, but dismiss the concern. Ewatomi is too proud to admit that her plain little sister had stolen her betrothed's attention.

LATER, A TENSE BUT CALM TITUS ARRIVES AT MY CHAMBERS TO DISCUSS THE plans.

"What happened to your face? You know what, never mind, I do not wish to know. Pack your trunks," he directs, gesturing to both of us. "A small caravan will escort you to Ameci at first light. It's all we can spare. Please also pack your preferred instruments of defense."

"Will Hanya come with us?" I ask.

"No. No servants. It'll be hard enough getting you two out discretely as it is," Titus explains, strained. "She's much safer here in the Palace than in her village by the wall. I will make sure she's okay. She'll be in the servants' quarters until you return."

"No, Titus, I did not mean that I wanted a servant to travel with me," I correct. I remember the servants' quarters quite vividly and cannot imagine Hanya staying there. "Please, put her somewhere else. Someplace more comfortable."

His face softens. "As you wish, Daughter of Chieftain, but be ready. Ewatomi and Farida are in the wind, your father has retired to his shelter, and I'm arranging your travel as quickly as I can."

As soon as the door swings shut, Kala dramatically announces, "I'm not going to Amęci."

"What? What do you mean?" I ask, only half-listening. "We have to go."

"*You* have to go. *I* need to go home and warn my parents. We use a different defense against the Outlands magic, so there is not a solid wall around Väike. No starling posts. No militia to speak of. All of our recruits are bound to the militaries of other clans in exchange for protection. Where do you think the refugees will go once Kähari turns them away?"

Kala's eyes and nose are red from crying and her gorgeous, dark eyes are flat. I have never seen her like this. "You can't go—you won't be able to leave. Maybe we could send a letter by a messenger."

"If they won't open the gate for me, they certainly won't—"

"I will find a way." I grab a piece of parchment from the desk and dip a pen.

"What are your parents' names then?"

Kala looks crossed. "I've told you their names a dozen times!"

"Well, do you want to fight with me about what a selfish prick I am or do you want to save your parents' lives? Priorities, Kala!" In mock exasperation, I tap the parchment with the pen.

"I'll write it, you boiled-brained beast," Kala grumbles, taking the pen and parchment and sitting down at the table.

Eyes intent, Kala begins writing furiously. Meanwhile, I drop into the pillowed chair next to her and stare out the window. In the far distance, I can see seemingly infinite lights from travel torches waving just outside Kähari's elaborate gated entrance.

"There are more than yesterday," I comment in surprised alarm. "A lot more."

"Here." Kala folds the parchment and hands it to me. "Väike is a three-day ride at least on the stable roads. How will we find someone who will take it?"

I purse my lips and tap my chin thoughtfully. When I don't know an answer, there is always one person who certainly will.

Titus sighs and clicks his tongue.

"That's easy. The Ojo who warned of the water crisis. He has been suspended by the Order since that time he testified in elder council." He barely looks up from his tablet as he scribbles something down. "No one will touch an Ojo, and he'll be desperate for coin by now. You compromise your values if you're hungry enough."

Servants hurriedly mill around the kitchen behind him, packing provisions for the evacuations. "He is still here in Kähari, I'm fairly sure," Titus adds.

"Where can we find him?" I ask eagerly.

Titus winces. "Not a place you should go."

"Please, Titus. It's for Kala," I beg. "I need to help her warn her family—that Ojo knows who I am. I'm sure he will—"

He waves away my plea. "I'll tell you as long as you never tell your mother, come back straight away, and promise to take a guard. There are only a few guards left at the Palace, and you will need one who can be discreet for the right price."

"And believe me, you will need discretion," Titus adds mysteriously.

"I can trust you not to tell my mother?"

"Darling, I've seen you sneak out of the Palace daily and haven't breathed a word. I know you'll do what you want regardless—you always have and somehow, you're still alive."

I grin. "Titus, that nearly sounded like a compliment."

"It wasn't one." He groans and rolls his eyes. "Go, Daughter Maze, and if you do not come back alive, I will pretend this conversation never happened."

Far from the Palace and the south end of the Kähari wall, the brick road becomes a dirt one and runs beside a quarter mile of a curiously obscured marketplace of mind-altering substances, a nightly rest on flea-ridden beds, and sex for those willing to pay for it. Dried-out gardens lie covered in ash from the warehouse chimneys that huff black smoke all day and night long, but the buildings boast splotches of bright hues—blue, purple, red, orange, and yellow. At the center, the bluestone statue of a tiger, for which the alley is named, glares down at all who pass.

I pull the hood tighter over my head, mostly so I will not be recognized as my coach pulled by two thick camels bumps along the road. My guard, Abrar, riding a warcat, helpfully follows at a distance. It is an expensive trip—all the coin I paid for the silence of Abrar and the driver, who didn't understand why I wanted a coach instead of riding my beloved Helissi. But in the coach, I could be an anonymous, wealthy patron of the immoral arts.

People are drunk and friendly in Tiger's Pass. Nobody pays me any mind as I look for the Toja House, rumored to offer the most beautiful, exotic harlots in all of Kähari, and the strongest booze (lose a day in the Toja, the saying goes) too. According to Titus, the Ojo called Mezu has not-so-discreetly been holed up there for days.

From the street, Toja resembles a purple-colored hovel, but inside the interior is dim, brassy, and beautiful with elegant window dresses, thick carpets of fur, and candles everywhere. A handful of young men and women in richly-hued gowns and tunics smile and flit around like hummingbirds, pausing only for a moment at each potential client before moving on. A handful of musicians play soulful horns in the corner. One of the players meet my eye and stares so intently that I am immediately uncomfortable. Then, a young man, faintly handsome, also meets my eye and approaches with a drink in hand.

"Welcome to the *Toja*, darling girl. What's your pleasure?" he whispers, too close to my ear, and I am embarrassed to admit that a brief heat moves through my body. Or was it my magic? Sometimes I struggle to separate the two; they tangle.

"I'm looking for someone," I reply, stepping back a bit, and pushing the goblet away.

"Not for, um, pleasure. He has long, matted hair and a scar over his eye, down to his cheek," I hastily add, using my finger to demonstrate.

The young man straightens up and turns off his romantic charm as quickly as he turned it on. "Are you one of his wives?" he asks carefully.

"No, no. Certainly not," I reply, startled, pulling out a silver coin and pressing it into his palm. "I have a job for him. That is all."

He bites the coin with his stark white teeth and shrugs. "Upstairs. Third floor, fourth door on the right."

I walk up the winding staircase, ignoring a couple intertwined by every limb on the gold-colored rail. I also ignore the grunts and groans as I carefully count to the fourth door. Am I curious about what is happening inside the other rooms? Sure, I am *very* curious about what the morally ambiguous got up to doing, but I am here for Kala. For once, I will be selfless because it is the right thing to do. For once, tonight I will help people instead of hurt them (or help them to help myself). Fourth door on the right, I found it. I take a deep breath and just let myself in.

In retrospect, that was a terrible mistake.

"Good glory!" I cover my eyes.

Startled, Ojo Mezu curses and pushes the white-haired, buck-naked, winged Faerie from his lap. As she goes stand, she stumbles over her long hair and curses as she hits the floor and scrambles away into the hall.

"Who are you? Are you from the order?" he asks gruffly. "Do I have a mission?"

I pull off my hood. "Of sorts."

He raised his eyebrows. "I remember you, Daughter of Chieftain. Curious girl from the woods with no will to live. Stupid girl who admitted to her father that she went to the Outlands."

"Indeed." I nod, pleased that I am so memorable. "I need you to deliver a message in Väike."

"Well, one, I'm an *Ojo*—not a messenger," he grumbles, grabbing his drink from the nightstand and tossing it back. "Two, you shouldn't be here. Aren't you twelve?"

"I am much older than twelve, *you* are unemployed, and I've got six gold pieces for the job," I offer cheerfully. "Three now and three when you return with proof that the message was delivered."

"Six pieces. I'm intrigued." Mezu raises his thick eyebrows. "What's the message?"

"I've written it down, but it's private. Don't open it." I brandish the envelope.

"To a lover?" He smirks and his dark eyes meet mine.

The tip of my ears pinken. "Do we have a deal?"

"Show me the gold," he instructs, looking skeptical.

I place the coins on the table, and he gathers them with his long elegant fingers and holds one up to the dim candle light.

After a long silence, he grunts a reluctant reply, "Deal."

"You'll ride tonight," I demand, tucking my coin purse back under my cloak.

Mezu stands and towers over me. "I'll ride tonight, little bird."

"You won't be seen or intercepted."

"Now you insult me."

"Not my intent." I pull my hood back on. "Just a happy coincidence."

KALA THANKS ME PROFUSELY WHILE HER LARGE DARK EYES BLINK AWAY OBVIOUS tears (that I pretend not to notice). It will do no good to fall to emotional pieces. With no time to spare, we scramble to finish packing the trunks. I am not exactly sure what to pack for Amęci, which is infamous for its cold climate. I am fairly sure none of my thin jumpers and dresses will be enough. Perhaps I can layer them several times over?

"Titus issued us some coin," Kala reminds me as she folds her things into her red trunk with the gold buckles. "We'll just have to buy a few things when we arrive."

"What do you think it's like?" I ask, curiously, shoving my own trunk closed.

"It's so odd how you don't really have seasons here. It snows sometimes during Väike winter," Kala says wistfully. "There's all different kinds of beautiful snow. When my brothers and I were young, we had a lot of fun with it, and mother would make candy in it—from tree syrup. Dribble it into fun shapes..."

Kala trails off and clears her throat.

"I'm sorry that you didn't get to go home for Onyanka," I offer, feeling terrible. "Truly."

"I'm sorry for all of us." Kala glances over at me, her silky dark hair spilling over her shoulders when she moves. "I don't think this is the Onyanka many of us imagined. The chieftain has retired to his storm shelter, for gods' sake, so clearly, the council expects things to get much worse."

"Clearly."

Finally, only hours before sunrise, we retire to our beds for the last night in the Palace for a while. We leave for Amęci at first light.

I struggle to sleep for so many reasons. The stricken look in Ewatomi's eyes haunts my guilty conscience. I worry about the evacuation to Amęci. What is it like in the land of ice? When would we return home? Once we do, it will be impossible to sneak into the hidden library—once the refugees are dealt with, the Palace will be crawling with even more guards than usual. How would I ever master—

Exhaustion wins.

I AM IN A MEADOW. ABOVE ME, A SKY FULL OF STARS. WHEN I MANAGE TO TEAR my eyes away from the beautiful sky, my grandmother stands in front of me. She looks bright and youthful, no cane, hunch, or limp. "Funani," I cry.

I run into her arms and breathe in my grandmother's sweet honey scent, the smell of her favorite soap that I took for granted.

"Oh, Maze, love," she whispers into my hair. "I need you to wake up and run."

"What? Why?" I pull back from our embrace.

"I need you to wake up and run now," she repeats, more urgently. "For god's sake, never ask *why* when someone tells you to run."

I glance over my grandmother's shoulder and glimpse three sets of eyes in the nearby forest, staring at me. The eyes belong to three tall, thickly muscled and hairy, angry-looking men with glittering armor and hard eyes. Though they are men, they also resemble wolves. My skin goes cold. Growling, they begin slowly moving towards me, but transforming at the same time, morphing into big, black, snarling wolves.

"Mazzie, run," Grandmother Funani advises again before she vanishes. *Run.*

I abruptly back, stumbling and running as fast as my legs can carry me.

I WAKE MID-SHRIEK AND PUT MY HAND TO MY CHEST AS I TRY TO CATCH HER breath. An alarmed Kala swiftly appears at my side. "Maze, are you okay——"

We both freeze at the sudden sound of crash, clattering, and shouting in the hallway. Kala tip-toes to the door and peers through the crack in the door jamb. I climb out of bed and follow close behind. Immediately, Kala jerks back and flips every lock tightly closed. Face ashen, she turns back to me. "We need to go. Get dressed. Grab some coin for your pockets."

"What?"

"We've got to go. Now," Kala hisses, as she shoves a chaise in front of the door. "We can't wait for the caravan."

"Uh, right." Heart racing, I scramble over to my trunk and start shoving things into a canvas bag. My brush, coins, salt soap, spare jumper. I drag on a jumper and a cloak.

Then, I rush to peer through the crack in the door. I can make out several masked people, clad in black. Skilled killers. One attacks a member of the royal guard with a machete——the guard counters and leaps aside only for his life to be ended by another of the masked attackers, who decisively thrusts his saber into the man's side. As my eyes nearly meet his terrified eyes, bulging from his contorted face, I back hurriedly away from the door.

"I think those people in the hallway mean to kill you," Kala replies grimly as she jams things into her own satchel. "Your mother said if anything were to ever happen, it was my responsibility to get you to safely to Amęci."

"What about my father?

"He is in his bunker. He'll be fine. Hurry up."

Was it a coup? Was it organized, revenge-seeking Ganju refugees? Why would Kala be tasked with protecting me? I have so many questions, but fearfully recognize it is a terrible time to hazard a prolonged conversation.

Kala unlocks the large windows and pushes one pane open. Chilly night air rushes in. "You have got to go. I will meet you at the bridge before the mountains. Do not stop for anything until you get there."

I pull my canvas bag onto my back and climb out the window as I've done many times before. The practice will help tonight.

"What about you?" I ask before starting to scale the thick vines.

"If it is a coup, I have no power to speak of. I'll be fine—I just want to slow them down. Go," Kala says confidently, closing the window.

"Kala," I try again.

Kala moves away from the window, and I hear the lock click.

Moving fast and ignoring the stinging cuts to my hands, I scramble down the vines and cut through the gardens. In the distance, I hear a mob at the wall, drunk with anger and shouting. I wonder how close they might be. Heart in my throat, I reach the barn and Helissi's green eyes meet mine in the dark.

"Come," I whisper. My panther lumbers up, and I climb on, nudging him forward into the night. My black warcat moves quickly and quietly, a significant stealth advantage over a horse. We keep to the woods. In the distance, I hear dogs barking. Wood splintering. Screaming. About halfway between the Palace and the mountains, the road abruptly turns from stone to sand and dirt, which shrinks hastily next to the river. Atop Helissi, I arrive at the bridge and carefully wade, warcat in tow, underneath to wait for Kala.

As I lean against the bridge's mossy underbelly, I worry briefly about how long I have to wait and what it means if Kala is terribly delayed.

You know what it means, my heart counters gently.

The sun begins to rise. Soon, we will not be able to move under cover of darkness. What if Kala does not appear at all? What if Kala was wrong about those men, and they did not care if she was noble or not?

Then Kala appears, rowing a small boat down the slow river. When she sees us, she smiles in relief and climbs out of the boat. My face nearly explodes in a relieved grin until I notice blood twisting down Kala's arm and the front her jumper. "What happened?"

"Oh." Kala looks down at her clothes and shrugs. "I mean, it's not *my* blood."

I frown. "I have questions."

Kala shakes her head. "Later. Let us get out of here first. The mob is moving closer. It is complete pandemonium. We need to get to Ameci."

"What about my father?"

"From what I gathered in my short interaction. they haven't found him. They likely never will with so few people knowing the location of the shelter. He is fine, but we will not be if we do not leave *now*."

We climb onto Helissi, who continues taking us farther away from the Palace, deep into the brush, and then mountains.

"We should've sent help to Ganju," I complain as we follow a mountain stream. "And we should have investigated the disappearance of the Tofuli tribe. I can't explain it, but I feel they're connected."

"Clan leadership royally messed this up," Kala corrects me. "Besides, we do not know who those killers were. Perhaps there is a third crisis altogether—maybe a coup, taking a chance during a moment of weakness."

"You sound like my grandmother, ever the conspiracy theorist. My father is well-loved in Kähari. There were not even any protests at his selection—an achievement he totes to this day."

"But those people did seem to know the Palace," I admit. "They moved so quickly."

Kala does not reply.

The sun does not show its bright face that day. Instead, dawn brought heavy clouds carrying cold rain, which loosen their wrath in full, and the chilly air that coats and squeezes our lungs. The droplets burn my cheeks.

"This is a good thing," Kala manages through chattering teeth after we'd walked in the downpour for hours. "They w-w-on't be able to see us, and o-o-ur tracks will be washed away. Maybe the predators will let us alone."

I groan at her optimism and pull my cloak tighter around my shoulders. "Who cares if they can't see our tracks if we catch our death?"

Helissi growls his agreement.

"We're not going to die, Maze. Where's your Kähari s-s-spirit?" Kala, whose skin looks grayish, gives me a half-hearted grin.

"Dead," I reply bluntly.

CHAPTER
TEN

Climbing skills are not required to cross the thick mountain range separating northern Kähari from the Outlands. Käharians marked a cave path, allowing the knowledgeable to easily pass through. An outsider would walk in circles, drown, or die on the dangerous peaks scraping the blue skies. The path has the added benefit of helping us avoiding the apex predators—lions and wild dogs—who lurk on the lush mountainside (although one must stay vigilant for cave-dwelling crocodiles).

Surprisingly, Kala expertly navigates through a shadowy labyrinth of passageways and several yawning entry points through waist-deep water. Fortuitously, we do not encounter any dwarves, known to mine diamonds and respond grumpily to unexpected guests, and the rain dribbles to a stop as we reach the other side. Just beyond the mountains, recolored to crimson, gold, and sapphire from years of absorbing Outlands magic, lies a peaceful greenish-yellow plain underneath a blanket of stars. Farther north stands a dense wall of gleaming trees.

We are in the Outlands. The full moon shines on it. It is as safe to cross as it will ever be.

With Kala's arms wrapped around my waist, I spur Helissi north, towards the Ameci star, arguably the brightest star in the realm and a brilliant method of navigation in a place where landmarks are unreliable markers. As we travel, the barren plain of the savanna slowly shifts into foothills and enormous, vibrant green trees. The footpath disappears. In the far distance, smoke twists from the occasional cookfire, a mark of a clan or family, probably mage, living far from civilization.

Wild beasts roam, some harmless like the wildebeests, some well-teethed with sharp claws like the saber-toothed tigers and wild dogs, which we have luckily not confronted yet. The Outlands is uninhabitable land, decreed as much by the realm's Congress of the Great Clans, for no further development (though a few have tried). We struggle to find stable roads and sometimes fall into paths where the brush and weeds have been flattened by the footfalls of beasts.

Cut off from the Kähari network of caravans, it will take several days, perhaps weeks, at a fast pace to reach Ameci through the Outlands (this is an optimistic prediction). We also do not have protection from the changing elements, so we will have to move without delay before the full moon wans and the Outlands shift on us. It will be harder to travel through Outlands in a swamp during a lightning storm. Or a desert in a drought.

"We need to stop," I confess, fatigue raking my body.

Visibly stunned by the concept that we would need any rest at all, Kala consults a map detailing the stable lands and paths. "There is a work house by the Najura lake, which is known to be fairly stable—besides growing and shrinking in size. We can spend a night there to gather ourselves and start fresh," Kala finally concedes.

"Unless she has a bath, there will not be *anything* fresh about me in the morning," I complain, adjusting myself on top of my panther's bare back.

Miraculously, we find the work house—a weather-beaten barn surrounded by tall stalks of purple corn, a hoard of ugly, winged cats, and overfed field rabbits. 'Clean bedding for a night of picking of corn,' the painted sign states. Easy work, I thought naively while praying the owner will accept coin instead.

An Outlands woman opens the door. Immediately, I wonder if she identifies as a witch. First, she wears all black from turban to boots, an amulet in the shape of a saber moon hangs around her neck, and silver bangles around her wrists and ankles. Second, sharp herbs permeate the air around her. Third, while it appears the area around her fields is beginning to sink into the expanding lake, her farm seems solidly afloat.

Her cloudy eyes linger briefly on Kala's bloodstained clothes, but she does not ask any questions. Instead, she grumbles something about 'strange clan folk' and pointedly warns us against Helissi eating any of her goats. We offer coin for the bed, but Leines refuses. Our great clan coin has no value to her.

While Helissi rests in the barn, Kala and I work together in the moonlight, filling buckets and crates with corn. As it turns out, it is not easy work at all. The fatigue off the last couple of days clings to both of us like a heavy blanket. We stumble around the field like two drunkards, looking for the lingering kennels. While we work, I worry. Is my father okay? Did Ewatomi and my mother make it to Ogun safely? What of Hanya? Or is everyone dead, and are we the only survivors left to tell the tale? My body starts to seize in panic, so I focus on the task at hand. *Corn. Corn. Corn.* I drop the crumbling ears in the basket resting on my hip. My breathing slows back down, but the worry faintly persists in the form of a fluttery heart.

For supper, Leines cooks a legume stew served with a sourdough flatbread. She offers Helissi dried bush meat and pointedly warns us (again) against letting him eat her goats. I (again) agree to those terms and hope Leines isn't too attached to the emerald-colored rabbits.

Most of her seasonal help moved on, Leines explains. The crop is not as good because of shifting lake, which shifts more magic-saturated soil into the fields. For another, with the strong economies in Kähari and Ogun, fewer people are looking for work in the Outlands. Occasionally, there is a mage, usually on the run. Leines says she prefers mages because they work hard, but they usually move on after just one night.

"You're not afraid of them?" Kala asks curiously.

Apparently, Kala cannot tell Leines is a witch. I wonder why she can't see it.

Leines ladles up the stew into tin bowls. "I'm only afraid of whatever is *chasing* them."

Then, Leines handled more of the harvest herself this year than ever before—she is getting older, and it is a large farm. Her partner died decades ago in a futile skirmish with long-horned hyenas in the Outlands, and her six children grew and moved to Ogun or Kähari. For "better lives," she grouses bitterly as if this were a terrible offense.

But enough about her, Leines concedes after talking all through the entire supper. Not that I mind. I am exhausted and not thrilled at the thought of social interaction with a stranger. For me, conversing is more difficult than picking the corn.

"You girls are from Kähari," Leines observes, as she clears the tin bowls. "That's the only place they wear those brightly colored jumpsuits. *Clan girls.* Just over the mountains, eh?"

I nod, beaming with indoctrinated Käharian pride. "It's lush, lots of palms and white sand and gardens and lakes...and the architecture. It's like it's one with natu—"

Kala jabs me in the ribs with a short elbow.

"It's fine," I finish feebly.

Leines's eyes scan us carefully. "A bit young to be on your own."

She probably sees a lot of runaways, but maybe not many young women with coin in their pockets. I glance at Kala, who returns a look of warning.

"We are just on a little adventure," Kala replies casually, standing to help her clear.

"Aren't telling me, eh?" Leines grins, showing dark gaps in her smile. "It's all right. You're not the first mysterious lot to pass through here, you know. Just the other day, I saw Kähari's *noble guard* ride through here. Full armor, phoenix banners, and all. Took most of my good corn. Where were *they* going, you think?"

I opt to shrug. "Haven't any idea. Not our business of course."

"That's a nice warcat, you got. Must've cost quite a bit of coin for a pet like that," Leines tries again.

"My grandmother found him when he was just a kitten. He'd been left to die," I lie.

Helissi was a gift, but from my father for my birthday in his first year of Chieftain. Truthfully, it is not a proper gift for a chieftain's daughter (warcats are for warriors and guards), but I begged and he relented. He sent an advisor to buy Helissi from a breeder in the Outlands (exposure to magic that makes the cats grow large—some even grow wings), and proudly presented me with my cub. It is easily my favorite childhood memory.

Adding honestly, I say, "He's no pet though. He is my companion and familiar, and he can come and go as he pleases. He chooses me."

"Well then, odd that you are not with your wonderful grandmother and family to celebrate Onyanka." Leines stares us down with her bulgy eyes.

"My grandmother is dead," I reply bluntly.

"We are family. This is my sister," Kala adds coldly, tiring of the woman's nakedly transparent attempt to interrogate us. "We're traveling to visit family in Ameçi, but have met with some delays with our transportation, so we have taken to foot."

I avoid the witch's eyes and focus on my tin mug as they dart back and both between us, taking in Kala's darker skin, my lighter skin; Kala's long silky black hair and my cloud of curly coils. Her thin lips twist. We smile, wide and innocent, at her.

Clearing her throat, Leines drops the rest of the dishes in the soapy tub of water. "Well, you did the work and earned your beds. Bathe and wash your things. I'm not your mother, but I can't have you leave here smelling as ripe as you do. The wet room is in the back."

I WAKE THE NEXT MORNING FROM UNEASY DREAMS AND NUZZLE UNDER THE covers to protect from the chilly draft skipping across the bed. The cool blue light of the morning's wee hours skirts through the curtains and the walls and floor, prompting me to drag myself from under the course duvet. In alarm, I notice the unfamiliar walls and the dirty floor. I am not at home.

The last two days slam into me like an angry bull. Swallowing hard, I turn over and see Kala, long hair was tangled and everywhere, curled up next to me. She snores peacefully—for now.

With a yawn, I stretch and hear my painful toes crack. Sitting up, I glance blearily around the threadbare bedroom. Helissi, who we snuck inside, curls in the corner sleeping as serenely as Kala.

Someone softly knocks on the door. Wincing as my scabbed over feet hit the floor, I open it to Leines.

"Merry Onyanka," she cheers, waking Helissi, who growls in annoyance. "Up! Come!"

Over a plate of runny breakfast eggs, Leines gives us gifts of dried fruits and sings tribal songs in an unfamiliar language; very different from the Onyanka I have come to expect; but more welcome than the inquisition from the night before. Kala's eyes dart, untrusting of the old woman's sudden cavorting. "I haven't had guests on Onyanka for years," Leines declares brightly.

"Not since my youngest son moved to Ogun for a job—in an iron mine. Those jobs pay well, he said. I'll visit all the time, he said. Nothing pays better than clean air, fresh food, and a sky full of stars if you ask me." Even though no one asked her.

After breakfast, Kala hurries us out, begging forgiveness of a disappointed Leines. She generously offers a small crossbow, candle lanterns, provisions, and supplies, which we accept. I will need to remember to mention Leines to my father, so that she can be thanked properly.

When I offer coin, Leines demurs. "I have all that I need. Praise the gods, old and new, you can only expect so much reward in this life."

WE RIDE THE WELL-RESTED HELISSI FOR SEVERAL HOURS THROUGH THE savanna on what we hope is a stable road. We stop to camp on a peak near a narrow river, just before a slowly shifting mountains slope.

"When traveling across the Ohia Realm in the Outlands, at least three things are necessary. Coin, a weapon, and a full moon," Kala observes. "Coin because you can buy yourself out of some trouble—hunger, lack of clothing, transportation, or shelter, and the weapon for trouble with little chance of peaceful negotiation. Full moon so you don't disappear into a pit of quicksand or a shifting river."

"You certainly seem quite knowledgeable about the world for a Väike girl," I quip.

"You'll be kinder to me or you'll starve, your grace," Kala warns, and then proceeds to use a couple of stones and some twigs to spark a fire.

Removing the crossbow from her back, Kala examines it for a moment before hoisting it at eye level and wandering into the thick knee-deep brush. With careful concentration, Kala squints through the sunlight, points the crossbow at a tree, and pulls the trigger.

Crack! The arrow slams into the tree. Upon impact, a belligerently squawking flock of glittering golden buzzards rises from the tree in a bright cloud. In a swift motion, Kala leans back, catches one in her sights, and sends it diving back to the ground. Then Kala retrieves it and proceeds to expertly de-feather the thing with a hooked knife.

I stand there, dumbfounded. "Where in the *realm* did you learn to do all that?" I ask as Kala slides the naked bird onto a splint and puts it over the fire. "You're a wild one."

"Don't tell me a fisherman's daughter doesn't know how to prepare a simple bird," Kala laughs lightly, wiping her hands on her jumper.

"I've been daughter of a chieftain longer than I was daughter of a fisherman. And furthermore, naturally no, but I know how to skin a fish," I reply defensively. "So, where are we going to sleep? Do you have mysterious wood-crafting skills?"

"Sorry, no. We will sleep outside under the stars," Kala says, as if this was a perfectly acceptable idea. She sips from a leather pouch filled with water, courtesy of Leines. "There isn't another workhouse or village for several miles. So, it is the ground or we can keep moving."

I shudder. "My bottom is shouting at me with all sorts of profanity, and my legs are yelling even louder."

"I mean, I'm curious now. What are your ass and legs saying?"

"Can't quite make it out, but I can tell that they're conspiring against me."

"Ah, a coup by your limbs. So, we sleep here."

"Sleep *outside?* We'll get eaten by a lion! Or one of those river crocodiles." I shiver, stroking Helissi's silky black fur. Helissi shifts his head in my lap and gives me an empathetic look. "What about the wild dogs?"

"We sleep outside in Väike all the time—without a gigantic, friendly panther nearby. Minimal predatory attacks, I assure you."

"You seem very sure of that. Also, *minimal?*"

"I am sure." Kala turns the buzzard on the splint. "We'll be fine; there are more desirable targets here," she repeats, sounding a little less convinced.

I pull my knees to my chest and stare at Kala with questions swirling in my head. For instance: what happened back at the Palace? Did Kala kill those attackers like she killed that bird? Who else has she killed? But most importantly, will the stars protect us from oversized, saber-tooth tigers?

I want to ask all those questions and about a dozen more, but stay silent because I am afraid of the answers. Instead, I ask something more benign.

"How did my mother come to meet you anyway?" I ask, watching for a reaction that does not appear. "She never told me."

Apparently, it is not as benign as I thought.

Avoiding my eyes, Kala pulls a few more dried branches and brush into a pile. "It is a very long story."

I pointed out, "We have a lot of time and no men, music, games, or acrobats to pass the time. I'd like to hear it."

"Buzzard?" Kala offers, gingerly removing the roasted bird from the fire. "It is hot."

"Is it good?" I ask cautiously.

"It is buzzard and it is hot." Kala holds out a leg.

My stomach turns looking at it. "I'll just gather some brush for the shelter and dream of cake."

THE SUN BEGINS TO SET, THE SKY BECOMING A GERANIUM PINK. WE ARE finishing our (awful) buzzard supper when Kala's eyes widen and Helissi lifts his head and snarls menacingly. A solemn howl pierces the air. It sounds like a wild dog, not far from where we sit. Fear crawls on my skin and magic swirls into my throat. Kala's face turns ashen as she looks around.

"It is a wild dog," Kala confirms.

"Helissi is easily four times its size."

"It is never just *one* wild dog," Kala replies, pulling up crossbow and cocking it.

I flinch when the dog howls again. "How do you know it is after us?"

Kala continues to peer. "Have you seen *any* other animals, besides birds and rodents?"

There is the howl again; closer this time.

"Up that tree." Kala points. "Bring the lantern."

I urge the Helissi towards the large, gnarled tree shimmering with silver leaves. He does not climb—the branches would never support his weight; instead, Helissi confidently prowls around the base while Kala and I scale the tree. I grip every handhold so tightly my knuckles turn white and my hands sting and bleed. I do not slow; a brief pause could mean my death. We climb well up in the tree before I expel a shaky breath

Mere breaths later, wild dogs bound out of the shadows. 'Wild dog' seems like a benign name for these frightening creatures—I see three wolf-like creatures with a stag's haunches, cloven hooves, a lion's neck, tail, and breast, badger-shaped head, mouth opening right back to the pointed ears, revealing ridges and rows of jagged teeth. My breath comes faster and faster. Perhaps they started as wild dogs before the magic twisted their bones for generations. Now, they are something quite different. Something absolutely visceral.

The pack gathers at the tree, circling slowly below as Helissi growls, roars, and bats them back with his large paws. They back up, and then one of the dogs, with white markings around his eyes, howls again. I jerkily pull myself onto a thick branch. The dogs rush around, and I cringe as they jump at us.

"More are coming," Kala grunts as she settles herself onto a thick branch. "Hurry, open the lantern."

The lantern shakes because my hands are trembling, but I manage to open it, and Kala jabs the hilt of one of the arrows inside. Flames lick up the arrow as she places it back into the crossbow and fires into the pack below. The pack leader howls angrily, lunging backward.

Another dog leaps to attack Helissi, and I scream, covering my face with one hand and reaching with the other. Peering through my fingers, I see magic explodes from my fingertips, bloody from racing up the tree, and into the wild dog's heart.

The stunned dog falls over, dead, just before it reaches Helissi, who snarls and hisses. I gaze shakily at my fingers. I do not completely understand it, but I have magic, and I can make it do things. I can control death, but it requires sacrifice. Blood. Pain. Anger. Fear.

I worriedly eye at Kala, but she focuses on the others. Narrowing her eyes on the targets, Kala repeats her fire-arrow sequence twice more. Soon all the dogs are dead and burning on the ground, emitting a most unbearable smell. "It is an old Väike trick. When they smell the burning flesh of the others, they keep their distance." Shouldering the crossbow, Kala begins to shimmy down the tree. With a quaking body, I follow.

"When they would stalk our grazing livestock, we would burn a bone from a wild dog. Their fur makes a warm coat. They don't taste too bad either, when they are properly seasoned," Kala adds.

I laugh nervously. "Call me cracked if you'd like, but put me in front of a beast like that, and it does not occur to me to do anything but escape for my life. The last thing I'm considering is its potential for feast or fashion."

Kala pauses in confusion over one of the dogs, the one that my magic killed. She pulls a burning arrow from another one and jams it into the dead dog's flesh so that it begins to smolder. "Helissi must've gotten this one."

Running my hand through my hair, I shrug and mutter vague agreement.

Kala confesses sheepishly, "I think you are right about a shelter though."

I glare at her.

SOME HOURS LATER, THE SOUND OF SINGING BIRDS GENTLY LURES ME AWAKE. I open my eyes wide and stare into the pale, morning sky. Around me, the sticks and palms forming our temporary shelter look to be undisturbed. It appears we have not been eaten, which is a gratifying surprise.

However, I am disappointed at my lack of dreams. I want to see my grandmother again. I cannot shake the feeling that—even though I was unable to summon her memory—my grandmother is watching and protecting me. Maybe the dream the night of the raid was not just a dream but some kind of 'visit' from my grandmother. Maybe my grandmother had paranormally visited the workhouse woman as well; overnight, Leines went from surly and suspicious to nurturing and helpful. It is a comforting thought (but possibly a fantasy).

With a groan, I roll over groggily on the wet grass and pull myself up and out of the shelter. Kala, who apparently needs very little sleep, perches by the fire, frying eggs from who knows where and laid by who knows what. Probably some three-headed vulture. I observe a pile of reddish-pink fruit and waxy green pods, surely a result of a recent rifle through the grove. With her other hand, Kala examines the wrinkled map.

"I would be dead if not for you," I realize. "Or at least very hungry. Why did you pass the berries—just there?"

I point to the blue ones oozing their sugar sap and dotting the nearby brush.

Kala smirks. "You're right, you would be dead. You can't navigate your way out of a crate, and those berries are poison. Good rule of thumb: if the birds and bugs want nothing to do with it, neither should you."

Kala glances at me and grins even more widely. "Fun hair."

I glance sidelong over in the river at her reflection. My thick hair billows around me like a lion's mane. "Thank you," I reply sarcastically. "I've used only the best products—sweat, mud, fresh, enchanted rain water."

"I wasn't making fun that day, you know. I really do like your hair. It is like a crown." Kala looks back down at the map. "Mine being so fine and thin."

"I know you weren't making fun. Unfortunately, we both lack charm." Sighing, I sit down next to her. "What do you think is happening back home?"

Kala exhales and avoids my eyes. "Whoever those people were, there weren't too many. I'm sure—I hope—the noble guard overtook them quickly once they returned to the Palace, and they were taken to the Iboji or killed on site. They had the element of surprise and inside help. Your chamber was first at the top of the stairs. Bad luck, I guess."

"Were they refugees? The leaders of the coup?"

"I didn't exactly interrogate them during my expert blade play and daring escape, but I'm sure your family is fine. Your mother and Ewatomi are safely in Ogun. Your father had already retired to his bunker," Kala adds when I do not respond. "Regardless, your parents would want us to make it to Amęci."

I stare into the fire, watching the flames lick the air. As Kala expounds upon the plan for our journey, my body grows warm, a little too warm. A wave of nausea courses through me, and I put my head between my knees, waiting woozily for vomit that never comes. Instead, ghostly whispers fill my head, and a vision takes me.

The tent is on fire.

It licks up the sides of the thick fabric, forming a tomb of black smoke. Outside the tent, screams and the clash of the Kaharian guard against some unexpected faction. I hear the clang of the blades, smashing of flesh, and sounds of death.

I crawl from the tent. Through tearing eyes, I manage to make out some of the fighting. The enemies are men (or possibly very tall, broad-shouldered women) in black cloaks. Skilled. Quick. They use blades and crossbows as they take out members of the guard one by one.

I try to stand but choke for air. The smoke keeps me on my knees, wheezing. Around me, the fire blazes across the corpses. One of the men in black notices me, and his eyes narrow through the sit in his mask as he raises his iron crossbow. One arrow whistles past. Another finds its mark with a thud in my chest. I press one palm to the wound to no effect—blood pours through my hands. With a gurgle, more blood spills from my mouth, the world darkens, and my body begins to shudder.

"Maze. Maze! Please, Maze."

I gasp as I come out, lying on the ground in the dirt next to the cookfire. For a moment, I lie looking up at the sky, paralyzed with fear as my heart careens against my chest. A scream sits like a lump in my throat. "Breathe," Kala urges, dabbing at my bleeding forehead. "It must be another one...of your attacks. I don't know what we'll do about them out here with no tonic—"

"The Kähari advisor did not make it to Amęci. Reinforcements are not coming," I rasp, gulping at air. "They were attacked, a fire—"

"What?" Kala looks baffled, gazing around in confusion and seeing only a windy but otherwise peaceful day; our cookfire burned to only a few lingering embers.

"Maze, we haven't seen the caravan. It was just a dream."

I drag my fingers down my cheeks. "It wasn't a dream, and I can prove it."

WE BRISKLY PACK UP CAMP AND DESTROY ALL EVIDENCE OF OUR SHELTER.

Atop Helissi, Kala and I head through the woods, making a beeline to a greenish watering hole as a pack of hairy emerald wildebeests make an equally frantic escape in the other direction. As Kala shouts her dissent, I push Helissi faster, my ear nearly touching the black fur of his neck. Kala's arms tighten instinctively around my waist. We tear around the bend at full speed, kicking up clumps of dirt from the forest ground. The hair rises immediately on the back of my neck as the arid smell of smoke meets my nostrils.

"Good glory!" Kala cries, leaping from Helissi.

Flames roar across the convoy's campsite. Burning Kähari banners flap in the wind, and the rancid smell of burning flesh hangs in the air. The convoy's size and breadth surprises me—I did not realize that my father sent so many men to deliver the message. He must have been concerned about an attack like this one. With my heart in my throat, I look around for survivors. Yet, the only sound returning to my ears is the fire's crackle as it burns through the dry underbrush.

Kala covers her mouth with her sleeve. "What happened? How do we put it out?"

"We pray to the gods and ancestors for rain," I cough through the thick, black smoke. "Come on. We've got to get downwind."

"There are *people* over there," Kala protests hoarsely. "We've got to help them."

"No, they're all dead," I reply firmly as I drag Kala back atop Helissi to guide us away to a safe distance. "Five guards and the advisor. We cannot stay here."

"Maze, *how*—" Kala begins but apparently decides it is better to just follow away from the smoke and goes silent.

We ride atop Helissi in horrified silence for a long time. When we finally speak, Kala and I briefly debate telling someone of authority what we saw but think better of it. Whoever had murdered those people intended for the fire to erase all of the evidence. If word spreads that we know what happened, we will become evidence to erase.

ALONG THE STABLE PATH, THERE IS A SMALL OUTLANDS VILLAGE CALLED NSA only miles away. To me at least, it became clear now that Kähari is a target for someone and becoming increasingly unlikely that it was a group of starving refugees that stormed the Palace. It was—they are—something more sinister and calculated.

We amble down the street of Nsa; Kafu territory, ruled loosely by a Giant tribe too proud (or smart) to join a clan. I am taken aback by the size of Nsa; there appears to be thousands of the Kafu tribe, varying in coloring, height, and weight—a literal ecology of people. The Kafu people stand (overall, with a few exceptions) notably tall with long elegant necks, wear plain clothes in grays and browns, and decorate their skin with gold-colored tattoos and piercings that twinkled.

Some young women tend to a herd of three-horned goats while the thick-browed young men manage the crops. A contingent of older men and women gather around an exuberant marble game. Children run around enthusiastically, laughing, and shouting—completely immersed in a game that seems like nonsense to anyone but a young child. A few older girls watch like lionesses to make sure no one wanders.

I do not see any exquisite stone buildings or brass monuments—just a few farms and thin trees stand tall enough to scrape the clouds; rows and rows of elevated houses built from crisscrossed logs; and at the center, a village square with some limited opportunities for commerce. Apparently, foreign travelers are not unusual in Kafu, being the most substantial village between Kähari and Ameci and a common trade route stop. Still, we stand out. We are two young, fairly small-statured women, who (thanks to the horrifying stench) clearly have not bathed recently, traveling atop a warcat usually reserved only for the active military or a noble of power in a great clan. Kala and I do not expect, given our current circumstances, we will be welcomed respectfully. At the very least, we will be too memorable.

I send Helissi to hunt in the nearby wood, and then we disguise ourselves in masculine fashion (with the help of some old clothes Kala buys off a down-on-his-luck farmer) before entering the lone, unnamed tavern for supper.

It is crowded, nearly every table occupied with merchants, townspeople, and passing clan patrolmen drinking firewater and talking loudly as if they want everyone to hear their conversation. The tavern and its inn are known as a safe resting place for travelers—for mages and non-mages alike. Several different languages, modern and ancient, abound. However, the racial and social tension is unmistakable once my eyes adjust to the dim candlelight. The humans are armed to the teeth.

"I am getting used to looking hideous in public," I comment lightly, catching a glimpse of myself in the plate's reflection. My hair is tucked into a gray turban, and I wear a faded tunic with my jewelry hidden in the pockets of my trousers. "I do not even mind. It is very freeing so long as I do not have to stand beside my sister while my mother offers her sharp comparative commentary."

Kala snorts a half laugh, but her eyes are distant.

We buy spiced beans and curries and honey wine for a single copper coin—a bargain! I tuck in hungrily and looked up to find Kala staring at me. Her eyes dart around, scanning for eavesdroppers.

"Are we not going to talk about the fact that you passed out and, upon waking, suddenly knew that the Kähari convoy—miles away—had been attacked?" Kala asks.

"I thought I smelled smoke," I try. "And I had a *feeling*—"

"And then you *knew* they were all dead."

"I passed that judgment based on a lack of screaming as they laid in flames."

"Don't lie to me. We were nowhere near them. How did you know? Are you a seer?" Kala lowers her voice even more. "Are you a *witch*?"

"Of course not. Wow, have you tasted the beans?"

Kala is relentless. "Maze, just tell me. How long have you known? What can you do? Do your parents know?"

From Kala's stirred face, I can tell Kala has been dubious but now feels confident she discovered something remarkable. It is impossible to deter her for much longer.

"I'm obviously breathless with excitement to answer *all* of your questions. After curry; this is a really good curry," I reply through a mouthful of food.

Kala glowers at me.

I protest, "Kala, we have not had seasoned food in days! Remember the buzzard? It still haunts my bowels."

Kala crosses her arms and tilts her head to the side.

I drop my utensils and pause feasting. "I am not a witch. I am not a seer; I do not see the future, obviously or I never would have tasted the buzzard."

"But?"

"But, while there is not a way to verify it, I may be a descendant of the Kipporah tribe. The visions started when I was young; I practiced suppression and managed to control my communing until recently."

"Kipporah...Death Elves that practiced necromantic magic. That tribe thought to be extinct," Kala recites. "Humans called them *Borabus*. Zombies."

She pressed her lips closed at my expression.

"Well, I am not undead and the tribe is gone mostly, as far as I know," I say casually, as if talking about what gown I might wear to my Hathi. Perhaps that would normalize it for Kala.

"So, you're some sort of reaper carrying lost souls to the ancestral realm?"

"No, not like that exactly. I see and feel death, if that makes sense. I can control some of it, but I barely understand it despite living with it my entire life," I reply honestly.

Shocked, Kala puts her face in her hands. "I cannot *believe* you are part Elf. I thought perhaps that you had a pinch of low blood to explain the episodes your mother described..."

"There is nothing *low* about my blood or anyone's blood, for that matter," I dissent.

Nose wrinkling, Kala peers out from the gaps in her fingers. "Do your *parents* know? Certainly, your mother..."

"My mother knows. After my first vision, she threatened me. I don't know if she knows exactly what it is, but she thinks it's dangerous."

"Because you could be killed for it! Or worse." Kala shudders.

I clear my throat uncomfortably before tucking into my curry again.

"You have to stop, Maze. It is *blood magic*. It is a sin and against the law." An ashen-faced Kala leans forward.

Heat burns in my face. "It saved our lives," I protest angrily. "My grandmother visited my dream to warn me about the Palace attack. My vision warned us that the Kähari convoy was dead—"

I stop; probably not a great time to mention killing the wild dog with an emotional thought. Kala thrusts her chin forward. "You cannot *control* it. That makes it dangerous."

I shrug and cross my arms.

"I am not being fair." Kala swallows and stares at the floor. "We should not have anything between us. We need to trust each other if we are to survive this."

I raise my eyebrows in surprise. "Do you also have ma—"

"No, of course not. I'm as dully and plainly human as they come," Kala retorts.

"Mm."

"But your mother is paying me an unusually high stipend to be your lady." Kala bites her lip and her voice cracks. "She said she wanted to protect you."

I blink and wrinkle my nose.

"She never said exactly why," Kala hurriedly adds. "She always worried about you. Now I wonder if this is why. Ewatomi doesn't have special abilities?"

I frown. "I suppose not. I mean, I've never asked. I wasn't even sure I had it to be honest. I assume Ewatomi does not. My mother *likes* her." A pit grows in my stomach as I slowly push lukewarm beans around my plate. "Why would my mother choose you?"

This time, Kala answers directly.

"In Väike, I am known for my skill with a blade and bow. Your mother thought that might be useful. I also speak several languages, and she thought I might recognize words from your epileptic fits, which I now realize are not epileptic at all."

I fold my arms across my chest.

Kala clears her throat. "If you can see the deaths of the people in the convoy, could you see who killed them?"

"I only see what the dead and dying see. The killers wore black masks. One of them had yellow eyes and what looked like a necklace of teeth around his neck. But you're a hypocrite," I accuse. "You berate me for my magic, but now you want to use it?"

Kala flinches and bites her lip as if experiencing a small spasm.

Changing the subject, I suggest, "Do you think we could send a letter to my father? They have post starlings."

There is no post station in the Väike or much of the smaller Outland villages in the north or south, for instance. Sometimes the birds disappear traveling through the Outlands. So, I am amazed to see a busy starling post in Nsa's village square.

Thinking, Kala exhales and shifts in her seat. "If you try to send a letter to Amęci, they'll—whoever they are—might learn we're out here if it gets intercepted. Kähari is still compromised even if the raid has been quelled."

"Maybe I could write to my mother...or Ewatomi in Ogun." I wince. "Perhaps she can find a way to get word to my father about his advisor."

Kala shakes her head. "I wouldn't risk it," she replies. "Right now, we're Kähari's only chance at calling on reinforcements."

"So, we're alone," I say, uneasily. "Perfect."

"When we make it to Amęci, we won't be," Kala declares confidently.

FOR A FEW MORE COINS, WE RENT A SMALL ROOM RIGHT ABOVE THE TAVERN. Kala wanders out, promising to return with a plan and Helissi (if she can sneak him in). I sink into an exhausted heap on the dusty wood floor. So much has happened in such a short time. The reveal of an ill-judged romp soured my budding relationship with my sister. I was attacked and driven from home—not the Palace really, which was never really home, but Kähari. I spoke to my grandmother, albeit abstractly. Kala knows my deepest secrets.

I do not know if my father is alive, though I guess he likely is. I worry about Ewatomi and mother. After all, they set out to travel on a stable road to Ogun; what if they encountered just as many obstacles as we have?

Regardless, Kähari changed forever the night of the raid. It will never be seen as the quiet, peaceful nation again. Survival distracted me, but now that I sit still, my blood runs cold and I fight for my limbs to relax. My fears, thoughts, and intentions stumble over each other fighting for my attention. I wipe my eyes and with a damp finger and then carefully draw the symbol for Kipporah in the dust—the circled dot (the eye) with the horizontal wave above and below. A hum in my body cradles me gently and croons comfort. My father lives. I am sure.

Then I speedily wipe the symbol away with my fist. Though I loath to admit it, maybe Kala is right; it *is* dangerous to dabble in things I do not understand. *I killed that wild dog.* Yes, it saved Helissi, but I did it almost involuntarily. My emotions, *my blood*—drove my magic. If I am upset with Ewatomi or mother or a stranger, will the magic well up in me again? Ignoring it will not work either. It is inside of me, twisting and pushing to escape.

"I have good news, but it's going to cost us." Kala returns to our room with Helissi lumbering in behind her.

"The innkeeper is okay with Helissi being in here instead of the stables?" I ask, yawning and sitting up in the bed.

"I thought it better not to ask." Kala spreads her map onto the nightstand and smooths out the wrinkles with her palms. "There is a caravan headed this way carrying salt from Osanyin. It was originally headed to Kähari, but has been diverted and instead is headed to Ameci."

"It will pass this village tomorrow morning," I catch on, following Kala's finger path. "We could go with the caravan. It'll be so much safer and faster. We'll beat the moon shifts."

"All of that," Kala confirms. "But it is expensive, and we don't have much coin left. Do you have that necklace from Bosede's family?"

I redden. "Yes."

"We'll need to sell it to the salt traders for safe passage to—" Kala stops when she sees my face. "What's wrong?"

I flew too close to the sun. I want to confess. Instead, I blink away the tears burning my eyes and unlatch the necklace. Why *am* I still wearing it? I lost my *sister* over the blasted thing. Even as I experience those rational thoughts, I also think back to that night in the kitchen with Bosede. How happy and content I felt and how badly I want to feel that way again.

Loved. Special. Perhaps my head is just spinning from sleeplessness. We need the money.

"Nothing." I drop the heavy necklace on the table with a clunk.

CHAPTER
ELEVEN

he Outlands stretch out several hundred miles to the north and south, and even farther to the east and west. Towards Amęci, the rosy sun lifts into the sky and casts lanky shadows on the hundreds of camels and outsized coaches in the salt travelers' extensive caravan. No one trusts anything more than a sturdy camel in the Outlands; the weather and terrain changes too quickly once the moon wans. Stiflingly hot to blistering cold. Dry winds to heavy rains. Rocky and rough, hardened sand, muddy swamps, rainy forests—the Outlands is an eclectic collection of terrain. In such a place, camels are the most more reliable transportation.

Kala hires one of the larger, nicer coaches, and I nearly weep in relief. I am tired of walking and broken from sleeping on the bare ground. Frankly, the transient life we have been living since that night at the Palace is horribly stressful. I could never be a nomad or live in the Outlands. I've gone soft living in the Palace as the Chieftain's daughter.

"Go on, Helissi," Kala urges, pushing the large, reluctant panther into the coach. "You're riding today."

Helissi wanders over and puts his large head in my lap, and I rub him behind his rounded ears. Kala shoves our parcels under the seat and sprawls into the seat across from me.

"It's very nice," I comment, looking around in admiration. There are two small cots on one end and a bin, stocked with provisions purchased in Nsa. The coach has windows of thin green glass and a small, separate compartment upfront for the driver, herding the train of camels.

Windhoek, the chief of the traders, knocks on the coach door and then lets himself inside at Kala's half-hearted, encouraging wave. We both look skeptically at the tall, pale-skinned, muscled man with a shiny bald head and several distinctive scars visible through his shabby clothes.

"Rare for young women such as yourselves to travel this way," he observes, seemingly without any evident ill will but it felt creepy nonetheless. "But coin's coin, eh?"

"We appreciate your accommodating us at this juncture," Kala replies, looking very worldly and utterly bored with the conversation. "We hope to be leaving soon."

"Of course. Just wanted to welcome you and let you know that there will be one more stop between here and Amęci—a tiny little village called Zouérat. *Hostile* mage tribe. I recommend minimal contact unless you want to be turned into a toad or something." He shrugs. "Other than that, welcome to the salt road."

We chorus awkward thank-yous until the door shuts behind him.

"One of us should stay awake at all times," Kala announces suddenly, staring at the door. "I chose this coach not for its comforts but because of all the locks. But—"

"Oh, yes, certainly." I nod, also staring at the door. "Say no more."

THE CARAVAN PASSES SLOWLY THROUGH A DENSE, NEWLY FORMED AND brilliantly green rainforest. For miles, I cannot see anything living besides prismatic frogs and thick snakes slithering up into the trees. Thunder rolls and the rain passes through the sun and forms a frothy rainbow. The camels trudge diligently through the mud quietly through the day and into the night.

To my immense relief, Helissi handles the travel nicely—by sleeping through it. He curls in one corner, a large black slumbering mass. Too tired for conversation but too full of adrenaline to sleep, Kala huddles in a chair biting a nail until it bleeds. She rocks a little. I have been selfish. Kala also does not know what happened to her family. The refugees could have reached the Väike by now. I hope Ojo Mezu delivered the letter.

We move rapidly moving north and wind whips the coach. The heat I've known my entire life *gone*. A chill sets into my bones, and I shake and shiver now and again as our clothes are too thin for the north. I hope will be able to find my godfather quickly lest we freeze to death once reaching Ameci.

"Are there spirits in the coach with us now?" Kala asks after a spell of being unnaturally quiet.

"I don't know. I haven't asked. Wouldn't want to sin and all that."

"I don't know if I'd be able to stop myself, to be honest," Kala admits, looking back out the window. "I'd be so curious every day."

"I have been trying to understand it more. There are books in a hidden library in the Palace."

Ever the scholar, Kala is excited immediately. "Go way out—a hidden library? Where?"

"My grandmother mentioned it before she died, and a spirit called Adin told me how to find it. He's been helping me." I sigh. "I thought if I could find the Trench…"

Kala blinks. "You think the *Trench* is real? Now, I'm sure you're cracked."

"I have nothing else to go on," I complain glumly.

"Wait, wait, a spirit in the Palace," Kala pauses thoughtfully. "Could you reach him from here? If you had to call on him? Could he tell us what's happening at the Palace?"

"I've never done anything like that." I bite my lip. "I don't know if it works that way...but I suppose it's possible. Maybe in a dream, like how Funani came to me, but I did not summon her. She just came."

Kala's eyes are wide with excitement.

"Go to sleep," she begs. "Aren't you curious?"

"What about all the blood magic and sinning and the utter damnation of my soul and all that?" I sigh. "Besides, how can I sleep now? I haven't slept deeply since we left. I'm too…"

"Scared," Kala finishes for me. "I know. I'm terrified, to be honest."

Grimly and somewhat dramatically, I declare, "I don't know if I'll ever sleep again."

I sleep, dreaming of Kähari and the Palace grounds.

The waning moon passes slowly overhead. I sit on a stone bench, waiting for someone but not sure who. I curl my palms into my purple gown of fine silk and a partially braided turban in an eye-catching yellow and purple print on my piles of black, coiled hair.

Bosede appears next to me on the bench. He leans towards me. His bright blue eyes darken. He offers his hand, and I take it. Bosede leans in and kisses me gently. Then he presses me against a tree and kisses with more urgency, harder. I struggle to focus, but the garden around me disappears into delicious warm waves that drift all the way down to my toes.

"Sorry to interrupt," a grim voice says.

With a little pop, Bosede promptly vanishes and Adin, looking very much alive, stands in his place. He crosses his arms over his broad chest, and, somehow, his mask looks even more ominous than before. "Any progress?" he asks.

"Not as much progress as you've made finding me."

"Chaos awaits. Have you determined your place in the prophecy?"

"I haven't—the Palace was attacked. For the time being, I've abandoned my task."

For a second, his figure stands perfectly still and unblinking. I stare back, trying not to show any fear (even though I am terrified). Shadows play across his face, and his gaze bright and haunting. He smiles slowly. "I have figured out your role."

I swallow hard. Caught in his gaze, I move forward unconsciously, but jump back as though being near him burned me. In the glitter of his eyes, I see an unfamiliar, vengeful ugliness and something else I can't quite make out. Something feels off. This is not my friend. Dark shadows gather behind him, a chill envelops me, and there is the steady rhythm of the warm, wet breath of a creature (that I dare not look at) behind me.

"You are her. She is you. The girl who ends the realm."

"You are not Adin." Feeling magic swirl in my chest, I take a step forward and peer at him. "Who are you?"

With a gasp, I wake up and nearly fall out of my chair. My heart pounds, and my entire body soaked with cold sweat. I'd thought my dreams were a safe place to explore my power, but I fear I may be wrong. I glance at Kala, slumped over in her chair and snoring softly. The light of a full moon washes through the windows and over the polished wood floors. The coach is still; we are no longer moving.

I peer out the window. We arrived at Zouérat, I assume, after seeing a modest honza (a meditation house for Zouérat tribe witches and wizards that I have only seen in books). People from the caravan busily water, feed, and rest the camels while the local mages eye them suspiciously, leaning against their iron blades.

"Kala, wake up," I say, shaking my companion's arm. "We're in Zouérat."

Kala jolts awake but does not care one bit about Zouérat.

"Did you talk to Adin?" she asks. "When you were asleep? I tried to stay awake but—"

"I thought it was at first, but it was not Adin. It was someone or something else intending to kill me."

"Can you be killed in a dream?" Kala wonders uneasily. "Did they say why?"

"It didn't want me to know why. It wanted me to think it was Adin."

"And you're sure—"

I shake my head. "But it wasn't him. Adin helps and protects me. Besides, spirits don't have hell dog familiars. Whoever they were, they were powerful. Maybe more powerful than me. They controlled the dream, and somehow, they know I trust Adin."

"Is there a chance it was just a nightmare?" Kala asks cautiously.

I pause, wrong-footed. "I mean—I guess."

Eyes widening, Kala stands up. Helissi raises his head, preparing to defend me. "Did you tell it where we are?"

I rack my brain, trying to remember. "I don't think so. In the dream, we were standing on the grounds of the Palace in Kähari."

"Okay, good. That could mean anything." Kala chews on her lip before saying. "You can't sleep again until we get to Amęci."

I scoff. "First of all, what? Second of all, why?"

"If you dream about the caravan or our location or our plan—whoever this was, they'll know where we are and try to stop us." Kala digs through one of the parcels for the coffee beans Leines had given them. I press the bag against me. "I shouldn't have encouraged you. This was a bad idea. Maze, I'm sorry."

I sigh and relent, putting one of the coffee beans in my mouth and wincing at the bitter taste. "I need to go for a walk or something. Stretch my legs."

"Windhoek said they are hostile here against the members of the great clans."

"Forgive me if I don't believe the rantings of that bigoted pox." Shuddering, I toss back the rest of the coffee beans into my mouth and chew grimly. "I won't be long."

Like many of the villages in the Outlands, Zouérat is modest with wooden houses dotting the rippling green hillside. There are plenty of people on the roads, but whenever I get close, they quickly move out of the way or pull up their hoods. I pass through a lush courtyard and up some stone steps to visit a tiny shop selling bread, meat, and beer. A kindly old wizard minds the shop, which stands mostly empty. I watch enviously for a moment as he freely uses his magic to shift the bread through the brick fire ovens. He does not speak a common tongue, but accurately translates my vague hand motions and begins to prepare a basket of goods.

"Oy, witch in the blue cloak," calls a dwarf sitting on a bench by the empty bar.

The dwarf has clumps of dirt in his bushy black beard, tunic and trousers, as if he'd spent the day digging in mud and dirt. "Did you come in with that Skull?"

"I'm sorry. Who? Windhoek?" I ask, surprised anyone would address me. I am not sure if I understand him; he has a strange accent and dialect. "I'm traveling with the caravan, but I wouldn't say I know Windhoek personally—if that's what you're asking."

"Good. Windhoek is a murdering prick. Can't trust a Skull." He chugs his beer and whips the droplets from his beard with the back of his hand.

"Skull; what does that mean?"

"Violent human guerrillas. They call them Skulls because they're kill mages and collect their skulls and bones as trophies."

My lips press into a thin line as particular visions come flooding back. Kala and I had been right to lock the door. Does Windhoek know who I am? Unlikely. He does not seem particularly bright, and I do not have any distinctly Elven features like the pointy ears or the long, glowing hair. Besides, what would he want with me with an entire village of witches and wizards within reach (though, perhaps, he knew better than to take on a whole village of people free to master their magic living in the paranormal Outlands)?

"That's gruesome," I reply cautiously. "I may have read about them, except they called them vigilantes. They went after dangerous mages, it said."

The dwarf snorts. "Of course, it did. You know, the Skulls murdered an entire tribe of dwarves once. Bet you didn't learn that. They didn't get me, but that's no victory."

"During the Chaos?"

The dwarf has a faraway look in his eyes. "Chaos never ended. Some of them—they're still out there, a wild little army. Some are in the Great Clans in positions of power."

I frown thoughtfully.

"Psst!"

Tensing, I swish around to see Kala hovering in the doorway of the shop. She seems afraid to venture inside and shuffles nervously from one foot to the other. "We'll miss the caravan."

The old wizard utters something in his ancient tongue as he limps over to hand me the basket. I give him silver coins, and he counts them carefully before nodding. As we rush back to our coach, Kala admonishes me for going so far. I counter that I smelled bread baking, and Kala reluctantly concurs that fresh bread is worth an extensive search operation.

Kala pauses and sniffs. "Is there magic in this?"

Oh, definitely. "No, of course not," I scoff.

We climb back into the coach and slide the door shut. Kala flips all the locks. "What did you say to that dwarf?" Kala inquiries, narrowing her eyes.

"He mostly spoke to me."

"You need to be more careful. That dwarf is a Crow. Didn't you see the feather on his coat?" Kala unwraps the brown bread and begins carving it up with a pocket knife, sending delicious flakey crumbs scattering everywhere.

"A Crow?"

Kala taps her foot and expounds. "Outlanders who torture and kill humans. You would do well to avoid them. Look for the feather next time and then keep your distance."

I scratch my cheek. Two warring factions: Skulls and Crows. *Chaos never ended.* Bands of bones and teeth; it could have been the Skulls that attacked the women's village in the knife-prompted vision. From what I saw, it could have been Skulls that burned the Kähari caravan—but *why?* Someone might be trying to kill me; perhaps it is the Skulls—except I cannot imagine they would be reckless enough to attack a Palace in a clan nation and, if they hate mages, there would not be one among them. Kala, who is irritated with me, ignores my manic twitching.

The caravan passes through the rest of Zouérat, seemingly without incident. but not long after the caravan resumes its route, the Outlands take a wild turn. The weather turns increasingly cold and dry. In the patchwork of stable homesteads and villages along the way, the inhabitants wear elk garments, coats of reindeer, cloth leggings, and boots to their thighs. Eventually, an icy wind strikes against the coach and snowflakes swirls against the windows. After what seems like days, we see bright lights in the distance.

Amęci.

The camels, apparently unfazed by the cold, trudge all the way to the imposing ice-stone gate. The members of the Amęci guard, custom officers, wear gray reindeer-skin uniforms, cloth leggings, and animal-hide helmets and masks, covering most of their faces (except for the eyes) that decorated in elaborate blue, white, and navy beading.

Kala and I watch nervously from our window as the guard begins to carefully search the caravan and the traders. Eventually, they knock briskly on the door of the coach, and Kala nervously opens the door. The icy wind snaps at our faces as we step outside.

"We'll need your documentation," one of them says, scowling.

He glances at the growling Helissi in the corner. "His too."

Kala tries to reason with him. "This is Daughter of Chieftain Oko, Mäzzikim *Ka* Kähari, and her warcat, Helissi. I am Kala, her companion. Kähari is overrun with Ganju refugees, and the Palace was attacked—"

The guard chuckles and nudges the guard next to him. "Daughter of a Chieftain, eh? A noble riding in a salt caravan with no guards, servants, or banners."

"It's true," I try, but I am immediately cut off.

"If Kähari had been attacked, we would've heard."

"We had to leave in the dead of night," I protest as my arms are roughly pinned behind my back. "Please, you must grant us an audience with the Chieftess Udo Olokun *Ka* Ameçi. She can explain everything. Oy!"

I watch, distressed, as a guard shoves Helissi from the coach with a boot and fires his weapon at the him until he snarls angrily and bolts. My magic bubbles up, but I fight it down. Exposing myself now could jeopardize all of us. Still, I recoil as Helissi runs at full-speed back in the direction from which we came. His large paws toss up snowy clouds as he runs. My second instinct is to call him back, but I hold my tongue. Helissi is smart and strong, and he was born and bred in the Outlands. He can make his way back to Kähari if he desires.

I cry out as the guards drag me from the coach. Relief at reaching Ameçi fades. My nerves rattle around in my chest. I barely feel the bitter cold as it bites at my face. Mercifully, an officer hands us fur-trimmed deerskin coats and boots and watches, weapons trained, as Kala and I shakily put them on. This is probably what mages who aren't part of a noble family go through every day. Here in Ameçi, I am nobody.

I plead, "Please, if we could just see the Chieftess. She'll clear up everything."

"You and everyone else."

A few other cries of alarm pop up and down the caravan as a few others are less-than-kindly yanked off camels or out of compartments.

"Windhoek didn't say we'd be stopped and arrested," Kala grumbles as she slumps next to me in the wagon with the other nervous detainees. The guards chain our wrists and ankles to the iron benches. "Could've mentioned it when he was counting our coin."

"I didn't even realize there *were* travel papers," I admit quietly. "I've never traveled to another clan nation."

"But you've gone beyond Kähari's western barrier—did you not pass through customs to go into the Outlands?" Kala whispers.

"I know a way."

Kala sucks in an uneven breath. "Then I wonder if others know too."

The wagon lurches forward under the power of two heavy-set reindeers. At first, it seems we are entering a wasteland of snow and ice, glittering as the moon passes overhead. Just beyond a low ridge of hills, the bright lights of Akoma, the capital city of Ameci, shine. The border wall, built primarily by the founding mages, is enchanted, and the ice shifts slowly, molecule by molecule, into a patchwork of images, showing images of the people who built it and scenes from the long days and nights it was constructed—a visual history reminding all of everyone that humans and mages worked together to build safety.

I am happy the mages had such foresight; in case humans have short memories.

Meanwhile, the other two detainees whisper about me without realizing I sit among them.

"I'd know her if I saw her. Spent some time in that court. Odd, slight thing. Of course, the older sister is the beauty. She's to be wed to the son of the Chieftain in Ogun," says a bearded man shivering in a thin blanket. "Soon, I hear."

"You think it was really Mäzzikim in that caravan? What do you think she's doing here?" an older woman asks, creasing the deep worry lines in her face. She is dressed more appropriately for the weather in a layered cloak of fur. "Bad enough that Ganju has fallen. Kähari now, too?"

"Ganju has fallen?" Kala asks in alarm. I shoot her a stern warning look.

The woman nods, looking at Kala. "Smells of death there at every turn. Anyone who could still walk—left it. Fat lot of good it'll do them though. Did you hear what happened to the refugees in Ogun? Ruddy evil monsters, those Oguns!"

"You think everyone is monstrous," replies the weary bearded man.

"Then I suppose they all are because I'm only reporting the facts," the older woman says primly before shifting the conversation. "Perhaps they sent Mäzzikim to make an alliance with Ameci."

"Nah, wouldn't have. That poor girl—rumor amongst the help is there is no love or trust lost between her and her mother, and the father barely knows she exists. Rumor has it that she's not even Farida's child," the bearded man answers gruffly.

I nearly tumbled to the floor when the wagon hits the next bump. I dig my fingers hard into the bench below to steady myself and move my feet closer to the warm brick.

"Careful, girl," the woman advises unhelpfully, turning turned back to the man. "Well, wherever she is now, she's surely getting a better welcome than us," she sniffs

Kale exchanges a bemused glance with me.

Ameci is home to intricate architecture, towering temples, and cosmopolitan air. It is the 'Land of Ice and Winds,' and the landscape indeed looks as though it had been shaped by the wind sweeping through Ameci for centuries. Ameci supports itself by supplying the purest water to the rest of the realm. Now lavish palaces and stone towers, fortified by ice, mark the early water barons' healthy fortunes, who tapped the realm's liquid gold. The homes and businesses are a mosaic of colored tiles, glazed over from a recent snowfall. More modest homes resemble wide, circular tents set upon wood platforms and covered in felt or hides. Nature has been relatively well-honored—fir, pine, and birch trees line the roads and surrounded everything.

Sleds and buggies with slides and something called running boards zip through the streets, pulled by enthusiastic teams of reindeer. There is even a trolley, announcing its presence with a large bell as it guided along by something called *hydropower*. It is like magic. Not surprisingly, Ameci is also a hot spot (pun very much intended) of education, sponsoring the most prestigious universities for history, science, and medicine in the Ohia Realm.

Suppose it was not apparent from the ambitious superstructures in the skylines. In that case, there is prosperity in the fashions—the richly-colored deerskin skirts and waistcoats were thick and long, fur and beads trimmed everything. I have never seen anything like it. For a brief moment, I forget I am on my way to a prison cell and find myself fixated as a giddy tourist. Then, Kala sits up rigidly and blinks.

"Letaro! It's Letaro! Look, in the marketplace," she hisses, nudging me with her shoulder. I twist to see, and sure enough, there he is—trademark mirrored glasses and all—heading towards the marketplace with a silver walking stick.

"Letaro!" I scream, trying to stand, but my chains yanked me back into place.

"Quiet, or I'll cut out your wagging tongues, you cockroaches," snaps the grumpy guard at the head of the prison wagon.

The outskirts of the laborer village catch my attention as I peer through the prison wagon's grimy barred windows. There are manufacturing plants, brick factories splashed with brightly colored paint, spewing plumes of what appear to be steam clouds from their stacks. Closer to the capital, I see the workhouses; generally, places for people just getting their start or down on their luck. Even those buildings are kaleidoscopic and picturesque; the snowy yards warm with small children at play with their sleds and imaginations.

Further, into a wealthier area, we ride past brilliant temples, schools, a serene quad, and a steamy blue lagoon, where people of all shapes, sizes, genders, and colors swam and played.

Then the wagon enters the capital, where people have an even better class of residence. A lot of them likely worked as advisors or owned one of the water dispensaries. Some perhaps were previously chieftains or chieftesses (now simply nobles). There are gated parks with pine trees and winterbells, well-endowed schools and academies, and theater houses and taverns at every corner. At the top of the hill, I see the Palace—an outsized stone mansion hugged by a thick line of pine trees covered in twinkly lights.

The wagon slows, the reindeers clomp to a stop. The guards open the doors and yank us out, and we are marched towards a plain-looking gray stone building, the detention lodge. Despite our tearful protests, Kala and I are separated and examined by doctors. My assigned doctor, an ancient woman with gnarled hands, works briskly, peering, checking, prodding as I shiver. The doctor pauses for a moment as she examines my back. I know she sees my guards. She asks if it hurt when she pressed; I say no.

"Significant scarring," the doctor mutters, jointing something down on a tablet.

"Oh, those. I got them from my warcat," I answer nervously.

She gazes at me, knowingly.

"You put that on." The doctor turns away to clean her tools.

I pull on my issued fur-lined gray wool leggings and supple knee-high black boots. Itchy and constricting, but I can admit it is much warmer than my own clothes. When I finish, the doctor rings the guards to take me to my cell.

CHAPTER
TWELVE

hey won't let me out.

Inside the cold stark white cell, I can hear the heavy steps of the guard's boots as he makes his rounds. Outside, the sun rises, casting pale beams of light through the green glass and bars across my windows. There I sit, muttering to myself, with my arms wrapped around my knees. Without sleep, every thought is fuzzy, and my brain trips over itself.

Surely, I will die soon—hopefully.

I squirm and chide myself for the negative thoughts, but they keep crowding in. *This nightmare will never end*, my subconscious tells me. *You will never see your father again. You will never see Kähari again. You should give up.* I feel my magic dwindle into a tiny flutter as I take short, quivering breaths. Overcome, I cry into my threadbare pillow for a spell, which isn't entirely helpful. My eyelids are swollen and red, and I panic no one will be able to identify me.

I think wistfully of home with its soft pillows and blankets and the gauzy curtains hanging around it like hazy clouds. Will I ever sleep in it again? Perhaps not. Nocturnal visions aside, my grandmother us to joke that once you were an adult, you never slept because you have the problems of the world upon your back, and you would fuss to yourself at night trying to fix them.

Then I realize something important that brings hope. I feel my magic, dimly, but no visions come. No one has di in these halls, and I refuse to be the first.

THE GUARD'S BOOTS COME TO A STOP OUTSIDE MY CELL. I STIR UP WHEN I hear him fiddle for his keys. He opens the door to the cell, and I nearly faint with relief when he bows, looking sufficiently humbled. He releases from Kala from her cell down the hall, and then escorts both of us to the Palace. We follow the guard silently into an elegant parlor of white and gold upholster chairs and small pines decorated with small twinkly lights. These lights turn out to be lightening bugs drawn to the bark of the maple-coat trees. The shivering Kala chooses the chair close to the hearth. I choose a chair by the window so that I can look out across the dome roofs of all the multicolored awnings and streets of bluestone snaking around them. White mist drifts up from every chimney as the Amęci people warm their bodies and cook their suppers.

"Chieftess Udo *Ka* Amęci," announces a young man's voice.

Both of us immediately stand in respect.

The Chieftess Udo eschews the bright whites and silver clothing that I expect expected of the Amęci clan. Instead, the tall, slender albino woman drifts into the room a deep royal blue-colored gown with patterns of gold stars and a gold headdress with multicolored beads that trailed down and twisted into her yellow-white coiled hair. I notice her hands are coated in heavy gold rings as she gracefully sits down across from us.

"They said someone was impersonating Daughter Mäzzikim Ka Kähari; I told the guards that couldn't be true. I ordered your release as soon as I heard. I'm so sorry for the poor treatment you received upon arriving at our gates. We've had some trouble lately, and we are exercising caution," Chieftess Udo says in a tone mixed of surprise and regret.

"We understand," I say, even though I don't.

"I've asked my men to search for your warcat," she added, preempting my question.

My shoulders sagged slightly. "Thank you."

Chieftess Udo says, "Please join me for a hot cup of honey ale. Then we'll sort your rooms. Some proper clothing. I imagine you're exhausted from travel."

"Thank you, Chieftess," Kala replies gratefully; I echo her.

"It is unusual, is it not, to travel without a party?" Chieftess Udo asks, as a maid carefully fills our mugs. "And such a long way," she adds in fully naked suspicion.

"I know our visit is unexpected, but we have sensitive information to share," I say, catching Kala's eye and shake my head.

With a frown, Chieftess Udo dismisses the servants and then gestures for me to continue.

"It is rumored that Ganju has fallen," I say carefully. Chieftess Udo blinks in surprise.

I continue, "While I can't confirm that rumor, I can confirm the refugees were turned away from Ogun have descended on Kähari and—by now—possibly Väike. Things have become violent, and my father says we need reinforcements from Amęci before things worsen."

Udo raises her perfectly manicured eyebrows, purses her lips, and drinks from her goblet. "Oko needs soldiers. How many?"

"As many as you can spare. I don't really... I'm not sure to be perfectly honest."

Chieftess Udo blinks. "Daughter Mäzzikim, are we at war? War can take many forms. They can be violent and bloody, but it can also be a quietly growing faction of descent. It all ends the same."

I am honest. "We're not at peace, Chieftess."

Chieftess Udo narrows her eyes and squints at me. "Who is the enemy? Why did your father send you and not an advisor? Where are your guards?"

It is an excellent question. Who *is* the enemy? I pause and circle my mug's rim with my finger. "There was a caravan that carrying one of my father's advisors who was supposed to make the request. They were slaughtered and burned."

With a set jaw, Chieftess Udo stands up and paces in front of the large windows.

Then, Udo bellows for her assistant. "Logos, sound the bells. Close the gates. Assemble council of elders now."

Logos nods and departs as speedily as he came.

"Please, could you help me find my godfather too?" I ask. "My mother asked that I find him once I arrived."

"Of course," Chieftess Udo replies absently. "I will call him to court tomorrow. In the meantime, I insist you stay in the manor for your own safety. I'll send word to your parents that you have arrived intact, more or less."

Before Kala and I leave with a kindly older servant, Chieftess Udo says, "Your parents…they are from a fishing village in Kähari. Is that right? I don't remember exactly."

I open my mouth to respond, but Udo blunders on.

"No matter. There isn't any stigma from that," the Chieftess adds unconvincingly. "None."

In the guest quarters, furniture gleams of polished pinewood, and huge paintings (called *watercolors*) in wide, gilded frames hang on the walls, cream-colored curtains draped at the windows, oil lamps, and a bright floral pattern carpeted the floors. Outside the glass panel windows, a gentle snow peacefully swirls.

"You're safe now," the servant woman, Mate, says gently as she guides us inside.

When I see my reflection in the wet room looking glass, I recoil at the stranger staring back at me. My dark eyes are haunted, wide, bloodshot, and rimmed with dark circles. Dried-over cuts mark my face, and my wool dress hangs from my alarmingly thin frame, and my hair—

As if on cue, Mate walks in and pulls one of my shaking hands tightly in hers. "All will be well after a nice bath."

Mate is a brilliant woman; I melt into the fragrant bubbly water. Once I am wrapped in a warm robe, Mate brings fried cakes drizzled with honey sugar, which I eat like a ravenous beast, and a bound, warm brick for the end of my bed. "It is an old but effective tradition. Feels lovely in a cold bed," she explains.

As she braids my hair a curious Mate asks, "How did you come to be called Mäzzikim?"

I answer, "My mother says it is an old family name."

"Hmm," Mate replies.

"Why? Does it have some meaning?"

An ancient one, Mate reveals, a meaning that surely my mother did not mean for me. When I press, Mate admits that 'mazzikim' in an ancient language means invisible demon, an annoyance, or danger. I am left dumbfounded. Did my mother hate me from the very moment I was born, so much so that she literally named me an *annoyance*? I thought my mother hated me for my visions, my awkwardness, my lack of beauty—I had a thousand explanations for why she might not like me and spent much of my life trying to change my fate with her. Was I doomed from the start?

Sometime later, a doctor visits with a tonic for sleep, which calms my complicated thoughts. Next to Kala, who refuses to leave my side, I fall asleep between clean bedsheets for the first time in days and vow never to take that glorious feeling for granted again. I sleep deeper than the dead.

THE SHOCK SINKS IN THE FOLLOWING MORNING. NOW THAT I AM SAFE, I AGAIN fret over the safety of my family. My father is alive, I am sure, but is he in danger? Did my sister arrive safely in Ogun? The bits and pieces I've learned about Ogun aren't sitting well with me, and I worry my sister is about to make a horrible mistake.

Perhaps? Of course, she is making a horrible mistake, the little voice in my head admonishes. *And you're running out of time.* To do what, I wonder.

At the breakfast table, Udo explains that Letaro had come to the Palace, concerned that the prisoners arrested outside Amęci were victims of mistaken identity (Kala looked noticeably pleased that he'd heard her voice—and recognized it—after being gone so long). His absence from Kähari is partly her fault, Chieftess Udo admits. She'd called Letaro back to Amęci when tensions around Ganju started bubbling over. Although, apparently, Letaro had already been keen on returning before she reached out.

"Letaro is one of my most trusted advisors," Chieftess Udo says. One of the servants pours hot tea into their ceramic mugs. "He is a brilliant historian and has experience with these types of conflicts. Wars are won by the historians, clerics, scribes, and strategists," Udo continues as she slides her cup closer to her. "Every ruler worth their crown knows that."

I say nothing and pretend to be interested in servants serving plates of duck eggs and smoked salmon. I wonder why Udo allowed one of her advisors to leave Amęci to tutor me. Was she hoping to influence my father?

"I know you're probably thinking that the whole thing could've been avoided by extending a waterline to Ganju," Chieftess Udo says shrewdly. "It is really not that simple. It was about more than water."

"So, everyone keeps saying." I reply, fighting to keep my tone light as my magic flutters against my fingertips. "Anyway, I assumed Letaro rushed back here to be safe with his family."

"Letaro's family lives...*lived*, I suppose if the rumors are true, in Ganju," Chieftess Udo corrects, sipping her tea. "But as far as I know, he hasn't been in contact with any of them in years. Decades, even."

"I thought he was from Amęci?" Kala mirrors my confusion.

"Letaro isn't Amęcian. He is Ganju," Chieftess Udo answers with a bark of laughter. "You can't tell by the nose? It is so—well, never mind that. He immigrated here as a young man—under asylum—after they took his eyes for pursuing and reading materials forbidden under Ganju law. His own family turned him in."

Chieftess Udo notices my mouth agape. "You honestly did not know?"

Kala shakes her head in horror. "I thought he was *born* blind. What was he reading?"

"Literature about the ancient tribes and their demigods—he wants to understand the world we live in today. He warned this day was coming."

My mouth falls open. "You allow the study of all of those things?"

"Of course. It is encouraged and supported for each citizen. Every bit of the past—even when it is horrifying, disheartening, and embarrassing—is important to understand, accept, and apply conceptually to the future. It is the only way progress is made. If you do not turn on the light, you cannot kill the cockroach hiding in your house."

Chieftess Udo pauses. "I assumed Kähari was one of the more progressive clans? Is that a misconception?"

I fall into silence. Amęci remains an important ally for Kähari, one we cannot afford to lose—especially now. Udo needs to understand our commonalities and not see the differences.

"Not as progressive as Amęci, but certainly not as conservative as Ganju or Ogun," I offer carefully, wondering if she'd already heard otherwise from Letaro.

"Hmm," Chieftess Udo muses.

I stare at my plate.

"You know, every now and then, an ignorant fellow from another great clan will ask—why haven't there been any mages who made a *positive* contribution to this continent," Chieftess Udo begins, as if sensing my discomfort. "To them, I say extraordinary mages have existed in every generation. Every blessed one. But, like everyone else, their powers and personhood must be nurtured and recognized. Instead, most are forced into the shadows—their potential wasted because people were unwilling to see it, their optimism and innovation curdling into resentment and fear. Those mage people that persevered anyway were diminished and ignored by historians. You hear nothing of them, and that is by *design*."

Chieftess Udo looks at Maze thoughtfully. "Not here, Daughter Mäzzikim. Much like arrogance, intolerance is a habit of the ignorant."

CHAPTER
THIRTEEN

From breakfast onward each morning, Chieftess Udo keeps everyone in the Palace so busy with preparations for the march on Kāhari that we hardly have any time to think. She set Kala and I, separately, to various frivolous tasks—sending casual and cryptic letters at the starling post, getting fitted in cold-weather gear and gowns (it is frigid, so maybe this task is less frivolous), and tasting batches of provisions for the journey. She keeps us occupied and, at first, I assumed she aimed to distract us from our traumatic experience. Then I begin to suspect other motives. However, Kala and I have bonded tightly. With a simple exchange of glances, we send each other messages more effective than a starling post. One evening, we meet in the grand and gleaming kitchen for a brief, clandestine conversation.

"She doesn't want us leaving," I speculate to Kala in an undertone. Servants carrying trays mill around them. "I don't think she told my godfather know that I'm here."

"Maybe she's trying to keep us safe," Kala replies optimistically. "We don't even know what happened after we left."

"So, when *do* you think we'll go back to Kähari?" I ask, crossing my arms. "I want to know if my father is all right. I want to see if the Palace is still there. If my mother and sister... and Bosede —"

Kala's face registers shock and then suspicion.

"No - not - I am just *curious*," I reply evasively.

"You're lying," Kala says. "Something happened with Bosede."

My face pales and then reddens. Feebly, I squeak, "I don't know what you mean."

"Why do you want to go back anyway? Have you ever considered... that you live in a place where you can't be with who you want? That you can't even study what you want? That you can't do what you were born to do? You can't be who you are." Kala asks bluntly. "Well? Have you ever *really* thought about that?"

"It's home. I'm happy there."

As soon as I utter those words, I am unsure. Have I ever been happy in Kähari? Sure, one day I thought I would leave (perhaps find the Trench if it existed and other people like me). Spend more time exploring the Outlands. Study at a university. Travel the world.

But, beautiful Kähari remains my family's home and birth nation. I did find peace in my grandmother's home near the shore. I have a new appreciation for my nation and now that I've been forced to run from it— all I want to do is go back.

My heart inquires: *But are you happy? Or is it just familiar?*

Are you safe? My mind wants to know.

"Are you? *Were* you?" Kala debates. "You know, Ewatomi told me that your mother used to beat you. Because of your visions, I presume."

I startle. "What? How did she—?"

"Ewatomi did not know why. She does not know about the visions, but she knows your mother would beat you—and I quote—because you told *too many imaginative lies*."

I put my hand to my cheek, feeling my breath catch as the pain throbs under my fingertips. My mother's angry, terrified eyes fill my head.

"She slapped me, but it was only once—"

"Only once *that people saw*. I've seen the scars on your back," Kala says bluntly. "That's why I asked Ewatomi in the first place. You have markings all over your back."

My mind jolts back to the Ameci doctor who paused when she examined my back. I wonder if she could tell what the marks are. In confusion, I deflect, "But I thought *you* did not want me to practice my necromancy either. You called it blood magic and a sin."

"Because it *is* dangerous...especially out *there*," Kala makes clear. "You're safe here, Maze. I hope you understand that. You should stay."

I EXPERIENCED MY FIRST ENCOUNTER WITH DEATH WHEN I WAS SIX. OUTSIDE after supper, I pulled weeds from the family's vegetable garden. I heard the creaking of the swing—a rope and wood plank my father had hung from one of the trees—and thought it was Ewatomi. Instantly jealous—why had Ewatomi been let free from chores while I rooted around in the dirt, I rushed to the swing and froze mid-step.

There was another little girl on the swing, rocking back and forth. She looked sad, and there were some oddities with her quite nearly translucent clothing and complexion. I stared at the little girl as she swung back and forth in the tree, wondering if it was all in my imagination or a trick of the sun. I wanted to go find my mother, but worried if I did, the girl would disappear. Then, I blinked, and the girl disappeared.

I immediately ran to tell her mother, who at first exhibited confusion but then threw herself into passionate tantrum, shook me by the shoulders, and then slapped me so hard, in front of family and neighbors, that my ears rang. *Wicked child, wicked child!* The years muddle so many memories so well, but that one remains as rich and vibrant as the day it happened. It frequently replays in my nightmares.

Nearly an adult, I struggle to discern my visions from dreams or nightmares (although lately, it seems they are all nightmares). That night in Kähari, while we await word from my godfather, I have a dream so clear and vivid. In the dream, I walk along a coastal road in the cool blue light of dawn. Far ahead lies the shadow of an unfamiliar fishing village. My grandmother shimmers into being in front of me, pulling me gently into her arms. I collapse against her in the throes of heaving, painful sobs.

"Daughter Maze, wake up."

I open my eyes to the guest chambers in Amęci. Kala stands above me, her dark, straight hair braided into two long lines down her back, courtesy of the patient and talented Mate. Even though it is dark and hours before sunrise, Kala wears a navy dress with fur trim, looking much like a noble herself.

"You were crying in your sleep."

Wincing in embarrassment, I wipe at my damp cheeks with my sleeve. "About what?" I ask hoarsely.

"Psh, I don't know. It was your dream." Kala sits on the bed. "I think they're going to leave soon for Kähari. A couple squadrons from the Amęci military."

I sit up, now wide awake. I struggle to remember my dream, but it is already fading away. "We need to find out."

"What was in your dream? Did you...see Adin? Or whatever is impersonating him?"

"I don't think so, but I don't really remember... I feel like I would."

I try to slide out of bed, which sits higher off the floor than I am accustomed to and wind up in a heap on the floor. "Ow..."

"I'm judging you right now," Kala comments, glancing down at me.

DAWN THE NEXT MORNING FINDS KALA AND I STANDING ON ONE OF THE balconies looking down at a couple of rows of Amęci military in their slick uniforms and helmets. The highly trained men and women carry crossbows or blades; on their backs, heavy, black-clad metal sticks called clubs. They carry and fire and swing their weapons with frightening precision. They plan to transport the squadrons along the coast (skipping the uncertainty of the Outlands given the waning moon) using military warships, large, grayish black with voluminous sails, which have been under development for the more significant part of a decade.

"I think if Amęci ever wanted full control of the realm," Kala says thoughtfully. "They could have it."

I say nothing, but silently agree. None of the other nations—besides possibly Ogun—could come close to Amęci's military might. I ask Kala if Chieftess Udo has sent for us; she hasn't and my suspicions grow.

Amęci's selected squadron spends the greater part of the morning enjoying a farewell parade and cheers from the citizens of Amęci. The general feeling seems to be one of relative confidence; how hard would it be to stop a small rebellion of starving refugees? They would go to Kähari, show their strength by securing its borders, and that would be the end of it.

Kala and I take turns watching from the balcony for a spell and wait for Chieftess Udo to send for us. When we did not hear anything by the afternoon, I set out to find her. I want to go back to my father in Kähari. I want to hear see his face and hear his voice.

Unfortunately, the only one she could find was Chieftess Udo's extremely attractive but extremely annoying assistant Logos. He is in less than a helpful, saucy mood.

"As you might imagine, Chieftess Udo is very busy," Logos says absently as he scribbles something on his tablet. "I'm not sure I can find a time—"

"I am the Daughter of Chieftain Oko Mäzzikim *Ka* Kähari," I declare firmly, holding my chin up. "And I *demand* an audience with her."

My power show does not have the desired effect; he pauses and forces a withering smile. "Oh, do you demand it, your grace? Well, in that case, what is it regarding? Your companion, Kala? Udo thought she'd be happy."

He grumbles under his breath. "Never satisfied…"

"Happy?" I ask, puzzled. "Happy about what?"

"Her parents. They're here," the assistant says, returning his gaze to his tablet. "From Väike. Look nothing like her, for what it is worth, but genetics are a strange thing."

A chill that has nothing to do with the ice storm outside moves me. "What?"

"They're *here*," he repeats, sounding annoyed. "They're in one of the village inns getting settled for a few nights, courtesy of Chieftess Udo's coin."

Kala did not mention that her family had arrived in Amęci. Did she even know? How did they get here? I stare there like a baffled fool while Logos scribbles something again with his odd-looking pen.

"Your godfather—when he heard of a girl that matched your description, apparently, he went to a village, where you must've stopped at one point. I don't know all that you have been up to in the Outlands…"

"Anyway, he is returning to Amęci now that he knows you have arrived safely. Chieftess Udo would prefer you stay in the Palace but—"

"He is?" I say in surprise. "I thought he couldn't be reached, nobody told me."

"It was no easy task." He shrugs. "Do you still need an audience, your... grace?"

I frown. "I mean...I do have a few questions. Will we be leaving with the squadron? Has she heard from my father, Chieftain Oko?"

Logos laughs and then catches himself when he sees my expression. "Oh, sorry. But sweetheart, no. You will stay with your godfather until it is safe to return to Kähari."

"And if I don't want to do that?"

"Have you celebrated your Hathi?" He raises his eyebrows and examines me crassly.

"I'm old enough; my mother is just reluctant. Surely some kind of exception can be made due to all of the chaos."

Logos shakes his head definitively. "Chieftess Udo won't do anything against your parents' wishes or your clan's backward traditions. Foreign diplomacy, and all that."

"Your grace," he adds almost as an afterthought.

ONCE AGAIN, KALA AND I SEPARATE—THIS TIME, IN TWO DIFFERENT AMĘCI villages, but it was hard to hold that against Chieftess Udo, who seems genuinely happy that she connected us with familiar faces. Kala has a reunion at an inn with her parents. A village away in a tavern, I reunite my godfather, who I haven't seen since I was a small child. He is much older now with little gray hair curling from every spot on his body. I can hardly see his face, but for the beard, but every age spot, glance, and movement are familiar. Dwen Sofah is a childhood friend of my mother, and one of the few people she trusts.

"Mazzie," Dwen exclaims in his naturally gruff voice. "Long time since I saw you, eh? Thank the gods you're all right. How's your *mother*?"

"If travel went well, in Ogun with Ewatomi. Preparing for the wedding," I reply, staring uncomfortably into my tea.

All around us Amęcians laugh, sing, and enjoy heaping plates of fish and lamb (or bear, perhaps?), beans, and hot cakes. And all of them look perfectly warm, which didn't make sense to me. I am so cold even my magic is shuddering.

"Ah, your time will come," he replies, mistaking the cause of my glum face. "Buck up."

"I'm just cold, but it is nice to see a familiar face," I answer. "How come you didn't come to Ewatomi's Hathi or engagement festival?"

"That's prime fishing time, girl—before the snow and frost sets in. Besides, your mother knows I don't care nothing for that mess. Bunch of strumpets strutting about like it means something," Dwen counters, tossing back his firewater with one large swallow.

I raise my eyebrows in amusement.

He wipes the droplets from his graying beard. "Come on, I'll take you to my house."

Nervously, I get up to follow him. I worry maybe Chieftess Udo may not trust this man. Perhaps she intentionally delayed connecting me. It does not seem like she holds my parents, my mother in particular, in great esteem. Then, I chide myself for being paranoid. He is Dwen, my godfather. I have known him since childhood. If I cannot trust him, could I trust anyone in this country?

I shiver in my gray fur cloak and beaded hood, courtesy of Chieftess Udo, as I follow Dwen through the streets of the small village, lined with tiny, domed houses promiscuously close to one another. I see an elaborate but small temple and a hot house filled with fruit-bearing plants.

"I-is it m-m-uch farther n-now?" I manage, clutching my arms to my chest for warmth.

"You southerners—can't handle no kind of weather," Dwen chuckles.

"You're fr-from the s-s-outh," I protest.

"Not no more, but lucky for you, my house is right here."

Dwen's modest, cozy-looking house is charming and blue with a bright red door, and there were more rooms (and wet rooms) than expected based on the outside. He even has a spare room prepared for me with appropriate cold-weather attire hanging in the closet, which I find presumptuous and weird. "Your mum told me that you were coming," he says when he sees my face. "Told me to make sure you had everything you needed for a long stay just in case."

"How long exactly?" I ask nervously, looking at the overstuffed closet.

I pull out a fur-trimmed reindeer hide dress with an oversized underlaying of white skirts, a beaded belt, and a matching beaded hat. I see a pair of boots, thigh-high fur-trimmed and elaborately embroidered. Even the earrings are trimmed with fur. I groan internally. It will take time to get used to all the heavy clothing. Not that I want to get used to it.

"Don't know. Month." He shrugs. "Whenever it's safe to go back."

A month? I grimace.

"Does she know I'm here?" I ask.

"Ah, well, I've written her a letter, but it could be awhile before it reaches her. Tea, girl?"

"Is my father alive?"

"That's not something a peasant like me would be privy to know," Dwen replies good-naturedly. "But if I was a betting man, I'd guess that Oko's got more lives than that cat of yours. Where is Helissi?"

"Udo has men looking for him," I reply vaguely.

For the rest of the evening, Dwen fusses, pouring several mugs of tea, asking how I feel, and reassuring me about my father but also requiring me to explain again and again what happened the night of the Palace raid. My magic stirs quietly in my stomach as I talk.

"Insane," he keeps repeating. "Insane. Never heard of anything like that happening in a noble house. In a damn Palace. Insane."

Finally, after eating a bite or two of his disgusting vegetable stew and more awkward conversation than I could bear, I beg off to bed to my room. It is warm and comfortable, though the carpet and the furniture have seen better days. A couple of faded paintings hang above a crackling fire in a navy-marble fireplace, and snow swirls casually outside the window. All things considered; it is peaceful, but then I hear a click.

My honeymoon of trust and security with Dwen ends when I twist the knob and find it locked from the outside. I shake it to be safe, and chills settle in my belly. Not unlike my mother, my godfather prepared a well-appointed prison cell for me. Perhaps he means well, but suddenly everything feels a little colder and darker. My magic rattles in my bones and hums.

I listen for a while as my godfather prowls around, downstairs and then upstairs to his own room. Sighing, I change into nightclothes and slippers, climb into the bed, and blow out the candle in the lone lamp. Except I cannot sleep—I am paralyzed with anxiety. Panicked thoughts zoom through my head running into bits and pieces of memories moving at a frenzied pace. On top of all of it, discomfort in this strange place—this nation, this strange home with a stranger.

I *need* to talk to Kala.

When a clump of snow hits the window, I jerk upright. It has to be Kala. Apparently, we connect more cosmically than I thought. I hurry to the window and look out, but cannot make out much in the swirling snow. I take a forgotten pin out of my hair and jam it into the lock of my door. Clearly my godfather underestimated my ingenuity, *and* the number of pins it takes to tame my hair. With some twisting, I open the door, smiling with satisfaction when I hear the click. Then I quietly pad downstairs to my godfather's kitchen.

Someone catches my wrist in an iron grip and covers my mouth with his free hand. My magic rushes from my heart to my fingertips.

"Don't scream," Ojo Mezu commands in a whisper.

I nod angrily and twist away as he loosens his grip.

"What are you doing here?" I hiss at Mezu, clutching my chest and exhaling. "How did you get in here? How did you find me?"

Mezu smirks. Though his tattoos are hidden by heavy clothing fringed with fur and he'd shorn his dreads, he still makes an imposing figure.

"I delivered the message. Followed Kala's parents here. You owe me some coin. Did you think you could run from me?" growls the surly Mezu. "I need it now."

"I—" I wince. "See...about that. I don't have it anymore. I used it all to get here, but I wasn't running—"

Mezu taps the table with a long finger. "That's not precisely how debts work..."

"Oh, hush, I'm a daughter," I whisper back, dismissively. "I'll get you double the coin once I'm back in Kähari. Besides, what do you need my money for? You're an Ojo. People give you free things everywhere you go—for your service to the realm."

"Not anymore. The Chieftain of Ogun made sure of that," he scoffs, gesturing dramatically and chuckling darkly. "Now I am Mezu. A man of no nation, of no clan, of no purpose."

It occurs to me that Mezu has been drinking. Probably for a while.

I jump when I hear a shifting upstairs. "Be quiet," I warn. "You'll wake my godfather."

Mezu rolls his eyes and then pulls up his sleeve. I suck in my breath. His arm looks raw and red; it is a stark reminder that he—despite his size and demeanor—is little more than bone, meat, and blood just beneath his skin. His *Ojo* tattoo—the cross of triangles—is gone.

"Does it hurt?" I manage to ask.

"Not in the way you think," he grumbles, wincing and shoving his sleeve back down. "Have you got anything to drink?"

"How did Gye get you banished as an *Ojo*?" I ask in curiosity. "I thought Ojos were Ojos for life. It is an institution separate from nation politics."

Mezu hesitates for a moment. "The Tofuli elfin tribe...the one that disappeared. I had assumed that it has something to do with the water crisis—it happened so close to the river. Perhaps desperate Ganju venturing too far."

Mezu pulls a bottle from my godfather's shelf and poured a splash of vodka into a tiny glass. Then, shrugging, he pours a bit more. "Want any?"

I shake my head.

"I returned to that campsite several times. Tried to convince people to come sees the damn thing so that they would understand that the settlement was abandoned involuntarily. I finally convinced your father to send his scouts with me. But when we got there, all evidence of the camp disappeared, and my integrity was called into question."

His jaw twitches. "At first, I was told there just weren't any missions for me. Eventually, the Ordered stripped my designation."

For a flash of a moment, Mezu looks lost, young, and suddenly not so frightening, but his eyes blaze when he continues his story.

"A month or so later, I went back...and there was a mining platform. An illegal mining platform—raised by the Ogun."

My blood runs cold. "What? Are you sure?"

He swigs down the rest of the vodka. "Gye's handiwork is very distinctive. Excessive amounts of iron. I think...he either had them murdered and disposed of... or..."

"Or what?"

"The Trench."

"The place where mages live? It's real?" I say in surprise. "I knew it! Where is it?"

"*Live* puts it kindly. The place where everyone of known magical genetic history is *imprisoned* in an anti-magic aura is more accurate," he corrects bluntly, waving a finger.

"What?"

Mezu sighs. "I know where the Trench is, and I have no idea where the Trench is."

My eyes go wide and my mouth slackens. "Because it's always changing. *The Trench is in the Outlands*," I finally realize. That is why my grandmother's story changed each time; she was trying to give me a clue. Why didn't she just say it? I bit my nail, thinking back on my conversations with her. All of those stories. Were there other answers in them?

"It's late, little bird," he says finally. "If you don't have the coin..."

"I'll get it. I'll get it tomorrow," I promise hastily, having no idea where I will find the coin by then. "But can you tell me—is my family okay? My sister, mother, father?"

He stands up and pulls on his hood. "Yes," he says simply, opening the back door.

"Thank you, Mezu," I sigh gratefully, as a chilly wind blows through the kitchen and leaves me shivering.

"I wouldn't be so relieved about that if I were you," he replies cryptically before closing the door behind him.

For a while longer, I lie awake staring at the ceiling with too much to unpack. *The Trench is real and it's in the Outlands.* If anyone can be believed, certainly a former Ojo. They know everything about the realm; every corner, every custom. Though clearly the *Ojos* aren't as powerful as I once thought. Mezu certainly had been acting in the interest of the realm, yet his power was stripped from him as soon as he reported wrongdoing by one of the more powerful nations.

My family is alive, which I suspected, but I worry anew about the fate of my sister, who bunkers with such a corrupt, violent nation, and betrothed to a noble family with questionable motives. I hypothesize that my mother, at some level, must have known. Is that what Mezu meant when he said he wouldn't be relieved about my family being alive?

My mind swirls for hours; circling around the same thoughts and back again.

Eventually, fatigue takes over and the room around me fades away. After floating in darkness for a spell, I find myself standing in a new place. It is a dream, I decide. Not quite a vision. It has a hazy feel about it, like the details are not quite complete. Still, I worry I will run into whatever tried to kill me before. Could I die in a vision? I have no idea. I hope not.

I am no longer in my bed in Dwen's little house. Instead, people fill the temple around me. Pious robed people; heads bowed and chanting prayers to Ogun and the other realm's other demigods. Priests and priestess, all in white, file to the altar; I immediately follow with the staff in hand. I am one of them, filled with excitement and joy. It is a selection ceremony, I realize. We will announce the next Father or Mother of Ogun. Suddenly there is shouting outside. A low murmur of concern fills the temple.

Maybe it is not a dream at all, but instead an ancient memory—but triggered by what? My thoughts are mixing with the memory. I cannot remember this happening before. I do not know if it is a good thing. Probably a bad thing, given the way things seem to be going.

One of the priests puts his hand on my arm and hisses in my ear. "We must go. Now."

The wooden doors slam open. Masked men enter roaring and brandishing iron blades. People scream and flee. In the chaos, some are cut down. But the men are not focused on the people; they want the holy congregation.

I run with the others but it is too late. There are too many of them. The man who had whispered in my ear—he is sliced in half, a frozen look of terror on his face. His blood splatters onto me and floods the floor. Then his killer turns on me, and before I can move, he whips his sword around and a naked hot pain blazes through my gut. Gasping for breath, I fall to my knees in a puddle of my own blood. I drop the staff; it hits the floor with a clang and rolls under the pew.

With a little shriek, I shoot up in bed, gasping for breath as my magic vibrates through my body. I gulp down air and focus on the room to calm myself. It is her godfather's house, and I am in his spare room. The sun fills the cold, unfamiliar space. Two windows. Two doors; one to a closet. My heartbeat slowly returns to normal.

It could not have been a dream, but something must've triggered it. It is too random. After I try whispering my incantation but no spirit appears, I climb out of bed and search the room. Coming up empty, I wander down the hall to my godfather's bedroom, which luckily is empty. He must be downstairs, but I rush my search. Finally, tucked deep behind a trick wall in the closet, I find a wooden box that was almost humming with enchanted energy.

I lift the lid. Inside, wrapped in wool cloth, is the staff. It has seen better days. The gold staff is rusty and dusty and several of the little gems are gutted or missing, but it is unmistakable from my vision. Ogun is a monarchy. They no longer follow the religious foundations of the great clan nations; the same foundations that had ensured peace in the realm for several centuries. But I doubt many know that the monarchy had been created by a brutal, bloody force.

I glance around the closet. There are a lot of items in here; each humming with a magic, with souls. In fact, it reminds me of my own trove. Whispers fill my head. I do not block them; I listen. Souls cry out in warning. I whisper my acknowledgment and my world shifts.

Suddenly, I am with the Ameci warriors as they advance to Kähari. In the distance, a wall of warriors, clad in tunics and armor of crimson, emerald, and midnight-black, carrying banners with a gold eagle emblem. Not Ganju; Ogun. Shock rockets through my body.

I blink and jerk. The enemy is Gye Nyame. Does his influence extend to the man downstairs frying hot cakes and bacon? The priests and priestess in that temple died a long time ago, but Dwen has the staff. My mother might've trusted this man, but maybe that is a reason I should not. At best, he is no different from the dubious merchants in Arufin; at worst, Dwen is an killer who treasures his trophies.

I have to tell Chieftess Udo what I know: Death is coming for the Ameçi. For the first time in my life, I think my magic has *predicted* death. Maybe I can stop it.

"Everything all right up there?" he calls. He must've gone to "unlock" the door as he does not seem surprised by my wandering around, which meant he never intended for me to know he locked it in the first place. Abruptly, I shut the box.

"Uh, yes, just looking for a wetroom," I call back. "Thought I'd take a long, warm bath."

"Don't take too long then. The bacon will be cold."

Whoever the man was downstairs, he is not Dwen—or at least, not the Dwen I thought I knew. *Get out.* My mind and heart are in agreement.

After piling on clothing, I wander into the wet room, turn on the bath water, and lock the door, and pull it shut. Then I tip-toe down the hallway to my room to hurriedly gathered some things, including a small, gray crossbow loaded with red-tipped arrows that I'd found strapped under my godfather's bed. I have no idea how to use it, but hopefully Kala will figure it out if the need arises. As quickly and quietly as I can, I pry open the green-glass window and climb onto a tree. As I shimmy my way down, I mourn that I can no longer call on Helissi.

I try a jog, but abruptly slow in all the slushy snow.

I curse, and an alarmed-looking white hare rushes out of my way. It will not be long before Dwen notices I am missing. I need to find Kala, but would Kala even leave Ameçi now she has reunited with her parents? As I pad towards the village inn, my magic buzzes in my gut again. I cannot give up. If the evil spreads, just like it did centuries ago, even Ameçi will not be a safe haven—not if the power concentrates in the 'less progressive' houses.

Less progressive is polite. Ganju, Ogun, and Kähari; all three nations rule in varying power-hungry, bigoted, ignorant, short-sighted, and cruel ways. I need to convince my father that this thinking is dangerous. After all, he values Chieftess Udo as an ally, and it would be in the interest of Kähari; the Ameçi and Kähari armies together could soundly defeat the Ogun and restore a *true* peace.

Better for some is rarely better for all, a little voice reminds me as I hurry across a bridge. There are people—humans— in Kähari who benefit from the current system, and they will be less enthused to fight against it unless they see something in it for them.

How about peace, my heart offers kindly. *You are a naïve cow,* my mind complains.

It is idealist, I know, and likely more complicated, as everyone loves saying. Yet, I have woken up from the false sense of peace that I'd enjoyed throughout my childhood.

I will never go back to sleep.

THE VERY KIND INNKEEPER RINGS KALA, WHO MEETS ME IN THE ADJOINING tavern. She looks rested and happy, so naturally, I am racked with over guilt about asking her to give it all up. I tell Kala about the vision in the Ogun temple and the staff. Mezu's appearance. Her theories. Kala listens patiently, nodding now and then in between sips from her tin mug of coffee. The pan-fried cakes between us go untouched.

"We need to go back to Kähari," I announce finally.

Kala's face drops. "Maze…"

"I need to talk to my father. I think the Ameci are marching into an ambush," I hurriedly add. "The Ogun—something is happening."

"Maze—"

"Kala, I need to tell Chieftess Udo. The Ogun hoped to weaken Kähari; that's why they didn't tell us the refugees were coming. The attack on the Palace was orchestrated by people who knew the inside of the Palace well, not a bunch of starving refugees. The Ogun are there, waiting for the Ameci. There will be no safe place. This is a coup—more than a coup!"

Kala bites her lip. "The Ameci are halfway to Kähari by now. Couldn't we send someone to warn them? There are advisors, Ojos—"

"I'm not even sure if my godfather is who he says he is. Who else can we trust?" I demand. "The Ojo who discovered that lost tribe was promptly dismissed from the Order."

"My ears are burning."

Kala jumps as Mezu appears by our table. I am not surprised to see him. I don't think he cares about collecting money from me. I am the only other person who has seen the campsite and can collaborate his story; his path back into the Order.

He has dark circles under his eyes. Had he been following me since last night? Frankly, I do not care if he has. I feel a strange comfort as soon as I am in his presence.

"*Gods*, who in the realm are *you*?" a flustered Kala asks at the same time. "This is a private conversation!"

"I am Mezu. Perhaps the little Mazzie bird has mentioned me?" He smiles at me.

"No, I haven't. Kala, this is Mezu, a *former* Ojo. He's a churlish, stalking git with questionable timing. He's the one who carried the message for your parents—and alerted my father to the missing Tofuli tribe."

"Churlish, stalking—it is fine, I'll allow it, sweetheart." Rolling his eyes, Mezu turns back to Kala. He pulls a chair from a nearby table and sits down. "I can help you reach the Ameci army. I'd go on my own, but they won't listen to me—I'm 'disgraced,' but they'll listen to Daughter Kähari."

"She shouldn't go anywhere *near* Kähari," Kala insists. "Her mother beat her, forced her not to talk about... basically pretending she didn't exist—obviously favoring her older sister—" A flustered Kala stumbles over the explanation as she struggles not to expose too much information to a near stranger.

"Kala," I cut in to argue, but Kala races on, now addressing Mezu directly.

"In Kähari, anyone known to be a mage, caught practicing, or even *reading* about tribal magic is shipped off to an asylum, prison, or executed— the latter of which is much kinder."

"That's precisely why my mother was trying to protect me," I snap.

"She hardly let you leave the house once Funani passed," Kala shoots back, finally looking at me again. "She wasn't protecting you—she was protecting herself."

A flash of grief hits me hard. "How can you possibly know her intentions—"

"She said she hired me to protect you, but she awfully suspicious that you might be searching for other people like you—especially after discovering that tribe missing in the Outlands."

"*My* discovery," Mezu corrects needlessly.

"She told me to report back on your every move," Kala claims, rolling on. "She said it was to protect you, but I started to doubt it immediately. You were right – on *the very first day*."

"I didn't do it," Kala adds quickly when she sees my face. "Not when I started to realize…not after I saw…"

My head swirls with contradictions. My mother hired Kala to spy on me, but was it just because she was overprotective? Or were there more nefarious reasons for shutting me up and keeping me close until she could marry me off deep in the north?

"Mazzie, you told me that you have been waiting to leave Kähari your entire life."

"Maybe my mother did want me to marry someone from Amęci because she said Amęci was more progressive. She was just trying to protect me." I hear myself, and I do not even believe it.

"She was protecting Ewatomi's marriage to Bosede—and the alliance with Ogun by shipping you as far north as possible. Your status implicates the whole family," Kala snorts in disbelief. "But sure, yes, what a loving and caring woman. I'm sure she meant well when she put those marks on your back."

When I stiffen, Kala adds, "Helissi did not do that."

Kala leans closer. "I fought off those masked men. They intended to kill you. They dressed as Skulls, an easy cover, but they *weren't* Skulls. To our knowledge, only two people alive knows *what you are*. I am one of them. The other is your mother."

I draw in my breath sharply, as if hit in the chest with a hot shot from a crossbow. Reading my mind, Mezu shakes his head. Then he gestures to the tavernkeeper for amber beer awhile an obviously frustrated Kala shrugs and lapses into an awkward silence.

"You're safe here," Kala adds with finality.

"We're safe here *now*," I point out. "But not if the Amęci fall to Ogun. Kala, we have no choice—"

"We don't even know if the Ogun—"

"I don't normally agree with little birds, but…she's right," Mezu replies, offering me an easy nod. "If the Amęci fall to Ogun—to Gye—the realm will descend into chaos. Again. There is no telling who will be left standing this time."

Kala stares at us in silence for several moments, tightening and loosening her hands on the table. "Please, Kala—Chieftess Udo can't fight the enemy if she doesn't know who it is," I beg. "You have to let me go."

After another long beat, Kala relents. "We need provisions. Weapons. A map. A coach and some work animals, if we can swing it." Kala ticks off on her fingers, and then her eyes light up. "Letaro! He might be able to help us. He'll know where the Amẹci army is. He is Chieftess Udo's trusted advisor. They must have a stable route they're taking."

I smile through tears. Kala places my hands over mine, wraps her fingers.

"Oh, how sweet," Mezu grumbles sarcastically.

"I cannot ask you to leave your parents," I say quietly, ignoring him. "You can go home. I cannot ask you to go with me."

"Then a good thing you don't have too. I've volunteered, and we're not doing it without you, Matza the git," Kala replies reluctantly, looking at Mezu again. "You're coming, too."

"*Mezu*," he corrects, looking annoyed. "And I'm not—"

Kala ignores him and continues on. "Honestly, we were lucky to make it here alive. We had no idea what we're doing. That caravan carried us through the worst of it and then we got arrested at the border like a couple of fobbing jolt-heads. We need you—Ojo or not."

"Yes, so, perhaps you should avoid drinking yourself into a stupor and disappearing into the pleasure house," I warn Mezu.

Kala raises her eyebrows at me.

"Actually," Mezu says, flashing his exceedingly annoying smirk. "That's *exactly* where we need to disappear. Your godfather will be here any moment, and he did not look pleased about the flood in his house."

CHAPTER
FOURTEEN

he next day is busy—for everyone except me. My only role: Remain out of sight. Kala rushes off to consult with Letaro and Mezu tucks me away in a pleasure house, well-known for its discretion, a village over. Then Mezu dashes off too so that he can make arrangements for our travel and gather supplies. Well, he dashed off in that brooding way of his, anyway.

Mezu is right about one thing: I know my godfather will never look for me in the pleasure house. That said, I could do without all the naked bodies, loud groans, and curse-laden language so early in the morning. I keep to the parlor, where the old biddy of a madam counts her take and then counts it again (and again) for good measure. Without prompting, the madam talks about all the tricks she used to turn and how men used to beat down the door for a night with her. I nod politely and wish I knew a wee bit less about the old woman's genitals.

Kala eventually returns with maps and supper in hand. Visibly brightened, she tells me about Letaro's office, lecture hall, and research lab at the university; how it is chock full of books that are illegal in Kāhari and Ogun (and Ganju, if it still exists). Over warm meat (of mysterious origin) and fried potato patties, Kala explains that Letaro had tried to get them to see at least part of the truth for themselves without speaking it to them directly, which would've been dangerous for them all. He even grudgingly admitted that they were open-minded students, Kala adds with delight. He'd half-expected that we would report him for being too radical.

"Of course, I wouldn't," I say through a mouthful of food. "I invited him for that reason."

"Your mother found out what he was teaching us and asked him to leave. The only reason he was able to leave with his life was because of his close connection with Udo," Kala adds carefully. "And Udo only conceded to his teaching post in Kähari with the hopes of influencing you and, subsequently, your father."

I clear my throat and redirect Kala to the matter at hand, and Kala notes that Letaro wanted to be careful not to discuss confidential military action with her, but could reveal what anyone who once served might know: the army left precisely one day ago, and it generally stops twice in a stable place on route to Kähari, a four-day journey for that large of a squadron. Chieftess Udo herself is leading the army along with two of her most decorated generals and a handful of war advisors. After some hesitation, Letaro gave Kala two old maps from a previous skirmish with two areas circled.

About a third of the military remains behind to protect Ameci nation from any other threat that may arise, and Ameci has alliance with several of the smaller clan nations nearby. "Only Udo's defense advisors have the authority to direct the rest of the army in Chieftess Udo's absence," Kala explains further. "To move them in would be an act of outright war; he can't do that without proof of need."

"So, we either need to prove that the Ogun intend to ambush the Ameci so reinforcements are sent...or we need to find the Ameci army and warn them so that Chieftess Udo can plan accordingly," I finish, but shrug with skepticism. "Why did he help us? What are we, two young women, to an advisor of Chieftess Udo?"

"Ironically, I think it is because he didn't believe me. He probably thinks we're cracked. What, is he going to send Ameci's remaining military because you had a vision? But on the off-chance you're right..."

Fair enough. "Did you hear if..."

"Your godfather, or whoever he is, *is* looking for you. Pretty hard, sounds like. Everywhere. Just like he traveled all the way to that village before. Happily, the authorities won't help him for another day as it was clear that you'd left intentionally. As long as we slip out early tomorrow, he won't find you." Kala looks around. "Where's Mezu?"

"I don't know. You can count on him to show up exactly when you didn't even know you needed him," I reply "Must be Ojo nature."

"Mm," Kala muses thoughtfully. "Well, we should try to sleep...who knows what tomorrow will be like. And to be safe..."

Kala pulls out a little bottle of sleep tonic and shakes it. "Can't have you getting murdered in any nightmares."

I WAKE THE NEXT MORNING, WRAPPED IN AN ITCHY BLANKET ON THE PARLOR room floor. A sliver of sky slips in between the ornate, heavy curtains. Everything is quiet, save for a couple of bashful patrons tip-toeing out; and the 'clink, 'clink,' 'clink' of the madam counting her coin.

Quite an odd year it has been—it finds me in a pleasure house for the first time in my life and then for a second time in a completely different nation. Neither time pleasurable in the least.

Kala sleeps on the velvety couch next to me, breathing slowly and deeply, her midnight-black hair scattered around her, forming a halo-like headdress. I wonder what it is like to sleep and dream without learning every horrible secret of the realm and worrying about being killed. It must be nice.

I stare at the beautifully painted ceiling. Less than a month ago, I shared heady kisses by candlelight with a man who makes my heart skip whenever our eyes met. It seems like a different life. Now I am estranged from my sister and forcibly been separately from my parents. I escaped death and traveled across the realm, through the Outlands, with another girl whom—at one point—I hated. Now I cannot imagine life without her.

Over the course of it all, I discovered more about my childhood home. I did not realize the extent to which my comforts—even the ones I enjoyed before we became a noble family—had been built on the bones of others. How could my mother allow the continued discrimination knowing that her daughter could be a victim of it? Is my mother complacent in the abuse as long as our family is shielded from it?

I know the answer to that question, even if I am not ready to face it. The scars on my lower back, so purposefully, horrifyingly placed so I cannot see them. With some twisting, I manage to get a glimpse of them, dozens of white lines, long healed from the bleeding, crossing upon my skin. My mother is not complicated, misunderstood, or well-meaning. It feels better to think that, but it isn't the truth. My mother knows exactly what she is doing.

I cannot let that consume me—not now. Anger will only cloud my judgment, my intention, my magic, just as the grief after my grandmother's death once did. Although, I have to admit—my grief since her death has shifted. It is still excruciating, of course, but it happened for a reason. I'd treated necromancy as a queer hobby. When there was no one to share it with anymore, I tried to shove it down and make it disappear, but it wouldn't. It couldn't. It is in my blood. Whether I am half, part, or one drop, I am mage—a gifted necromancer from the ancient Kipporah Elven tribe's bloodline. I can spend my life embracing it or falling into madness within my own head.

"Where's Mezu?" Kala asks sleepily as she sits up and stretches her hands over her head. "No matter how fast of a ship he's managed, we need to go soon if we're going to beat the army to Kähari."

"Gathering supplies," I answer, sitting up and wrapping my arms around my knees. "Where do your parents think you are?" I ask curiously.

"They trust I'm where I need to be," Kala replies vaguely. "Do you think your godfather is still looking for you?"

I pull back on the knit hat and stuff my hair inside. "Yes. He will search high and low for me—I'm sure at my mother's command. But by now, he'll have no choice but to assume I'm long gone. Vanished in the Outlands."

Kala winces. "Honestly, I can't believe we're doing this. Can you? We should be studying in your chamber. Good glory, why are all the adults such idiots?"

I laugh at the absurdity of it all. "I've never liked people, especially those of age. Cocky, stupid bunch of shitters, if you ask me."

"Maze?" Mezu opens the parlor door. He notices Kala and dismissively points at her. "And you, I guess. Let's go."

"Rude, Mezzio," Kala sniffs, tossing her hair over her shoulder. "I was just coming to not completely dislike you."

But we both follow him.

Apparently, Mezu is less enthralled with our plan for ground travel (not that we realized there is another option). We will never beat the Amęci to Kähari on the ground, he insists, particularly when they were using water vessels. But Amęci does have a type of rapid-speed water vessel, built unusually narrow so it can travel along the rivers instead of the oceans. The Outlands rivers are not fixed, but the water vessel, built on solid science and alchemy, moves so swiftly, it should not matter. Experimental, Mezu warns, but he knows friend who is a commander. Given all of their technological advances, I wonder how primitive the Amęci find Kähari. Very, is my guess.

"This is a terrible idea, and we're both going to die," Kala boldly declares as we trudge through the snow in an open field toward an icy river. "I hope you know that."

"You seemed excited by the idea earlier," I reply cuttingly. I imitate Kala's earlier shrill inflection. "Oh, wow, I had heard rumors. Wow."

"I do not like your tone."

"That's okay. It was for my own enjoyment," I reply cheerfully.

Before she can properly retort, Kala's eyes widen. The water vessel appears larger than four Outlands wooly elephants, made of heavy wood, painted pitch black with volcanic-glass windows, with a triangle-shaped reflective sail. It sits like a slumbering beast at the edge of the rushing river while Mezu speaks to another man in low tones in front of it.

When Mezu sees us, he jogs over through the snow.

"I didn't tell him where we were going or why, so be careful about what you say," Mezu warns us. "The moon is waning, so the Outlands will be shifting. It could be a rough ride."

Kala narrowed her eyes. "How rough?"

"We'll live," Mezu says vaguely, turning back to the water vessel. "This craft has only the basics. No weaponry. A bit cramped."

"What a glowing endorsement," Kala mutters.

Mezu taps his nose. "Ah, but it flies like the wind—even the Outlands quakes that rippled into the sea will not shake us."

AFTER A NERVE-WRACKING JOLT, THE WATER VESSEL ZIPS THROUGH OUTLANDS via a wide river, which meanders this way and that. The water vessel moves so fast, the villages along the river's edge blur. At night and at top speeds, the ship appears virtually invisible in its black and reflective coating, like a ghost.

"Udo will have my head if she thinks her big project has been compromised," the ship's commander Boa says cheerfully with a pipe hanging out of the side of his mouth. "And if you think *Iboji* is bad, you haven't seen anything until you've had a stay in *Ewone*."

"What's Ewone?" I ask, waving away the man's pipe smoke and coughing pointedly.

"The prison in Ameci," Mezu answers curtly, looking out the window.

"They put us in a cell when we arrived—"

"A ministry holding cell, I bet. Practically a Palace in comparison," the commander crows. "In Ewone, you wish for death every moment of every day."

A greenish Kala sits in the back, clutching a burlap bag full of vomit. She observes with suspicion, "You seem to know quite a bit about prisons."

"Mm." The commander takes out his pipe and wags it at her. "Quite certain that the three of you don't want to get into a game of questions, eh?"

Kala only grunts and dry heaves. The commander shrugs his shoulders and blows a few perfect plumes of purple smoke before glancing at Mezu. "An *Ojo* saved my life once you know. I was facing down a massive rong—"

"Wait."

With fear rising up my throat, I lean forward in my seat and close my eyes. In my head, all I can hear are screams and the whistles of blades and arrows in the air. People dying in anguish. It's too late.

"Slow down," I advise urgently. "Or stop somewhere east of here. Now."

My fear catches on with the others.

"What is it? Maze, what do you see?" Kala demands to know.

"Yah, we still a good twenty miles from Kähari, but we'll be there soon," Boa comments, flipping a couple of switches and looking at his map. "This river connects with the sea. We will loop around and hit the beaches."

"I know but—"

Suddenly something slams against the side of the water vessel, shaking it violently. Immediately, Kala begins rapidly praying to the gods (new and old, I notice warily). Only Mezu remains stoic.

"We've been hit!" the commander calls back, reaching for his harness.

Personally, I find the terror in Boa's eyes to be a little unnerving. "Don't know by what. I've got to take us—"

The water vessel lurches, and my heart does the same—right into my throat. Still, I do not feel death coming for me. I will survive this disaster, but not everyone will.

"The Ogun and Ameci are fighting right near us—the Ogun ambushed them before they could reach Kähari," I shout over the noise of the churning, water-powered engine struggling to propel forward. "We are in an Ameci ship; they think we are the enemy."

"How do you—"

We are hit again and, with the second jolt, sent spiraling and reeling towards the shore. Boa slams forward against the windshield. Kala sobs hysterically as Mezu reaches over the commander to grab the controls. I pray, gripping my restraints so tightly that my knuckles turn white. Water begins seeping into the cabin, soaking my furry Ameci boots.

The water vessel hits the sand and rocks with a loud crash and ear-splitting screech as it drags and flips, whipping us around violently. It finally slides to a stop, upside down, just before reaching the edge of the peaceful lapping sea.

I realize I have been screaming the entire time and try to gulp down air. Kala whimpers somewhere behind me. With some effort but very little optimism, I reach over and press my fingers into the commander's neck, whose glassy eyes gaze at nothing. Blood oozes from a wound on the side of his head. I sit back, defeated and sad. Mezu grunts in pain and releases himself from his seat restraints. With a thud, Kala does the same.

I fumble for the lever and release myself onto the sand. I vomit twice and then fall shakily onto my back. Above me, the stars glitter across the sky. As I catch my breath, I recognize this small part of the sky; the same sky I have seen nearly every day growing up, tossing out fishing nets with my father.

"We're in Kähari," I wheeze, pulling off my sweaty cloak. "He did it."

Nearby, Kala lets out a low moan and wipes at the bloody gash on her forehead. She gazes at the blood on her fingertips and vomit on her jumper as she utters, "I think...we should leave water travel to fish. Is the commander...?

"Boa. He's dead," Mezu interrupts, and he glances pointedly at me. "Let him be."

"What do you mean by that?" I ask defensively as I sit up.

"I'm going to bury him so that he can rest peacefully with the ancestors." Expressionless, he looks at me again. "Let him be."

Kala hangs her head in despair. We have seen so much violence and death. Could we ever go back to the simpler life we knew before? Or would we be forever haunted by everything?

Anyway, Mezu has nothing to worry about because I do not *want* to speak to pilot's spirit or relive his death. I was so focused on saving Kähari and the Amęci that I did not bother to retain his name. I doubt he has nice things to say to me.

After gingerly removing Boa's body, Mezu examines the water vessel. "Iron arrows from a rapid-fire Agnar shooter," he confirms, shaking the heat from his hand. "We were taken out by the Ogun."

"That means..."

"It means you were right. The Amęci are already nearly here," he confirms grimly. "Ogun responded to our water vessel with hostility, so I'd say that the Ogun have already descended upon the Amęci forces long before they made it to the Kähari gates."

"So, what should we do now?" asks Kala, who has come to the same grim realization. "We have to stop this fighting before it becomes a war."

"I ... don't know," I reply, at a loss.

"You do know," Mezu corrects bluntly as he washes off sand and blood in the shallow surf. "This is *about* you. I know you are Kipporan Elf. At least in part. A death mage. It's painfully obvious. You are complete shit at hiding it."

I blink in surprise and take a step back.

"The Kipporah did not just disappear. They were systemically hunted because they can learn every secret of every being who ever died in the realm. You could expose the Ogun."

"Use your power and ends this before Chaos rears its head," Mezu finishes.

I know a spell, but it is blood magic. Surely, I will face significant consequences. In magic, you cannot make something from nothing. Even killing one wild dog left me feeling drained. It will cost blood. If I take a human life, what will happen to me?

"There aren't a lot of options, Maze. Ameci were expecting to tame a small rebellion of starving refugees and instead they're facing war-ready, bloodthirsty Ogun. In an ambush," Mezu points out gruffly, as if he hears my thoughts.

"Maybe you could find Bosede," Kala suggests practically. "He could end this. Don't use magic that you don't underst—"

"Now, why would the Son of Ogun listen to..." Mezu raises his eyebrows and then leers. "So, you *have* taken a lover."

I flush.

"You couldn't say anything because it was also your sister's lover. Tsk, little bird. *The scandal*, Daughter Mäzzikim," he finishes, tapping his lip with his finger.

"All right, enough of that," I snap, turning back to Kala. "I need to talk to my father."

"I'll go to the Palace and see if he's there," Kala offers, ashen-faced. "Primarily because I could use a doctor."

"You go with her," I instruct Mezu. "If you find my father, tell him about Gye Nyame."

"I will take Kala. But, if I had to guess, your father is not at the Palace."

My eyes narrow. "Ojos never guesses."

A slow smile crosses Mezu's face. "Chieftain Oko, along with his advisors, is somewhere he can strategically see the battle. It is impossible the scuffle has escaped his notice." He scans the skyline, and his gaze lands on the northern mountains. "There."

CHAPTER
FIFTEEN

he long expanse of the land I know well stretches out like a dark, twisting shadow. The violent skirmish between the Ogun and Amęci has already taken a toll on the Outlands just outside of Kähari. As I climb higher, I can see the fires burning through trees and the screams and shouts echoing in the distance. By now, all of Kähari must know war is upon them. Whose side would my father choose? Not Ogun. *Never* Ogun. I can hear the Ogun army chanting as they move closer to Kähari's gates.

I run up the path in darkness as light rain drizzles down. I reach the top of the first hill, and hike up my heavy Amęci dress before digging my hands and feet into the mountain, finding a foothold, and then scaling carefully to the next ledge. It is as high as anyone needs; I can see well beyond the Kähari border. Panting, I climb over the ledge. Dark clouds loosen their wrath in full, leaving my filthy, uncomfortably warm clothes sticking unflatteringly to my skin. Once I reach the top of the peak, I do not see my father. Perhaps Mezu is inaccurate in his speculation.

Biting my lip hard, I continue my search. The mountain sides are notoriously unsafe, and thought to be fairly overrun with wildcats, who often war with the antecores. The latter feature sharp, flesh-tearing tusks and sharp hooves. Both species fiercely defend the mountains.

A low moan cuts through the darkness. I freeze. My magic is my only weapon here, and I barely know how to use it. I struggle to focus my eyes in the darkness, searching for a pair of murderous, beady eyes leering in the brush. Instead, my heart stops.

"Father!" I scream, rushing to his side.

The Chieftain Oko *Ka* Kähari lies unnatural and akimbo in a pool of warm blood, which leaks from his mouth. I press my ear to my chest. I exhale deeply when my father gasps shallowly. Perhaps there is still time to get him to a medicinary. I put my hand in his, and he squeezes tight.

"Mazzie, you are...alive," my father manages between gulps of breath with his dark eyes full of relief. "Ogun—"

"I know. Shh."

I reach for the wound. When I find it, I work carefully; my fingers stained with blood. I remove a piece of shrapnel and then another and another. Some horrible Ogun weapon, I am sure of it. My father does not even flinch as I root around in his flesh.

"No, Maze, your mother," he whispers.

"I know," I shush, stroking his cold cheek in what I hope feels comforting. "You're going to be fine," I lie. His death is coming, I know it now. We are so far away from any medicinary or village clinic, which will not be able to handle the wound besides. His pain rattles in my bones.

"All this time, I did not know. I am so sorry," he wheezes.

I smile, wobbly, back at him through tears. "Did not know what?"

Suddenly his grip slackens, and his eyes glaze over.

My chin drops to my chest. For a moment, I sit in the rain, mud, and my father's blood, knees to my chest, feeling sick and disoriented. I close his eyes. Despair and anger churns inside of me, and the strong spark of my magic fills my body.

"Mäzzikim."

My heart stops again. Don't panic. Stay in control. Harness the magic.

I slowly stand and turn to see Bosede, emerging from the mountain fog and brambles with the slow assurance of a native snake. His eyes are bright and wet. None of this was his idea, his eyes suggest. An Ogun saber, forged in iron, dangles at his side.

For a moment, neither of us moved.

"I thought I'd never see you again," he admits finally. "I'm so glad you are alive."

"Are you?" I ask.

Caught in his familiar gaze, I move forward unconsciously but jump back. Shadows play across his face, and his blue gaze was bright and different. There was something new there, as if he had become another person in the few short weeks that we had not seen each other. Or perhaps I am seeing him for who he is? Still, lightning zips around my stomach. He stares back with the same intensity, and it hums in the air between us.

"We're powerful, the two of us," he says.

Suddenly I understand our connection. We do share something. Kipporan blood. Could we be related? My stomach rolls in discomfort at the thought. Then, I recoil further. Bosede—not Gye Nyame—killed my father. Swallowing a mouthful of bile, I take a step backward. "What have you done?"

"What your mother and my father knew had to be done. We made a sacrifice for the good of the realm."

"Does your father know what you are?" I ask, hoarsely.

My suspicions further stain the dwindling chemistry between us. He raises his iron saber slightly. I am the only thing standing between him and the throne of two powerful nations. If I am not with him, I am against him.

"I chose not to be a demon," he declares bitterly. "It is a choice."

"We're not demons, Bosede," I try desperately, and then amend, "At least, *I'm* not. You don't have to—"

"You look human. You pass, like me." His nostrils flare slightly. "But we are *not* human, and the age of magic has ended with the Chaos."

He laughs darkly. "A good Elf is a dead one. It's what my father always says."

"You say his words like you believe them."

"It is for the good of the realm, Maze." Rain drips down Bosede's sharp cheekbones and his chin. "My father will grant me the throne, and when Ewatomi and I join our nations—"

"So, it is a coup," I spit in disbelief. "Gye sent you to do his dirty work."

"There can be no peace as long as mages with dangerous magic walk in this realm," Bosede counters with a scoff. "We will be the greatest empire that ever existed; the first empire in the age of men. The Iron Empire."

I shiver against the rain.

"We thought for sure that *Ewatomi* was the mage. A girl that beautiful surely must've made some deal with a demon." Bosede shakes his head, ruefully. "So, imagine my surprise tonight when Ewatomi told me that *you* were the mage. A twist!"

"Ewatomi doesn't know!"

"I happened to mention you on the night of her Hathi. In her jealousy, she complained you're an 'odd little duck' who claimed to talk with ghosts when you were young—until your mother made you stop." He shrugged his shoulders. "I figured out the rest."

I flush and stare at the ground, collecting my anger. A twist to me as well. I thought that night was a genuine connection, but it was a strategy; his opportunity to redirect his affection to the right target, and I kissed the snake in the mouth. I cannot believe my lips were ever upon this foul excrement of a human. I must take care to be more selective in the future, if I have one.

"If he knew, my father would want you dead. I do not want to kill you."

"But you will anyway."

"One realm. Think about it. Maze, you want peace—*this* is how you achieve it."

I glance at my hands, covered in my father's blood. Inspired, I smear it on my cheeks. Bosede looks alarmed as I smile widely. I feel my power erupt, take root, and spread all over my body. It is a tingle then a pressure. I will not need any words; I do not need a blade. Instead, I focus on what I want to happen, pray for it to come. My breathing deepens, my muscles steel, and my eyes narrows. I upturn my palm, and the magic twists and sparks like lightening.

"I do want peace." I focus on his throat, dragging my fingers closer together.

Bosede drops his saber and grasps desperately at his throat. His eyes bulge as he chokes, he staggers and then collapses at my feet. I force the magic onto him as he gasps and wheezes. "If you use your magic, you could defend yourself," I remark casually.

As his skin begins to purple, I close my palm.

The light leaves Bosede's blue eyes. I sigh, rubbing at phantom pain—Bosede's pain—in my neck. I have ensured my father will not be trapped by the bęsan; with his murderer gone, he will transcend to the ancestral realm. However, I am not finished with the Ogun.

Taking a deep breath, I walk back to the ledge. Shakily, I lift my hands to the heavens and shout an enchantment into the rain. *Focus.* I have long odds of success, but I hold my breath.

The air remains still, and I drop my hands. I managed the wild dog and Bosede, but I suppose it was arrogant to think I could harness and direct magic advanced enough to strike several hundred warriors at once. Perhaps my sacrifice is not great enough. Now, the Ogun will easily take Kähari; Amęci too—this night will mark the end of the Great Clans and the beginning of the Iron Empire, even with Bosede dead. Defeated, I hang my head, watching as the raindrops dribbles down off the tip of my nose and onto the grass.

But then the sky grows even darker, and the wind swirls and spins so hard it nearly tosses me off my feet and into the slick mud. Fighting to get on my feet, I try to ignore the thumping of my heart as the spirits that linger in Kähari rise from their rest. *Souls of prey.*

There are ghastly cries and moans. Wispy white shapes begin to form and move. Many of the spirits are men, women, children struck down during the Chaos centuries ago. By a horrid twist of fate, their spirits had lingered in the realm waiting for bęsan—the karma—to set them free. And, how delightful, the Ogun are an old enemy; their rage would turn the Ogun army into an ocean of blood. They swirl from the ground, lift ancestral weapons buried beneath the dirt. Off they set—to hunt down the Ogun and drive them from Kähari land.

Not Kähari land, my heart corrects, *Kipporan land.*

My father's blood served as the sacrifice for Bosede's life, but I have nothing left to trade the universe for the Ogun army. I am the sacrifice. My brain swells against my skull, and legs and arms cramp. I fall to my knees and struggle to breathe.

You can't give up now, my heart pleads.

A stringing heat blazes through my body. I press against cool, wet grass for relief. Nausea rises in her throat; and I fight to swallow it down. I wonder, dizzily, if I am dying. Death feels alarmingly close. The sky spins above me.

This is the way my life ends.

This is how I die.

Then it hits me—this is the impact of hundreds of Ogun lives ending at once. I scream as their terror and pain blasts through my blood and burns and blisters my skin. The air shifts uncomfortably, and then everything goes black.

I WAKE UP WITH A POUNDING IN MY HEAD THAT THUMPS AND BUMPS LIKE THE drums at celebrations. I hear voices echoing in my head. Celebratory voices, but hushed like the wind. *Spirits.* Then silence, followed by the chirp of curious birds who do not have the faintest idea of what happened. Something warm and wet presses against my face. With some effort, I open my eyes and find myself staring into the green eyes of an old friend.

"Helissi," I breathe, wrapping arms around my panther, who gently pulls me into a seated position. The big black cat purrs and nuzzles against me; I rest against him, feeling a security that I have not felt in days.

"You found me," I whisper into his fur.

Gingerly, I peel myself off the ground and glance around. How long have I been out? I am a wee bit concerned about conjuring an army of the dead and then sleeping through the battle. Seems like a bad practice, but things *seem* peaceful. The sun lifts into the pink sky. I can hear birds chirping, even louder now. Everything is still and calm. Even in the far distance, I do not see any fires.

I glance to where my father fell. Despite all of the blood and the gaping wound, he 'sleeps' peacefully on the grass. Kneeling by him, I say another prayer to Kipporah for his quick ascension. He deserves better than being trapped between the realm of the living and the dead. He deserves to rest with the ancestors in paradise.

I glance over where Bosede had fallen. His iron saber lies cradled in the sodden grass. Before climbing onto Helissi's back, I jam it back into his cold palm and close his fist. I do not want there to be any doubt about who killed Chieftain Oko *Ka* Kähari.

"You and your clan will pay for what you've done, Bosede," I declare, staring down at his body in cold anger, daring his spirit to confront me. Satisfied that the monster is dead, I turn to Helissi. "Let's go."

ATOP HELISSI, I TRAVEL THE FAMILIAR ROADS BACK TO THE PALACE. THE SKIES arching above, pink bright and green land, floating peonies, pushed by a coastal breeze—the prolific beauty of Kähari hides all of its darkness, all of its secrets.

As I pass through the first village, it is clear the skirmish beyond Kähari's borders ended. Everyone in Kähari, flushed with excitement and relief of having avoided the worst of it, whisper theories about what finally drove the Ogun back from Kähari's gates. Small crowds of people cheer when they see me—Daughter of Chieftain— Mäzzikim *Ka* Kähari, whom everyone had apparently assumed to be dead somewhere in the Outlands after the Palace raid. I attempt to smile, turning this way this way and that, but staying alert. Among the people, Ewatomi is the favorite—the bright shining star. But right then, I am the survivor.

Would they feel the same way if they knew what I'd done? In one night, I helped steal a military-grade water vessel, sailed across the realm at incredible speed, crashed on a Kähari beach, participated in a murder plot against the next-in-line for the Ogun throne, and literally cast death upon another nation's army. I smile with pride—internally of course, so as not to *look* prideful. Must remain humble. Or at least give the appearance of being humble.

When I reach the Palace, I find it terribly disturbing that nothing has changed besides a new door (apparently, the old one had been splintered and ripped from the hinges by the intruders). That was the only visible difference anyway—other than the seemingly excessive number of grim-faced guards, carrying rapid-fire shooters instead of blades, matching around at the ready. When I enter, the guards and servants swarm immediately (not a massive surprise as I am caked in mud, vomit, and blood). Titus looks incredibly happy to see me and envelops me in a relieved hug (despite the stench and questionable bodily fluids).

"I knew you were alive. Thank the gods! I knew it! I knew it," Titus keeps saying in relief.

I leave behind a sticky blotch on his bright blue tunic with gold embroidery I peel away. "Sorry about that," I manage through relieved laughter.

"Well, you will certainly need to wash more than your hands for supper this evening," he quips, guiding me by the arm. "But good glory, I am so glad you are okay. Kala said—but she also said *she* was all right, and I saw her arm and her face, so I wasn't sure—"

Where's—"

"The raid was subdued soon after it started. Your father survived it, but isn't home," Titus explains quietly as he escorts me back to my chamber. "He's dealing with political matters. He is meeting with Ogun leadership in Barack."

I grimace but do not correct him.

"Besides, all the men connected with the raid have been...dealt with," he continues.

I grimace again. "Who were they?"

Titus sighs. "Unfortunately, they were very tight-lipped even after being subjected to our most, uh, effective techniques. We know nothing for sure but...the general consensus is that they were *not* Ganju. Some sort of radical group, we think. Not sure why we were targeted."

"Interesting."

"Security has been stepped up quite a bit of course," Titus adds quickly to reassure me. "The Palace guard on duty that night have been let go because the *other* general consensus is that someone who knew the Palace let them in."

"What matter is my father contending with now?" I pray my face does not betray me.

Titus continues, "Chieftain Gye Nyame offered to talk to him directly and confidentially, and choose the mountain location for privacy. I don't suppose you heard...?"

Gye Nyame lured my father to the mountain, and then sent his son to kill him.

"That the Ogun ambushed the Amẹci, who were coming to our aid, not far from our gates?" I finish wryly. "Long story, but I may have heard a thing or two. Do you know why?"

"The Ogun are claiming *they* came to subdue the Ganju refugees and mistook the Amẹci for them."

"Titus, that is the weakest bunch of bollocks—"

Shushing me, Titus cuts in, "Mazzie, I don't believe it either. I have my suspicions. As does Chieftess Udo. Unfortunately, we are implicated in them. She believes that they might have been led into a trap—by you, by us."

"What? But that's not true!" I insist, face reddening.

Without Amẹci, Kähari stands significantly weakened—in trade, in war, in standing in the realm. If the Ogun return to try again, it is unlikely Kähari can hold them back. "That's why we rushed back—I worried the same. I wanted to warn her."

He shrugs. "It's not your fault, Daughter Maze. The Ogun were playing a more advanced war game than us. We still do not have news from the front; we do not know what drove the Ogun back. Nevertheless, Udo is *furious*. Not a wonderful emotion for an ally to be feeling."

"No. Not at all," I agree.

"It has been one disaster after the other," Titus sighs. "Ever since the Ganju refugees."

Unbelievably, I nearly forgotten about them. They were the spark that set my life ablaze.

He reads my face. "Dead, Daughter Maze. Buried or crow's feed at this stage. Well, the majority of them. Some went back into the Outlands, but with the waning moon…"

"Your father has certainly begun to rethink his military strategy. Our military is too small to defend our people. Our weapons are outdated. If either Ogun or Amẹci had decided they wanted to take us as a colony, it would not have been challenging. On the contrary, it would have been embarrassing."

"I can imagine."

"Peace is in being prepared," Titus adds after a beat, taps his chin thoughtfully. "That's ruddy brilliant. I'll have to write that down…"

Frowning, Titus catches himself. "I don't know why I'm telling you all of this. But you seem...different. Older...or something."

"Disillusioned. Disillusioned is the something," I say wearily.

"Well, I knew you and Kala survived the raid and the Outlands. I just knew it," Titus declares triumphantly. "We sent out search parties, but they returned without you. It was agonizing, waiting to know. Eventually, we heard from Chieftess Udo, but—"

"Are my mother and Ewatomi in Ogun?" I ask, even though I know the answer.

Titus frowns. "They returned after the raid was subdued. With the moon began to wane, the Outlands proved too volatile for the long journey to Ogun. Your mother said she sent word to you via starling to Ameci."

"Did she?" I utter icily. "I must have missed the letter."

Titus clears his throat. "Ewatomi was set to marry Bosede this evening in a private ceremony and leave for Ogun permanently tonight. Your mother insisted on it as soon as the bride prize was settled."

"That does not even follow Kähari traditions!" I shake my head in amazement.

"Farida has been scattering money and promising favors to anyone in noble positions who will continue to support Ewatomi's marriage to Bosede after this Ogun fiasco. I strongly suspect that the wedding was supposed to occur before the attack."

I am not sure I'd call a thinly veiled act of war a 'fiasco,' but I have other problems to address; problems named Ewatomi and Farida. "You suspect treason. A coup."

Titus holds up his hands. "You said it. *I've* said nothing of the sort."

A memory rumbles in my mind. *He is noble, wealthy and... he is noble and wealthy.*

Titus never liked Bosede. "Of course not."

"I'll notify your mother and sister that you have returned home."

"No." I abruptly change direction and head for Ewatomi's chambers instead. "I'm going to go see Ewatomi and deliver the happy news myself."

"Er, Daughter Maze—don't you think you should...maybe bathe?" Desperately, Titus calls after me. "Put on some fresh clothes? Eat something...?"

"No."

"Good glory, why not?"

"Because I do not want to do that, and a wise woman once told me that I should do what I like when I like. Now, could you please ask one of the servants to make sure Helissi is fed and watered? He's back in the stables. If you see Kala, tell her I've arrived and please send her to my chambers straight away," I order. "I want to see her."

"Yes, your grace," Titus replies, dumbfounded.

I STALK THROUGH THE HALLS, MY PERSON IN COMPLETE DISCORD WITH THE Palace. More than ever, I clash with the ornate paintings and the lush carpets. The servants look at me with a mixture of pity and curiosity on their faces. They all know my mother thinks I am a useless thing, incapable of serving any interest. They've always looked at Ewatomi differently; since childhood, the Kāharians thought Ewatomi was beautiful, charming, and deserving of a noble status.

I just saved their *lives*, but I am still the family's insubstantial runt.

Nodding at the guards lingering outside Ewatomi's doors, I open the door and march inside. Ewatomi redecorated in the short time I was away; each room awash in Ewatomi's favorite color (a very particular pink-peach) and gold and floor-to-ceiling windows festooned in cream-colored curtains.

"More," Ewatomi demands as her harassed-looking servants rush to paint glittering gold tips to the ends of her enormous hair. "I want Bosede to see me and think of the sun."

Her eyes go wide with surprise when she sees me in the reflection of her looking glass.

Ewatomi gasps, whipping around. "Oh, Mazzie, I thought for sure you were lost in the raid—Praise the gods!"

A wonderful actress, that Ewatomi. I force a withering smile that I know does not reach my eyes. "Leave us," I command the servants, who look as startled as Titus did by my tone. "I would like to spend some time reuniting with my dear sister."

Glancing nervously at each other, the servants hurry from the room, and the smile, along with any suggestion of a happy, sisterly reunion, dissolves from Ewatomi's face.

"What do you want, you rank clay-brained whore? As you can see, I am very busy." Ewatomi turns back to the mirror and pats her cheeks with pink blusher. "Did you recently bathe in elephant dung?"

"What are you *doing*, Ewatomi? Do you have any idea what happened outside Kähari's wall yesterday?" I sputter. "The Ogun attacked Amęci. They violated the sacred peace agreements of the Ohia Realm—and you are still marrying Bosede?"

When Ewatomi does not reply, I embellish, "People are talking. They're calling it *treason*."

"That is all utter hearsay until the Order of the Ojo and Congress finish their investigation." Ewatomi corrects, shrugging and patting some more rouge on her cheeks. "In the meantime, I'm getting married and claiming my throne."

"I assume you know," I say flatly. "You know Bosede planned to kill our father, and the meeting with Gye Nyame is a trap. What were you newlyweds going to do after that? Have *our* religious congregation killed so they could never select another ruler after you?"

"Of course, not, how—" Ewatomi clears her throat and stammers. "Father didn't understand. Maze, Ogun and Kähari *together* against the Amęci—things are changing. I will be an *empress*. In other parts of the world, Bosede said—"

"Bosede is dead and he planned to kill you as soon as he claimed Kähari," I spit out, and then watch with satisfaction as Ewatomi's mouth sags open. "The Ogun have been driven back. Your little coup has met its deserved end."

My older sister turns and stares at her reflection in shock and horror. "You are lying."

Vaguely alluding to my necromancy, I coolly reply, "You know I am not."

Trembling, Ewatomi presses her fingers to her temples.

"You will be hanged when the people of Kähari find out what you've done. You *and* mother," I add, crossing my arms. "Unless you both leave now. I can do you that act of charity."

Ewatomi's face twists with anger. In one fluid motion, she pulls an iron saber from the sheath by the vanity and swings expertly for my head. I flinch, and try to duck.

Clang!

Ewatomi's saber connects—not with my flesh, but with Adin's ghostly war blade. Ewatomi shrieks in surprise. Of course, Ewatomi cannot *see* Adin or his blade. Instead, it appears like some invisible force preventing her from reaching me. Ewatomi's face shifts from anger to fear as she struggles against it.

"It's true." Ewatomi is ashen. "It's true. You're a filthy *mage*."

I am feeling less charitable. *Destroy her*, a little voice in my head insists. I fight against my emotion so I do not lose control of my magic; it is burning in my blood.

Sweat beads along Ewatomi's forehead as she pushes harder against her blade. "I didn't mean to tell him. I didn't know what I was telling him. He tricked me!"

"I agree, they used you and I feel sorry for you."

"I don't need your pity or charity," Ewatomi declares.

But, losing steam against Adin, Ewatomi drops her sword to the floor with a clatter. She scoops it back up and drops into a fighting stance.

"Argh!" Ewatomi whips it back and swings again, but she is no match for Adin's sword skills. With just one hand on the blade, he stops it again. Ewatomi is a shallow worm with more ear wax than brain matter.

"What do you plan to do once you kill me in your chambers? Mop up the blood and hide my body in a closet until your wedding is over? Drag me past the guards in a garment bag?" I laugh darkly. "You're not making sense."

"I am under no obligation to make sense to you or anyone else!" Ewatomi spits, pushing harder against her blade. "I will not lose what I've fought for—I will do what I need to do, and I'll worry about the mess later."

"I can kill her," Adin offers kindly. "You just say the word..."

"Please, go. Start over someplace far away," I beg Ewatomi. "Take mother with you. It is only a matter of time before the elder council—"

"If father is dead, mother leaves, and I am not crowned, you won't be able to stay in the Palace. You're too young. They'll *never* crown you—not for a breath," Ewatomi threatens, catching her own. "By law, the priests and priestesses must choose another ruler. You'll be toiling in a workhouse or stinking of fish."

"Better than hanging in the square," I shoot back at her. "I am giving you a chance to live. Maybe you won't be an empress, but you'll be alive."

My words hang in the air. We stare at each other in a long, uncomfortable silence. The only sound is of birds bickering outside; I wonder if they are sisters too.

"What about you?"

"I know things that others don't. I need to stay and set things right."

"Mother promised me a real throne; she promised me an empire," Ewatomi finally admits morosely, sinking in a cloud of dress. "What do I do now?"

"I do not care," I grind out, as Adin chuckles with dark satisfaction behind me. "Once people realize what happened... I see your death if you stay here, I promise you. Go, leave Kähari. Take mother with you."

She nods in defeat. After grabbing a handful of her brightest gems from her dresser, Ewatomi decisively pulls up her skirts and rushes from the room. She does not offer to write. She does not wish me well. She does not look back. Yet, my heart startles by the words I utter next.

"Follow her," I instruct Adin quietly. "Make sure she leaves the grounds. If she tries to implicate me to anyone in the Palace on her way, kill her."

Adin nods slowly. "With pleasure."

AFTER WAITING FOR A BEAT, I LEAVE EWATOMI'S CHAMBERS AND MAKE A beeline for my own. I pray Kala is inside, and my prayers are answered. Kala, clean and in a freshly-laundered yellow jumper, sits by the fireplace with her knees huddled up by her chest. She looks like a new person, save for her arm, carefully wrapped in tight bandages. Kala stands up gingerly.

"Your grace," Kala says teasingly, offering a tiny bow. Her hair hangs down like a silky curtain. "How might I be of service?"

"Shut it. Kala, thank goodness you're all right!" I exclaim, embracing my friend and holding on tight. "Your arm...will it...?"

"Heal? The doctor thinks so." Kala offers a small smile. "What happened? I heard that the Ogun left in defeat. Did you find your father? Have you spoken to your mother?"

I pause, grappling with how much to say. "My mother and sister are leaving Kähari. If I am lucky, I will never see either of them again."

"Leave? No, I don't think so," Kala shakes her head. "I just spoke to the Chieftess. She came to your chambers and babbled something about having to face her sins and pay for what she's done. I assume she means she'll be—"

No. I know my mother. Fiercely proud. Immensely concerned about her image. Terrified of any scandal to the point that she lashed my back, with no remorse, to prevent it. Leaving Kala mid-sentence, I hurry from my chamber, bursts past the guards and race up the winding staircase to the first floor of her mother's chambers. Then I dash through her library and dressing room. My boots pound across the floor, chest tightening as my breath grows scarce.

I storm onto her balcony and see her, balancing gracefully atop the railing. She hears my calls and glances over her shoulder through a curtain of her long, dark hair. She smiles, looking resigned. I freeze as an iciness starts at my fingers and moves up my arms. My mother must know my father is dead, the Ogun have been driven back, and Ewatomi's engagement teeters on the edge of falling apart amid the news that the Ogun attacked an ally and attempted a siege of Kähari, Amęci, and the Outlands. It will only be a matter of time before someone sees her hand in all of it. She does not intend to be punished for any of it.

There can only be one reason I hear my mother's thoughts.

I take another careful step forward and hold up my hands. "Please, don't. Just—"

"I did it for Ewatomi. All of it. And I do not regret it," the Chieftess Farida *Ka* Kähari states plainly, staring out at the sky. She looks down at the people milling below. "If you are a mother one day, you will understand."

"Will I? I'm your daughter, too!" I snap angrily. "Have you forgotten that?"

"Oh, Mäzzikim." she clicks her tongue and laughs softly. "No. You are not."

My heart stops.

"You're a river foundling, Mäzzikim," my mother quips into the breeze. "One that I would've gladly tossed *back* into the waves if your idiot of a naive father hadn't been so pleased to find you—after all *my* alleged failed attempts to give him a second child. Mine. He blamed me." She sighs. "*Men.*"

"That's not true."

Oh, darling, my heart sighed sadly.

"I tried to love you, I did, but you are cursed—you cursed our family, this nation, and the realm. Oko thought you were a blessing, but you were not, and then he thought the throne was a blessing, but it was not. We were given all of it so that it could be taken from us! My son who died before he even left my body. My eldest daughter, to whom I have dedicated my life and given up my partner for, has abandoned me, and my youngest daughter, who I graciously took in—she is actually the *daughter of death.*"

I flinch at the onslaught, but my mother's eyes wildly dart and her tongue is unrelenting. "Yes, I see it now! I must have offended the gods by allowing you to live. They gave me everything, so they could take it away. So that I could feel loss more *deeply* and *profoundly* than I ever might've understood."

"You have done quite a bit of mental acrobatics to somehow blame your treason on me," I manage to heatedly reply. "It was wrong."

"Only wrong if we lost. Mazzie, without power, without wealth, this life is as tedious as a sandy nail in your sandal," my mother notes thoughtfully. "You'll learn that one day soon."

"Get down," I demand, inching forward again. "Please."

"Silly girl, I know *you're* not afraid of death," she teases before letting herself fall, a satisfied smile still plastered across her face as she drops out of sight.

Simultaneously, I collapse to my knees and shudder uncontrollably as shock courses through me. It is too much. Thoughts in my head spin and churn like a tornado, and my magic, my being is lost in it. I am paralyzed. It is too much. It is too much.

Kala appears out of nowhere. Without saying anything, Kala wraps her arms around me and tucks her hands mine. There is screaming (some may have been mine), shouting and chaos around them as others realize what had happened, but Kala and I stay here, twisted together, for a very long time.

CHAPTER
SIXTEEN

he Chieftess Farida *Ka* Kähari died. No doctors were called, only corpsmen to collect the body and servants to wash away the blood from the walk. As if sensing the mood of the clan, the weather turns bleak and foggy.

Titus and Kala, with the help of a few guards, eventually extract me from the balcony and lead me back to my chamber. Titus barks orders to the servants that I do not hear. I barely feel Kala's hand on my shoulder. I only hear the blood pounding in my ears and see my mother's mocking grin whenever I close my eyes. It is too much.

It is. Just. Too. Much.

A servant brings me some mint tea, which soon goes cold in my unmoving hand.

"Daughter Maze, I am sorry to bother you. But have you seen Ewatomi? Daughter Maze?"

Titus's voice tumbles around my head. I know this voice. He is speaking to me. I should answer. Kala pokes me in the shoulder. I blink but avoid Titus's eyes. "Ewatomi... I last saw her in her chambers, getting ready for her wedding ceremony. Not too long ago."

Kala meets my eye. I know Ewatomi already fled the Palace—without our obviously implicated mother, who did it all, even sacrificed her own partner, to help Ewatomi. Ewatomi indeed is a soulless wench, I think bitterly. I am glad I am unrelated.

Titus continues talking. "I worry that Ewatomi will learn the news in a most ...inappropriate way about her mother—if I do not find her first."

Puzzled, a rare emotion for him, Titus bites his lip. Finally, he says, "My problem, not yours. Kala, could go to the medicinary? She might need something for the shock."

"I'm fine, really," I insist, trying to look more alert and shifting upward.

Titus exchanges concerned glances with Kala. "You've yet to be examined since your travels, which, by the look of you, were quite intense. I will send a doctor. If you'll receive him?"

"Of course," Kala replies quickly before I can protest.

"With Ewatomi missing, the wedding is delayed, obviously," Titus adds, mostly to Kala as they make their way to the door. "...not a surprise considering the skirmish... and Bosede hasn't shown...what a disaster."

Oh yes, the wedding will be very, very delayed, as the partner-to-be is dead and rotting on a mountain peak and the treasonous bride-to-be has fled the country. It is a bigger disaster than Titus knows.

THE RAIN BEATS CONTINUOUSLY AGAINST THE WINDOWS FOR THE NEXT FEW days and the wind howls against the Palace stones. The doctor visits my chamber, grimaces while he cleans my numerous bruises and cuts, puzzles over my blistered skin, and offers a salve that is not nearly as effective as what a healer in Omiki could offer and does nothing to cure the deep abrasions in my mental and emotional facilities. I fall into a depression, wondering if I really am wicked and cursed.

Perhaps Oko wasn't my birth father, but he rescued me, parentless and afloat, from a river. He had *chosen* me. Even though his partner saw me as an interloper –a curse—intruding on her family, Oko stayed committed to caring for me. I use my grief for my father, whose death had yet to be discovered, to feign grief for my mother. It is horrible and effective.

The nation immediately descends into mourning. The servants cover Chieftess Farida's portraits in sheer dark drapes and remove the generous sprigs of lavender and golden roses, replacing them with white roses and black hollyhock. Farida's remains are placed in a closed casket and set in the grand hall, surrounded by candles and flowers. Titus sends letters to Farida's family and friends, Congress, and others—while simultaneously engaging the guard in a fruitless effort to send word to Chieftain Oko.

Back in my chambers, Kala fusses over me, probably because I stay slumped in a chair, wrapped in a thin blanket, and staring unblinkingly at the unlit fireplace. Kala offers tea, chocolate, a second blanket, and a bath. I have not bathed since I returned to the Palace (in my defense, I was instructed to wait until my wounds healed).

"Just a quick one," Kala begs, peeling the sticky blanket off me. "You'll feel so much better once you wash off all of the...of...once you wash," she hastily finishes.

I relent, and a gleeful Kala rings Hanya, who appears with a robe and bath stones. Without feeling much of anything, I sink into the large marble bath, filled with blue perfumed clouds floating on the surface. It stings my skin, but I close my eyes and lean back. Then, I shoot up when I hear a little cough.

"Sorry," Kala whispers from her perch atop a wicker basket in the corner of the wetroom.

"I can bathe on my own, you know," I snap. "You needn't hover. My mother can't pay you anymore, obviously."

Kala looks as though she's been struck. "I'm not here because of the coin."

"Bollocks, you aren't," I grumble, shrinking deeper.

Crossing her arms, Kala sits up a little straighter. "Well, I'm not leaving you, no matter how villainy you get. You're not drowning on my watch."

I raise my eyebrows.

"Now, please bathe yourself—your smell is infecting my very soul," Kala sniffs, covers her nose with her mouth and grimaces.

I snort, which set us both off into a strange fit of giggles.

Ewatomi is still missing after fleeing the Palace, and now, it seems, people realize that Chieftain Oko and his two personal guardians had also been missing for far too long. The search extends to the capital and the other villages. It will not be long before they search the caves and the northern mountains. I am confident that the discovery of the bodies of the Chieftain Oko *Ka* Kähari and the Son of Chieftain Gye Nyame Bosede *Ka* Ogun will take a few more hours at most. I fight the urge to run away. I do not want to leave Kähari so soon after Ewatomi and raise suspicion of foul play by the entire family. Perhaps if I wait, it will imply my innocence, the lone innocent survivor of the noble family.

I am innocent, in a sense. I didn't lay a hand on anyone. Demon's in the details.

Maybe I am a coward, but I do not want to be considered a suspect in Farida's death—not that it would matter if I am held accountable for all the Ogun deaths—or Bosede's. I wouldn't live long after that. They can only put me to death once. Though, perhaps, they would choose more painful means based on the number of crimes. No sense in risking that. I have enough problems.

Hanya pauses in her work. "What is this?"

I strain to see. "What?"

"It is a silver streak in your hair," Hanya comments in confusion. "It's odd, but quite pretty in a way. I can try to hide it in a braid."

I sigh. "Don't bother. I am tired of hiding."

The shock of Farida's strange death continues its icy grip on the Palace. The nobles are sullen and shaken, and Titus especially seems to be at a loss. He takes orders from the Chieftain Oko, certainly, but he considers himself an advisor for Chieftess Farida first and foremost. With neither of them around, Titus seems to be fighting to keep himself busy. He charges this way and that, directing the preparations for mourning, writing letters and sending starlings to the other nations, shouting demands at a servant who was unfortunate enough to cross his path.

No one seems to understand why Farida, beautiful, bright, and held generally in high esteem, had taken her own life. She married a decent man, who had the good fortune of being chosen as Chieftain. Indeed, Farida had been very blessed, especially as her eldest daughter, her beautiful pride and joy, planned to marry a noble of another clan nation that very night, and her youngest daughter—feared dead or lost in the Outlands— miraculously discovered alive that very day. Despite the apparent disaster with the Ogun, Farida petitioned hard for the wedding to go forward. Taken together, it begs the question: Did she take her own life? Or had someone taken it for her?

In my humble opinion, there is only one question: how horrible must Farida's crimes have been that she'd prefer to kill herself rather than face the courts? However, with Farida dead and Oko and Ewatomi missing, there is only one person left with anything to gain.

People begin to eye me suspiciously.

From the bits of information gathered from Kala, and from the reported gossip from Hanya, I gather enough hope that perhaps my crimes will go undiscovered. I pray and wait for word in near silence while Kala examines me with a suspicious eye, but does not press. Hours pass, but no new information on the subject on which I brood comes to pass.

When I am not huddled in a chair, I pace in my chambers in a state of high anticipation. No one comes to arrest me that evening. There is also no word of Ewatomi or Oko. Finally, Kala forces me to take to bed.

"Better for the carpets certainly," Kala mutters, tucking me in tightly. "You're wearing a hole in the floor."

I glower at Kala from beneath the blankets. "I'm not a child. You can't tell me what to do," I say, sounding very much like a child.

Kala rolls her eyes and leaves the room.

Hours passes, darkness falls, but I lie awake staring at the murals on the ceiling. Then I feel a familiar chill. "Adin," I finally whisper into the dark once I was sure of Kala's snores in the next room. "Where are you?"

The air shimmers in front of me. Adin's tall figure appears. As a spirit, he never sleeps, and his eyes practically glows in the dark.

"What is it?" he asks gruffly from beneath his mask.

"Is she gone?"

"Yes."

"Adin, are they coming for me?" I ask quietly.

"Please, I need to know what is happening. What are they saying in court? At the ministry?"

"Rumors abound siege was planned by Chieftain Gye Nyame *Ka* Ogun, who is close to death. Quell. There are conflicting reports..." He trails off and looks away.

Heart pounding in her ears, I sit up and hug my knees to my chest. "Tell me, Adin," I insist. "I need to know."

"There is talk that Nyame *Ka* Ogun aspires to rule the whole continent, but he began to worry that the increasingly progressive nations would turn against him and his suspiciously-obtained monarchy and join forces with the small mage minorities that live in the Outlands. Shrinking his power."

A pit forms in my stomach.

Nodding, Adin continues, "The servants, when they think no one is listening, they're saying he ordered all the remaining tribes destroyed or forcibly relocated the Trench."

"The Tofuli tribe—"

"...was one of many," Adin says emotionlessly.

"What will happen...to Gye Nyame?"

Adin shakes his head. "The lives of mages no longer matter in the realm. They haven't for three centuries ago. There will be a brief morality-driven uproar. A call for punishment, although certainly Gye will find someone to take the blame for him. Maybe confounding trials, and then it will fade."

My mind flashes back to Ewatomi. *There's the issue of different... cultures, for one.*

"I'd wager good coin that the real reason that other clans didn't want to help Ganju is because the impoverished Ganju population was heavily mage. They saw it as a non-violent way to rid themselves of it. They spoke in euphemisms to help convince themselves otherwise, but I see it now. How could I be so blind to how awful things are?"

250

ADIN CONTINUES, "AMONGST THE SERVANTS, THERE IS A THEORY THAT YOU are cursed."

"Gods." I groan.

Adin does not reply.

Taking a deep breath, I put my head in my hands. "What can I do about any of it? I am nothing." I blink in realization. "I've got to get out of here before they decide that I killed Bosede. Or they decide to blame me for my mother's death. Or—"

"You just ordered an army of the dead to drive back the continent-hungry Ogun," Adin replies in disbelief. "You're hardly helpless."

"I couldn't even properly kill a spider before. I am stronger in the Outlands; stronger having been there, but I feel it wearing away." I climb of bed and scurry to my dressing closet. "Besides, I'll be hanged for being a cursed bastard mage and noble family impostor."

"You are being rash. I was wrong. You are more powerful here, so close to the throne. You are different from the little girl who demanded my attention in the grand hall," he advises.

"You heard Ewatomi. They'll never put me on the throne, even for a day." I stuff things in a knapsack and sling it over my back. "I am too young."

"Yes, and we know how plainly intelligent Ewatomi is," he replies dryly. "Not to mention how much she has your best interests in her cold, dead heart."

I protest, "You may see me differently now, but I haven't even had my *Hathi*. I'm considered a child in the eyes of the gods *and* the law."

"False gods. Bad laws. What of the allies you already have?"

"Kala can go back to her parents and her life—the one she had before she met me," I reply sadly as I open my window. "Who knows where Mezu is. You're dead. End of list."

Then Adin surprises me by nodding gravely. "I cannot force you to stay. You must choose your own path," he says cryptically. "Good luck, Mäzzikim."

I sigh in relief. "Adin, I will return one day, I promise."

Every time I've seen Adin, I have noticed a little more of him. More detail. More color. But still, there was one part of him that she had never seen—a fundamental part of him.

I pause. "Adin, can you take off your mask?"

He stiffens. "Kipporah warriors never remove their masks."

"If I do not survive whatever comes, I'd like to remember your face. I won't judge. I won't flinch. I promise. If I die before I return, I just want to be able to remember all of you as someone who is important in my life."

There is a pregnant pause before he reaches up and slowly removes the mask.

Adin Munduhaka looks nothing like I expect. His square face is framed by thick eyebrows—one scarred slice of skin in the very middle. He has full lips and the scruffy dark brownish beard of facial hair. His dark eyes scrutinize me, searching for a reaction.

I stand on my toes to place my hand on his cheek. Although I know I will not, I hope to feel the dependable warmth of skin against my palm. Dropping my hand in disappointment, I solemnly say, "You saved my life. I won't forget you, Adin Munduhaka *Ka* Kipporah. I won't forget what you've done or what I've learned from you. I will make sure you are remembered with honor."

"I will haunt you if you don't," he remarks warily.

CHAPTER
SEVENTEEN

set off again for the Outlands, but more carefully than I did after the raid. Things have changed. There are Kähari guards everywhere, pacing, marching, looking tense, and brandishing their weapons. But I know the Palace better than they do—every hidden hallway and lesser-used path. Dressed as a servant, I escape the Palace with ease and then move strategically through the gardens and the brush until I reach the stables.

I whistle low and a pair of green eyes immediately meets mine. Growling, Helissi lumbers from the barn. I thank Titus internally; Helissi looks alert, well-fed, groomed, and positively ready to take off at full-speed into the night, which is precisely what I need him to do.

I decide to pass through the mountains. After all the recent skirmishes, Kähari's front gate will be thick with patrols. At the same time, I have to be careful not to draw attention *to* the mountains—lest the bodies be discovered while I am close by. Luckily, Helissi needs no lessons in stealth. The big cat drifts easily and quickly through the forest.

I have not been riding long when I suddenly shiver from an unnatural chill. I slow Helissi and wrap my cloak more tightly around me. A light rain starts misting, obscuring the path. I groan internally; I have not reached the mountains yet.

Then I notice a large, leafy hardwood tree offering pockets of shelter.

"Come, Helissi." I guide Helissi underneath and climb off. As the rain begins falling harder, I look up and realize not a single drop is touching us.

"What in the…is this a magic tree then? Brilliant luck finding it, then."

"Mäzzikim."

Startled, I turn around. A woman, wrapped in a gauzy white and maroon tunic, steps down from the dark sky like a predatory bird. She wears a golden turban and collar. Her eyes, nearly black and deep set above high cheekbones, bear into me.

"Kipporah?" I squeak in disbelief and kneel. I peer up through my hair, not believing what I am seeing. Was it a dream? A vision? A leftover effect from a recent tonic? I curse myself for overindulging in so many. If it is real, why would I see Kipporah? Why now? Is Kipporah angry with me? Will she strike me down now for calling upon the dead to fight my battles? Perhaps send me to a fourth realm to be nibbles for hell dogs?

Still, Kipporah says nothing. I cannot feel my feet, and my throat goes dry.

Helissi growls defensively but quiets when Kipporah holds up a hand and wiggles her fingers. Slowly, he curls into a ball and immediately began snoring.

"Where are you going, Mäzzikim?" Kipporah asks, her voice elegant and tone peaceful.

I look up cautiously. "To find the Trench and help the mages."

Kipporah smiles knowingly. "I have seen the misery of the mage in the Ohia Realm. I see their suffering, and I have been waiting for one blessed in my likeness to be strong enough to rescue them," she says, smiling kindly. "I want you to bring them into their rightful ancestral place in the realm, but you are going the *wrong* way. Or perhaps I should say…running away?"

I flush. "But—"

"You must return to Kähari. Tell the great clans that our people—all people—must be freed, and the other mages—they have been divided against each other. You must unite them. It is the only way you'll be able to enter and escape the Trench."

"I can't go back to Kähari," I object. "I have done some terrible things. My parents are dead; the latter's suicide might still be pinned on me. I cast out Ewatomi. I am nothing. *Less* than nothing if they find out that I'm not even human—"

"I will be with you," Kipporah promises, her eyes sparkling. "As I have always been with you since you were a mere twinkle in your father's eye. I blessed you with strength and power. I will protect you, and you must go back."

"How do I know you're real and not some figment of my tonic-ladened imagination? Or worse, an enemy sending me to certain death?" I challenge.

My tone sounds more brutal than I intend, but my skepticism bursts wide open. It is a gross understatement to say I've had far more than my share of bad luck lately.

Kipporah raises her eyebrows but smiles. "Generally, I like a young woman who questions everything and trusts no one."

I yelp at the sudden pain in my wrist. In horror, I turn it over to see my flesh reddening and burning to form the circled dot (the eye) with the horizontal wave above and below. It glows in gold once it settled, and the pain (but not the shock) subsides.

Bile rises in my throat. "What—?"

"I am Kipporah, and you will trust me. Now they will *know* that you are a mage. *My* mage," Kipporah says with satisfaction. "You will no longer hide who you are and you will serve me as intended. It is your destiny."

I pale. "No, please, I'm terrified and exhausted. I could've died a hundred times in as many days!"

"But did you die?" Now, Kipporah sounds annoyed with me.

"No, but—"

"I personally believe a wee bit of terror is actually quite motivating, so long as you channel it towards your bravery, and quickly," Kipporah replies without sympathy.

"But I have questions," I protest. "Farida wasn't my real mother, and Oko wasn't my real father. Who are my parents? If you are the goddess of death—"

"Are you questioning me again?" Kipporah thunders.

I hold up my hands to placate her. "No, not, of course not. More of a request, if it's possible. I just thought, *as* the god of death—maybe you could show me."

"Better." Kipporah inhales and, chanting, moves her palm in a slow circle before snapping her long fingers.

I stare, entranced, as a misty image appears.

"Is that my real mother?" I question in awe. "My *mother?*"

High cheekbones. Bright, determined eyes. Her eyes are like mine. Her coiled hair billows around her like a lion's mane as she runs with a basket clutched in her arms. Her body wrenches and twitches as it is hit with arrows, but she does not break her stride or lose her grip. After smearing her blood on the infant's face, she reaches the river and pushes the basket into it. Dropping to her knees, she sobs and appears to pray as the basket pitches in the gentle surf.

My eyes widen with a horrible realization.

"It is my mother's knife," I breathe. "Was the infant me? Why don't I remember?"

"Oh yes, that *is* surprising; infants are renowned for their memories," Kipporah says impatiently, as it all vanishes into the air.

I shrink back.

"With the last of her magic, your mother imprinted on you and the knife—she only intended to imprint on you, knit her soul to yours so that she could stay with you and protect you, but magic is not so neat as that. She imprinted on both and the knife was the other piece you needed to bring the pieces together."

"Can I speak to her?" I ask desperately.

"You speak to her every day," Kipporah replies frankly.

"I don't know what you—"

Kipporah's month twitches. "Amaka Sakwe, your mother, is in your thoughts; she is in your heart. That tiny voice in your head telling you to do the right thing? The strength that you feel right as you are about to give up? That is your mother."

"*Amaka Sakwe.*" I try my mother's name in my mouth. It floats out as if it has been there my entire life and a magical warmth fills my belly. It is the most magic I have felt since the night in the hills.

"That means my birth name was Nuri," I realize. "How will I—"

"I personally would rather be talking about how to save the realm rather than your identity crisis. Read more books, you'll have less questions," Kipporah says in annoyance.

"And my father?" I ask nervously.

"Not much I can say about him, I'm afraid, because he is alive."

I am stunned. "What? How? Where? Why hasn't he come looking for me?"

"Again," Kipporah begins impatiently. "He is *alive*. Not my area of expertise. But I can show you what he looked like—he was in one of your mother's final thoughts."

Kipporah raises her palm.

This time, a man appears; tall, thin, and surprisingly dark-skinned with long and stark white hair, and gray eyes. When he smiles, dimples— my dimples—appear in his cheeks and chin. I stare, mesmerized. I've seen him before, of course, in the vision, but I didn't know he was my father. It is different now. Kipporah snaps, and he is gone. I exhale a shaky breath.

"You can spend years, decades even, wandering around in old memories. You will waste away at it and make none of your own. You need to look forward, Mäzzikim. You have these visions and this magic for a purpose beyond your enjoyment, beyond quenching your curiosity," Kipporah counsels.

"I hoped it would ground me; knowing where I come from," I reply hoarsely, reeling.

"I do not want anything to ground you. You are one of the realm's last hope for peace."

Not very reassuring for the realm, in my opinion.

"I can only appear to you twice more. If you see me a fourth time, it means you have finally—for better or worse—experienced your own death," Kipporah warns. "And the realm has died with you."

I inhale nervously.

"Go. Fulfill your purpose. Together, we will rise."

With a crack, Kipporah vanishes, and the rain streams through the leaves, soaking me to the bone.

CHAPTER
EIGHTEEN

Back in my chamber, I peel off my wet clothes and slide between the covers on my bed. I stare into the dark, thinking about my conversation with Kipporah. It feels like I am watching a play of myself. As my play's supposed protagonist and leading lady, I should show bravery and compassion, but all I do not feel it. I do not know what to do or where to start. Without my grandmother, I do not know to whom I can speak. As my mind sought escape, I sink into sleep.

I wake up late the next morning with the previous evening rolling over me like an ocean wave. I look at my arm and wince when I see the mark still seared into my skin. I had hoped last night was a dream, but it pains to the touch. A cold chill with hints of nausea passes through me, and I pull the silky sheets to my chest.

"Adin," I whisper my magic into the dark.

Adin is already there, waiting. "You've returned, Mäzzikim."

I hiss excitedly back to Adin. "Adin, I saw Kipporah. She told me that I belonged here."

"Mm," Adin replies vaguely, not sounding surprised in the slightest.

Frowning, I sit up. "You white-livered rat!" I accuse playfully.

A sharp rap on the chamber door startles us both. I hear Kala climb out of her bed to answer it. "Go, get out of here before Kala thinks I'm mad," I hiss as I pull on my robe and lay back down on the bed to feign sleep.

"Far too late for that."

"Adin!"

Adin disappears with a quiet shift in the air as Kala opens my bedroom door.

"I've got biscuits," Kala announces happily, revealing a stack in a warming cloth.

"I'm not hungry," I reply, pulling my covers back up to my chin. "So, if you don't mind...go away."

"This one here has chocolate and rum inside," Kala counters.

Suddenly Kala sniffs the air, frowns, and glances around the room. She spots my wet cloak, clothes, and muddy sandals. "You left last night. Where did you go? Maze, it's not safe to leave without your guards."

"I'll eat the biscuit if you don't ask any more questions," I offer, sitting up.

Kala cheerfully hands it over. "I thought perhaps we could play a game of mancala today. Get your mind off things. I found marbles and a board."

"I don't want to play."

"I don't much care what you want today. We're playing, or I will happily resume my questioning."

"I thought we had an agreement," I grumble through a mouthful of the chocolate biscuit.

"As Titus would say—oh, honey. No."

We are not playing mancala long (or well) when there is another knock on the door. Unfortunately, it is not a servant carrying more warm biscuits. Instead, it is Titus with deep and pronounced dark circles under his eyes. He has news. We settle into the receiving room to hear it.

"We have received a distressing post starling from the Barack village near the mountains," Titus proclaims solemnly.

My shoulders rise to my ears.

"Maze, your father, Chieftain Oko *Ka* Kähari is dead."

Kala gasps in shock and grabs my hand.

"His body—and that of his guards—was discovered in the mountains by dwarves. There will be an investigation and tribunal, of course—"

Kala meets his eyes and shakes her head at him, ever so slightly.

"I'm so sorry, Daughter Mäzzikim," Titus adds sadly, bowing his head. "I know this is particularly hard for you, so soon after losing your mother and sister missing. I can't imagine the terrible pain...and Funani...alone in this world..."

Kala glares at him, making a slashing motion across her neck with one of her hands.

I drift off in my head as Titus rambles on. Oko not my birth father, Farida was not my mother in *any* sense of the word, and Ewatomi is not my sister (I wonder if she knows that). I do not know if I should feel loss or betrayal, so, naturally, I feel both. However, I have no tears left to offer. Instead, I will feign shock, I decide. I should probably hurry and do it. They're watching me for a reaction, and I certainly do not look like someone who just found out her father was dead.

Shakily, I stand from my place at the table. Some of the small mancala stones scatter slightly. I draw in what I hope sounds like a surprised breath, and then exhales. The grief will come, I know. The grief will come and consume me like a monster. For now, I must focus on survival.

"Where exactly? How?"

Kala shoots me an odd look. Perhaps I need to further hone my acting skills.

"A dwarf found him on the highest peak of the mountain."

Titus stares at the ground. "The Ojos think he was lured there along and then killed by an Ogun—based on the wound. His other guards were found dead nearby. The wildcats got ahold of them, though. Gruesome sight."

"Titus," Kala hisses, scolding. "Gods, help you."

What about Bosede? Did they find Bosede? I bite my lips closed.

"We'll need to make arrangements," Titus explains. "Two internments; I cannot believe Kähari has lost its Chieftess *and* Chieftain and its provisional successor. This is unprecedented."

Kala's hand lands on my shoulder. "You should sit down, Daughter Maze," Kala says gently. "I'll ask Hanya to fetch you some herbal tea and calming tonic."

To my immense relief, Kala looks at Titus and asked (in a way) precisely what I want to know. "Have you any more news? If not, I think Maze needs to rest."

Holding my breath, I wait for Titus to mention Bosede's body too. Instead, he bows, again offers condolences, and leaves the room.

A seed of fear sprouts in my belly. Could Bosede possibly be alive? His death replayed in my head. No, it wasn't possible...Was it? No, definitely not...I saw the life leave his eyes...

No, if anyone knew death, I do. Bosede is dead.

Once the door firmly closed behind Titus, Kala declares miserably, "I'm so sorry, Maze. I can't believe it! I wish I could take all of this away from you."

I know she means it. Surprise tears stream down my face as Kala embraces me in a hug. The source of the surprise—how fond I've become of Kala. Not by blood, but we intertwined as sisters. Against my will, I discover myself sobbing inconsolably. I've gone soft.

"You don't deserve any of this. I am sorry," Kala whispers into my hair.

Kala guides me to a chair and then builds a modest fire, even though the room is already warm. "So, your father was on the peak as Mezu suggested." Kala asks, tossing in twigs, which crack and spark as they catch fire. Then, she set to work picking up the marbles. "Did you get to speak with him? I assumed not, but you never said..."

Color drains from my face. "Did you tell anyone that I was in the mountains?"

"No. Of course not."

"I spoke to Bosede." I hurriedly add, "He's dead, but you can't say anything."

Kala's mouth sags open. "Bosede's dead?" she whispers, wide-eyed.

"I thought so. Yes. Probably, but he could be alive. Maybe."

I suddenly have second thoughts about letting Ewatomi go free. What if Bosede and Ewatomi have run off together to gather strength, and then launch a counterattack on Kähari? A little knot forms in my chest. Kala is having a similar panicked reaction for an entirely different reason. She grabs me by both shoulders. I wince against the pain triggered in my arm. "What happened in the mountains?"

"I found my father, dying—Bosede killed him."

Kala's mouth sags open. "That's an act of war! Why didn't you say anything?

"Because Bosede is dead too."

Kala frowns. "Right, okay, I have more questions."

"I killed Bosede," I confess hoarsely.

"How? Bosede is a trained warrior, and you didn't even have a weapon." Kala presses her fingers against her lips in confusion. As the answer dawns on her, Kala's eyes widen.

"You used magic," Kala accuses, taking a step back. "That's why you didn't tell anyone."

"Don't look at me like that! Like I'm some ill-tempted, hell-hated demon," I retort sharply. "Bosede killed Oko, and he meant to kill me. I was defending myself!"

Kala takes a deep breath and gathers her words. "Someone with less scruples than you, couldn't they easily use that power for more nefarious purposes? Wouldn't the realm be safer without it?"

I grind my teeth for a moment. "Well, you'll be happy then that there is perhaps one less—Bosede was a mage of Kipporah. He thought himself a monster, and he became one."

Kala's mouth twists into a bow as a long uncomfortable silence stretches through the room, during which I fume silently. Kala will never understand what it is like to be hated for being who she was born as, I realize. We would always have that wall between us. Perhaps it would thin over time as we better understood each other, but it will be there.

"Magic is *pure*, Kala. It is a part of nature. People can corrupt nature, just as humans have cut down trees to fashion a crossbow or gone deep into the ground, further than it is safe to breathe, to gather iron ore and shape a blade."

My nostrils flare. "I'm proud of what I did. I stopped a coup against the throne."

"History shows that too much power in too few hands—"

My grandmother's words ring: history is kept by those with access to the fastest pen and the darkest ink. I tire of the argument and interrupt Kala. "Hanya's taking far too long with that tonic. I'll fetch it myself."

Kala nods and lapses into resigned silence. I wonder if our friendship can survive these difficult conversations. It does not seem likely. I pull on a robe and leave the chambers, slamming the door behind me.

As I HEAD TO THE MEDICINARY (TWO GUARDS FOLLOWING IN TOW), MY MIND spins. Was Bosede alive? He couldn't be, could he? I saw the light leave his eyes. I felt for a pause. And how could anyone survive being strangled that long in a death grip? I have another theory; maybe someone moved the body to hide his crime. Kala is right; the murder of a Chieftain is an act of war—if one could prove that an Ogun wielded the weapon.

Or maybe he's just not dead. I am tops at coming up with conspiracy theories.

"I should've cut off his head to be sure," I mumble to myself.

I arrive at the medicinary and request a sleeping tonic from the standing doctor, but not before hearing the rumors circulating amongst the servants. In fact, the clan practically hums with a curious and feverish mood; Kähari has not seen such a public scandal or tragedy for centuries.

"Did you know?" and "Did you hear?" everyone keeps asking. They lower their voices when I get closer, but I can still hear them. Both the Chieftain Oko and Chieftess Farida dead within a day's time, they point out. One murdered by an Ogun weapon; another by suicide. The eldest sister ("the beautiful one?"); Yes, she's *missing*.

Suspicious isn't it, Käharians muse, that Ewatomi disappeared shortly after the blood-thirsty Ogun were battered back. Some speculate that Ewatomi might have run off with Bosede, choosing her suspect betrothed over her motherland of Kähari.

Foul, they declare. Foul indeed, I silently agree.

How did the Ameci—who were outnumbered and outgunned—pull a victory off? Some of the warriors whisper about 'invisible forces' protecting them. Some say they saw a mist rise from the ground that choked the Ogun, but (curiously) not the Ameci. Some say they could hear the fog screaming. Of course, in return, they receive disbelieving expressions and nervous glances—was it blood magic? On orders from the elder council, the guards begin raiding the homes of suspected mages in all the Kähari districts, turning nothing connected to the alleged crime but arresting thousands. I could not stop them. My age prevents me from temporarily ruling Kähari.

Did you hear? Did you know? Hushed whispers hover everywhere, especially inside the Palace, where the council of elders are locked in constant bickering and investigations. I wonder if I will be invited to the table for the discussions. Perhaps they are letting me grieve.

Or, perhaps I am under suspicion.

With tea and tonic in hand, I shut myself back in my chamber bedroom with the doors locked. I do not wish to hear any of it. Kala avoids me for a while, probably wary of offending me again. Good. I do not want to fight with her either.

Time ticks slowly by. That evening, I near wear a path on the floor pacing in my bedroom. I want to talk to Adin, but I know Kala might hear and disapprove. I want to speak with my father. I want to go back to the hidden library to read the tomes, but I know guards follow me everywhere I go, and if discovered, all the books would be burned. At this rate, I will never be able to read the tomes again. I am trapped. Trapped in my head. Trapped in my chambers. Trapped in Kähari. I scratch at my skin until it bleeds.

I worry about Imvula and wonder where the former house girl and her family went. Perhaps Ameçi or farther abroad. I cannot shake the memory of my disturbing jaunt into the servant's quarters, with its tight hallways and foul, musty air—the smell of people who worked from sunrise until long after the sun set. I do not know how they could stand it, but I suppose they were doing it to survive. Some of them, they had no choice. Completely oblivious, I lived right over them. Right over their pain.

The only difference between people living underneath the Palace and I—luck. I am lucky that my mother outran those attackers. I am lucky that a river crocodile did not eat me for breakfast. I am Oko plucked me from the river and convinced Farida not to throw me back Luckier still, my family joined the ruling class. I lived a life of privilege that other mages did not even have a chance of experiencing.

To stop the crippling guilt, I prepare my own sleep tonic, pouring the hot water over the herbs in my tin cup. I grasp it in my hands, relishing for a moment in the warmth that it brings. I sit in front of my window and sip as I watch the waves in the distance lap at the sandy shore. The same waves that had been there a year ago. The same waves from before my birth, and will be there after I am gone. As the tonic settles into my stomach, I force myself to change into nightclothes and climb into bed.

Ask Adin for help. There must be other spirits connected the Palace. There must be a way to get the tomes. That is my last thought before going to sleep. I do not dream.

CHAPTER
NINETEEN

n my mind, I envisioned—once invited as a courtesy—I would sit towards the back of the room during investigative tribunals. After some debate (mainly over my tender age), the Kähari Council of Elders agreed I should play Ewatomi's role in my eldest sister's absence. Representing the highest noble of Kähari, I sit at the head of the room. I am a fawn among apex predators in a magnificent chamber.

The chamber for the Kähari Council of the Elders enjoys soaring ceilings, sandstone pillars, flags from the various districts and villages, and rows of long tables with high-backed, elevated chairs. In front of each member, parchment, pens, place cards for votes, and a small burnished gold bell. I am infinitely grateful Titus sits on my right. To my left, there stands a large, glossy podium for testimonies. Aides, advisors, and pages stand at the ready.

We do not wait long for the arrival of the legate and headman of Ogun. I twist my hands nervously in my lap as he enters the council chambers. Wawauda, a stout man with a large gray beard, had been Ogun's ambassador for years. He is the best, they say, having graduated from the Witwaters where he mastered several languages (modern and ancient alike) and evidently learned how to bend people to his will with his scholarly but approachable candor.

Generally, conversations between legates and national royalty are friendly and diplomatic. Given the circumstances, I strongly suspect that would not be the case today.

After greeting several councilmembers Wawauda seems to know personally, he sits at his place at one of the tables. He smiles thoughtfully at me as I pretend to be pay rapt attention to my fingernails.

Titus clears his throat. "Let's begin."

A female Ojo called Feechi with broad shoulders and a shiny bald head testifies first. She went to Barack to investigate once the bodies were discovered. She speculates that both Oko and a noble member of the Ogun army traveled to the highest peak to watch the fighting or perhaps negotiate privately (Titus confirmed the latter without naming Gye, which puzzles me).

"Something went awry, and the Ogun attacked Oko," Ojo Feechi states frankly. "There was evidence that Oko tried to fight back, but he still got the worst of it—being shot by an iron shooter at close range. The Ogun must've survived the fight with minimal injuries and fled. This is my report: I am declaring it an ambush."

I feel a little burst of relief. There had been no witnesses.

Titus calls Wawauda to testify. With some effort, the portly man lifts himself out of his chair and lumbers to the front of the room.

"Greetings, Council of the Elders *Ka* Kähari," Wawauda says, as if he just popped by for an afternoon chat. He looks at me. "Forgive me. Should I say Chieftess? Or…your grace? Chieftess Regent—?"

I am not swayed by his charm. "Thank you for joining us, Wawauda. Daughter Mäzzikim is fine," I grind. I nod curtly at Titus. "Please, continue."

"Of course, your grace." Titus clears his throat. "Wawauda, we would like your testimony to focus on the manner at hand: the attack on the Ameci warriors, known allies to both nations, just beyond Kähari's gates."

Wawauda bows. "I regret the mistrust the recent events have created. I assure you; Ogun did not take any intentional hostile actions against either clan."

"You formed a blockade to prevent Amẹci from coming to our aid against the Ganju refugees," one elder protests. "And you appear to have a concentration of well-armed military forces very far from Ogun—"

"You conspired with the chieftess and murdered the chieftain of Kähari!"

Wawauda shrugs his shoulders. "Assumptions, accusations, insinuations."

"An attack on the Amẹci is an attack on all clan nations," another member of council blusters. "You won't talk your way out of this one, Wawauda."

"It is regrettable. The incident, I mean. However, the Chieftain Gye Nyame was unaware that the Amẹci were even coming to Kähari. If that had been communicated—"

"You saw their banners. You knew who they were."

"It was late evening. Very dark. An honest mistake. Frankly, your protests offend me."

"What does Chieftain Gye say of this?"

"I will not offer his opinion. The man is quite ill and trying to regain his strength before Congress. But if I may offer my own, the real danger is the demonic mage that set a plague upon the Ogun army. While a handful of Amẹci were lost in the scuffle, we lost over three hundred men."

Gye Nyame illness is his alibi. No wonder Titus did not name him. Best not to lob any accusations that would not stick. I wonder who Titus thinks went to the mountains on Gye's behalf. Does he suspect Bosede?

Wawauda snaps his thick fingers. "Like that. Gone. It is an abomination," he thunders.

A brief silence fills the room.

Titus, speaking out of turn, shoots back, "An abomination, much like our chieftain being murdered by one of your men?"

Not just any man, I want to shout, but I could implicate myself. I do not think Kipporah intended for me to return to Kähari to be imprisoned or killed.

"That is nothing by a vile rumor being spread by an ill-guided Ojo, an institution that I question more and more by the day."

Wawauda glances at Ojo Feechi, who glares back at him. "But I do agree with your search for the instigator of such a horrible crime. Are you getting this down, Titus?"

Titus looks up from his scribbling. "Please only address the members of the elder council and her grace," he states primly.

Sighing as if he were about to address inattentive children, Wawauda folds his arms across his chest and says, "Ogun does not typically interfere with the doings of another nation. However, we did believe that we could curry good favor with Chieftain Oko if we assisted with the Ganju situation. Unfortunately, we've only learned that we should've kept our noses to ourselves."

"So, you *deny* that Ogun has committed a hostile act."

"Again, I understand that this matter is unprecedented. If that were true, we would not expect to escape punishment. We believe in the noble powers of the realm. We believe in the justice of the law."

Several heads in the room bob up and down in agreement.

Wawauda pauses and folds his hands in front of him. "That said, if we are punished for a crime that we did not commit, *that* would be a hostile act and end all agreements detailed in the peace treaties," he finishes icily.

A threat, I realize as I look at the nervous faces of the elders around the room. A confident threat considering Kähari's powerful allyship with the Amęci. Ogun has no qualms about attacking other clans—they'd just proved it. If they act with hostility, war will spread quickly. Even if it is expediently quelled, a lot of people will die—and will it end quickly? Amęci has considerable weaponry. Did Ogun also have an arsenal of weapons?

"If you aim to punish hostility, which I assume you do, you need to find the murderer who killed three hundred Oguns before he escapes abroad."

Wawauda opens his portfolio and pulls out a document. "Ogun is issuing a request that this happens as soon as a successor of Kähari is named, and that the criminal is extradited to Ogun when the investigative tribunal has concluded."

He walks up to Titus and hands the document to him with a wink. "I regret I had to travel here under some terrible circumstances. I will see you lot at Congress soon."

"Wait, one more question for the record," an elder calls out. "What of Bosede? He was traveling to Kähari for his wedding to her grace, Daughter Ewatomi. Has he returned to Ogun?"

My shoulders involuntarily tense.

"As we'd hate to assume foul play, we imagine he has run off with that ill-breed, idle-headed goblin of a Daughter."

I sharply take in a breath, and my mouth sags in shock. Other faces reflect my disbelief. I have never heard anyone speak so disrespectfully about a royal, and from a man known for his diplomatic candor. If he declared such things in sacred halls, the rumors on the streets in Ogun must be much worse. "You're out of line, Wawauda," I admonish bluntly, clenching my fists.

He bows his head slightly. "I speak from the frustration in my heart we all share."

Bosede must be dead. He would have returned to his throne. He did not love Ewatomi, and she did not love him. They both loved coin and power. The very thought of them running off together, in disgrace, to live in near poverty in the countryside—laughable.

Then, where is the body? The seed in my stomach sprouts.

"Ewatomi could be a victim of foul play," the councilman offers weakly.

Wawauda laughs dryly. "Come now, Ekon. Even you don't believe that."

"Lies, lies, so many lies," he murmurs in such a way that it hangs in the air and slowly floats down upon us. After bowing with false ceremonial pomp, Wawauda strolls from the room. No sooner than the large doors swing shut do the enraged members of the council turn inward to argue.

"We must find the man who killed the three hundred. Our auxiliary forces cannot hold back Ogun aggression," one says with conviction, his nostrils quivering. "

"Come off it, whoever it is, he is a hero," a councilwoman angrily counters, leaving some members recoiling. "Even if we cannot prove it, we all know the Ogun aimed to overtake the Amęci and Kähari."

"Whoever it is—he is not *human*. Three hundred Ogun and Ogun only, in an instant! And the dead, not a mark on them. It is certainly blood magic, and we cannot show tolerance for that. The list of mage classes it could have been is quite long."

You would not know enough about the ancient tribes to know which one, I think bitterly to myself. Perhaps if Kähari allowed a proper, uncensored library or comprehensive education for all. *That's the spirit*, my heart cheers. *Your naivety excites me*, my mind jibes back.

"We will have a doctor examine one of the Ogun victims," Titus broke in, jotting down notes. "Maybe that will shed light before we spill more blood."

A doctor will find nothing. A healer would find everything. For once, I am grateful for my clan's bigotry.

I TWITCH FOR THE REST OF THE DAY. THE MEMBERS OF THE ELDER COUNCIL look so nervous and frazzled. They bicker, exchange well-founded suspicions, and some strange and unreasonable theories, but they cannot seem to decide what to do next. Finally, council ends, and I return to my chambers for supper. I avoid the dining room and the kitchen—I cannot stand the looks and the whispers. If no one found Bosede's body, at least one other person out there knew he had been killed. After all, they hid the body. Why? I don't know, but it worries me.

Hanya puts down my supper tray on my sitting-room table and promptly reviews the gossip amongst the Palace staff. "Killing the Chieftain of another nation," Hanya declares in disbelief.

"Your grace, if it can be proven through investigations, we will go to war, and war is awful. I hear there is less bread, for one thing."

"Truly grim, I'll light a prayer candle," Kala replies sarcastically.

Placing a tray in front of Kala, Hanya sniffs dismissively. "Daughter Maze loves bread. Thought *you* would've known that." Kala glares at her, pursing her lips.

"What about my mother? Was there any talk of her?" I ask, swirling but not touching my spiced garlic lamb. "And my sister?"

The members of council determined that Farida killed herself to avoid punishment. Of what, they weren't certain—but suspected that the Chieftess knew what had happened in the Outlands and why, and perhaps played a featured role in it. They also theorized Ewatomi fled in embarrassment with Bosede after learning his clan led a failed attack against the Amẹci. After all, she is implicated in treason. If she turns up, she will be tried for it, which is reassuring. Perhaps Ewatomi will keep her distance from both Ogun and Kähari.

"Can't say for sure anyone really believes it," Hanya says. She accepts my bread offering. "But," Hanya adds through a mouthful. "Everyone just wants things to go back to the way they were."

LIFE CANNOT GO BACK TO NORMAL—NOT FOR A LONG TIME. THERE ARE TOO many loose ends. Too many unanswered questions. Or, as Wawauda said, *lies, lies, so many lies.*

A week after the death of Chieftain Oko and Chieftess Farida, Kähari still lacks a ruler—a vulnerable position considering Ogun's pending threat. Preparations are quickly made for a selection rite on top of planning for two mourning periods. All the bells in the temples ring each morning and then go silent as the priests and priestesses gather to pray for guidance. It might be days; it could be months before a new ruler is identified.

In all the preparation, the search for Ewatomi is slowly abandoned, and rumors continue to swell about her role in all the recent death. How much had she known? Is she a traitor? I did nothing to dissuade them. Ewatomi is an ill-nurtured traitor, the worst rank of humankind, and if they stay focused on her, they will lose sight of me.

But a new rumor, which Kala brings to my attention, surfaces. No longer the 'heroic survivor of a terrible tragedy,' I am called a 'cursed girl from a cursed family' in all the papers, even the kinder ones. People are restless to see me removed from the Palace and a fresh noble family installed.

"Exactly how bad is it?" I ask, unsettled by a particularly vicious article. I much prefer learning about history, so I have never read newspapers much before. This is a poor time to start.

"I'd say prepare-for-pitchforks-and-torches bad," Kala replies honestly, picking up another one. "Look, at least the *La Mation* says you should be 'pitied for being related to a sanguine sponge of a father and two brazen-faced weasels'—you know, that sounded better before I read it out loud. Never mind."

Kala drops the paper as if it spontaneously caught fire as I wonder what the griots are rhyming with "brazen-faced weasels" in their song stories.

"You can go home to Väike," I admit in glum defeat.

"You don't have to stay here either," Kala reminds me. "You might be the only person who knows the truth—but you can't take on the realm."

Kala picks up all of the newspapers and tosses them into the fireplace, where they crinkle and blacken into ash. "I'm going to write Chieftess Udo, requesting asylum for you in Ameçi. They have several universities there...and hot springs...and..."

Kala babbles on, but I am not listening. Naturally, as a well-practiced procrastinator, I do not have a plan for addressing the court. I'd hoped Kipporah would give me some sort of sign, but so far, nothing. I wish I could go back to the hidden library.

I hear the door slam. Kala might've left to get letter writing supplies or maybe a book about Ameçi. Frankly, I do not care. The wonderful silence washes over me. For the first time in a long time, I decide to unlock my room of treasures. The room feels strange and cold. Everything is still stacked neatly, but coated with a layer of dust and cobwebs.

Frustrated, I wander into the middle of it and sit down.

"Well, this was an excellent plan, I am inspired already," I sarcastically quip to the room.

I lie back on the floor, not caring that my backside now carries a white film of dust. The realm is doomed. Surely Kipporah had made an epic mistake giving me a task of this magnitude. I stare at the mark on my wrist. I'd seen it before, of course, in the tomes about Kipporah. But where else? Kipporah's words return to my mind: The other mages—they have been divided against each other. You must unite them. Together, we will rise.

I close my eyes, searching inwardly for my magic.

One of the boxes rattles from its pile and falls to the floor. I jump up in alarm. It couldn't possibly be a coincidence. Could it? I venture over and pick it up. With some effort, I lift the lid. Inside the box on a little bed of cotton lay the knife with the engraved wooden handle. The knife I bought from the street vendor before I sat down for a meal with my grandmother for what I did not know would be the very last time. It feels like a lifetime ago. I was so different.

I stare at it a long time, turning it over in my hands. My mother's knife; she died with it in her pocket, too weak to use it to defend herself after using her magic to save me. She must have known a small knife like this one would not offer much defense. She carried it for another reason. If I could just understand the significance of the vision or the symbols.

Refocusing, I examine the markings, which I previously ignored, but nothing jumps out at me. They still mean nothing. They still look unfamiliar. My magic sparks and then trickles away. It has been weak since the night in the mountains. Perhaps I have exhausted it, like a muscle.

"I could use something less cryptic. Perhaps a book for reference," I call to the empty room. Silence. Sighing, I drop the knife into my dress pocket. Maybe something would come to me later.

"Maze! Maze!" Kala hisses from the front room.

"What is it?" I ask as I enter the sitting room. "Oh...gods!"

Mezu slowly limps in; Kala smartly covered him in a servant's gray servants tunic and hooded cloak, but struggles under his arm to hold him up, and I scramble to help.

"Shh, Hanya will hear. Come on, no one can find him here," I point out as I guide them to my 'treasure' room. We manage to slide him awkwardly onto the ancient chaise by the window. A cloud of dust rises from it as Mezu settles in heavily.

"What happened to your leg?" I ask in horror.

"What is this room?" Kala asks, looking round in curiosity.

"Why do you two ask so many damn questions? Get me something I can use as a bandage and some alcohol! Now, please," Mezu manages through a mouth twisted in pain.

The enterprising Kala rips cotton fabric from the skirts of an old gown and manages to scrounge up a forgotten bottle of fire whiskey. Feeling a little paranoid, I pull my curtains shut.

"How did you get past the guards?"

"I have my ways, lovely," he grumbles. "Nobody died."

Mezu pulls up his pant leg, and I barely hold back a squeak. I exchange a worried glance with Kala as Mezu, grunting, wraps the bandage around his knee. Blood seeps through his fingers. "That looks quite awful. You might need to go to a medicinary," Kala timidly suggests.

"Or straight to the corpsman," I grumble, only half-joking.

"I'm a banished Ojo posing as an official Ojo. I would be arrested immediately and get a new address in Iboji."

"If we're going to hide you here, we need an explanation," I insist with irritation. "Why did you come *here*—of all places?"

"Helped you get back to Kähari, didn't I? Don't you owe *me*, then?"

I cross my arms. "Helped yourself as much as us and nearly killed us in the process, so I think we're even. What happened?"

"Mäzzikim, your voice grates like a whip," he complains, reaching for the fire whiskey and taking a deep swig.

"What? It's *pain medicine*," he counters when I glare at him.

I look at Kala, who glances curiously around the room and avoiding my eyes.

"You can start talking or I'd be happy to call the guards and let them know that there is a strange man in my chambers," I warn.

"Fine, fine." Another long swig. "I followed your precious Kala to the Palace, saw to it that she got inside, and then I went into the Outlands."

"You...were in the Outlands? In the midst of the fighting? Why?" Kala asks in disbelief. "That's stupid. An idiot's masterpiece, in fact."

"Good to see you too, Kalacat," he groans, leaning back against the chaise and closing his eyes. "Good on you, Mazzie, by the way, for tossing the Ogun."

My mouth falls open.

Kala's eyes widen, and she whips around. "It was you? *How?*"

"Mezu, how did you—Kala, I did not know if it worked, honestly. I sort of lost consciousness right after I conjured it," I divulge, as an exasperated Kala drops her face into her hands. "What was I supposed to do? Let the Ogun destroy the Ameci and take Kähari?"

When I notice Mezu grinning wickedly, I add, "Don't listen him. He's just trying to pit us against each other."

"It didn't work *exactly*," Mezu cut in. "It—"

Seeing Kala's aghast face, I hold up a finger and shake my head. "You still haven't explained your leg. Stay to the subject."

"I'm getting to it. I was wounded while fetching this…"

Mezu reaches into his knapsack, and then tosses me a familiar large wooden doll with yellow dress and broken glass eye. My body goes cold as

I hold the doll again. I slowly exhale, trying to force my mind to keep the anguished screams away.

"I buried it near the campsite in case Nyame disturbed the campsite remains. It's one of my exhibits in my case against Nyame."

I raise an eyebrow. "To help you get your Ojo status back."

Mezu ignores me. He takes another swig and shakes his head his disbelief. "Nyame has four blood-hungry yankas guarding his illegal mine. I didn't think those existed anymore."

"I can't be the only one in the room that doesn't know what a yanka is," I declare, crossing my arms.

"It's sort of like a dragon," Kala quips intelligently.

Oh, so I am. As I am the ignorant one here: Can a yanka breathe fire?" I ask, thinking that maybe it was not a dragon in the vision; perhaps it was a yanka.

Kala corrects herself. "I meant only *superficially*. A yanka is an outsized reptile. Really long neck. Usually lives near rivers. Really gnarly teeth."

Kala's eyes drifts to Mezu's leg. "They can grow as large as ten men."

"If Gye Nyame is using mage animals, then he is preparing for a war against the remaining mage population and anyone who defends them. He must know he doesn't stand a chance with crossbows and sabers. That is why that horrible Ogun legate was so forward at elder council," I surmise darkly, crossing my arms over her chest.

"Could be," Mezu replies vaguely before looking me in the eye. "But whether or not I have my title, I am dedicated to this realm. I don't want to see it destroyed."

Kala and I both quiet for a beat.

"Kala, go fetch some pillows and blankets for Mezu," I command. "Ask the kitchen to send up fish and bread, could you please?"

Kala nods curtly and leaves the room.

"You won't be here when we wake up, I assume," I say quietly. "You disappear so quickly, sometimes I think I've imagined you."

Chuckling, Mezu closes his eyes.

"How did you know it was me?" I ask.

"I suggested it." He winces. "I haven't been entirely forthright with you."

"You're a mage," I guess quietly.

"My great grandfather descended from a tribe of warlocks. Not long after my mother died, my father noticed I had certain abilities and sent me to an exorcism camp. I got away. For awhile, I lived in Dragon's Pass as a coin boy in a popinae. When the Ojos came for selection…I used my power of suggestion so that they would choose me. I knew it was wrong; against the will of the guards, but I wanted a family—a brotherhood. I prayed to the gods, promising I would never use it again if I could be an Ojo."

"But you did—you used it on *me*." I hugged myself trying to figure out how I feel about it. Gods, the power of suggestion—an incredible and dangerous power, but what is his price? There is always a price of magic. "You *used me* to kill three hundred Ogun."

His gaze meets mine. "You wanted to do it, and it needed to be done."

"If we're partners in this, maybe you can help me." I clear my throat and take out the knife, which warms from its magic, and flip it around to the symbols. "If you could just—"

"No," he states firmly. "I made a terrible mistake, and I am sorry for it."

I frown. "But you're *not* an Ojo anymore."

"Perhaps in title, but they can't take my distinction from me. I may have forced my way in somewhat unethically. I survived every trial without using magic, and I was anointed by the gods. I'm meant to only help you—only help anyone—when I think it serves the greater good of the realm," he lectures.

"I *am* trying to help the realm. With Ewatomi's disappearance, I am being watched too closely, but I know what is happening and I want to expose Gye Nyame and the Ogun—"

"I'm sure your intentions are pure," he begins.

"Stop," I cut him off angrily, tossing the doll with a clunk at the foot of the chaise. "Why would you even come? Why did you come to *us* for help if we weren't going to work together?"

"I didn't come for help. I came to say goodbye to this short, but exciting dalliance."

I snort. "Dramatic, aren't you."

Mezu opens his bright eyes again. "A long time ago, I used to fight the monsters no one wanted to fight. It used to be the ones you could see—imps, gremlins, ghouls."

He continues after a long swallow from this whiskey bottle; he shivers slightly as it burns his throat. "Now I fight new ones, and they're invisible—greed, bigotry, rage, fear. Do I get a pat on the back, a roof over my head for a night, a pile of gold coins, and a pint of fire water? Nah."

"I swore an oath too, but I'm doing puzzles in the dark."

"I saw what happened to the Ogun," Mezu discloses. "A haunting of souls—you turned nearly three hundred of their men into dust, practically in your sleep to hear you tell it! Have you ever really thought about it since?

I am amazing, an amazing sociopath, or both. Heat floods my cheeks. "It's magic, I hardly know how it works, and in my defense, there's been quite a lot happening—"

Mezu grunts in pain. "Yet, none of it surpasses the hundreds of voices you silenced in one instance. You are magnificent. Maybe the most powerful mage I've ever met."

"You say it like an insult. *You* put the suggestion in my head," I protest, practically spitting in disbelief. "Now, you're judging me?"

"I don't judge you for it. I admit my part, but it was like unchained chaos. That kind of magic—it comes at a price." He raised his eyebrows. "What is the price?"

I press my mouth into a thin line. The blood of a chieftain; that was the price.

Without waiting for an answer, Mezu continues, "Your destiny will guide you to where you need to be, but I can't be part of it. I have my own course."

I retort, "You are as useful as bare trees to a starving giraffe."

His eyes flash and his lips curve into a smile. "I do enjoy your way with words, but you *will* forgive me. I'll keep your secrets; you'll keep mine."

Protests die on my lips and I squeeze my eyes closed against his gaze. "You're doing it *again*," I bite at him. Already, I feel the memory of what he said fading. I press my palms to me head, trying to force it to stay inside. I am left with the emotion, anger, without knowing the cause.

Mezu chuckles.

Seething a bit, I turn on my heel and leave the room. I am still glowering in the sitting room when Kala returns with the supper tray of fish, bread, and mangos.

"Did he die while I was gone?" Kala asks with concern, seeing my disgruntled face.

Slumping into a chair by the fireplace, I grunt, "No, not dead. Just a git."

Kala smiles a little, but her eyes are distant. I know she is thinking about what I have done, wondering how she should feel about it. For now, she does not bring it up. "Well, you should always give an Ojo a hot meal and a warm bed. Even the gits. Go to bed; I'll care for him."

At Kala's insistence, I reluctantly take the sleeping tonic and climb into bed. A little part of me hopes I will not wake up. Or that I would wake up, but and discover that everything is all part of a really long nightmare. At least I knew Mezu would be gone in the morning.

The next morning, Mezu does not disappoint. On my sitting room table sits three gold coins.

CHAPTER
TWENTY

Clad in our mourning attire, Kala and I sit outside by the umagodi field in the fine spring weather. The field sits empty, of course; no games will be played during the requisite mourning period, and the tournament has been indefinitely postponed pending investigations. Instead, we watch the slow-moving train of mourners from other nations leaving the guest houses and entering the Palace to pay their respects at the catacombs (I avoid the catacombs for obvious reasons). Eventually, I will have to enter. For now, I garner enough sympathy to do as I please. As one might imagine, there is quite a lot on my mind.

"You've been very quiet," Kala prompts.

What I can I say? I am pondering important questions. For instance, I am not sure if I am a hero or a villain; I am sure Kala is wondering the same. I do not know if I can—or should—do what Kipporah asks of me. I do not know where I will live once the religious congregation chooses a ruler for Kähari. How will I access the hidden library if I do not live in the Palace? How will I ever learn to use my power without it? Where is my father? Will I ever sleep again? Perhaps most importantly, am I Mäzzikim or Nuri?

"I was thinking I'll never get married," I reply out loud, picking a piece of lint off my black gown and flicking it into the wind.

Kala blinks in surprise. "Of all things—*really*? *That's* what you're thinking about."

"Well, maybe to a really old man," I amend.

Kala plays along. "Old and very sick."

"Yes, so sickly. That's how I like *my* men. Close to death."

Or dead. I flush a little, thinking about Adin.

"I wonder if Ewatomi knew...that Bosede..." Kala trails off. "It just seems so—"

Suspicious. And (the smarter) half the country agrees with Kala.

"I know," I agree, feeling weird about keeping such significant secrets about my family (or lack thereof) and Kipporah's appearance from my friend.

I briefly consider telling Kala everything right then, but the ridiculous, rambling speech dies before passing my lips, and I choose instead to focus on an albino woman wearing a ruffled black hat at an odd angle. I thought for a moment it was Chieftess Udo. I must write her and tell her my side. I hope she believes me. Considering she rushed back to Ameci, I am not feeling wonderful about my odds.

"With Farida and Ewatomi gone, who will speak at the selection rite after the transfer of power?" Kala asks suddenly. "Will it be you?"

Ah, maybe that is it! I can address the court and the people of Kāhari during the selection. Plead on behalf of the people trapped in the Trench. Speak out against the injustice against mages across Kāhari and the realm. In poor taste, sure. Wrong time and place, of course. Would people throw things? Likely. Would those things be hard? Possibly. But when else will I have the opportunity to speak to most of the nobles and clan about the Trench? I could deliver an impassioned speech from the lone survivor of a fallen family. Yes, that is it. It will be brilliant!

"I'll talk to Titus," I decide, brightening.

Kala looks understandably puzzled. "Maze, you literally hate people. And speaking. And doing things."

She is right. I hate all of those things.

"It would be an honor," I lie breezily.

THE MOURNING PERIOD ENDS. THE SERVANTS SET TO WORK CLEANSING THE house; scrubbing the floors, washing the linens, airing sheets, beating the carpets, polishing looking-glasses, taking down paintings of the noble family. Dusting away the death. Every piece of wood furniture polished to the brightness of the sun. Every vase and pot teeming with vibrant flowers. Pillows perfectly fluffed. The Palace hums with new life and hope.

The Elder Council of Kähari seems anxious that the traditions of Kähari rule be perceived as seamless. The people should see a chieftain or chieftess selected immediately, just as Oko had been selected over a decade ago. There must be appropriate celebrations, despite the recent gloom. "There has been too much death...too much *change*," Titus insists to me, after he describes the elaborate banquets, inter-district umagodi skirmishes, and parades that he planned. "We must put it behind us."

Easy for Titus to say—he is not the one that lost his entire family in the course of a day. Although I must admit, today I am almost numb to the pain. I feel...free.

Half a dozen servants walk by carrying bundles of wild flowers to place all over the Palace. As I sneeze, I note to Titus that the Palace has begun to look like a garden.

"Good. The coin lady will call me a cutpurse and slit my throat, but people must see that order has been restored," Titus declares confidently.

"I understand." I walk briskly to match his pace. "Has the holy congregation selected...?"

"No, no, of course not," Titus retorts, distracted as he glances down at his list.

"Don't you remember your father's selection? The bells will toil again once that happens for an entire day. It's actually quite annoying, to tell the truth. Ding dong, ding dong, you'll get sick of it too. Just wait. It could take a bit. A few weeks... months...and with you too young to assume power in the meantime, things are a bit complicated..."

Trying to muster up courage, I follow him like a lemming. Finally, Titus pauses.

"Darling, I don't want to be *that* person—but have you made other living arrangements? There is a good chance the new ruler of Kähari won't want you living under his or her roof. I can find you a lovely place nearby or in Natal. Maybe with a small garden?"

I scoff. "With what coin? I had planned to take up residence under a bridge."

"Mäzzikim *Ka* Kähari, darling, you are a wealthy noble. By abandoning her duties as your father's successor, Ewatomi has abandoned her claim to your parents' assets. Your mother stockpiled quite a bit, and now it's all left to *you*."

He sighs. "I'm quite jealous, to be honest."

I scowl at him.

Titus hastily adds, "Of the coin, not all the death, of course."

Oh, the irony. Ewatomi and Farida would be so angry, and, of course, I find that part to be the most delightful. "I can live alone?"

Dreams can come true!

"You'll need a legal guardian, of course—at least until after your Hathi. I suppose you can determine when you're ready for that as your parents cannot."

Titus clucks his tongue. "I'll help you make proper arrangements, call the coin house—after the selection. I daresay my plate is full at the moment."

He looks at me pointedly.

"Thank you. But, uh, I actually wanted to ask you if I could speak at the selection rite...for the transfer of power," I force the words out hurriedly before I lose my nerve.

"Oh, honey, no. You'll be there for the transfer but you cannot speak."

I stare at him.

Titus winces and pats me on the shoulder. "I'm sorry."

"Why not?"

"Nothing personal. It's just—given, uh, your status...it has to be a priest or priestess or someone of distinguished who has. It cannot be you," he sputters.

I shrink in disappointment. In other words, anyone but the cursed girl from the ruined family. I am indeed the last bit of gloom lingering in the Palace.

"You understand." He lowers his head. "I'm sorry."

I hear something and strain to listen. Others in the hall do the same, looking around for the source. A servant shouts, "Do you hear that? I think it's—"

"Gods...the bells!" Titus shrieks, turning his attention to the nearest servants who shrink back in alarm. "Praise be, it *is* the bells!"

"The bells! Everyone, hurry! It's finally the damn bells!"

"Ding dong," I mutter under my breath. I need another plan and fast.

THE SELECTION RITES ARE ALWAYS HELD IN THE LARGEST HOLY TEMPLE IN THE nation, an extraordinarily elaborate white and gold fortress with gleaming spires scrapping the sky. It holds ten thousand people easily, Titus told me once. Being the remaining member of the most noble family in our nation, I am ensured a good seat right in front, and, of course, I chose Kala to sit beside me.

The festivities commence in the evening under a serene night sky thick with stars. After hours of grooming, Kala and I travel from the Palace to the temple atop a camel-drawn coach, at the head of a grand parade with bands of horns and drums and dancers twisting, shaking, bucking in their violet and gold fringe costumes. Crowds of people, cheering and celebrating, line the street. The excitement is infectious. Despite my nerves, I find myself clapping to the music, laughing nonsensically with Kala, and waving to the crowd. The little girls in particular watch with awe and bright eyes and hoped that *they* could be the next daughter of the Chieftain *Ka* Kähari. I imagine that the aspirations of the older and wiser people might be more tempered, given what happened to my family.

"Selection doesn't look like *this* in Väike. This clan throws a great party, I'll give you that," Kala admits reluctantly, a moment later.

"Wait until you see the rest before you rush off for Ameci's hot springs," I tease.

"Whom do you think will be selected?" Kala tosses petals from the window. "Perhaps a happy old man with a beard who smiles and laughs and brings joy back to the clan. Or maybe a young woman—with long white hair and progressive ideas for education, science, and the arts."

Tonight, a new chieftain (or chieftess) will install himself at the Palace, and I will be degraded to the condition of a visitor and then an interloper. I remember meeting the former royals when we arrived. They treated us with civility but little excitement—understandable. My mother pressed them to know what it *felt* like, but they politely demurred and wished us luck. They moved quickly, before the end of the season, and y mother immediately carried forth her redecoration of their rooms. I believe they resettled in the capital; I plan to settle at some distance from the Palace; an incredibly far distance.

I peer at the crowd. Underneath the gaiety, I see the suspicion and questions on their faces. They needn't worry, frankly, I can barely wait to be unseated and fade into obscurity.

"I do not think the religious congregation is particularly imaginative or adventurous," I answer Kala. "I just know it won't be me and that's all that matters."

When we arrive at the temple, servants rush to put down rugs so that my noble feet do not touch the ground before I enter the holy house. Accompanied by several guards, we make our way up the stone stairs, into the temple, and to the very front row of pews. I carefully lift the beaded skirts of my dress to avoid tripping. When I reach my seat, I am relieved to have arrived without falling over, but now feel very self-conscious about my large headpiece, which certainly is obstructing someone's view of the altar. I do not need to give people more reasons to dislike me.

I admire the gold-hued stature of the founder of Kähari with her arm and fist outstretched with a phoenix clawed to her knuckles. In her other hand, Kähari grips her staff of life and fertility. As the legend goes, at the end of the Chaos, several tribes wandered for thirty days in the chaos of the Outlands. Then a woman and prophet called Kähari who led her people to a stable land by the sea with fruit-bearing plants and fresh water, saving the tribes from starvation. For that, Kähari was declared a demigod, and the tribes banded together and built a wall around the stable land to form the nation of Kähari. I have seen the statue many times and did not realize how much Kähari resembles Kipporah superficially. I wrinkle my nose with suspicion.

"I've never seen a selection rite up close. I've only ever been outside. The largest temple in Väike only holds one hundred or so," Kala whispers in my arm.

A priest with a long white, coily beard strolls onto the altar. It is so quiet in the temple; we can hear the gentle swish of his long purple and gold robes. He speaks at length about the tribes wandering in the desert and finding hope. While carefully avoiding anything specific, he implies that Kähari is facing dark times (eyes boring into me as he says this), but can hope for a fertile future if we keep faith in our divine founder.

A familiar rotund priestess with a bright white smile joins the priest on the altar. I recognize her from my late grandmother's temple.

"My people...Kähari's people... Kähari has spoken to us and she speaks clear! Be blessed, children of the clan! Bring light and joy to your homes," boomed Priestess Umbomi, gesturing dramatically with her hands. "A new Chieftain *Ka* Kähari is born *today*."

I stifle a groan as Umbomi starts the slow process of blending together the dried flowers, dirt, and water in a bowl to form a brownish gray paste. Looking stoic, the priest stands next to Umbomi and waits. And waits. His nose twitches a little.

"What is she doing?" Kala whispers in frustration.

"They'll put a mark on the forehead of the person they think has been chosen. If it turns gold, it is a sign from the gods that the person is the next ruler of Kähari. If it stays brown, then they must return to prayer," I whisper back.

"Kähari first did it—from her death bed—to bless the next ruler."

"So, this might all be for nothing if it doesn't turn?"

"They've only gotten it wrong once, and that holy congregation was hanged for conspiracy," I answer, wringing my hands in my lap.

"Oh..."

As the murmurs of the congregation grew louder and more impatient, the priest clears his throat loudly. "It is time," he articulates meaningfully.

Looking annoyed at being interrupted, Umbomi ceases stirring the paste.

"Daughter *Ka* Kähari Mäzzikim, as the remaining member of the former Kähari noble family, please join us at the altar for the transfer of power," Umbomi says with reluctance.

Kala squeezes my hand as I stand. I walk gingerly to the altar, painfully aware of every judging eye in the temple glowering at my back. With some effort, I kneel before the priest and priestess and wait for Umbomi to name the successor. A rush of emotions and questions hit me. Who would be chosen? Would they suspect me of foul play against the family or the Ogun? Would they be even more determined to stamp out magic? My position—daughter of the Chieftain—has been my shield. Wealthy, noble or not, I will soon be as vulnerable as any other mage in Kähari, and here I am—about to demand that the mages be freed. To calm against a rising wave of anxiety in my stomach, I close my eyes and focus on my magic, beating like butterfly wings against my heart.

I flinch in surprise when Umbomi's warm fingers press against my forehead and cheeks. There are loud gasps in the room (one of them is mine). Mutters and whispers turn into full on disbelieving chatter and scattered shouting. Then there is a long pregnant pause as if all the air sucked from the room. Breathing hard, I gaze up at Umbomi, who is smiling with satisfaction over her perfectly orchestrated dramatic twist.

"No!" I exclaim in alarm.

"Rise, Chieftess Mäzzikim *Ka* Kähari."

"No," I hiss more forcefully, touching my cheek as I stand. I look at my shaking fingers, smeared in shiny gold paste. "I'm not old enough. I'm not eligible."

"Kähari tells no lies, young one," Umbomi whispers gleefully to me.

"No. This is a mistake," I whisper desperately to Umbomi.

"Kähari has spoken; let her will be done," Priestess Umbomi continues to boom as she takes me by the shoulders and turns me around to face the congregation.

You're the only one who didn't see this coming.

"Praise be! Long may she reign," Umbomi shouts to the rafters. Her voice hammers my ears, and I want to sink into the floor and disappear. I hear whimpering; I think it is me.

"Get the crown," Umbomi hisses at the skinny priest as she pulls the decorative headpiece off my head.

The priest hurriedly comes over with the crown of selection—in all of its spiked and glittering glory—and places it atop my braided locks. My eyes stay on the congregation, who are displeased by this odd turn of events. Horror, shock stains their faces. To the men, I am a woman. Despite having a female founder, a single woman hasn't been selected to rule Kähari in decades. To the women, I am an unworthy girl who hasn't even celebrated her *Hathi*. To every gender in between, to the older and wiser, I am too young and inexperienced and hail from a cursed family. To the nobles, I am not one of them. To the poor and desperate, I robbed their opportunity to rise. The stony silence strangles me; the mark on my wrist starts to inch, and my left eyelid starts to twitch.

As the congregation collectively bows and begins to pray, a heavy blanket of doubt weighs down on me. After taking a couple of deep breaths, I meet Kala's eyes. Kala smiles. As the selection prayer concludes, Kala begins applauding and others dutifully follow. Soon the applause thunders through the temple and through the streets of Kähari. I wonder if Mezu is somewhere among them or if he would learn about it by post starling as he scuts around Ogun. Either way, he will likely be in shock; now I am in the position to help him. I can't be gleeful about it though; I'm terrified. I wish to go back in time to my bath, during which I felt excited about dining, dancing, and escaping scrutiny that comes with being the daughter of a Chieftess. I planned to quietly continue my search for the Trench—for answers. How would I do any of that now?

I swallow hard and rub my sweaty palms against my skirts. Sparks of magic travel through my body and prickle at my fingertips. I close my eyes against it.

When I open my eyes, I see spirits. Some wispy and white. Others nearly in full color, but still translucent. Warriors in ancient armor. Young children. Kipporah Elves, but also various nations of Dwarves, Trolls, Giants, Faeries. The lost souls whose bodies broke to build this very temple. In near unison, they solemnly raise their fists to their hearts.

Adin is right. Kähari is a well-haunted country.

As the ceremony takes places around me, my mind runs on a continual loop of questions. My selection, it could only be part of a plan (but what god in their right mind would put an uneducated young mage woman on the throne at a time like this one? At a time when elements are ripe to boil over into a second Chaos?). There has to be a purpose. What is my purpose? Can I figure it out before they turn on me? I will have mere days to determine a strategy.

There were over four hundred common and tribal languages spoken in the Ohia Realm, I cannot not string together enough words together in any language to properly express my terror. In spite of this, I know my people are depending on me. I may not win, but I will fight.

It is a slow journey back to the Palace. As soon as the news dispatched, every citizen in Kähari pours into the streets, shouting and crying in unison; so loudly, it can probably be heard in the darkest corners of the Outlands, reaching the ears of every clan and tribe. "Long live the Chieftess! Long live the Chieftess!"

Despite a warm rain washing over the evening, the crowd had grown too large for the royal guard to disperse or travel through it, so instead they escort Kala, Titus, and a few scattered members of council, religious congregation, and. I along the southern edge of Kähari, keeping distance from the main roads and rivers.

I am still stunned into silence and Kala seems at loss for words too. I am returning to the Palace, having been granted great power and responsibility—regrettable, but there it is. I do not understand how it fits Kipporah's plan. I do not know how Kala and I will act toward each other now. I do not know if she'll evens stay. Finally, it seems that no matter how often or industriously I try to leave the Palace, something drags me right back (with nary a possibility of a happy return). Others examine me for a reaction, but I do not know if I should smile—would that look less than humble—or if I am betrayed by the fear in my head. The caravan travels in near silence, save for the navigation from the guard.

When we finally reach the backwoods of the Palace, north of the river, the pink moon shown above us. A young member of the royal guard opens the door to the coach and offers a hand, cautiously, as if he thought it might offend me. I tuck my face down, but take his hand, which steadies my shaking legs.

"Your majesty," he practically whispers.

"It is rude to stare," Kala puts in bluntly, taking me by the arm and shoving past him. "We will be in her chambers until the excitement dies down. Is that all right, Titus?"

Still looking stunned himself, Titus's head bobs up and down.

INSIDE MY CHAMBERS, I TWIST A SPOON INSIDE A CUP OF COLD TEA.

"Did you," Kala begins apprehensively, sitting across from her. "Could you even—"

"I do not have the powers of mind or elemental control, Kala. I did not choose this," I reply hoarsely, losing my breath in my rush to defense. "Believe me: More than anything, I do not want this."

"I do, *and* I believe that is why you were chosen. Just as your father was chosen. Neither of you want power; it is why the power was safe in your hands. It is the will of the gods," Kala replies, her face earnest in the candlelight. "You will save the realm, Maze."

"At what point can I live by my will?" I moan and rub my eyes with my forefingers. I glance at my crown, which sits gleaming at the end of the table. "No one expected this, no one of influence wants it, and there will be madness."

"A right spectacle," Kala assents straight away, grimacing.

"Tomorrow, a lot of people will come to talk to me. Most will not be friendly." I scratch through my sleeve at the burning mark on my wrist. "If I am discovered—"

Putting her fingers to her temples, Kala exhales slowly. "There is something else. Someone passed it to me during the ceremony."

Kala pulls out a piece of folded parchment and slides it across the table to me. I open it hastily, and my heart tumbles into my sandals. Although unsigned, I immediately recognize the curved letters and trademark heavy ink. My fingers tremble as I strain at the short scrawl in the feeble candlelight:

DEAR MAZZIE,

I'VE DONE IT AGAIN. I DRASTICALLY UNDERESTIMATED MY OPPONENT. STILL, I PREFER MY LONG ODDS TO YOURS. WHEN YOU SEE ME NEXT, TREAT ME AS YOU WOULD AN EMPRESS. TREAT ME AS A JEST, I WILL ENSURE THAT I HAVE THE LAST LAUGH.

LIVE, CHIEFTESS, FOR NOW.

WITH MY DEEPEST RESPECT,

E.

Just below her signature, Ewatomi drew a skull with gaping black eyes burrowed deep into the parchment. I exhale a rattling breath as I finally realize the living haunt me too.

THE END

HAUNTED

CPSIA information can be obtained
at www.ICGtesting.com
Printed in the USA
BVHW050802231222
654910BV00006B/450

9 781735 664132